WORLD OF CHANCE

"This is Burning Bright, heart of the Game, where the best clubs and the best players—the great notables—live and work. I'm not missing this chance. Chances like this are only once in a lifetime—"

When spacepilot and ambitious young game designer Quinn Lioe gets shore leave on Burning Bright, determined to play the Game at its brilliant center, she unwittingly walks onto the battlefield between two great empires, human and alien. The fate of fortunes, and the future of empires, turns on her.

"Intricate and cleverly developed."
—Science Fiction Chronicle

Tor books by Melissa Scott

Burning Bright
Dreamships

BURNING BRIGHT

MELISSA SCOTT

TOR®

A TOM DOHERTY ASSOCIATES BOOK
NEW YORK

BURNING BRIGHT

A Tor Book
Published by Tom Doherty Associates, Inc.
175 Fifth Avenue
New York, N.Y. 10010

Tor® is a registered trademark of Tom Doherty Associates, Inc.

ISBN: 0-812-52175-7
Library of Congress Catalog Card Number: 93-18412

First Tor edition: May 1993
First mass market edition: May 1994

Printed in the United States of America

0 9 8 7 6 5 4 3 2 1

PART ONE

DAY 30

Quinn Lioe walked the galliot down the sky, using the shaped force fields of the sails as legs, balancing their draw against the depth of gravity here in the planet's shadow. Stars glowed in the mirror display in front of her; spots of dark haze blocked the brilliance of sun and the limb of the planet, so that she could see and read the patterns that gravity made in the vacuum around her. The low-sail, under the keel of her ship, vibrated in its cup: the field calibration had slipped badly on the journey from Callixte to Burning Bright, would have to be adjusted before they left orbit. She sighed, automatically easing the field, and widened the cross-sails' field to compensate. Numbers flickered across the base of the mirror as the ship's system noted and approved the changes; she felt the left cross-sail tremble under her hand, as its draw approached the illusory "depth" of hyperspace, and shortened it even before the warning flashed orange and red across her screen. The galliot continued its easy progress as though there had been no chance of grounding.

"Beacon," she said to the ship, to traffic control waiting somewhere ahead of her in the parking pattern, and a moment later a marker flared in the mirror's display, ahead and slightly to the left of the galliot's course. She sighed, wanting to hurry, wanting to be done and parked and free for the five days or more that it would take to recalibrate the fields, but disciplined herself to safe and steady progress. The galliot crept forward, sails beating slowly against the weak currents of hyperspace that were almost drowned by the local gravity. Her hands rested lightly on the controls; she felt the depth of space in the pressure of the sails, saw the same numbers reflected in the slow swirl of the currents overlaid on the mirror's mimicking of reality.

At last she brought the galliot to a slow stop almost on top of the unreal marker, and shortened the sails until the system gravity took over, drawing the ship neatly into the designated space. She smiled, pleased with her precision, and kicked the lever that lit the anchor field. Lights flared along the mirror's base—familiar, but nonetheless satisfying—and the ship said sweetly, "On target. Anchorage confirmed."

"Nicely done," a familiar voice said, and Lioe glanced over her shoulder in some surprise. She hadn't heard Kerestel enter the pilot's dome, had thought he was still back in cargo space sorting out what had and hadn't gone on the drop. *And, to be fair, cleaning up after the bungee-gars.*

"Thanks," she said aloud, and ran her hands across the main board, closing and snuffing the sail fields. She set the anchor field then, watched the telltales strengthen to green, and turned away from her station, working her shoulders to free them of the night's—*morning's,* she corrected silently, *it was the beginning of the new day on Burning Bright*—painstaking work. "How's it look back there?"

"Bungee-gars," Kerestel said. He leaned against the hatchway, folding his arms across his chest. His hands and bare arms were still reddened from the embrace of the servo gloves he used to move the canisters that held the cargo safe during the drop to the planet's surface. "Gods, they're a grubby lot."

Looking at him, Lioe bit back a laugh. As usual, Kerestel was wearing a spacesuit liner, this one more battered even than usual, the long sleeves cut off at the shoulder to make it easier to work the servos. He had stopped shaving two days into the trip—*also as usual*—and the incipient beard had sprouted in goatish grey tufts. The hat that marked him as a union pilot—this one a beret of gold-shot grey brocade, pinned up on one side with a cluster of brightly faceted glass—perched, incongruously jaunty, on his balding head.

Kerestel had the grace to grin. "Well, you know what I

mean. And Christ, the pair of them couldn't make up their minds what was to go in the drop—if they had minds."

Lioe nodded, and turned to the secondary board to begin shutting down the mirror. Bungee-gars, the hired hands who rode the drop capsules down out of orbit to help protect particularly valuable cargoes from hijacking after landing, were generally a difficult group to work with—*you have to be pretty crazy to begin with, or desperate, to take a job like that*—and the two who had come aboard on Demeter had been slightly more bizarre than usual. "What I don't care for," she said, "is running cargo that needs bungee-gars."

"You got a point there," Kerestel said rather sourly, and Lioe allowed herself a crooked smile. Cargoes that needed bungee-gars were valuable enough to hijack in transit as well as at the drop point, and the free space between the Republic and the Hsaioi-An was loosely patrolled at best, with no one claiming either jurisdiction or responsibility. She shook the thought away—there had been no sign of trouble, from Callixte to Demeter or after—and keyed a final set of codes into the interpreter. Overhead, and across the front of the dome, the tracking overlays began to fade, first the oily swirls that showed the hyperspatial currents, and then the all-but-invisible blue-black lines that showed the depth of realspace. The stars blazed out around them, suns strewn like dust and seed, tossed in prodigal handfuls against the night where the plane of the galaxy intersected the mirror's curve. Then the shields that cloaked sun and planet vanished, and the brilliance drowned even the bright stars. Lioe blinked, dazzled, and looked away.

"But if they'd only make up their mind," Kerestel said, and Lioe frowned for a second before she realized he was still talking about the bungee-gars. "You probably felt it, Quinn, they kept changing which capsules were going, so by the time they'd decided, the whole ship was unbalanced. I'll bet money that hasn't helped the low-sail projector."

"I didn't feel we were off alignment," Lioe said. "She handled fine, and the projector didn't feel any worse than when we left Demeter. You did a good job, Micky."

She saw Kerestel's shoulders relax, subtly, and realized that he had been looking for that reassurance all along. She hid a sigh—she liked Kerestel well enough, liked his ship even better, but his insecurities were wearing—and said, "Speaking of which, have you scheduled the repairs?"

"Yes." Kerestel's face brightened. "The yard says they can take us into the airdock tomorrow, and they'll tear down the projector right away. The whole thing, including recalibration, ought to take about eight days. Not bad, eh?"

"Not bad," Lioe agreed. *Not bad at all, especially when it happens over Burning Bright.* "I thought I'd take off, go planetside," she said, carefully casual. "You're not going to need me up here."

Kerestel frowned slightly, said, after a heartbeat's pause that seemed much longer, "You're going Gaming, right?"

"That's right." Lioe bit her tongue to keep from adding more. *This is Burning Bright, heart of the Game, where the best clubs and the best players—the greatest notables—live and work. I'm not missing this chance. Chances like this are only once a lifetime—*

"It's a game, Quinn," Kerestel said.

"And it's one I'm very, very good at," Lioe retorted. She grinned, forced a lighter tone. "Christ, Micky, it's not like I'm quitting."

"One of these days, though," Kerestel muttered, and Lioe reached across to touch his shoulder.

"Not likely, and you know it. Piloting's a steady living, and I'm not stupid." *I had to work too hard to get the apprenticeship, coming out of Foster Services; I'm not giving that up anytime soon.* But that was none of Kerestel's business; she forced the smile to stay on her lips, said, "All I'm saying is, I think I'm going to spend the repair break planetside. All right?" She could force the issue, she knew—they were both union, and the union gave her the right to move off the ship anytime it was anchored in orbit for more than five days—but she liked Kerestel too well to use that lever unless she had to. *And besides, he's getting old, one foot on the retirement line. I don't want to hurt his feelings.*

Kerestel nodded, reluctantly. "All right," he said, and then made himself sound more enthusiastic. "And good luck with the Game."

It was those efforts that made him worth working for,

even if he was getting old and querulous. "Thanks," Lioe said, and retreated to her cabin to collect her belongings.

It didn't take her long to pack: her jump bag was easily large enough to hold a couple of changes of clothes, plus her Gameboard and the thick plastic case that held the half-dozen Rulebook disks. She seized a hat at random, this one black, with a wide brim, shrugged on a jacket—her favorite, heavy blue-black workcloth with a flurry of Game pins across the lapels—and tapped into the local comnet to find a taxi-shuttle to take her across to the customs station. Kerestel was nowhere in sight when it arrived, and she hesitated, but called her good-byes into the shipwide intercom. There was no answer; she shrugged again, caught between hurt and annoyance, and pulled herself through the transfer tube to the taxi.

The landing check was strict and time-consuming. The officer on duty went over her papers with excruciating care, and ran the Rulebooks through a virus scan twice before grudgingly allowing her to carry them onto the surface. She made the orbiter with only minutes to spare, and collapsed into her seat, resolved to sleep for as much of the descent as possible.

She woke to the unfamiliar noise of air against the orbiter's hull, sat up in her harness to see fire rolling across the viewport. The orbiter bucked and fought the sudden turbulence, and then they were down into the atmosphere. Servos whined underfoot and in the cabin walls, reconfiguring wings and lifting surfaces, and the orbiter became a proper aircraft, banking easily against the heavy air that held it. The engine fired, a coughing explosion at the tail of the taxi, and the craft steadied further, came completely under control. Lioe released the breath she hadn't realized she'd been holding, and craned her head to look out the viewport again.

"We'll be landing at Newfields in about fifty minutes," the steward said, from the front of the cabin. "It's day thirty of High Spring, the end of High Spring—that's day ninety-four of our four-hundred-day year. Burning Bright has a twenty-five-standard-hour day, and you should program your chronometers accordingly. If you are keeping Greenwich Republican time, the GRTC factor is eighty-eight

B-for-bravo one hundred fifty-two. Ground temperature is twenty-three degrees. If you need any assistance, or further information, please feel free to ask. Your call buttons are on the cabin wall above your head.''

No one seemed to respond, and Lioe turned her head back to the window. Clouds flashed past beneath them, thin wisps that only partly obscured the glittering water. Burning Bright was mostly water; the main—the only—landmass was largely artificial, the new land built on the inner edges of the giant atoll's original islands, guarded from floods by a massive network of dikes and storm barriers. The city of Burning Bright—city and planet shared a name; the two were effectively identical—was one of the great engineering achievements of the nonaligned worlds: *even in the Republic, and even in Foster Service schools,* Lioe thought, *you learn that mantra.* And it was pretty much true. In all the time she'd spent in space, piloting ships between the Republic and the nonaligned worlds and Hsaioi-An, she'd never been anyplace that was at all like Burning Bright.

"Can I get you anything?"

Lioe looked up to find the steward looking down at her, balancing easily against the movement of the orbiter, one hand resting on the back of the empty couch beside her. She shook her head, but smiled. "I can't think of anything, thanks."

The steward nodded, but didn't move. "I couldn't help noticing your pins."

Lioe let her smile widen, grateful she hadn't had to set up this encounter herself. "I saw yours, too." She glanced again at the pair of Game pins clipped just below the company icon: one was the triangle-and-galaxy of the Old Network, but the other was unfamiliar. "Local club?" she asked, and was not surprised when the steward shook his head.

"Actually, it's a session souvenir," he said. "It was a Court Life variant, run by Ambidexter about five years ago."

"I think I saw tapes of that," Lioe said, impressed in spite of herself. The steward didn't look old enough to have been playing at that level five years ago. "That was the one that featured Gallio Hazard and Desir of Harmsway, right? The one that really made Harmsway a Grand Type."

"That's right." The steward glanced quickly around the cabin, then lowered himself into the couch next to her. "I'm Vere—Audovero Caminesi."

"Quinn Lioe." They touched hands, awkward because of her safety harness.

"You wouldn't be the Lioe who wrote the Frederick's Glory scenario," Vere said.

"As a matter of fact, I am."

Vere grinned. "That was a great session. There's been a lot of talk on the net about it, I'm still trying to find someone at the club who'll run it. Are you going to be doing any Gaming while you're here?"

The conversation was going just the way she'd hoped it would. Lioe said, "I was hoping to. I don't know the clubs, though."

Vere spread his hands. "I can give you some names, if you'd like."

"I'd appreciate it."

"There are really only three clubs that are worth your while," Vere said, lowering his voice until she could just hear him over the noise of the engines. "Billi's in the Old City, Shadows under the Old Dike in Dock Road District, and the Two-Dragon House, in Mainwardens'." He grinned suddenly. "I think Shadows is the best of the lot—it's where I play, so take it for what it's worth."

Lioe smiled back. "What's the setup like?"

"They're all about the same, really," Vere answered. A chime sounded from farther forward in the compartment, and he lifted his head to look over the seatbacks for the source. Lioe followed the direction of his gaze, and saw a call light flashing above one of the seats. Vere grimaced, and pushed himself to his feet, but leaned down to finish what he had been saying. "Shadows has newer machines, but they're not state-of-the-art. Billi's was that maybe four, five years ago. Two-Dragon is pretty standard stuff, a little older than Shadows."

"Thanks," Lioe said, and Vere smiled down at her.

"Don't forget me if you run an open session."

"I'll keep you in mind," Lioe said, and meant it. She would be needing good players, if she managed to persuade a club to let her lead sessions, and anyone who could play for Ambidexter was good enough for her. It was just a pity Ambidexter himself was no longer in the Game.

She turned her head to the viewport again, was startled to see how far the orbiter had dropped. The water was no longer just a blue haze, had gained a crumpled texture, and flecks of white dotted the metallic surface. Burning Bright City was just visible in the distance, if she craned her neck, but mostly hidden by the orbiter's nose. The craft banked sharply then, showing her nothing but the brilliance of the sky, and when it steadied onto the new heading, Burning Bright lay spread out beneath the orbiter's wing. It seemed very small at first, an island split in three by a forked channel, but then the orbiter banked again, losing altitude, and she began to make out the smaller landformed islands that made up the larger masses. Most of them were thickly settled, furred with brick-red buildings, light glinting occasionally from solar panels and interior waterways. Only the high ground at the outer edges of the islands remained relatively uncrowded. She frowned idly at that, wondering why, and the speakers crackled at the front of the cabin.

Vere said, "I've just been informed that we are starting the descent to Newfields. We should be on the ground in about fifteen minutes."

The orbiter canted again as he spoke, and when it came level again, Lioe was looking at a scene she recognized. Twin lakes lay to either side of a piece of land like a small mountain, falling steeply to the sea on one side and more gently into settled country on the other. That was Plug Island, where the first-in settlers had first dammed the shallow lagoon to create more land for their growing city. Double headlands cradled each of the lakes; the desalination complex and the thick white walls of the tidal generating stations that closed each lake off from the sea gleamed in the sunlight. Outside the generating stations' walls, surf bloomed against the storm barriers that defended the Plug Island lagoons; it frothed as well against the base of the cliffs to either side. They were coming into Newfields. Even as she thought it, the orbiter rolled a final time, then steadied into the familiar approach. They flashed over the clustered houses of the Ghetto where the off-worlders, and especially the hsai, lived—still on the inner edges of the island, overlooking the land, away from the sea—and then dropped low over the administrative complex. The orbiter touched down easily on stained and tire-marked pavement, and she leaned back in her couch, no longer watching the blocks of warehouses that flashed past beyond the empty field. *Not long now,* she thought, *not long. I'll find a room in the Ghetto, and I'll call some clubs, and I'll have a Game to run.* She smiled, losing herself in a dream.

DAY 30

The ambassador to Burning Bright knelt in his reception
room, facing the hissing screen. A few check-characters
crawled across the blank grey space; the ambassador
frowned, seeing them, and glanced over his shoulder at the
technician who knelt in front of the control board.

"Sorry, Sia Chauvelin," the technician murmured, and
his hands danced across his controls. The characters vanished, were replaced by a single steady glyph: the link was
complete.

Chauvelin glanced one last time around the narrow room,
at the plain black silk that lined the walls, at the low table
with the prescribed ritual meal—snow-wine; a tray of tiny
red-stained wafers, each marked in black with the graceful
double-glyph that meant both good fortune and gift; a
molded sweet, this one in the shape of the *nuao*-pear that
stood for duty—laid out in the faint shadow of a single perfect orchid in an equally perfect holder carved from a natural
pale-purple crystal. His own clothes were equally part of the
prescribed ritual, plain black silk coat over the pearl-grey
bodysuit that served humans like himself for the hsai's natural skin, a single knot of formal ribbons tied around his left
arm, the folded iron fan set on the bright carpet in front of
him. He glanced a final time at his reflection in the single
narrow window, checking his appearance, and found it acceptable. It was night out still, the sun not yet risen; he suppressed a certain sense of injustice, and glanced again at the
technician. "Is everything ready?"

"Yes, Sia Chauvelin."

"Then you may go." Chauvelin looked back at the screen, barely aware of the murmured response and the soft scuffing sound as the technician bowed himself out and closed the door gently behind him. The remote was a sudden weight against his thigh, reminding him of his duty; he reached into the pocket of his coat to touch its controls, triggering the system. The hidden speakers hissed for a moment, singing as the jump-satellite bridged the interstellar space between the local transmitter and an identical machine on maiHu'an, and then the screen lit on a familiar scene. Chauvelin bowed, back straight, eyes down, hands on the carpet in front of him, heard a light female voice—human female—announcing his name.

"Tal je-Chauvelin tzu Tsinra-an, emissary to and friend-at-court for the *houta* of Burning Bright."

Chauvelin kept his eyes on the fan, dark against the glowing red of the carpet, staring at the five *n-jao* characters of his name carved into the outer guard. There was a little silence, and then a second voice answered the first, this one unmistakably hsaia, inhuman and male.

"I acknowledge je-Chauvelin."

Chauvelin leaned back slowly, raising his eyes to the screen. Even expecting it, the illusion was almost perfect, so that for an instant he could almost believe that the wall had dissolved, and a second room identical to his own had opened in front of him. The Remembrancer-Duke Aorih ja-Erh'aoa tzu Tsinra-an sat facing him in a carved chair-of-state, hands posed formally on the heads of the crouching troglodyths that formed the arms of the chair. His wrist spurs curved out and down toward the troglodyths' eyes, their enameled covers—done in a pattern of twining flowers, Chauvelin saw, without surprise—glowing in the warm lights.

"This person thanks his most honored patron for his acknowledgment," he said, in the hsai tongue that he prided himself on speaking as well as any jericho-human, any human born and bred inside the borders of Hsaioi-An. "And welcomes him with service."

Ja-Erh'aoa made a quick, ambiguous gesture with one hand, at once accepting and dismissing the formal compli-

ments. The stubby fingerclaws, painted a delicate shade between lavender and blue to match the enameled flowers of
the spur sheath, clicked once against the carved head, and
were still again. Chauvelin read impatience and irritation in
the movement, and in the still face of the human woman who
stood at ja-Erh'aoa's left hand, and braced himself for whatever was to follow.

"I would like to know, je-Chauvelin, what you meant by
this report."

For a crazy second, Chauvelin considered asking which
report the hsaia meant, but suppressed that particularly suicidal notion. The Remembrancer-Duke had shifted from the
formal tones of greeting to the more conversational second
mode, and Chauvelin copied him. "My lord, you asked for
my interpretation of what the All-Father and his council
should expect from the elections. I gave you that answer."

"You recommended that we support, or at least acquiesce
in, Governor Berengaria's reelection." Ja-Erh'aoa's hand
moved again, the painted claws clicking irritably against the
troglodyth's low forehead. "Am I mad, or do I misremem-
ber, that she supports the Republic quite openly?"

Chauvelin winced inwardly at the mention of memory—
ja-Erh'aoa implied that he had implied an insult—and said,
"It is so, my lord." He kept his voice cool and steady only
with an effort: he had known that this would become an
issue of *an'ahoba*, the delicate game of status and prestige,
but he had counted on ja-Erh'aoa's support.

"Then why should we not stand in her way?"

I gave you my reasons in my report, my lord. Chauvelin
suppressed that answer, and saw the faintest of rueful smiles
cross the human woman's otherwise impassive face. He said
aloud, "My Lord, the other candidates are not safe. They
either have no backing among the people who matter"—*or
among the people in general, but that's not something a
hsaia would understand*—"or are too young and untried for
me to suggest that Hsaioi-An place any trust in them."

"It is not expedient that we support Berengaria," ja-Erh-
'aoa said flatly.

"Then, my lord, it is as though my report was never

made.'' Chauvelin sat back slightly, folded his hands in his lap.

"Unfortunately," ja-Erh'aoa said, "your report has become common knowledge in the council halls. I have suffered some—diminishment—because of it. It is even being said, je-Chauvelin, that you are too close to the *houta* on Burning Bright, and would perhaps benefit from a different posting.''

"Do you question my loyalties, lord?" Even as he said it, Chauvelin knew that was the wrong question, born from the sudden cold fear twisting his guts. It was too direct, put ja-Erh'aoa in a position where he could only answer yes—and he himself was too vulnerable to that accusation to risk angering his patron. No *chaoi-mon,* citizen by impressment, could risk that, particularly not when he was born on Burning Bright and served now as ambassador to that planet— He silenced those thoughts, kept himself still, hands quiet in his lap, face expressionlessly polite, with an effort that made the muscles along his spine and across his shoulders tremble slightly beneath the heavy coat. He made himself face ja-Erh'aoa guilelessly, as though no one had touched his one vulnerable spot, pretended he did not see the Remembrancer-Duke's fingerclaws close over the troglodyths' heads.

"No one questions your fealty, je-Chauvelin," ja-Erh'aoa said, after a moment. "However, it is as well not to cause even the hint of a question.''

Bad, very bad, Chauvelin thought. He bowed again, accepting the rebuke, and said, "As my lord wishes.''

"I would also see to your household, je-Chauvelin," ja-Erh'aoa said. "I am concerned that this report has traveled so far outside my knowledge, and yours.''

Chauvelin lifted an eyebrow at him, stung at last into retort. "My household is well known to me, save the guest I entertain at your command, my lord.''

There was another little silence, ja-Erh'aoa's hands slowly tightening over the troglodyths' heads, thumbclaws perilously close to their carved eyes, and Chauvelin braced himself to offer his humblest apologies. Then, quite slowly, ja-Erh'aoa's hands loosened again, and he said, with apparent inconsequence, "How is your guest, Chauvelin?"

"The Visiting Speaker is enjoying the pleasures of the planet," Chauvelin answered, conventionally. *In point of fact, the Visiting Speaker Kugüe ji-Imbaoa je Tsinra-an, cousin of the Imperial Father, is spending most of his nights attending parties and most days sleeping off the effects of Oblivion. Even so, I may have underestimated him—or at least his household.* He made a mental note to make a second investigation of the half-dozen attendants who had arrived with ji-Imbaoa.

"You will convey our greetings," ja-Erh'aoa said, and Chauvelin bowed again.

"As my lord wishes."

Ja-Erh'aoa nodded, pushed himself up out of the chair-of-state, at the same time gesturing to the woman behind him. She said, in her clear voice, "The audience is ended."

Chauvelin bowed again, more deeply, hands on the floor, straightened slowly when the click of the room door was not followed by the static of a broken connection. Eriki Haas tzu Tsinra-an, ja-Erh'aoa's First Speaker, looked back at him without expression, came slowly forward to kneel on the carpeting in front of ja-Erh'aoa's empty chair. Chauvelin lifted an eyebrow at her.

"What's made this report so different from all the others? My lord knows what I think of Berengaria." He used tradetalk, the informal creole that was the common language of human beings in Hsaioi-An, and Haas's severity melted into a rueful grin.

"What makes it different is exactly what he said: somebody leaked it before it could be edited for the council. And my lord's right, you should check on how that happened."

"I fully intend to," Chauvelin said. "This is not the most opportune time to have a visitor."

Haas nodded. "The problem is, the je cousins have been getting a lot of attention at court lately—Norio Mann is a je Tsinra-an, and he's been the All-Father's favorite son since the petro strike on Hazuhonë. And the cousins are doing everything they can to consolidate their position."

Chauvelin nodded back, wishing—not for the first time—

that communications between the court on Hsiamai and the worlds outside Hsaioi-An were a little more frequent. "If I had known—" he began, and bit off the words. The rivalry between je and tzu lines of the imperial family—between cousin and direct-line family—was ongoing; if he couldn't anticipate particular events and shifts in favor, he should at least have made sure nothing in his report could have affected the Remembrancer-Duke's position in that struggle. *But I didn't count on his dumping ji-Imbaoa on me. Or his household.*

Haas smiled sourly. "For some reason, Tal, they've decided to pick on you—you are in an anomalous position, after all. And my lord is vulnerable through you, don't forget."

"I don't forget," Chauvelin said.

"Good."

"Tell me this," Chauvelin said, and in spite of his best efforts heard the anger in his voice. "Do you want me to retract my report? It's my best advice—my lord never used to prefer a political lie to common sense, but I am at my lord's command."

"No." Haas waved one hand in a hsaii gesture, negation and apology in one. "What's done is done. But you might look for some way to reaffirm your loyalties in public, Tal. My lord would find it helpful."

"I'll do that," Chauvelin said, a new, cold fear warring with the anger. He had earned his place on Burning Bright, earned the right to return to his homeworld, a favor almost never granted to *chaoi-mon,* and that did leave him open to just this accusation, that he favored his origins over the imperial clan that had adopted him.

Haas looked at him from under lowered lashes. "My lord is vulnerable through you," she said again.

"The threat was clear the first time," Chauvelin said.

"I hope so," Haas murmured, and ran a finger along the elaborate enameling that decorated the cover of her implanted wrist spur. The picture wavered and died. Chauvelin swore, and reached for his own remote, closing down the local connection. Check characters flickered across the screen, and then the wall went dead, a blank grey space at the end of the room.

Chauvelin sat staring at it for a long moment, mastering his anger, and the fear that anger masked. *So my lord will throw me to the wolves,* he thought, testing the idea, and found he could view it without great surprise. *So I will find a reason for him to have to keep me, and I think I will begin with finding something, or something more, to discredit ji-Imbaoa. Not that that will be that hard, or particularly unpleasant.* He pushed himself slowly to his feet, wincing a little at the ache in his knees. Outside the window, the sky had lightened visibly, the sky even to the west, over the city, showing clear signs of dawn. There was no point in going back to bed—the conference had been scheduled at ja-Erh-'aoa's convenience, and he himself had other appointments later in the day. Better to eat—*assuming the kitchen staff is awake, which they had better be*—and then take steps to deal with this.

He returned to his own rooms to change clothes, discarding the unflattering bodysuit and heavy coat with a sigh of relief. One of the servants—the hsai preferred living beings to mechanicals; service given and received in kinship was the glue of their society, and this morning Chauvelin was oddly comforted by his place in the hierarchy—had laid out everyday clothing, shirt and plain trousers, and a less formal coat of green brocade. The fabric was of Burning Bright weave, shot through with strands of the iridescent pearl-silk rendered from the discarded shells of the sequensa after the more expensive paillettes had been cut, and he hesitated for a moment, wondering if it would be more tactful to wear something less obviously identified with his world of origin, but then shrugged the thought aside. The damage was done; it was better to pretend he hadn't heard about the rumors. And besides, the cool drape of the fabric was a reassuring luxury. He slipped it on, running one hand down the unshaped lapel just for the feeling of the heavy silk under his touch, and left the room.

The sun was fully up now, the rising light pouring in through the seaward windows, casting long shadows toward the city below the Ghetto cliff. The breakfast room, over-

looking the gardens that dropped in terraces toward the cliff
edge and the Old City, was pleasantly shadowed, only the
food tables softly lit by the stasis fields. Chauvelin smiled
with real enjoyment for the first time that day, and crossed to
the tables to pour himself a cup of flower-scented tea.

"Sia Chauvelin."

He turned to face the speaker, recognizing his steward's
voice, and saw a second person, jericho-human rather than
hsaii, standing beside the steward, so close and so exactly
even in the doorway that their shoulders touched. The
woman was part of ji-Imbaoa's household, and Chauvelin
set the tea aside untouched.

"Yes?"

"My lord wishes to speak with you," ji-Imbaoa's servant
said, her voice completely without expression.

"The Visiting Speaker has only just returned from the
city," the steward murmured, under lowered lashes. Her fingers curled with demure humor as she spoke.

Chauvelin lifted an eyebrow, his mind racing. *What the
ninth hell could ji-Imbaoa want, at this hour, when he's
bound to be hung over, or still drunk, if I'm particularly un-
lucky? I should change to wait on him, but I'll be damned if
he deserves the honor*— "The Visiting Speaker will have to
pardon the delay," he said, and indicated the informal coat.

"My lord will excuse," ji-Imbaoa's servant said, still
without expression.

"As the Visiting Speaker wishes," Chauvelin said, and
could not quite keep the irony from his voice. "Iameis"—
that was his steward, who bowed her head in acknowledgment—"you'll join me for breakfast after this. We have
some things to discuss."

"Yes, sia," the steward murmured, and stepped aside.

Chauvelin looked at the other woman. "Lead on."

He let her conduct him through the ambassadorial palace,
as was proper, for all that he knew the building far better
than she ever would. She stayed the prescribed two paces
ahead of him and slightly to his right, unspeaking, and
Chauvelin watched her back, rigid under the black tunic, and
the short swing of her left arm. A conscript's mark was tat-
tooed into her biceps, just below the fall of the cap sleeve.

Chauvelin felt his eyebrows rise, controlled his expression instantly. *Why would anyone be stupid enough to trust ji-Imbaoa with pressed servants? Loyalty can only be created by favor, not by fear—though some of my own first masters were no joy to serve, but nothing like him.* He filed the observation for later use, and braced himself as the woman came to a stop outside the door of ji-Imbaoa's suite. They were technically Chauvelin's own rooms, by virtue of his rank as head of the ambassadorial household, but Chauvelin himself rarely used them, since any visitor of higher rank could usurp them. Ji-Imbaoa had taken particular pleasure in moving his household into the rooms, and Chauvelin had had to keep a sharp grip on his temper to keep from betraying the existence of a second group of rooms. Ji-Imbaoa would have been happy to move in there, at the expense of his own comfort, just to win a few points in *an'ahoba.*

"The ambassador Chauvelin," ji-Imbaoa's servant announced to the invisible security system, and the carved and lacquered doors swung open.

The Visiting Speaker Kugüe ji-Imbaoa je Tsinra-an stood in the center of the suite's reception room, feet firmly planted on the silk-weave carpet that lay before the chair-of-state. *At least he hasn't chosen to take the chair,* Chauvelin thought, and suppressed his anger as he saw the mud on ji-Imbaoa's feet, caked between the claws and trampled into the carpet. It was a familiar way of showing power, but Chauvelin added it to the Visiting Speaker's account: the carpet was too beautiful to be treated as part of *an'ahoba.*

"Ts'taa." The word was untranslatable, carrying contempt and impatience and a concise statement of relationship, superior to inferior. Chauvelin raised his eyebrows, hoping that ji-Imbaoa had finally made a mistake—he and the Visiting Speaker were too close in the hierarchy for that to be anything but a deliberate and deadly insult—and realized with regret that ji-Imbaoa was addressing the woman servant.

"You are careless, and slow, and I am diminished by your habits." Ji-Imbaoa glanced sideways then, toward Chauvelin, and added, *"Chaoi* have so much to learn."

He had used the shortened term, the one that had once

meant "slave." The woman's shoulders twitched once, but she mastered herself, and bowed deeply. "I abase myself. I beg my lord's forgiveness."

Ji-Imbaoa waved a hand in dismissal, and the woman turned away, but not before Chauvelin saw the bright spots of color flaring on her cheekbones. *It's not wise—it's downright stupid—to abuse your servants to get back at your enemies.* He said, in his most neutral voice, "And yet the All-Father commends the practice."

Ji-Imbaoa's head lowered, suspiciously, but he said nothing. Chauvelin waited, running a quick and appraising glance down the Visiting Speaker's mostly humanoid body. Fingerclaws and spurs were painted a vivid red, the spurs protected only by a small cap of filigree-work. The bright ribbon clusters that flowed from bands around his upper arms, forming his only clothing, were badly crumpled, and Chauvelin glanced lower. The salmon-pink tip of ji-Imbaoa's penis was only just visible at the opening of the genital sheath: still drunk enough to relax some inhibitions, but sobering.

"I've summoned you because I've been hearing worrisome news," ji-Imbaoa said abruptly. *News you should already know about,* his tone implied.

Chauvelin murmured, "Indeed?" They were close enough in rank to omit honorifics in informal speech, and ji-Imbaoa had used the common forms.

Ji-Imbaoa's hands twitched, as though he regretted his choice, but he could not change modes without losing face. "You have an agent in the city, a *houta,* Ransome, it's called."

"Ransome is under my patronage, yes," Chauvelin answered. "He's been *min-hao* for some years." The gap between *houta,* nonperson, and client-kinsman was vast; Ransome needed the respect and protection of *min-hao* status.

Ji-Imbaoa flicked his fingers, dismissing the difference. "Decidamio Ghrestil-Brisch is showing a great deal of interest in him. I wonder why."

And so do I, Chauvelin thought. He said aloud, "There are a number of reasons that Damian Chrestil might be interested in Ransome, not least that Ransome's an imagist of some note in the city.''

''That may be,'' ji-Imbaoa said, ''but what I have seen is that Damian Chrestil—or that woman, his whore—wants very much to lure your agent back into the Game. Why would that be?''

''I don't know,'' Chauvelin said.

''Such pressure against an agent of yours, I'd think you'd want to know what's going on. They leave lures on all the nets, hints and pressures. It's not like Damian Chrestil to care about the Game—''

''Cella, his mistress''—Chauvelin laid the lightest of stresses on the word—''is a well-known Gamer, however, and Ransome was a notable for a long time.''

Ji-Imbaoa flicked his fingers again. ''I think it's worth investigation.''

Chauvelin sighed. ''So do I.''

''And I also think,'' ji-Imbaoa went on, as if the other hadn't spoken, ''that it would be worth doing what Damian Chrestil wants, if only to find out what's going on.''

''If it seems a reasonable risk,'' Chauvelin said softly. ''I don't send my people into difficult situations unprepared.''

''Of course, if he can tell you what they want,'' ji-Imbaoa said, equally softly, ''it wouldn't be necessary.''

''As you say.'' Chauvelin got a grip on his temper with an effort, knowing his anger was sharpened by fear. ''Will that be all? I have business this morning—''

Ji-Imbaoa cut him off with a gesture. ''There is one other matter. This Ransome: you say he's not *houta* but *min-hao?*''

''Yes.'' Chauvelin gave no other explanation, uncertain where this would lead.

''Then there is a matter of charges lodged against him on Jericho, which are actionable if he is *min-hao.*''

''At the time, he was *houta,* and served sentence on appropriate charges,'' Chauvelin said. *Not now,* he thought, *not now, of all times, to bring that up. Christ, it was fifteen years ago, and he spent time in jail; that ought to be over and done with.* But it had been a matter of *an'ahoba,* a game that Ransome played with regrettable skill and no status to match it—*and I should have known this would come up at the worst possible time. I can deal with it.*

"The larger matters still stand, in court record." Ji-Imbaoa made a small gesture, almost of satisfaction. "But I trust you will handle these matters appropriately."

"Of course," Chauvelin said, in his most colorless voice. *Twice in one day—that's twice someone's threatened me, and it's not yet midmorning. Not one of my better days.*

"I am sure," ji-Imbaoa said, and gestured polite dismissal. Chauvelin bowed his thanks, and let himself out into the hallway.

He made his way back to the breakfast room through corridors that were slowly filling with people, responding mechanically to the respectful greetings of his household. *Three things,* he thought, *three things I have to do. Find the weaknesses in ji-Imbaoa's household so that I can counter his threats, find out who leaked this report of mine, and then find out why Damian Chrestil wants Ransome back in the Game. And why it should worry ji-Imbaoa so much. Which means I will have to talk to Ransome: it doesn't do to have him keeping secrets from me.* He paused in the door of the breakfast room, mentally reordering his list, then went in to give orders to the waiting steward.

DAY 30

Damian Chrestil woke to sunlight and the steady sway of the
john-boat against the forward mooring. The stern tie had
parted in the night. He was certain of it even before he
stopped blinking, and moved his head out of the thin bar of
sunlight that shone in through the gap between the snuggery's canvas top and the side of the boat. He was angry
even before he remembered what lay next to him in the
bunk. It was his fault, the stranger's—he had been the one to
place the stern tie—and he propped himself up on one elbow
to study the situation, and the body beside his. He couldn't
remember the stranger's name, nor very clearly why he had
picked him up the night before; whatever had been interesting or endearing had vanished with his clothes. *Slumming,
certainly*—and the stranger turned over onto his side, dragging the thin sheet with him. That was quite enough, especially now that the inevitable headache was starting behind
his eyes. Damian kicked away the rest of the sheet and
reached for his discarded clothes, wriggling awkwardly into
briefs and shirt and trousers. The stranger—*whoever he is*—
was lying on top of the storage compartments. There was
nothing useful in them, not in a borrowed boat, but Damian
added the extra inconvenience to his account anyway, and
crawled out of the snuggery to deal with the stern tie.

Luckily, he had had the sense to pick a quiet lay-by. The
john-boat was swinging only sluggishly, the soggy impact of
the hull against the piling barely audible over the gentle slap
of the water, not even enough to bruise the paint. He made
his way aft along the sun-warming decking, and as the boat

swung in against the pilings, caught the dangling ring and made the tie fast. He stood there for a moment, balancing automatically against the deck's gentle heave, and blinked up at the sky and the white-hot light. The john-boat lay at the bottom of a blue-toned canyon. Shadowed factory buildings rose six stories high along either bank of the canal, their unlit windows showing only blank glass. This was not a delivery-way; there were no lesser docks or vertical line of gaping doors beneath an overhanging cranehead. It was just a traffic alley, not much used—it might even once have been a natural stream, by the gentle curve of its banks. The rising sun was pouring down from the near end of the channel, a wedge of almost solid light that turned the murky water to liquid agate. No one was moving on the narrow walkways that ran alongside the factories; no one else was tied up to the mossy pilings, or tucked under the cool shadow of the piers. He made a face—the heavy sun was doing nothing for his head-ache—and went forward again, shielding his eyes from the shards of light that glinted off the water.

The stranger was still asleep in the snuggery, face now turned to the empty pillow beside him. Damian Chrestil squatted in the entrance to the cavelike space, staring into air turned honey-gold by the worn cover, and felt a detached malevolence steal over him. Why should *he* sleep, when Damian himself was awake, and feeling unpleasing? There was nothing in the round face and showily muscled body that aroused the least compassion; his thin mustache was in-tolerable. *I must give up slumming,* he thought, and leaned sideways to release the lock that held the cover's frame erect. He caught the nearest hoop as the wind took it, guiding it down onto the deck. The frame folded neatly, as it was supposed to, with only a soft creak from the well-oiled mechanism, and the cover collapsed into a rumpled U-shape at his feet. The stranger slept on.

Damian stood for a moment longer, glaring down at him, automatically tugging his own thick hair into a neat queue. He remembered perfectly well *how* he'd acquired the stran-ger—he was a bungee-gar, and C/B Cie., the holding group that managed the Chrestil-Brisch import/export interests, had successfully received a shipment of red-carpet, the fun-

gus that fed the family distilleries. Red-carpet was expensive
enough on its own, especially on a world that had few native
sources of alcohol, valuable enough to justify employing
bungee-gars, but it had also served to cover the two capsules
of lachesi that had traveled with the declared cargo. Oblivion
was made from lachesi, and Oblivion was legal inside the
Republic, but the Republican export taxes on drugs were deliberately high. Evading those duties not only increased his
own profits, but allowed him to do favors for two important
parties, one in the Republic, the other in Hsaioi-An. And that
was how Burning Bright had survived free of control by either of the metagovernments: the web of favors given and
received that made it entirely too dangerous for strangers to
interfere in Burning Bright's internal politics. It was never
too early to start collecting favors, either, not when he intended to be governor in five years.

The stranger shifted uneasily against the mattress, drawing Damian out of the pleasant daydream. His head was really throbbing now—*Oblivion and bai-red rum, not a wise
combination*—and he wondered again why he'd invited the
stranger aboard. He was decent-enough looking—a dark
man, young, canalli dark, with coarse waves in his too-long
hair, heavy muscles under the skin, and buttocks Damian
could vaguely remember describing as "cute"—but not
cute enough, not with that silly mustache shadowing his full
mouth. He hadn't been that good a fuck, either: if the previous night's performance had represented his sexual peak, his
future partners were in for some serious disappointment.
Damian slipped his foot under the sheet, flipped it nearly
away. The stranger rolled over, groping blindly for it, mum-
bling something that sounded regrettably like *darling,* and
fetched up with his shoulder resting on the edge of the boat.
Damian Chrestil smiled slowly, and stepped onto the bunk
beside him, his feet sinking only a little way into the hard
foam of the mattress. He dug his foot under the stranger's rib
cage, saw him start to roll away automatically. The stranger's eyes opened then, a sleepy and entirely too cocksure
smile changing to alarm as Damian tipped him neatly out of
the boat. Instinct kept him from yelling until he surfaced
again.

"What the hell—?"

"Rise and shine." Damian smiled, some of his temper restored, and turned his attention to the mess in the snuggery.

The stranger trod water easily, shaking his hair out of his eyes, but knew better than to try to climb back aboard. "What'd I do?" he asked plaintively, and pushed himself a few strokes farther down the channel, out of reach of the cargo-hooks racked along the gunwales.

Damian paused, the stranger's clothes in one hand. He had them all now, except for one crumpled shoe, and he found that almost in the instant he realized it was missing, tucked in between the mattress and the bulkhead. He rolled them all together into a compact ball, and tossed it, not into the canal as he'd intended, but up onto the walkway between the pilings. It was not, after all, entirely the stranger's fault.

"I have work to do," Damian said.

For an instant it looked as though the stranger might protest, but Damian scowled, and the other lifted both hands in dripping apology, the water drawing him down for an instant.

"Fine." The stranger stopped treading water, lay back, and let the current take him, exerting himself only when he spotted the splintering ladder nailed to one of the piers.

Damian turned away, his mood lifting, and stepped out onto the narrow bow platform to loosen the tie there. His headache was fading now, in the morning air, was just an occasional pang behind his eyebrows. He could hear splashing as the stranger hauled himself up out of the canal, but did not bother to watch, walked aft instead and loosed the stern tie. He pushed hard against the piling, edging the stern toward the main current, and stepped down into the shallow steering well to hit the start sequence. The engine whined, then strengthened as the solar panels striping the deck woke to sunlight and began feeding power to the system, supplementing the batteries. The john-boat had already caught the main current, was drifting stern first toward the shadow of the factories. He swung the wheel, felt the rudder bite, tentative at first, then more solid as the propellers came up to speed, and eased open the throttle. The john-boat slowed even as the stern, the steering well, slipped into the wall of

shadow. He felt the sudden chill on his shoulders, was
blinded, looking out into the light, and then the propellers hit
the speed that counteracted the current. The boat surged
back into the sunlight, the water churned to foam in its wake.
On the walkway, the stranger was shivering even in the sunlight, stamping his feet to let the worst of the water run off
before he pulled on his clothes. Damian Chrestil wondered
again, briefly, precisely who he was, and opened the throttle
further, letting the pulse of the engine reverberate between
the factory walls.

It was good to be back on the canals again, if only for a
few hours, and he gave himself up to the pulse of the steering
bar and the kick of the deck beneath his feet. You never really lost the skill, once learned; would always be able to run
a john-boat, but it was good to feel the old ease returning. He
grinned, and gave his full attention to the delicate job of
bringing the boat out of the alley and into the feeder canal
that led down to the Factory Lane and the Inland Water.
There wasn't much traffic yet, none of the swarming mob of
gondas that would fill the lane and the service canals in an
hour or so, carrying midrank workers to their supervisory
jobs. The water buses that carried the ordinary workers to
the assembly lines had been and gone, were tied up in the
parking pools along the edge of Dry Cut to wait for the evening shift change. He reversed the propellers, cutting speed,
and slipped the john-boat into the buoyed channel, bringing
it neatly into line behind a barge piled high with shell scrap.

A light was blinking amber in the center of the control
panel, had been for a few minutes, since before he left the
feeder canal. He eyed it irritably, but knew he could not ignore it any longer. "Check-in," he said, and the screen lit,
the compressed in-house iconage skittering into place in the
tiny display. He scanned it quickly, still with half an eye on
the traffic in the channel, saw nothing that required his instant attention. He was about to switch off when the string of
messages vanished, and a second message replaced them:
*Jafiera Roscha received third endangerment citation; please
instruct.*

Damian Chrestil stared at the message for a long moment,
all his attention focused on the tiny characters, and had to

swerve sharply to avoid a channel buoy. He knew Roscha,
all right: one of C/B Cie.'s better john-boat drivers, competent, aggressive, not one to ask awkward questions when she
had a job to do. She was also what the canalli politely called
accident-prone, except that she usually caused the accidents.
He shook his head, said to the speaker mounted just below
the screen, "Check in, direct patch to the wharfinger. Autho-
rization: Damian Chrestil."

There was a moment of silence as the system hunted for
an unused uplink, the hissing static barely audible over the
engine and the rush of water along the hull, and then the day
dispatcher said, "I'm sorry, Na Damian, but Na Rosaurin's
on another line. Can I give her a message, or will you hold?"

"Give her a message," Damian said. "Tell her to find
Roscha and bring her in. I want to talk to her. And get me a
copy of this endangerment complaint."

"Absolutely, Na Damian." The dispatcher's sharp voice
did not change, but Damian could imagine the lifted eyebrows. "I'll pass those messages to Na Rosaurin, and put out
a call for Roscha."

"Thanks, Moreo," Damian said, and added, to the system, "Close down."

The system chimed obediently, and a string of icons flickered across the screen, their transit too fast to be read.
Damian glared at the now-empty screen for a moment longer, then made himself concentrate on the increasing traffic
as he came up on the buoy that marked the turn onto the Inland Water. He would deal with Roscha later.

The Water, the massive deep-water channel that bisected
Burning Bright, was as crowded as ever. Enormous cargo
barges wallowed along in the main channel, warned away
from the faster, lighter john-boat traffic by lines of bright-
orange buoys. Dozens of tiny, brightly painted gondas
flashed in and out of the double channels, day lights glittering from their upturned tails. Damian swore at the first to
cross his path, matching his words to the jolting rhythm of
the swells, and felt the john-boat kick as it crossed the
gonda's wake. He lifted his fist at the gonda driver, and got a
flip of the hand in return. He swore again, and swung into
the lane behind a seiner, its nets drawn up like skirts around

the double boom. It wallowed against the heavy chop—
Storm was only two days away, and the winds had already
shifted, were driving against the current, setting up an
unusual swell. The seiner's holds were obviously full: on its
way back from the sequensa dredging grounds off the
Water's Homestead Island entrance, Damian guessed, and
throttled back still further to clear its heavy wake. It was
likely to be the last cargo they'd see for a few weeks, until
Storm was past.

Even at the slower pace, it didn't take long to come opposite the mouth of the Straight River, and he slowed again to
thread his way sedately through the bevy of smaller craft that
swarmed around the entrance. The main wharfs loomed
beyond that, massive structures filling in the bend in the
bank between the Straight and the channel that led to the
Junction Pool and the warehouse districts beyond. He felt a
distinct pang of regret as he edged the john-boat into the
channel that led to his own docks—*if not for business, and if
not for Roscha in particular, he could have spent more of the
day on the Water*—and transformed it instantly into anger. It
was time Roscha learned her lesson: that was all. He edged
the john-boat between the barges tied up at MADCo.'s end-
of-dock terminal, and let himself drift down easily, nudging
the boat along with short bursts of power, to fetch up against
the worn padding almost directly beneath C/B Cie.'s antique
ship poised against a flaring sun. A familiar face looked
down at him—Talaina Rosaurin, one of the wharfingers—
and a couple of dockers ran to catch the lines.

"Morning, Na Damian. I've the day's plot set up, and
Roscha's on her way in," Rosaurin said.

Damian nodded in acknowledgment, and leaned sideways
to catch the webbing that covered the fenders. He held the
john-boat steady with one hand and tossed the stern rope up
onto the dock. The nearest docker caught it, began automatically looping it around the nearest bollard. "Thanks, Rosaurin. Finish the tie-up, will you?"

It was not a request. The wharfinger nodded, and dropped
onto the bow.

"I'll take a look at the plot as soon as I've seen Roscha,"

Damian went on, and swung himself easily up onto the dock. "Send her in as soon as she gets here."

"Right, Na Damian," Rosaurin said, but Damian was already walking away.

His office was in a corner of the main warehouse, insulated from the noise and smell of the moving cargoes by a shell of quilted foam-board, and well away from the wharfingers' station at the end of the pier. He threaded his way past the gang of dockers busy at the cranes unloading the barge that had brought the drop capsules in from the Zone, and glanced sharply into the open cargo space. He was moderately pleased to see that only two capsules remained to be brought onto the dock, and made his way past a whining carrier into the shadows of the warehouse. A pair of factors looked up at his entrance, and the taller of the two touched his forehead and came to intercept him, leaving the other to preside over the newly opened drop capsule.

"I'm sorry, Na Damian, but there's some minor spoilage in this shipment."

"How lovely." Damian bit back the rest of his response, said instead, "Finish checking it and give me a report. Is it TMN again?"

The factor nodded. "I'm afraid so."

"I need to talk to them," Damian said, and continued on toward the office. The door opened to his touch, reading his palmprint on the latch, and admitted him to the narrow lobby, empty except for the secretary pillar that guarded the inner doorway. The sphere that balanced on the truncated point of its slender pyramid glowed pale blue, tinged with green at the edges; threads of darker blue danced in its center, shaping a series of brief messages. At least two of the code-strings signaled longer messages backed up in the system—probably from his siblings, if they were sent here—but he stepped past the pillar into the inner office.

Behind him, the secretary said, in its cultured artificial voice, "Na Damian, you have messages waiting."

"Oh, shut up," Damian Chrestil said, and closed the door behind him.

He kept clean clothes in storage here, and there was a small but comfortable bath suite tucked into one corner of

the space. He showered and shaved, washing away salt and
sweat and with it the last holiday feeling of freedom, took
two hangover capsules, and dressed quickly in the shirt and
trousers and short jacket that he found in the storage cell. He
spent a little extra time coaxing his thick mane of hair into a
kind of careful disorder: he was vain about his hair, thick
and naturally gold-streaked brown, and the fact that it looked
good long did something to make up for the way the fashion-
able long coats sat lumpishly on his thin body. Willowy was
good, scrawny was not, and he was forced to dress accordingly.

He returned to the inner office, and settled himself at the
apex of the chevron-shaped desk. The smaller secretary
globe—really just an extension of the larger machine in the
lobby—chirped softly at him, and he swung to face it.

"Well?"

"You have mail in your urgent file."

"Well, isn't that pleasant," Damian said. "How many
items?"

"Two."

"Print them." Damian Chrestil ran his hand over the shadowscreen to light the various displays set on and in the
desktop, then leaned back in his chair as the tiny mail printer
whirred to life. It buzzed twice, chuckled briefly to itself,
and spat a sheet of paper with an all-too-familiar pattern.
Damian took it, scowling down at the dark-blue border
marks of a formal Lockwarden complaint sheet, and scanned
the sharp printing. Roscha, it seemed, had excelled herself—
or had she? He read the complaint a second time, more carefully, then set the sheet aside, frowning. The complainant's
name was unfamiliar, but he was a journeyman member of
the Merchant Investors' Syndicate, and the MIS was particularly hostile to C/B Cie. It would be nice to know just what,
or even who, had persuaded the man to file a formal complaint: the threat to throw him off the cliff face was not, on
balance, a likely cause, at least not in a bungee-gar bar like
the Last Drop. He fingered the shadowscreen again, putting
the complainant's name into a basic inquiry program, and
glanced at another screen, this one filled with the running
reports from the factors working on the cargo they'd col-

lected the night before. Roscha would have to learn better, however; for a start, she could pay her own fines.

"Na Damian," the secretary said. "Jafiera Roscha is here."

Damian paused, flicked a spot on the shadowscreen to mute the various displays. "Send her in."

The door opened almost at once, and a woman stood for an instant outlined against the lobby's buttery light. She was tall, and exquisitely built, her waist narrow between perfectly proportioned breasts and hips. Snug trousers and a dock-worker's singlet only emphasized that perfection; the light jacket that trailed from one hand was a shade of indigo that matched her eyes. Damian had forgotten—he always forgot, remembered again each time he saw her—just how striking she was, and despite the previous night felt a stirring of interest in his groin. Roscha came forward into the light, the corners of her wide mouth drawn down in an attempt neither to smile nor frown, and Damian slid the complaint across the desktop at her.

"What the hell was this?"

Roscha took it warily, studied the printed message, her eyes flicking back and forth between the paper and the other's face. Somehow, despite the hours she spent on the Water, she had kept her skin dazzlingly fair, the color of coffee cream; her red hair flamed against her shoulders, held out of her eyes by a strip of black ribbon. More black bands—braided ribbons or strips of leather—circled each wrist, and Damian recalled himself sternly to the business at hand.

Roscha set the paper carefully back on the edge of the desk. "I guess I had too much to drink last night."

"I guess you should be more careful where you drink," Damian answered.

Roscha shrugged, looking rather sullen. "There were a bunch of us, celebrating, and enough of us making noise. I don't know why they picked on me."

"Just accident-prone, I guess," Damian said.

Roscha looked away, not quickly enough to hide the flash of anger. "I just got carried away. I'm sorry."

"I don't pay my people to get carried away," Damian

Chrestil said. "I pay you to do your job, and do what I tell you. Not to go around collecting complaint sheets." He glanced down at the slip of paper again. "Do you even know this man?"

Roscha looked at the intricately patterned carpet, visibly mastering her temper. "By sight, mostly, and I know the name—he's in the Game, I've seen him playing on the nets. I did know he works for the MIS."

"Do you know what he does for them?"

"Works for one of the factors, I think," Roscha answered. "Computer jockey."

"Ah."

In spite of his best efforts, there was enough satisfaction in Damian's voice that the wary look in Roscha's eyes faded to something more like curiosity. Damian glared at her, and she met his stare with a stony face.

"They give you a choice," he said, after a moment. "Pay the fine, a hundred and fifty *real,* or take it to court. You'll pay."

There was another little silence, Roscha's too-large mouth thinning slightly, and then she said, without inflection, "I don't have that much in my account."

Damian looked at her for a long moment, and she returned the stare unflinching. A little color might have touched her wide cheekbones, but it was hard to tell. "All right," he said, and ran his hand over the shadowscreen. The second printer, the one loaded with draft forms, chirred softly under the desktop, and spat a slip of soft paper. "Here, give this to Rosaurin, she'll give you a voucher—and I'll stop you twenty-five *real* a paycheck to cover it. Agreed?"

"Agreed." Roscha still looked grim, but the tight set of her mouth eased a little.

Damian nodded, and slid the draft across the desktop toward her. Roscha took it, pocketed it without looking at the faint printing. "Right, then," Damian said, and the woman turned away, accepting that dismissal. Even before the door had closed behind her, Damian reached for the shadowscreen, raising the priority of his inquiry about the MIS complainant. A member of the Merchant Investors, even a low-ranking one, who was also a computer jockey and who

was around his warehouses often enough for Roscha to recognize him by sight, was a man who would bear watching. It
just might explain how local Customs had come to question
a shipment of his last month. On the whole, he thought, it
was worth paying Roscha's fine—he might not even bother
taking all of it out of her check.

He sighed then, and turned his attention back to the waiting messages. As he'd expected, his eldest sibling, Altagracian, the Chrestil-Brisch Pensionary, was at the top of the
list. Damian scanned the curt message—*call at once*—but
dumped it into a holding file without answering. Chrestillio
always overreacted; he could wait a little longer.

The secretary chimed again, and said, "There is an incoming message under your private and urgent code. Do you
wish to accept?"

Damian frowned, but none of his siblings had that set of
numbers. "Yes. Put it on the main board."

The central panel of the unimpressive triptych on the far
wall—*I should commission something better,* he thought, not
for the first time—slid apart to reveal the main screen, and a
moment later the connect codes streamed across the black
glass. The Visiting Speaker Kugüe ji-Imbaoa looked out at
him, heavy body framed by the curtains of an enormous bed.

Ambassador Chauvelin does well for himself, Damian
thought, and hid a grin. He said aloud, "Good morning, Na
Speaker. I trust everything's well with you."

"Na Damian." The Visiting Speaker was making an effort to be polite, unusual for him. Damian Chrestil waited
warily.

"You had some concerns about one of the ambassador's
agents," ji-Imbaoa said abruptly, and Damian glanced involuntarily at the security telltales embedded in the desktop.

"Na Speaker, our conversation was rather more
secure—"

"I have taken precautions," ji-Imbaoa interrupted. "My
end of this transmission is safe."

The hissing accent made the words even more of a rebuke,
and Damian frowned, looking again at the security readout.
"So is mine, but it's not a chance I like taking."

"You had been concerned about this agent, this Ransome," ji-Imbaoa went on, and Damian resigned himself.

"Yes. I was and am." *And I've been trying my damnedest
to get him back into the Game and off the main nets. The
bastard spends too much time on the nets, he's bound to see
what I've done to move the lachesi—*

"I have told Chauvelin that you want Ransome back in
the Game," ji-Imbaoa went on, "and that I believe Ransome
should do what you want—so that we can find out what you
are up to, of course."

"Christ." Damian controlled himself with an effort, said
only, "Don't you think that's a little obvious, Na Speaker?"
And what if he actually does find out?

"I rely on your bait to be good enough." Ji-Imbaoa in-
spected his fingerclaws, a smug and satisfied gesture.

"As I relied on you to get him off the nets," Damian
snapped. "Na Speaker, if you want this cargo that you've
invested so heavily in to get where it's supposed to be going,
Illario Ransome has to be distracted."

"I do not understand why he is so important." Ji-Imbaoa
sat down abruptly on the bed, flicked claws in impatient dismissal.

*Because he's the best netwalker I've ever seen. And he
plays politics.* Damian said aloud, keeping a tight rein on his
temper, "Illario Ransome is brilliant on the nets. He is also
an imagist, he taps all the nets, all of them, he goes trawling
for images for his story eggs, and he remembers everything.
He's the only person who would be at the right place at the
right time to spot the paper trail, and the only one who has
enough outside information to put the pieces together. Does
that make it clear?"

There was a little silence, and then ji-Imbaoa looked
away. "Still, you should have what you want. He should be
distracted, investigating your Game."

"I hope so." Damian paused, considering. It might work,
at that, might give him the time he needed to—adjust—the
customs nets to accept his new cargo. If Ransome did as he
was told, of course, and if Cella's scenarios were enough to
catch his eye . . . But Storm was coming, too, and the first
few days of Carnival were celebrated on the nets, as well as

on the streets. The two things together might be enough to let him get away with it. "Have you gotten the destination codes?"

"I am still waiting," ji-Imbaoa said. "I will pass them on to you as soon as I have them, you need not worry."

I always worry, Damian thought, but said, "All right. The sooner the better, though, Na Speaker, because without them I can't get this cargo into Hsaioi-An." He paused, seeing annoyance in the sudden clenching of ji-Imbaoa's hands, made himself add, "Thanks for dealing with Ransome, though."

Ji-Imbaoa's hands relaxed. "We are in this together, Na Chrestil. Now, I have had an active night, and wish to sleep."

"Sleep well, then," Damian answered, and cut the connection. He leaned back in his chair, ran his hand across the shadowscreen to close down the link. The triptych slid slowly back into place over the now-empty screen, and he stared at it for a moment. *I wonder what it would cost me to commission Ransome to do a piece to replace it?* he wondered, and grinned at the thought. *It might keep him busy for a while, and he'd be furious: it's an insultingly minor job. Hell, it might be worth asking just to see the look on his face.* He fiddled with the shadowscreen, filing the thought for later consideration, and touched another icon to bring up the rest of his mail. The secretary, programmed to be helpful, appended a to-do list as well. Damian considered it for a moment, and succumbed to temptation. Rosaurin wanted him to approve the next week's shipping plot, and that was much more fun than the painstaking records-melding that needed to be done. He pushed himself away from his desk and out the door before he could change his mind.

DAY 30

Ransome half sat, half lay in the chair that conformed itself
to his thin body, barely aware of the shifting cushions that
held him exactly where he wanted to be. Images filled the air
around him, ghostly yet substantial-seeming, all but blocking out the cityscape spread out below the loft windows. The
windows dimmed again, cutting out the sunlight—they had
been dimming steadily since sunrise, following the house
programming—but Ransome did not notice, lost in the flickering narrowcasts that held and surrounded him. The implants set into the bones at the outer edges of his eye sockets
caught and amplified the conflicting signals; his wire gloves,
thin and flexible and warm as blood, let him sculpt the space
around him, defining each unreal volume according to his
whim. The offerings of half a dozen different narrownets
danced in the air around him: Gamers to his left, four different sessions played out in as many different venues, three
old, pretaped, the fourth a late-night session that had
dragged on into the morning. Faces and streets and shadows,
culled illegally from the Lockwardens' security systems,
wove in and through the other images, overlaying them with
a bizarre patchwork of morning light and shade. The matching audio murmured on a dozen channels from the speakers
at the base of the room's walls, backing the images with the
solidity of sound. His attention was fixed on a single image,
floating overhead, at the apex of the cone of light and noise:
flickering market glyphs from the port computers spun in
delicate linkage, legitimate public numbers and private taps
combined into a single database, strings of numbers com-

bined into a dazzling three-dimensional shape that had a weird organic beauty all its own.

He let the shapes wash over and around him, put out his hand to draw in another narrowcast band. The air glowed briefly amber, control icons sparking in the system space that he had placed within easy reach, and then cleared again. A woman's face appeared, a mask of white paint and strong black lines and the vivid red of her mouth; he watched for a moment and pushed it away, to one side of the dancing market numbers. For a brief instant, his hand seemed to sink into the image, marring its edge, and then it moved, obedient to his touch. He reached again into the control space, found the symbols and the tool he wanted, and a second image, identical to the delicate, complex shape that was the graphic representation of the elaborate transformational database overhead, appeared in the air in front of him. He chose another tool, the wires of his gloves growing faintly warmer around his hands in confirmation of the choice, and then reached for the shape. He wrapped his hands around it, squeezed gently, compressing it, until it hung in a space no more than a dozen centimeters in diameter. Some of the delicacy had vanished in the compression, become little more than texture. He frowned, and reached for a second tool, used its all-but-invisible point to pry the numbers apart, untangling the channels, until the various strands were distinct again.

He lay back against the shifting cushions, studying the image, set it slowly rotating in front of him. The shape derived from those twining numbers would be the main focus of one of his story eggs, a commission for a Syndic of the Merchant Investors, a woman who lived and died by the movements of the trade that created the numbers coiling in the air in front of him. He reached for the face that hung in the air beside it, brought it down, until the strands of numbers slowly writhed behind the mask, like DNA beneath the skin. It was interesting, but not, he thought, what was needed now; it detracted from the bizarre beauty of the shifting numbers. He banished the face with a wave of his hand, leaving only the intertwining numbers, bronze and green and all the shades of metal, floating in unreal space. He smiled,

contemplating it, and reached into the control space to pre-
serve the image in one of the dataspheres waiting linked to
the main consoles. The sphere would store both the algorithm that transformed the numbers to this graphic and the
formulae for the connections to the financial nets—even the
private ones, one of which had been donated by the client—
that provided the raw data. All that remained was to set the
image into a proper casing, and that was already waiting,
ready on the shelf: a smooth, pale green egg the color of old,
well-weathered copper, with streaks and spills of stronger
green, and the ghost of the metal showing through. He
smiled, savoring the satisfaction of a job well done, and
closed the particular volume.

A voice that had been speaking from one of the floor-
mounted receivers for some time now, he realized belatedly,
was calling his name.

"—Ransome, I know you're there. I can see your taps."
There was a brief pause, and then, reluctantly, "It's important, I-Jay."

Ransome sighed, suddenly aware that it was morning and
that he had been awake most of the night, and that it was
Chauvelin himself who was making this connection, not one
of the apparently numberless ambassadorial servants. He
muted the remaining images with a wave of his hand, and
reached into control space to connect himself with the communications channel. "I'm here."

"About time."

The familiar face, elegant and worn and lined beneath the
brown hair just going cloudy with grey, bloomed in the air
above him. Ransome winced, and moved it to a less domi-
nating position. "I was working," he said, and winced again
at the defensive note in his voice. "What is it?"

Chauvelin smiled slightly, sourly, a faint quirk of one corner of his long mouth. "I need to talk to you—not on the
nets. The Visiting Speaker has come up with some interesting information you and I need to discuss."

"Fuck the Visiting Speaker," Ransome said, and
Chauvelin's smile widened into something approaching
humor.

"A privilege not likely to be granted." Chauvelin's smile

vanished as quickly as it had appeared. "Tell me something, why would Cella Minter want you back in the Game?"

Ransome blinked, wondering where this question had come from, and what it really meant. Cella he knew, both as Damian Chrestil's mistress and as an accomplished Gamer, but only from a distance. "I've no idea," he said, and then, because it was usually best to tell Chauvelin the truth, "I didn't know she wanted me back Gaming."

"So ji-Imbaoa says," Chauvelin said, and held up a hand, forestalling any answer from the other. Ransome grinned, and let him continue. "And so it looks to me, too, looking at the nets. I tied in to some of the club gossip boards. There's a lot of talk about Ambidexter, and usually Cella hinting in the background that he ought to come back to show people how his templates are supposed to be played."

Ransome shrugged, felt his face go wooden. "Ambidexter's dead—"

In spite of himself, the words came out bitter, and it was the bitterness that Chauvelin answered. "You're not dead yet. I don't have time for self-pity, I-Jay, I need your help."

Ransome lifted both eyebrows, a deliberate imitation of Chauvelin's gesture. "You must be desperate." He paused then, shook his head, shaking away the bad temper that was becoming a habit with him. "I'm sorry. I don't know why Cella would want me on the Game," he said again. "Unless it's something Damian Chrestil wants?"

"I'd say that was highly likely," Chauvelin murmured. "Which raises the question of why he would want it. And that is something I don't want to discuss on the nets."

Ransome made another face, though he had to admit the wisdom of it. He himself was not the only netwalker on Burning Bright, or the only imagist who tapped unlikely lines looking for good sources. "I suppose you'll want me to come to you."

"Yes." Chauvelin's tone blended forbearance and the resignation of an adult dealing with a child. "I think that would be best."

Ransome laughed, gestured apology, miming the hsai gesture that linked wrist spurs. The scars where his implanted spurs had been removed touched briefly, an odd, unpleasant feeling; he jerked his hands apart without finishing the movement. Chauvelin said nothing, did not move at all, as though nothing had happened, and Ransome said, "I'll be there in an hour." He knew he sounded curt, made himself add, by way of further apology, "It'll take me a while to pull myself together. I was up all night working on a commission."

Chauvelin nodded. "May I see?"

"It's a private commission," Ransome said, with genuine regret—Chauvelin was one of the very few whose opinions mattered to him—then grinned suddenly. "But I've done something for you, I'll show you when I get there."

"That will be the first good thing that's happened all day," Chauvelin said. He gave a twisted smile, as though he regretted the admission, and said, in an entirely different voice, "In an hour, then." He cut the connection before Ransome could respond.

Ransome sighed, staring at the still-busy images without really seeing them, then brought his chair upright. The net taps whirled around him, readjusting themselves to his position, but he waved them away, then closed both fists to shut down the system. Glyphs and code-strings flickered past, too fast to be understood at more than the subliminal level, and then the pictures vanished. Ransome sighed again, stretching, feeling the long night's work claw at his back, the old familiar ache in the bones and tendons of his hands. He peeled off the tight gloves, wincing a little, and set them aside. His chest was tight, catching in his ribs; he could hear the fluids at the base of his lungs, a harsh rasp that cut each breath too short for comfort. He reached instinctively for the cylinder of Mist, flipping it backwards to unfold the face-mask, but stopped abruptly. The red light glowed under the trigger button, warning him that he had taken a dose within the last two hours. He stared at it for a second, his mind forming a curse to override the fear, then made himself set it aside.

"Input," he said aloud. "Housekeeper systems." The words caught in his chest, the lack of air catching him by surprise. He coughed, hard, the spasm driving painfully deep. His mouth filled with phlegm that tasted like bitter copper; he spat it into a sheet of tissue, and saw the familiar thick white laced with a froth of red. That was answer enough. ''Cancel,'' he whispered, voice harsh and strange to his own ears, but the room responded calmly.

''Input canceled.''

Ransome scowled, hating the sickness, hating the fact that his systems remembered that choked voice as his own, and pushed himself up out of the chair. The injector lay on the shelf where he kept the story eggs' shells. He went to get it, feeling the too-familiar giddiness, laid the cold tip against the veins of his neck as he had been taught, where the skin was more or less permanently reddened from the injections, and pressed the trigger. The machine stung once, painfully, and he imagined he could feel the drug spreading like cold fire under his skin. The doctors swore it was a hallucination, a common side effect. It felt real enough, and he stood for a long moment, waiting, eyes fixed on nothing, as the chill spread through his chest and down his right arm, and the pain eased and his breath came easier, the rattling in his lungs fading slightly. It had been three years since the maintenance drugs, the ones that had kept the white-sickness at bay, had failed him, as he had known they would: five to seven years, he could expect the injections to work, and then he was dead.

Ransome stuffed the injector into his pocket, made himself shower and shave and find a clean shirt and jerkin, going through the motions until the fear and anger had retreated again. White-sickness was common in hsai space, a common killer of jericho-humans; it was also incurable, though onset and death could be delayed for decades with the right drugs. It was just his bad luck to have shared a cell with a carrier, back on Jericho. *My mistake to have been on Jericho at all, to have worked for the Chrestil-Brisch in the first place . . .* He shook the thought away, and glanced for a final time in his mirror. He was looking haggard—*too little sleep; nothing new*—but the hectic flush from the injection still burned on his cheeks, two ugly, fake-looking spots of red. The black jerkin and trousers and the loose white shirt had been meant to complement his usual bone-white pallor. He suppressed the instinct to rub his face, to scrub the red away, and

reached instead for the handful of carved stones waiting on
his workbench. He slipped those into his pocket, and left the
loft, double-sealing the palmprint lock behind him out of
habit.

His flat was one of a dozen in a converted warehouse, pur-
chased cheap by one of the artists' cooperatives now that
most cargoes moved through the new Junction Pool cargo
lifts rather than the long way around, from the ramps at Dry
Cut along the Old Coast Road that skimmed the cliff edge.
The old warehouse districts were no longer convenient, or
profitable; the buildings that had not been converted to other
uses—light manufacture, particularly, and in this district the
embroiderers' shops that made the embellished fabrics that
were Burning Bright's primary export product—stood
empty, their windows cracked, frames emptied by last year's
Storm. The lift was occupied, as usual—there were enough
heavy-materials workers in the building to ensure that the
single lift was always in use or out of order—and Ransome
made his way down the side stairs. It had been a fire access
once, running along the outside of the building, and the outer
wall was pierced at intervals by narrow panels of wire mesh.
The air that flowed in was soft and heavy with the salt smell
of the canals, and warm with the promise of Storm. There
were more signs of approaching Storm in the corners of the
stair, or at least of the Carnival that took up most of the two-
week period: a raki bottle stood empty on each landing, and
the lowest level, where the walls were solid to prevent unau-
thorized access, stank of urine. Ransome made a face, and
stepped carefully over the puddles to unlock the gate.

The alleyway was crowded with denki-bikes and two- and
three-wheeled velocks, the latter chained to anything sub-
stantial enough to defeat a standard wirecutter, the denki-
bikes clustered around the charging bollards, a blue haze
showing where the security fields intersected. Ransome
reached cautiously into the tangle of cables and locks to free
his own machine, and winced as the fizzing security stung
his fingers. Then he backed the bike out of the tangle—for
once without setting off someone else's security system—
checked the power reserve, and climbed aboard. The machine was woefully underpowered, for his taste, but it was

serviceable, and better than the tourist-trolleys. He edged the throttle forward—the bike whined and shivered—and let it carry him sedately into the traffic stream.

He took the short road to the Ghetto where Chauvelin lived with most of the rest of Burning Bright's noncitizen residents, skirting the cliff edge above the delivery basins of Junction Pool, then cutting straight through the industrial zone past the spaceport at Newfields. A column of smoke and steam hung in the distance, the winds slowly bending and fraying it to nothing: someone was saving money on launch costs, flying chemical rockets. The pilots who ran the orbital shuttle would be cursing, Ransome thought, and smiled.

The ambassadorial residence stood on one of the highest points in the Ghetto—on all of the Landing Isle, the largest piece of the original landmass: the hsai liked heights, and most of Burning Bright's inhabitants didn't care. The household staff had been told to expect him. Ransome paused at the gate only long enough to identify himself—most of Chauvelin's household knew him by sight, after nearly fifteen years in the ambassador's service—and then a pair of hsai servants came out of the main house to meet him. The male took the denki-bike, and the hsaii—Chauvelin's steward Iameis je-Sou'tsian, Ransome realized with some surprise—bowed politely.

"Sia Chauvelin has asked me to bring you directly to the garden," she said, in tradetalk, and Ransome answered in low mian-hsai.

"I'm honored by the courtesy." *And very surprised by it,* he added silently. *What the hells is going on, to make me rate this treatment?* He followed without question, however—he knew better than to ask that question—and je-Sou'tsian brought him through the sudden cool of a service passageway, bypassing the main house, and led him out as suddenly onto a path that ran between tall walls of flowering hedge. Ransome blinked, momentarily confused, then oriented himself. This was the maze, a part of the garden derived from hsai tradition, and one that Chauvelin rarely used. Je-Sou'tsian followed the turns without hesitation, however—*maybe it is true,* Ransome thought, *that there re-*

ally is only one pattern in use on all the worlds of Hsaioi-An—and let them out through a red-lacquered gate onto the carefully landscaped lawn of the upper terrace. Chauvelin was waiting a few meters away, seated comfortably in the shade of a bellflower tree, a luncheon tray beside him and a data manager resting in his lap.

"Na Ransome is here," je-Sou'tsian said, and the ambassador looked up with an abstracted smile.

"Ransome. Join me, why don't you?" To je-Sou'tsian, he added, "Thank you. That'll be all."

"Yes, sia," the steward answered, bowing, and backed away.

Ransome made his way down the terraced slope, stepping carefully around the elaborately casual plantings. He was very aware of the ambassador's residence looming behind him, the sunlight polishing the whitestone walls and glinting off the long windows. It felt unpleasantly as though someone were watching him, and he seated himself deliberately on the wall that overlooked the lower terrace. Chauvelin glanced up at him, gave a quick smile, and Ransome smiled rather wryly in return. If it had been the cliff wall, overlooking the hundred-meter drop to the Old City, he would never in a thousand years have settled himself there, especially with Chauvelin sitting less than two meters from him, and they both knew it.

"So good of you to come," Chauvelin said, with only the lightest note of irony.

Ransome let his smile widen. "I was working," he said. "What is this about Cella, and the Game?"

"That's the very question I'd like you to answer," Chauvelin said.

Ransome spread his hands—a human gesture, not hsai, and deliberately so. "I don't know. I've been out of the Game for three years, I barely pay attention to the Game nets except when I'm trolling for images. I don't know what Cella wants—except that if she wants it, Damian Chrestil probably wants it, too."

Chauvelin nodded slightly, though Ransome could not be sure if the movement was a response to his words or to

something on his screen. "I need to know why. Ji-Imbaoa
came in this morning—"

"Sober?" Ransome murmured, with just the right note of
shock, and allowed himself a brief smile when the word surprised a laugh from Chauvelin.

"Mostly so. At any rate, he came to me complaining that
Damian Chrestil is interested in you, via Cella—he knows
you as my agent, so don't ask—and demanding to know
why. When I checked him out, I found the same thing: lots
of agitation to get you back into the Game, and usually
Cella's at the back of it. I want to know what's going on."

"I told you," Ransome began, and Chauvelin nodded.

"I know you've been working. A commission for Syndic
Leonerdes, and that big installation for the governor. But I
need to know what's going on, I-Jay. Ji-Imbaoa—well, I
won't bore you with hsai politics."

"Bore me," Ransome said.

Chauvelin grinned, sobered instantly. "Suffice it to say
that ji-Imbaoa has more influence than he should, and he
wants this done. And that's the other thing I want to find out:
why the hell should he be so worried about Damian Chrestil?"

Ransome shrugged one shoulder. "Maybe they had a bar
fight, their tastes seem similar enough. Though I don't think
Damian Chrestil drinks quite so much."

"Let me put it this way," Chauvelin said, and his voice
was suddenly devoid of all expression. "Ji-Imbaoa is worried enough to remind me that, since I made you *min-hao*,
you could still face charges in Hsaioi-An, for lese majesty."

"Lesser treason," Ransome murmured, through lips
grown suddenly stiff and unresponsive, "but still treason."

"Just so."

They sat in silence for a long moment, the only sounds the
faint whistle of the seabirds and the whine of a denki-bike
passing in the street. Ransome slipped his hand into his
pocket, found the handful of carved stones he had collected,
turned them over one by one. He had been glad to be tried as
houta back on Jericho; insults up the social scale, from person to person or from *min-hao* to a person, could be construed as a kind of treason, and the sentences for that were

more severe than they were for theft. Insults by *houta,* on the other hand, were "no more than the barking of dogs," or so the hsaii judge had said through the human translator, and therefore didn't count against him. Unfortunately, the hsai had a very long memory for insults.

He slipped one of the stones out of his pocket, fingering the delicate features without really looking at them. His eyes traveled instead beyond the lower terrace, beyond the Straight River, where he thought he could see the bow of the Crooked River, dividing the Old City from the Five Points District. It was a trick of the light, he knew that, of the hazy sunlight and the water-heavy air, that turned all distances vague and soft-edged, drowned in a blue-grey haze like a watercolor wash. Even so, his mind filled in the outlines, drew a second steely curve beyond the more solid line of the Straight. Five Points proper, the five projecting pieces of cliff edge where the descendants of the city founders lived, lay beyond that curve, invisible, tantalizing, and the third of the points belonged to the Chrestil-Brisch. He had been there once, years ago—before Chauvelin, before Jericho, before he'd even thought of leaving Burning Bright, when he had still thought he could play certain games without penalty even though he'd been born poor canalli, child of a Syncretist Observant, playing games on equal terms with the second child of Chrestil-Brisch. . . .

He put that thought aside. Cella Minter was nudging him back into the Game, and the hand behind her was Damian Chrestil's: that was what mattered now, that and whatever hsai politics Chauvelin was tangled in. Chauvelin had been adopted into the tzu Tsinra-an, and was relatively a modernist and a moderate even within the moderate faction that dominated the court. But where he stood in the greater conflict that lay behind the factional quarrel, Ransome had never been completely sure. Hsaioi-An wanted to control settled space—the hsai needed to control settled space, because their culture could not admit that other species equalled their own; the whole elaborate fiction of adoptions and legal kin-species had been set up to allow the hsai to pretend that other beings were really a part of their own species. Chauvelin had embraced that fiction, heart and soul, or he wouldn't be here.

But he had been careful, all the years Ransome had known him, never to say whether he supported the wider definition of kinship, one that would eliminate the concept of *houta* and replace it with an acknowlegement of a basic kinship between all intelligent species, or the older, more conservative version. Most conscripts Ransome had known supported the old, narrow definition: why should others get for nothing what they had worked so hard to win? That sort of selfish self-aggrandizement wasn't Chauvelin's style—but then, it was equally unlike Chauvelin to keep silent even about risky political beliefs. More likely, Chauvelin had thought of himself as hsaie for so long that it no longer occured to him to think of himself as involved in that debate. Chauvelin had made one thing very clear. If Ransome didn't serve Chauvelin's interests, Chauvelin would no longer be able to protect him. That knowledge had a sour taste, and he looked away, stared over his shoulder toward the shimmering towers of Newfields. Even at this distance, he heard a rumble like distant thunder, and squinted skyward in spite of knowing better, looking for the pinpoint light of an orbiter already long out of sight. He looked back, dazzled—the sun was starting the decline over the highlands, turning the sky to a white haze—and saw Chauvelin looking at him.

"The sound of money," Ransome said, and deliberately turned his back on the port. Chauvelin lifted an eyebrow, visibly decided the comment did not deserve an answer, and returned his attention to the data manager that rested on his lap. The subject was clearly closed, or else, Ransome thought, even Chauvelin was a little ashamed of himself for this one. He watched Chauvelin work for a little longer, the long hands busy on the input strip, the grey-brown hair fading even more in the afternoon light, the slight, faintly quizzical hint of a frown as he studied something on the screen. Ransome did not like being ignored, did not like being ignored after being threatened, said, not quite at random, "Do you think it's wise to annoy Damian Chrestil?"

"Why not?" Chauvelin's voice sounded bored, his eyes still on the screen in front of him, but Ransome got what he was looking for, the subtle shift of expression that meant the ambassador was listening closely.

"He's not a fool," Ransome said. "Or a child. They say he'll be co-opted to the Select next year."

"Is that what they say?" Chauvelin did not move, but Ransome smiled to himself, hearing the slight change in tone. He had confirmed something that Chauvelin had suspected—and a seat among the Select, the elite advisory council that handled much of Burning Bright's foreign policy, was the first step toward becoming governor.

"Among other things." Ransome lowered his eyes to look at the carved head, pinching it between his fingers, glanced up though his lashes to watch Chauvelin's response.

"Well, that's what I pay you for," Chauvelin said. "And for finding out what in all hells Damian Chrestil wants." He leaned back in his chair, stretching long legs in front of him, and touched the manager's screen. The machine shut itself down obediently, its chime muted in the heavy air. He was wearing a hsaie greatcoat over plain shirt and trousers, a sweep of unshaped river-green brocade that set off the weathered ivory of his skin. His hands were starting to betray his age. Ransome looked down at his own fingers, saw the same lines and shadows starting, tendons and bones starkly outlined under the roughened skin. Not that he was likely to see the end of the process: by the time he reached Chauvelin's age—and there were not ten years between them—he was likely to be dead.

"Among other things," he said again, putting aside the familiar recognition, and tilted his head toward the terrace, toward the hardscaping he himself had designed. Chauvelin nodded, acknowledging the point, and by coincidence a breath of wind shook the bellflower tree beside him, bathing them both in its musky perfume. *It would have been a nice effect,* Ransome thought, *if I could've planned it.*

Chauvelin set the data manager aside on the stones of the wall, leaned back in his chair, taking his time. The sunlight cast a delicate pattern of shadow over him, pouring down through the bellflower's fan-shaped leaves and striking deep sparks of color from the draped greatcoat. Even in the shadow, the lines that bracketed his mouth and fanned from the corners of his eyes were very visible. The crows'-feet tightened slightly, a movement that might become either a smile or a frown, and Ransome bit his tongue to try to copy the other's silence, to keep from speaking too soon. The bell-flower's leaves rustled gently, and another orbiter rumbled skyward.

"I have to know what he's up to," Chauvelin said at last. "You're the best chance I have for that."

Do you mean ji-Imbaoa, or Damian Chrestil? Ransome wondered. *Or both?* He sighed, looked down at the sculpted head that still rested in the palm of his hand. *I would have done this anyway, regardless of threat or flattery—or love or whatever it is that's between you and me, Tal Chauvelin. For the love of this game that's better than anything the Game has ever produced.* "All right," he said, easing himself off the terrace wall, and reached into his pocket for the rest of the handful of carved stones. Chauvelin looked up, one eyebrow rising slightly.

"You said you had something to show me?"

Ransome nodded. "Hold out your hand."

Chauvelin extended one long hand, both eyebrows lifting now, and Ransome opened his fist, letting the stones—grey-silver, a shower of frozen mercury—fall into the other's palm. Several of them bounced away before Chauvelin could catch them, but he made no move to gather them, sat staring at the four that remained in his hand. Ransome watched him turn the carvings, roll them curiously beneath one probing finger, then lean to pick up the ones that had fallen, one by one, until he had them all. The delicate faces, some white as the hazy sky, one dark as slate, the others grey and silver, stared at nothing with knowing, provocative eyes. Chauvelin nodded once, silent approval, looked up at the other man.

"I thought I'd pave your paths with them," Ransome said, and, slowly, smiled.

There was another little silence, and then Chauvelin nodded again, this time in agreement. "How soon can you have it done?"

"And in place?" Ransome paused, thinking. The idea of paving the paths was new, had come to him on the denki-bike ride from his loft; he hadn't even begun to work out the quantities he would need, or the time it would take for an automated workshop to fabricate them from his models. "A week, probably—no, Storm's coming, everyone will be working on Carnival stuff. A week and a half, two weeks, probably. Give or take a couple of days."

"I want them in place by my party," Chauvelin said.

Ransome frowned for an instant: he had forgotten how late it was, that tomorrow was the last day of High Spring, and the date of Chauvelin's annual grand reception. "I don't know," he said involuntarily, and Chauvelin nodded.

"I know. But I'm willing to pay double costs, and a rush bonus on top of it, if you can find a way to get it done."

"I can try," Ransome said, absurdly pleased by the demand. There were a few places that might be able to do the production run on this kind of notice—stonecrafters didn't get too much extra business for Storm, unlike most artisans—and Chauvelin's own gardeners could handle the installation. . . . This was one of the things he liked without reservation about Chauvelin: when he played patron, he did it in grand style. *And the money wouldn't hurt, either.*

"I mean it," Chauvelin said. "Post the costs on the house net, I'll authorize the draft."

"I'll do it," Ransome said, and added, knowing the workshops, "if I can."

Chauvelin nodded, smiling slightly, and Ransome turned away, not waiting for the steward to take him back out through the maze, walking up through the garden toward the house and the well-watched passage to the street.

PART TWO

EVENING, DAY 30

Lioe started for Shadows just after sundown, riding the tourist-trolley to the elevators at Governor's Point, then one of
the massive cars down the cliff face to Governor's Point
Below. The cab stand was empty; when she consulted the
information kiosk, fingering worn keys while her other hand
rolled the old-fashioned ball that grated in its socket, she es-
timated Shadows was about twenty kilometers away. She
hesitated, wondering if she should try one of the other clubs
the steward—*Vere, his name was, Vere Caminesi*—had men-
tioned, but when she checked the kiosk again Shadows was
the closest. She sighed, punched in the codes that would alert
the velocab companies to a waiting fare, and lowered herself
onto a stone bollard that seemed to exist to keep the cabs
from getting too close to their prospective passengers. It was
getting cool, would be a chill night, by her standards, and the
breeze that swept up from the southeast raised goosebumps
even under her jacket. It carried the faint tang, damp and
salty, of the sea that was never far from anyplace in Burning
Bright; brought with it too a whiff of heavy foliage from
household gardens, the delicate mustiness that rose from
basements, and even a momentary sharp taste of the oil that
tainted the Inland Water, gone as quickly as it had come. She
cocked her head, listening, but could not hear the dull poly-
phony of the bell buoys that tolled to mark the channel. She
knew she should not be surprised—at this point she was almost as far inland as one could be and still stay on the Wet
side of the Old Dike—but she was oddly, vaguely, disap-
pointed.

The cab appeared a few minutes later, the whine of its motor audible well before it turned the corner. Lioe rose to her feet, slinging the bag that held her Rulebooks and Gameboard more securely over her shoulder, was aware of the driver's frank stare as he keyed open the door to the passenger compartment.

"Evening, pilot." He had a young voice, a cheerful voice, that went oddly with the lined and weathered face. "Where you bound?"

Lioe had almost forgotten she was wearing the hat, this one a small toque, suitable for Gaming, that marked her as a pilot of the Republic. "A place called Shadows," she said. "I'm told it's on Face Road, at the center of the Dike in Dock Road District?"

She was reciting the address from memory—no house numbers here, but all the buildings had names and were then placed within the district according to the nearest landmarks—and was relieved when the driver nodded.

"You're a Gamer, then."

"That's right." Lioe levered herself into the narrow pod. It smelled of smoke and fish, an odd, unfamiliar combination, stronger as the low door closed behind her.

"It's a good club, Shadows," the driver said. "Or so they tell me. I'm a home Gamer, myself." The engine whined as he stood on his pedals to get the cab moving again.

Lioe leaned back cautiously against the thin padding, feeling the vibrations of the little motor through the soles of her feet. The cab swung left in a gentle arc that brought them out into a larger trafficway—not a busy street, only a few other vehicles, velocabs and pushcarts, moving between the bollards that marked the edges of the road. They swung left again, the driver hesitating for an instant to gauge the faster stream of traffic on the wider street, and then standing hard on his pedals to bring the cab up to their speed. The cab slid neatly into a gap between another velocab and an empty flatbed carrier belching steam, but Lioe was looking at the shape that soared above the street, cutting off the sky. The Old Dike was festooned with lights, strings and streamers of them flashing in sequence to warn off wandering helio pilots, but they only seemed to intensify the black mass of the wall itself. More light like fog flowed along its top, fading into the sky at least a hundred and fifty meters above them. Lioe shook her head, amazed and wondering, and the driver shot her a look of triumph.

"It's something, isn't it? That's the Old Dike. The first-in people built it to reclaim the Old City."

Lioe nodded, still staring, barely aware of the other vehicles now crowding the road. "What's that on top?" she asked, after a moment. "Another road?"

"That's Warden Street," the driver answered. "Runs all the way along the Dike, from Lockwarden Point to the Governor's House. There's good shopping up there, the best shops in town for fashion, if you're interested."

"Maybe," Lioe answered. It must've been one hell of a project, building that, she thought, even if Burning Bright's first-ins were a different breed from the usual first settlers. Burning Bright had never been intended to be anything but an entrepôt—could never have been anything else, at least under human settlement, given the minuscule landmass—and the first settlers had all been merchants and bankers, bent on turning the planet's favorable position astride the main hyperspace channel between the Republic and Hsaioi-An into solid profit. And they'd certainly done that: despite the best attempts of worlds like Ky and Attis/Euphrosyne, Burning Bright remained the busiest transshipment point for goods going from one metagovernment to the other. Even in the first years, the settlers would have had the capital to bring in the best technicians to build the Dike.

Traffic was picking up, more and more vehicles cramming the road, and crowds flowed along the walkways outside the brightly lit shops. Only the foodshops seemed to be open, but light and bright snatches of music spilled from their doorways, clear notes like plucked metal strings. She heard laughter as well, over the constant rumble of the crowd and the traffic, looked instinctively to see a woman caught in the blue-white light of a store's display window, her head thrown back, hair spilling in untidy curls around a lined, handsome face. Her skirt—no one wore skirts in the Republic, except for ethnic festivals—was starred with little mirrors, reflecting the store's lights like chips of diamond.

And then the cab was past her, and Lioe resettled herself against the padding, wondering what she had seen. A shape flashed through the pedestrians, a man's head and shoulders moving with unnatural quickness above the people surrounding him, and then he shot between two men and a bollard, darting into the traffic stream on a battered bicycle. No one used bicycles much in the Republic, either.

The road rose ahead of them, and Lioe was suddenly aware, over the noise of the crowds and the snarling rush of the assorted vehicles, of the dulled, steady tolling of a buoy bell. She leaned forward a little, and the driver said, before she could ask, "We're coming up on the Straight now."

There were more bicycles in evidence on this stretch of road, and on the high-arched bridge, as well as cabs and three-wheeled cycles and a handful of the motorized denki-bikes. Most of the cabs and human-powered vehicles turned right or left onto the street that paralleled the as-yet-invisible river. As the driver stood on his pedals again to coax the cab up the steep rise, Lioe began to understand the reason. She could guess why there didn't seem to be many fully motorized craft on Burning Bright—fossil resources were scarce and inaccessible, electrics were still impractical for heavy loads, and solar was even less practical on something as small as a velocab—but it was still strange to feel the cab wavering from side to side as the driver added his muscle power to the engine's whining output. Strange, and somehow improper. Lioe was glad when the cab reached the top of the arch, and started the long glide down.

Across the bridge, the streets were quieter. The buildings turned blind faces to the road, and there were few pedestrians. Once or twice the cab crossed a wider street, both times with trees or flowers growing in a center island, framed by soft lights, and Lioe caught a glimpse of figures moving in that pastel radiance. More often, the cab flashed over the low hump of a bridge, and she saw shards of light reflected from the canal water less than two meters below. The driver—he had caught his breath, after the bridge—said, "This is Dock Road—Dock Road District, that is."

"Mmm." Lioe glanced from side to side, staring at the blank-walled buildings. Most of them seemed to be four or five stories high, made of something dark that might have been poured stone. Nearly all of them had lighter inclusions: a band across the front, or outlining a door, or defining the corners of the building, but there were no windows, or at least nothing she recognized as a window. She had thought the on-line guides had said that Dock Road was primarily a residential district, but these looked more like factories or warehouses than any house she had ever seen. And then the cab swept past a building with all its windows open, shutters folded back against the empty dark stone of the facade, a gate open too into a courtyard where people swarmed around a blue-lit fountain, and music spilled out into the quiet street. She craned her head as they slid past, and out of the corner of her eye saw the driver smile briefly over his shoulder.

They pulled up outside Shadows a little before the nineteenth hour. The club was a more ordinary building, three stories high with bricked-in windows and a brightly lit sign over the door, in a neighborhood full of buildings that had visible windows and doors that locked with metal grills. There was a food bar on the nearest corner—and a heavyset bouncer leaning his chair against the wall outside the entrance, so she shouldn't have to worry too much—and some kind of shop across the street, its display windows shut down for the night. She paid the driver what he asked and added the tip the guides had said was appropriate, then turned toward the club's well-marked door. The cab's motor whined behind her as the driver pulled away, but she did not look back.

After the glittering strangeness of the rest of the city, Shadows was refreshingly ordinary, another Gaming club like a hundred others she'd seen on other worlds. The door was painted with the images from hundreds of Gaming pins—conferences, competitions, specific sessions and scenarios, most of the Grand Types and even a few faces that had to be local favorites—but before Lioe could study them more closely, the door swung open onto a narrow hall.

The carpet was worn, with a few squares of a brighter shade of moss to show where the worst damage had been replaced. The white-painted walls were mostly empty, ex-

cept for a few display boards and a Gameboard under glass.
The displays were of sessions that had attracted attention on
the intersystems nets, and Lioe gave a mental nod of approval. There weren't many—there couldn't be many, if
Shadows was as new as the steward Vere had said, and it
was a good sign that the club hadn't tried to inflate its reputation by adding displays of merely local interest. The
Gameboard, the gleaming screen below it said, had belonged
to the club's founder, Davvi Medard-Yasinë. Lioe didn't
recognize the name.

The hallway ended abruptly in a softly lit lobby, walled on
three sides with multiscreen virtual-display-in-real-time
wallboards. Only four of the screens were displaying the
broadcast bands, and two of those showed the same session,
but telltales glowed green on a few of the others, and the
couches opposite those boards were occupied by people
whose faces were hidden behind the mirrored mask of their
shades. Telltales flickered on the temples of the shades, too,
indicating that they were tuned to a narrowcast from one or
more of the wallboards. There were smaller, lower-resolu-
tion VDIRT tables scattered around the rest of the lobby, but
not many of them were occupied yet. They would be busy
later, Lioe knew, when the main tanks filled up and Gamers
needed to kill a few hours between sessions. That is, if Shadows was like every other club in human-settled space. She
glanced one last time at the session playing on the screen
overhead—it was a Court Life variant, familiar iconography
identifying Count Danile and the Lady Hannabahn, but it
was impossible to follow the scene without the direct-line
voice feed—and turned her attention to the checkroom that
controlled access to the club's session rooms. A young man
was sitting behind its counter, Gameboard balanced in front
of him, but he looked up quickly as Lioe approached.

"Can I help you, pilot?"

"I hope so. Do you do temporary memberships?"

"We do." The young man touched keys on a terminal
tucked out of sight below the lip of the counter. "It's forty
real a week—we have a ten-day week, you know—and you
get all privileges except priority for limited-access sessions."

"So I can run sessions, if anyone's interested," Lioe said.

"Yes, no problem." The young man consulted his terminal again. "Can I get your name?"

"Quinn Lioe."

The young man looked up sharply. "The Lioe from Callixte?"

"That's right."

"I admire your sessions a lot." His clear complexion was slowly turning a delicate pink, and Lioe watched in fascination. "We just got a good tape of the Frederick's Glory session, downloaded from MI-Net a couple of days ago. It looks wonderful."

"Thanks," Lioe said.

"Are you going to be running any sessions while you're here?" the young man went on.

"I hope so," Lioe answered. "I was wondering who I should talk to about it."

"The night manager," the young man said, and touched keys on a different machine. "She can help you—and we're having a slow week right now, with Storm coming up."

"Storm?" Lioe had heard the term half a dozen times since landing, hadn't had the chance to ask what was meant.

"Yeah. It's our fifth season, lasts twenty days, about. There're so many big storms every year about this time that it makes more sense for things to shut down. So we hold Carnival." A tone sounded softly under the counter, and the young man turned away to touch some hidden control. The door to the inner rooms swung open.

Lioe turned, her idle question already forgotten, and found herself facing a tall, grey-haired woman, who held out her hand in greeting.

"Na Lioe? I'm Aliar Gueremei, *dit* Lia."

Lioe murmured a greeting, and clasped the fingers extended to her. Gueremei was weather-beaten, as though she'd been in space, but more so, her brown skin crossed with a web of fine lines and faint, bleached freckles. She wore coarse workman's trousers, but with an expensive-looking and impractically wide-sleeved jacket over it, clasped at the waist with a circle that glittered with tiny iridescent disks. Even if sequensa were less expensive on

Burning Bright, where the shells were seined and cut into tiny perfect shapes, they would never be cheap, and Lioe found herself revising her assumptions about Shadows and Burning Bright's Gamers.

"Come on into the back," Gueremei went on. "I know your work, from the nets, and I'm delighted you thought of coming here. Can I ask where you heard the name?" She palmed open the door as she spoke, and gestured for Lioe to precede her into the inner hallways.

"The steward on the inbound shuttle—orbiter, I mean—recommended you," Lioe said, "and then of course your name is good on the Game nets."

Gueremei nodded, though whether in agreement or thanks Lioe could not be sure. "Were you looking to run sessions while you were here—how long are you staying, anyway?"

"Probably about five days," Lioe answered. "The ship I was piloting for is down for repairs, recalibration of the sail fields. And, yes, I would like to run a session or two."

Gueremei nodded again. "I'll be frank with you," she said, as she led the way quickly through a maze of corridors. "We'd be very interested in your running something here. I've seen your Frederick's Glory scenario—and the Callixte board summaries, of course, the ones that went with the award—and a couple of others, and I'm very impressed."

"Thanks," Lioe said again, and waited. This was familiar territory, like the white-painted walls filled with quick-print sheets of network downloads, the padded doors and one-way glass windows that gave onto the session rooms, the banks of food-and-drink vendors tucked into every available alcove. Gueremei, or Shadows through Gueremei, wanted something, and the praise was just a prelude.

Gueremei touched another doorplate, this one badged with the Gameops glyph, and ushered Lioe into a crowded and comfortable office. The air smelled faintly of cinnamon, and there was a thin, dark-red stick smoldering in a holder on top of the VDIRT table that served as a desk. The chairs were Gamer's chairs, designed for long hours of relative immobility, and when Lioe lowered herself into the nearest one at Gueremei's absent invitation, she felt more at home than she had since she'd come to Burning Bright.

Gueremei settled herself on the other side of the VDIRT console, and unearthed a workboard from the mess of fax-sheets, quick-prints, Rulebooks and supplements, and a couple of expensive-looking Gameboards. She touched keys, peering down at the tiny screen, then looked back up at Lioe. "As I said, Shadows would be very interested in hosting you. There was word on the Callixte nets you had a new scenario in the works."

So that is the way things are going. Lioe smiled, and said, "Yes, I've been working on a new scenario—Rebellion variant with Psionics overtones, set on Ixion's Wheel."

"Baron Vortex's prison planet," Gueremei said, testing the words. "That sounds hard to pull off."

Lioe shrugged. "I'm using one of the rival claimants as a primary focus. I think that gives them enough firepower to stand a chance."

"Interesting." Gueremei glanced down at her workboard again. "If you were willing to give us an exclusive deal for the duration of your stay—and copies for later use, of course—we'd be willing to offer you twenty percent of the special-session fees."

"That's a generous offer," Lioe said automatically, temporizing while she sorted out the implications. It wasn't a bad deal at all, but twenty percent of fees was the standard rate, and if Shadows wanted to buy a copy of the scenario, they ought to pay more. "Still, I'd like a little more if you want to keep the scenario for your own use—either a higher percentage, or, better still, a flat purchase fee."

"That's hard to come up with when we haven't seen the scenario," Gueremei said. "We might be able to offer a slightly higher percentage, though, maybe as much as twenty-five percent."

"That really doesn't cover what I'd make from the nets," Lioe answered. "I'd need at least thirty-five."

Gueremei glanced down at her board again, shook her head with what looked like genuine regret. "I don't have the authority for that. What if you run the session here first, we'll give you twenty percent of the fees, and you'll be under no obligation to stay with us beyond tonight. If it's good, I'm sure Davvi—Davvi Medard-Yasinë, our principal owner—will want to purchase more rights."

And you'll have the prestige of having run the first session, whatever happens, Lioe thought. Still, it seemed worthwhile: it would be a nice bit of extra money, and there was a good chance she could sell the scenario afterwards. She nodded, and said, "What about players?"

Gueremei consulted her board, then touched the input strip to light a second screen under the surface of the VDIRT table. "Actually, we've a very respectable crowd in tonight. How many slots will you have?"

"Eight. Six-player minimum."

Gueremei nodded. "I can get you eight players, all rated A or higher. That's MI-Net rated, by the way."

Lioe nodded back, impressed in spite of herself. MI-Net was the toughest of all the Game nets, demanded the most from its players. "Then I'm willing. Twenty percent of the take, up front, and no strings."

"Agreed," Gueremei said, and, quite suddenly, smiled. "I'm looking forward to this, Na Lioe."

"So am I."

Gueremei fingered the workboard's input strip again, studied the results. "Room five is free for the night. It's a standard tech setup, Gerrish table, standard Rulebooks already in place, and we've got all six editions of *Face and Body* backed up on a separate datalink, so you get instant access when you need it."

"That sounds good," Lioe answered. She could feel the edges of her disks through the thin fabric of the carryall, wanted suddenly to get to work again. "When can I load in?"

"Anytime," Gueremei said, and pushed herself back from the table. "I'll get you started, then I'll see who's free to play."

"Excellent," Lioe said, and followed the other woman from the room.

Gueremei led her through a second set of hallways, and then out into a wider corridor where one wall opened onto a central courtyard. There were more VDIRT tables set out under the carefully tended trees. Lioe tilted her head, curious, and saw light reflecting from a glass dome that enclosed the courtyard. A group of players, perhaps half a dozen, were clustered around a bank of food-and-drink vendors: probably on intermission, she thought, and turned her attention to her own scenario. It was solid; if the players were halfway competent, it would go well. If they weren't—well, she would have to trust to luck and her own improvisational talents.

Gueremei stopped in front of a door marked with horizontal silver bands on a deep, brick-colored background, and laid her hand on the touchpad beside the lock. The mechanism hissed softly, and the door popped out from the frame. She tugged it open, and motioned for Lioe to precede her into the dimness. Lioe did as she was told, and swung her carryall onto the massive VDIRT table that dominated the space. She found the room controls, set into a dropboard at the session leader's seat, and touched the keys that brought up the lights. The room was just as it should be, banks of blank-faced processors, telltales red or unlit, and she settled herself in the heavily padded chair. The chair shifted under her weight, squirming against her as the oilcushions adjusted themselves to her body, but she was only dimly aware of the movement, concentrating instead on the panels that opened to her touch. She checked the air and temperature—*comfortable and stable*—and folded that board away, reaching for the table controls. The VDIRT display came to life under her fingers, the tree of lights that defined the library and display connections slowly changing from red to orange to yellow, and for a moment a faint haze of static filled the air above the center of the table. Lioe smiled, seeing that, imagining it filled with her own images, and touched keys to tune the system to her own specifications. A red light flashed instead, and glyphs filled the smaller, monitor screen.

"I need a password," she said.

"Sorry." Gueremei pulled herself away from the doorframe where she had been leaning, came around the table to lean over Lioe's shoulder. She touched keys; the screen, as usual, showed nothing but placeholders, but Lioe looked aside anyway, out of old habits of politeness. "I'm setting up a temp account for you," Gueremei went on. She worked one-handed, like a lot of older Gamers, using chord-keys to speed her input. "You can set your password now."

Lioe hesitated for a moment, then typed a single word: *hellequin.* The letters hung on the screen for a moment, and Gueremei lifted an eyebrow.

"What's it mean? If you don't mind my asking."

Lioe shrugged one shoulder, already regretting the impulse. It was no more than superstition that made her use that name; she should have known better. "It's my full name. Quinn's the short form." *It was the only name I could remember when the Foster Services people found me, the only thing I have that isn't theirs.*

"So." Gueremei nodded, and touched another sequence of keys. "Like Harlequin, right? You're all in," she added, and stepped aside.

"Thanks," Lioe said, and was glad to concentrate on the larger screen that windowed under the tabletop. Familiar glyphs and query codes filled the blank space, laid out in an outline form as familiar to her as the hyperspatial maps of a star system's deeps and shallows. She spilled the rest of her disks out onto the table's smooth, slightly spongy surface, and began slotting Rulebooks and databoards into the waiting readers. On the screen, glyphs changed shape, queries smoothing into acknowledgment as the VDIRT systems found the data they required and forged the links between them. More lights flared on the wall systems, the machines whirring slightly as they came on-line. Faces and shapes, familiar icons, began to appear in the haze of static.

"That's Desir of Harmsway," Gueremei said abruptly, and Lioe looked up in some surprise. "And Gallio Hazard. You did know they were local Types?"

"Yes," Lioe said, and wondered why it mattered. Notables generally didn't mind other people using their character templates—that was one of the definitions of a notable, someone whose characters were played by a lot of different people.

Gueremei's smile widened. "I think I'll definitely sit in on this session." Lioe looked at her questioningly, and Gueremei turned away. "Oh, don't worry, there's no problem. It's just they're Ambidexter's templates, and he hasn't played in years."

And in a situation like that, Lioe thought, *I bet there's one hell of a debate about how to play those characters. Oh, well, too late to change now.* She looked back at the screen, saw the stand-by symbol fade, indicating that file transfer was complete. The planning form for session parameters was flashing in the screen, and she touched a key to submit the various supplemental rules she preferred to use. Those slots lit, and vanished from the screen, leaving her with the bare bones of the situation. It was a convention of the Game that Baron Vortex, the villain who opposed the Rebellion and wanted to make himself Emperor, was involved in secret psionics research; it was also a convention that he controlled the prison world of Ixion's Wheel, from which no prisoner had ever escaped. She had combined the two, made Ixion's Wheel the center of the Baron's illegal research project— aside from the ethics involved, psions were illegal on the worlds of the Imperium—and then given the Golden claimant to the Imperial throne, Royal Avellar, a good reason to get himself sent to Ixion's Wheel. Avellar was a secret telepath, one of the last four survivors of a clone-group who had shared a telepathic link; and the one person who could restore his power, the electrokinetic Desir of Harmsway, was a prisoner in the research sections there.

"It looks good," Gueremei said, and Lioe jumped at the sound of her voice. An instant later, one of the printers whirred to life, spat a piece of paper, and Gueremei retrieved it. "I'll get you some players, then."

"Thanks," Lioe said. Her eyes were on her screens before the door closed behind the other woman.

Most of the relationships in the Game were familiar, formalized; everyone who played knew the characters and their backgrounds, and the pleasure of a session came from seeing how well a player could perform within those constraints. About half the characters on Ixion's Wheel were drawn from someone else's scenarios: Harmsway and Gallio Hazard from Ambidexter's sessions of five years ago; Avellar from an old, old session that everyone had said was wonderful, but no one had used; Lord Faro and Ibelin Belfortune from a session she herself had played on Demeter a few months before, whom she had salvaged from certain death because their templates were more interesting than her players had been capable of making them. The rest—the telekinetic Jack Blue, unofficial leader of the prison population; the Rebel technician Galan Africa, who hated blood telepaths, with good reason; the research scientist Mijja Lyall, part of the prison staff, living in fear that someone would discover her own low-level talent and transfer her to the experiment— were her own creations, but she had been careful to tie them to familiar places and characters within the larger Game. She studied the numbers for a moment longer, balancing skills and quirks and basic numbers, then touched the keys that dumped the templates to the system. A light flashed, con- firming her choice, and she turned her attention to the set- ting.

She had a good library with her, settings she'd laboriously compiled through her years of travel, walking through the various cities on all the worlds she visited with her palm- corder in her pocket, waiting for just the right combination of light and space, of architecture and atmosphere and atti- tude, that would make a perfect place in some Game. Ixion's Wheel had been harder to find than most, and she had had to transform her stored images more than usual, to get the harsh world suggested by the planetary statistics.

Frowning a little, she pulled her shades from the carryall, plugged the datacord into the socket on the temple, and touched the keys that opaqued the heavy lenses and dis- played the image directly in front of her eyes. She touched more keys, and the statistics for Ixion's Wheel hung in blank space: a hot planet, desert-dry except for sparse bands of grassland to the north and south. The prison complex lay just south of the dry line, in the softer desert; the port lay to its north, just far enough away from the complex to seem un- reachable. She had already pulled images for the prison— mostly from government buildings on Ardinée, a cheerless place if she'd ever seen one—but the port was less defined. And there wasn't much time: she would have to fall back on her old standby for hot planets, images taken on Callixte it- self, her home base.

She pulled that file, let it open, the images blossoming in front of her eyes. Plain, flat-fronted buildings painted in sweeps of shocking pastels floated against a multitude of skies. She picked a dozen buildings at random, pulled a port-and-city blank from a general pattern file, and began fitting the buildings into the open spaces of the map. A town, a port town, took shape behind the shades, outlines only at first, as she moved the buildings like the pieces on a chessboard, shuffling them for maximum effect. She rotated the image until she was seeing it edge-on, to view the skyline; then, as satisfied as she would be with this set of images, touched the controls to fill in the rest of the buildings. She chose a sky as well, the hot, thunder-hazed blue of Callixte's summer, and was pleased with the vivid splash of the painted walls against that metallic background. She replaced that sky with a storm, and watched the light bleed away into an ominous luminosity, the ramparts of cloud looming over the low roofs. It was good, an effect to be stored for later, but the first sky was the one she wanted now. She recalled it, and filled the empty space around the town with a generic grassland. It would do—nothing unique, and maybe not as good as some of her efforts, but it would do.

"That's very nice," Gueremei said, and Lioe jumped.

"I didn't hear you come in." She worked the toggle that cleared her shades, then dumped the cityscape to the main library.

"Sorry," Gueremei said, not sounding particularly repentant. "I've got a cast for you."

"Thanks," Lioe said, and held out her hand for the disk. Gueremei slid it across the table, and Lioe slipped it deftly into the last reader.

"You should be pleased," Gueremei went on. "I had to turn some people away. I've pulled you a good group, though, if I do say so myself. Roscha's a handful, sometimes, but she's a damn fine player, and she likes the scenario outline. I think she'll behave. Savian's a Republican, of course—" She stopped abruptly, bit off a laugh. "But so are you. I'd forgotten."

"That's all right." Lioe smiled, and did her best to hide

the excitement welling up in her, making her movements too quick and clumsy.

"So you'll be used to the style," Gueremei went on, as though the other woman hadn't spoken. She came around the curved side of the table, leaned over Lioe's shoulder to strike a chord of keys. "This is what I've done."

A secondary window bloomed in front of the main data-tree, displayed a double list of names. Lioe stared at it blankly, matching unknown names to the characters opposite. Roscha—Jafiera Roscha, who could be a "handful," according to Gueremei—would be playing Galan Africa: *not a bad part for a troublemaker,* Lioe thought. *At least there should be enough meat in it to keep her happy.* Savian, Peter Savian, the other Republican, would play Lord Faro—and a name seemed to leap out at her from the foot of the list: Audovero Caminesi, cast as the telekinetic Jack Blue.

She highlighted the name with a touch, and looked up to see Gueremei nod.

"He volunteered," she said, "and I like his style. You said you'd met." She paused, and when she spoke again, her voice was oddly formal. "Does this meet with your approval, Na Lioe?"

"It looks fine to me," Lioe answered, and swept the disks she had prepared for the players into an untidy stack. "Bring them in."

Gueremei nodded, stepped back to work the door controls. The door sagged open, and at her gesture the players filed into the room, carryalls and cased Gameboards in hand. Lioe looked up from her screen to watch them file in and take their places at the players' seats around the curved side of the table. A big bearded man came first, followed closely by a slimmer, hard-faced man with the silver disks of implant lenses gleaming in both eyes. They sat side by side, the bearded man grinning at something, and a young man in a supportchair followed them in. His thin wrists were heavy with jeweled bracelets, and there were more jewels in his ears. The silver-eyed man pushed one of the chairs away from the table, and the other eased his supportchair into the new space, murmuring thanks under his breath. A handsome, hook-nosed woman with an expensive Gameboard followed him, and then Vere, still in his steward's uniform, as though he'd come directly from Newfields. He glanced at Lioe with a smile that hoped for recognition, and Lioe grinned back at him, grateful for something like a familiar face. The striking red-haired woman behind him raised an eyebrow at the sight, her dark blue eyes, the color of the sea seen from near orbit, flicking up and down in insolent assessment. Lioe cocked an eyebrow at her, still smiling, and was rewarded by a faint, betraying flush of color: *not used to someone taking up her challenge,* Lioe thought, and filed the notion for later use. A slim man, with Asian eyes and implanted hsai spurs on both wrists, followed her, bony face expressionless. Lioe's attention was caught by the spurs—*is he hsaia, jericho-human, or adopted, or does he just admire the hsai principle of kinship?*—but pulled her thoughts sternly away. Politics had no place in the Game. That was only seven, and Lioe frowned. It would be hard to eliminate any of the characters—easier to be rid of two than one—and she glanced sharply at Gueremei, then back at the cast list. All the names were filled, so they were still one short.

"I've decided to sit in myself," Gueremei said. "I play under Fernesa—Gameop's privilege."

A mixed favor, Lioe thought. Gueremei would be good— you didn't get to be a Gameop without being at least a double-A player—but it was also a little unnerving, having her on-line for the first session. "Suit yourself," she said aloud, and Gueremei settled herself in the remaining chair.

"All right," Gueremei said, not loudly, but all attention shifted instantly to her. "This is Quinn Lioe, everyone, who wrote the Frederick's Glory scenario some of you played last week. Na Lioe, let me introduce your players. Peter Savian—"

That was the bearded man, sitting so close on her right that he could extend a hand, Republican-fashion. Lioe murmured a greeting, met and matched the pressure of his grip, and saw a new amusement gleam for an instant in his dark eyes.

"—Kazio Beledin—"

The man with the implant lenses touched his forehead, a

formal gesture that went badly with his crumpled, brightly dyed and patched shirt and dock-worker's trousers.

"—Alazais Mariche—"

The hook-nosed woman nodded very seriously, her fingers playing over the controls of her expensive equipment.

"—Vere you know, and Serenn Imbertin—"

"*Dit*—everyone calls me Imbertine," the young man in the supportchair said. Lioe nodded in acknowledgment, wondering if the chair were a permanent necessity. It was hard to tell—he was thin, certainly, but not wasted—and it was none of her business, in any case.

"—Garet Huard—"

The man with the hsai spurs looked up from his Gameboard to nod a greeting. He didn't have a hsai name—most adoptees used some hsai forms—and Lioe wondered again what the connection was.

"And Jafiera Roscha," Gueremei finished.

Lioe nodded to the redhead, startled again by the contrast between the woman's striking beauty and the aggression in her face.

"It's good to meet you," Roscha said, her voice low and unexpectedly musical.

"Thanks," Lioe said. She looked around the table, feeling the familiar excitement building in her, said, "Na Gueremei hás outlined the scenario to you, I assume?" Most of them nodded, but she continued anyway. "This is a Rebellion/Psionics variant, set on the prison planet of Ixion's Wheel. Baron Vortex has, unknown to anyone until now, been running a secret research project in the prison complex, trying to find a way to bring psis of all types under his personal control. You are all part of that project, either as prisoners or as part of the prison staff. One of you, however, has an ulterior motive: you have come to rescue an old friend and antagonist, now a prisoner, and in order to escape yourself you will all have to work together." She smiled then, and most of the players grinned back, even Roscha softening slightly, caught up in the preliminaries of the Game. "Assuming no one wants to back out, I have casting disks and the scenario supplements."

No one did. Lioe felt her smile widen even as she tried to

control it, and looked down at the display to check the cast list a final time. She dealt the disks around the table, and slid the session supplements after them. Huard, with his hsai spurs, would play the key role, Royal Avellar, potential if distant claimant to the Imperial throne; she wondered for a moment if he were really jericho-human, and if he was, what it would do to his play. Savian would play Lord Faro, Beledin the half-mad vampire Ibelin Belfortune—a good choice, given the visible chemistry between the two men—and Vere would play Jack Blue. Imbertine and the hook-nosed woman, Mariche, would play Gallio Hazard and Desir of Harmsway—not easy parts, requiring a lot of coordination, and Lioe hoped they had played together before. Roscha would play the technician Africa, and Gueremei would play Mijja Lyall. That was an interesting choice—Lyall was superficially a minor character, but could become pivotal if played right—and Lioe gave a little nod of approval. She fiddled with her own controls as the players slid disks and supplement boxes into their Gameboards, and linked the boards to the VDIRT table's main systems, bringing the prison complex into focus just above the tabletop. She kept it dim, the outlines vague and colors dulled, but she saw her players glance warily at it, assessing the setting. Savian ran a fingertip along the ridge of bone below one eye—there was a scar there, Lioe saw, faint as a thread against his brown skin—and studied the displays on his screen. Mariche busied herself with a pull-out input strip, typing something into her Gameboard, her face still and intent as she studied the shifting numbers.

"Is everything clear?" Lioe said at last, when the first flourish of activity slowed, and there were nods and mumbled agreement from the players. Even Roscha looked almost eager. Lioe glanced at her main boards a final time—everything was ready to go, all the linkages in place and the libraries on line—and looked back at her players, excitement coursing through her. This was what made the Game worthwhile, all of them gathered for the one purpose of playing her scenario— She put the thought aside and said, "Then let's go."

She reached for her own shades, settled the temples on her

ears. The broad double screen, dipping almost below her
cheekbones, stayed black for a moment, and then she adjusted the controls so that she was watching her players
through one completely transparent lens and watching the
Game they would create in the other, darkened lens. Savian
lifted a half-helmet, settled it very deliberately on his head.
The matte silver backing hid eyes and nose, but his mouth,
framed by the neatly trimmed beard, remained visible and
expressive. Most of the others wore shades similar to her
own; bands of black or grey plastic covered half their face,
turning them into icons of justice. Imbertine leaned back in
his chair, hands caressing the bright stones of his bracelets.
Looking more closely, Lioe could see the thin cables that
connected each one to the sockets of his Gameboard. She
smiled to herself, unable to resist prolonging the moment,
then touched her controls to bring a scene slowly into shape
in the players' view. The buildings of the prison complex,
blank grey walls, a single row of slit-windows visible just
below the tops of the buildings, grew more solid in the air
above the tabletop. The same image was reflected in her
shades. She touched controls again, and wind swirled around
the buildings, driving great sheets of sand against the
prison's force dome.

"Welcome to Ixion's Wheel."

EVENING, DAY 30

Ransome sprawled in his chair, caught in his web of images that all but blocked out the cityscape spread out below the loft windows. A solitary firework burst into a flower of golden rain—someone on the far side of the Water getting a head start on Storm—and he watched it fall and fade into a last trail of sparks, ignoring the dancing images. Most of them were Game nets—he was trying to do what Chauvelin wanted—but his heart wasn't in it. There was nothing new in the Game, had been nothing new for years, only the same sterile repetitions, theme and variations all gone stale with overuse. His eyes stole to the image sitting alone to the left of his chair, a direct feed from one of his dataspheres. The last of the tiny stone heads looked back at him, a faint, sly smile on its carved mouth. Idly, he reached into a secondary control space, flicked on the controls that would allow the Imani Formstone Works to produce copies of his originals. The head looked back at him, caught now in a maze of numbers and guidelines. It had taken him most of the morning to find a workshop that would admit it could do the job in the time required—and the hefty surcharge, twice what the job should actually cost, was the only reason the shop manager had agreed at all. But the ambassadorial accounting system had accepted the charges, and he was left to deal with the Game. Voices babbled from the floor speakers, no channel given priority; Ransome made a face at the noise, but did not bother to adjust the tuning.

A light flashed in communications space, and at the same time an identifying glyph crackled in the air overhead. Ransome sighed, recognizing the image—knowing too well that the caller was the kind who did not give up—and muted his images with a wave of a gloved hand. With the other hand, he reached into the main control space to connect himself with the communications channel. "What the hell do you want, Sanci?"

"About fucking time, Ransome."

There had been no delay. Ransome sighed again, shoved the familiar face—sharp chin framed by a short and tidy beard, eyes always slightly narrowed, as though he were looking into a bright light—to one side of the Game net images. "What do you want?"

"Have you been tracking the Game nets—the Old Network, by any chance?" Sanci smiled. "You might want to tune in."

"I doubt it," Ransome said.

Sanci's smile widened, and Ransome realized the other man was tracking his net hookups. "Someone's playing with your toys."

"What channel?"

"The mainline feed out of Shadows."

Ransome shoved Sanci's image farther to his left, reached into control space to fiddle with the icons hanging there. He opened a connection to the Old Network, not even thinking of the costs. Shadows was easy to find, its distinctive icon flashing to signal an interesting session in progress, and he brought it on-line, feeding the image into a small space directly in front of his eyes. Figures moved in an unfamiliar, cell-like room, altogether too like Jericho's prison system. He reached for the session précis even as he recognized two of the templates. Lord Faro was an old favorite, and so was Ibelin Belfortune, and if they both were there . . . He flicked the précis into prominence, skimmed quickly through the screen. Desir of Harmsway's name seemed to leap out at him.

"Who's running this?" he said aloud, and felt rather than saw the malice in Sanci's look.

"I knew you'd be interested in this one. And it's not a fill-in-the-background session, either. That's Ixion's Wheel you're looking at."

*I put those characters on Ixion's Wheel to keep them out
of other people's hands. And Desir of Harmsway is my character, my property—more than that, my creation. Who the
hell does this session leader think s/he is, using my persona
in a session?* Ransome bit back his instinctive reaction—
Sanci didn't deserve the satisfaction—and said again, "Who
is it?"

Sanci sighed, rather theatrically. "Woman named Lioe,
out of the Republic. She did the Frederick's Glory scenario
everyone was so hot about."

Ransome said, "She's good, or so I hear." His hands
were busy in the control space, expanding the picture, so that
hand-high figures moved in a cube of space half a meter
square.

"Good enough?" Sanci murmured, still with that knowing smile, and Ransome managed a shrug.

"It's possible, I suppose. I don't follow the Game that
closely these days."

Sanci sneered, but said nothing. Ransome hesitated, wanting to lie, to deny that he would follow this scenario now that
it had been brought to his attention, but knew that Sanci
would recognize the truth—knew too that Sanci would probably try to trace the taps, and blocking him was hardly worth
the trouble. *But I'll be damned if I'll thank him for this.*
"Good-bye, Sanci," he said instead, and flicked away the
other man's image. The movement cut the communications
channel as it sent the bearded face spinning, so that it turned
end over end three times before it disappeared.

The gesture had done something to soothe his feelings,
but Ransome was still frowning when he sat up fully. The
image-shell shifted with him, so that he looked down at the
narrowcast from Shadows as though it were a desktop
screen. He banished the rest of the images with a quick gesture, brought up the sound until he could follow the dialogue
in the little world that hung in the air in front of him. One did
not forget the Game, not when one had spent as much time in
its worlds as he had done, but one did get out of practice. He
scowled at the characters, reading the iconography of clothing and *Face/Body* numbers, and reached into control space
to tap the session leader's display bar. In the Game, Belfor-

tune and Lord Faro whispered together, fearful of interruption, and a familiar figure moved through the hall behind them, deliberately eavesdropping. *Avellar . . .*

He studied the string of glyphs and numbers that bloomed along the base of the main image, skimmed quickly through the overlapping screens to confirm what he suspected. The overall shape of the Game was almost as familiar to him as the layout of his studio, and it was easy to see where this scenario would fit into the whole. It was ostensibly a Rebel scenario, but it was tied both to the Psionics variant and the Rival Claimants offshoot of the Court Life Game—*and all of that done through Avellar and Desir of Harmsway, who was my character, and the situation between them was my invention*— Ransome reached out to expand the image, drawing out the details. Some of the players were old friends, old rivals in the Game—Peter Savian he'd known for years, and Kazio Beledin; Imbertine was another familiar name, as was Roscha, though he'd never met the latter off-line. But they were players, not session leaders: it was the leader who'd chosen to play with these characters—*my characters, and it should have been my Game. This Lioe's got nerve. . . .* He rolled the name over in his mind, recalling the little he'd heard. She was a notable-in-the-making, or so everybody said, a pilot out of the Republic, off Callixte, which was a good introduction in the Game . . . and her first name was Quinn, Quinn Lioe. He hesitated for a moment, running down the list of friends who still followed the Game and who would give information, and reached into control space to open another line. The Game session still swam in front of him, the characters murmuring to each other, and he pushed it aside to make room for the new image.

A disk of static appeared, a hazy oval that flickered through so many colors so quickly that the eye could only read it as grey: the system had made contact. "Hally?"

A face took shape, forming from the disk itself, so that it became a mask hanging in space, a face thin and rather fine beneath the canalli weathering. Earrings gleamed in both ears, and a fine chain—a datawire, Ransome guessed—ran from one particularly elaborate stud to a jewel-rimmed socket at the inner corner of his right eye. The iridescent strand seemed to glow against his pale brown skin. "Ransome?" Thin, delicately arched eyebrows rose in surprise, then contracted into a frown. "I'm watching a Game," Hally Ventura said, and broke off, seeing the face in his own screens.

"From Shadows?" Ransome asked, and was answered by a brief, lopsided smile.

"That's right. So what do you want to know about her, I-Jay?"

"What do you know?"

"About what everyone does. She's been a name on Callixte, everyone says a notable-to-be. And she's a pilot, union pilot, also works out of Callixte for that. Angele up at the port says her ship's in for repairs, and she's come to play. People've been at her to quit space, go into the Game full time, but she's not been interested."

"Piloting's a good job," Ransome said. "I'd think twice before I quit."

Hally shrugged. "She's very, very good at the Game." His eyes shifted, looking at something outside his own display. "Look, I-Jay, I want to watch this session. Was that all?"

"I just thought, if anyone knew anything, it would be you," Ransome said, and was rewarded by a quick smile: the apology was acceptable. "Thanks, Hally."

"Not at all," Hally answered, and the hanging mask dissolved into the oval of static. Ransome cut the connection.

The Game session floated back in front of him, expanded at a gesture to display its full detail. Belfortune sat with his head in his hands, answered, low-voiced, Lord Faro's questions. The tension between them was palpable: the players' affair had been over for years, but its memory still informed their play. Mijja Lyall, the scientist/technician, watched uneasily, her gaze flickering between the two men and the metal face that hung on the wall overhead. Baron Vortex, the Game's great villain, was overseeing this himself.

Ransome frowned, reached for the library icons, and had to shuffle access spaces until he found dead storage. It had been a long time since he had gone looking for his template libraries. He flicked them back into the working volume,

searched the most recent issues until he found Lord Faro's
listing. He had forgotten that Faro had become one of the
Baron's henchmen—that had happened almost two years
ago, just after he'd quit the Game. He leaned back in his
chair, the images tilting around him, and saw another firework flare through the pattern of the Game. *You couldn't ask
for better,* he thought, and reached for a hand-held remote to
summon the drinks tray.

The machine trundled over, the lid sliding back to give
access to the freezer compartment. Ransome chose abstract-
edly, opened the container, his eyes still on the session un-
folding in front of him. Faro was clearly torn between his
loyalty to Baron Vortex—a loyalty bought with fear and the
promise that Faro's lost estates would someday be returned—and his—*love? desire?*—for Belfortune. Belfortune
clearly shared both passion and fear, and Baron Vortex
watched from the wall. Lioe was handling him well, he admitted grudgingly. Too many leaders made the Baron too
villainous right from the start; Lioe was keeping him just
reasonable enough—though still with that edge of mad-
ness—that it seemed suicidal to oppose him.

Abruptly, he wanted to be there, at Shadows, watching
firsthand—or, better still, to be in the control booth with Medard-Yasinë. It was the first time in three years that he'd actually wanted to attend a Game, and his lips quirked upward
as he realized that at least he now had an excuse for doing
what Chauvelin wanted. He closed both fists, shutting down
the system—in the corner of his eye, glyphs tumbled head-
long as the slaved machines ran through their shutdown procedures—and reached for a stand-alone com-unit and
punched codes that would cycle through the helicab companies until he found one that could respond. It took perhaps
two minutes, the bar of light flashing in front of him, not
quite blocking his sight, and he spent the time searching for
his jacket and the cylinder of Mist he was forced to carry.
The com-unit beeped at him before he found the red-banded
tube, and he scrabbled impatiently for the hand-held unit.

"How can we be of service?"

It was a machine voice, or so the telltale at the base of the
unit said—it would have been impossible to tell from the

sound alone. Ransome curbed his impatience, and smoothed his tone to be as emotionless as possible. "I need transport to the helipad closest to Shadows—Face Road, by the center of the Dike in the Dock Road District. I think that's Underface."

"Just a moment, please." There was a little silence, not even the hiss of static, while Ransome scanned the cluttered space of his loft for the missing cylinder, and then the machine said, "Yes, Underface is closest. Your location code is Warehouse?"

"That's right." The cylinder was lying on the shelf beside the shell for the Syndic's egg.

"Thank you. Your helicab will arrive at the Warehouse helipad in fifteen minutes."

"Thanks," Ransome said, in spite of himself, in spite of knowing it was a machine, and broke the connection. He collected the cylinder, shoved it and his credimeters into the pocket of his jacket, and left the loft.

It took him almost fifteen minutes to reach the helipad— the computers were scrupulous in their calculations—and he barely had time to catch his breath before he heard the soft beat of the muted rotors. Somewhat to his surprise, there was a live pilot, who grinned cheerfully at him as she popped the passenger hatch.

"To Underface, right? Going to Shadows?"

Does everyone on the planet know about this fucking game? Ransome wondered. "Yes, to Underface—and, yes, to Shadows, too."

The pilot nodded, closing the hatch behind him. "I hear there's one hell of a session in progress there. You're like the fifth person I've dropped there in the last two hours."

"Really." Ransome settled into the center seat, the most comfortable of the three, and adjusted the door controls so that the whole panel went transparent, an enormous curved window on the city spread out below the cliff face.

"Yeah." The pilot manipulated her controls, and the helicab lifted easily, pivoting toward the cliff edge and the descent to Underface. She was on-line, Ransome saw, bound into the cab's systems so that her arms and legs seemed to end in the black boxes of the control consoles; more wires, a complex, braided band of them, fell from the junction box at the base of her skull. Her hair was shaved around that connection, but the rest of it fell in a scarlet tail from an untidy topknot. "I wish I wasn't working."

"You're a Gamer, then?" Ransome asked, and saw, too late, the pins studding her left sleeve. MI-Net, Court Life V, Vimar Nessen's Game, RedApple, Old Network, and dozens of others: she was a Gamer, all right, and a committed one.

She didn't seem offended, however, just shrugged that shoulder to make the pins glitter in the light from the instrument panel. "That's right."

"So what have you heard about this Lioe?" Ransome asked. This wasn't his style at all—this was the kind of information he preferred to find on the nets—but the chance was too good to pass up.

The pilot shrugged again, both shoulders this time. "What haven't I heard, really? Frederick's Glory got an A-double-star on Callixte, which those judges don't hand out like candy, and she wrote it. She's supposed to just be running a sample session for Davvi tonight, but what everyone's saying is that it's turning out to be something kind of special." She looked sideways, into the space that showed her the passenger camera view. "What I heard from one woman was, she's pulled one of Ambidexter's characters out of storage, playing him as a major character."

Ransome nodded, caught up in spite of himself in the old habits of the Game. "Desir of Harmsway. I was watching for a while on the nets."

"*Sha-mai.*" The pilot's curse was more admiring than anything. "Ambidexter's going to murder her. Very God, I wish I wasn't working."

Ransome gave her a bitter grin. If he'd ever wanted confirmation of how the white-sickness had changed him in the past three years, he had it now—not that he'd really needed it. Even a year ago, before the disease really took hold, she would have recognized him as Ambidexter, even if he hadn't been in the clubs for a year or so before that. . . . He shook the thought away, annoyed that he'd even acknowledged it, made himself pay attention to the pilot.

"That's assuming Ambidexter's still around, of course,"

she went on, quite cheerfully. "There was talk he was dead, not long back."

"I don't think so," Ransome said, with involuntary pique, and the pilot shrugged again. The helicab banked sideways into the airpath that paralleled the Old Dike; its lights, and the glow of the shops on Warden Street, filled the cab's interior with patches of bright color.

"The work on the nets under that name hasn't been very like him, that's for sure."

Ransome drew breath for an indignant response—*how dare she accuse me of not being myself?*—and stopped suddenly, wondering if this was Cella's doing. It wouldn't be unlike her, to whisper that he was dead, that his work was not his own. He opened his mouth, trying to figure out how to phrase the question, but the helicab tilted again, and he realized that the pilot's attention was once again on her craft. After a moment, his mouth twisted into a wry smile. That would be very like Cella, to assume that the rumor of his death would bring him back onto the nets—*and it would have worked, too, if I hadn't been so busy with other things.*

The helicab tipped again, responding to wind or air currents or an unseen traffic signal, and the door panel was filled with the city lights. Ransome stared, caught once again by the breathtaking beauty: the tidy geometry of the well-lit squares and canals of Dock Road, bounded by the twin lines of the Straight to the north and the Crooked to the south. In the distance, the broad triangle that was the landformed extension of Mainwarden Island jutted into the Water, dividing the massive stream into two channels. A line of light ran from apex to base, broke slightly at the edge of the low cliff that rose to Mainwarden Island proper: Compass Road, where the Lockwarden Society had their main offices. The Society's certification officers, the elite of the Wet Districts around the Water, generally lived in the tidy, decent neighborhoods to either side of that main thoroughfare. The Great Island light blazed at steady intervals from the tip of the Extension, directing the all-but-invisible traffic that filled the Water even at this hour.

"Coming down," the pilot said, her voice distant and professional again. The helicab straightened and slowed to hover, almost motionless. Ransome craned his neck to see through the lower curve of the door, and could just make out the blue concentric lines of the helipad below them. One band of light blinked, as though something had moved across it, and a moment later another one did the same. *Kids, probably,* Ransome thought, and in the same instant a strong white light flashed from the cab's underbelly, all but drowning out the landing lines. Ransome saw a last small figure scramble over the low barrier. The pilot smiled, and the helicab began to sink delicately toward the ground. They touched down almost without a thud, and the credit reader unfolded itself from the wall of the passenger compartment, beeping politely but insistently. Ransome fed his card through the reader, winced slightly when the total was presented, but touched the confirmation code without further protest. The door opened, and Ransome swung himself out onto the brightly lit pavement. The cab lifted away as soon as he was clear, trailing a diminishing cone of light.

It was not a long walk from the Underface helipad to Shadows, but Ransome felt his lungs clog and falter, stopped in the mouth of a half-enclosed courtyard to breathe from the cylinder of Mist. He grimaced at the bitter taste, grimaced again as the drug took hold, the cold pain clearing his lungs. He waited a moment longer, listening to a strand of distant music, a single violo drawn against the night, that floated down from somewhere above him, closer to the base of the Dike. The pain faded, and he kept walking. Shadows appeared out of the darkness a few minutes later, all its windows unshuttered and blazing with light, a suppressed excitement humming in the air around it. Even the food shop across the intersection seemed quiet by comparison, both the bouncers, conspicuous in their rusty black jerkins and studded wristbands, sitting comfortably in chairs just outside the doorway, a thermoflask on the ground between them.

There was no trouble gaining admission to the club, despite the crowd that overflowed from the main lobby into the access hall. Most of them wanted only to maintain their view of the large display screens, and were perfectly willing to let Ransome past as long as he showed no desire to linger. He fetched up against the far wall, beside the little office. The dreamy-eyed woman behind the counter only reluctantly took her attention from the display board balanced in her lap.

"What can I do for you?"

"Is Davvi here?"

The abrupt request raised her eyebrows, and then she frowned, visibly searching her memory to match the face in front of her. Ransome smiled, unable to keep the expression from turning sour, and said, "Tell him Ambidexter's here."

The dreamy eyes widened almost comically. "At once, N'Ambidexter. It's good to see you back again."

A few of the Gamers close to the desk heard the name even over the direct-input sound from the room systems, and turned to look. Ransome met the stares blandly, and turned his attention to the displays overhead. In the screens, Gallio Hazard confronted a figure he didn't recognize, an enormously fat man in prison clothes. Bricks and stones, a halo of debris, floated in the air around him, and Ransome realized that the fat man was a telekinetic.

"She is good, isn't she?" Davvi Medard-Yasinë had come quietly through the door that led to the session rooms, and smiled at Ransome's shrug.

"So far, yes," Ransome answered. "Look, Davvi, I need a favor."

"You can ask," Medard-Yasinë answered, but his smile widened.

"I want to watch, up close. Can you get me into the control room?"

"I figured," Medard-Yasinë said. "Come on."

He led the way through the door and into the depths of the club. These hallways were less crowded, but in nearly every side room a group had gathered around the VDIRT tables, and the same tiny figures moved in each tabletop display. The central courtyard was busier than Ransome had ever seen it, groups standing three deep at the larger tables there. Security was standing outside the control room, a thin unsmiling woman with specialists' badges on her shoulders, and the Gamers who had ventured into this area gave her a wide berth. They clustered at the far end of the hall, where someone had hooked a trio of series-linked Gameboards into a datanode, dividing their attention between the display screens and the door that led to the control areas. Medard-Yasinë ignored them, said something quietly to Security, who nodded and stood back from the door controls. Ransome waited while Medard-Yasinë keyed the entrance codes, looking politely down the hall away from the keypad. The people on the edges of the group looked back at him, frankly curious, and a couple of them put their heads together, murmuring to each other. Ransome smiled then, and a woman in the front row nudged the man next to her. Her voice carried quite clearly: "That's Ambidexter, I'm sure of it."

"You've been found out," Medard-Yasinë said cheerfully, and pushed open the door.

Ransome followed him into the control room, crowded with Gamers and display equipment. A massive VDIRT table, twice as large as most club models, dominated the room; the scenario played in the air above the tabletop, the images almost solid enough to block out the real objects behind them, and the virtual screens in the tabletop itself glimmered with technical displays. Ransome glanced quickly at them, skimming the lines of symbols, looked away again to scan the crowd. Most of the Dock Road notables were here, all right—and there were maybe a dozen of them; Dock Road was a Gamer's ghetto, especially around Underface— and the flickering tie-in lights on the wall consoles meant that a lot more people were tapping in through MI-Net. He looked sideways, at Medard-Yasinë, and saw a faint, feline smile of satisfaction on the other man's face. Ransome touched his forehead in acknowledgment, and turned his attention to the Game.

INTERLUDE

They crouched in the uncertain shelter of the cargo bay, hearing the clatter of boots on the walkways to either side. The overhanging shelves, piled high with crates, gave some cover, but they all knew that if the Baron's guards came out onto the center catwalk it would take a miracle to keep from being seen. Galan Africa/JAFIERA ROSCHA worked frantically at the powerpack of their only heavy laser, trying to mate a salvaged blaster cell into the nonstandard housing. Mijja Lyall/FERNESA crouched at his side, unable to concentrate on either the gun or on Jack Blue/VERE CAMINESI, who sprawled gasping against the nearest stack of crates. His bulk had displaced the lowest one slightly, and Gallio Hazard/IMBERTINE gave the whole stack a wide berth, kneeling well clear of its line of fall, his pistol drawn and cocked. He had laid the fresh clip on the decking beside him, ready for use. Lord Faro/PETER SAVIAN and Ibelin Belfortune/KAZIO BELEDIN crouched as always a little apart from the rest, Faro a little ahead of the wild-eyed Belfortune, as though he could somehow protect him.

"Where the hell is this contact?" Desir of Harmsway/ALAZAIS MARICHE hissed, his light pistol already drawn and ready. "Come on, Avellar, you can explain this one, too."

Avellar/GARET HUARD ignored him, went to kneel on the warped flooring beside Jack Blue. "How is it?" he said, as much to Lyall as to Blue, but it was the telekinetic who answered.

"Not so good." Blue's voice was thin and wheezy, and Lyall shook her head, reaching into the much-depleted medical kit.

"If you weren't so damn fat," Harmsway sneered, and Blue frowned sharply. A cracked piece of the floor tiling snapped loose and flung itself at Harmsway's face. He ducked away from it, but it still struck him a grazing blow along one cheekbone, raising a thin line of blood. Avellar snatched the falling tile before it could hit anything else.

"That's why I'm so damn fat," Blue said. The mass a telekinetic could move was directly related to his/her body weight; that he could throw even a kilogram, exhausted as he was, was the direct result of his obesity.

"Save your strength," Avellar said to Blue, and looked at Harmsway. "The ship is there, Desir, and my contact's waiting. Go right ahead."

Harmsway looked longingly at the cargo door, just twenty meters away across the width of the warehouse. It was even open, the ship's hatch gleaming in the loading lights, and he could feel that the last barrier was sealed only with a simple palm lock, the kind of thing he could open in his sleep . . . if he could only get there. His lips thinned, and he looked away.

"Avellar." Lyall's voice was suddenly sharp with fear, and Avellar swung to face her.

"I think—" Lyall began, then shook her head. "No, I'm sure. They've brought in a hunter."

Harmsway swore, and Hazard looked back over his shoulder at him.

Africa said, as if he didn't really want to know, "Hunter?"

"Another telepath," Blue said. "One who specializes in sensing out his own kind."

"How close?" Harmsway demanded, and Lyall shook her head again.

"I can't tell. He—she—it's shielded."

Avellar's lips tightened, and he looked at the two men who stood apart from the rest. Faro shifted his position slightly, almost in spite of himself, putting himself between Avellar and Belfortune. Belfortune did not seem to notice, but his free hand rose to the stained bandage on his left shoulder, pressed hard as though that would ease the pain.

Avellar lifted a hand and looked instead at Africa. "How's it coming, Galan?"

The technician shrugged, his hands never slowing on the balky connection. "We won't know until I try to use it. I think I've got it."

Avellar grimaced, looked back at Belfortune. "Bel."

"Let him be," Faro said. Belfortune passed his hand over his face, then reached for the gun he had laid beside him on the tiles. He still would not meet Avellar's eyes.

"Bel," Avellar said again. "We need you."

"There's nothing I can do." Belfortune spoke flatly, without lifting his eyes from the floor. His useless left hand was tucked into the front of his jacket, held as if in a crude sling.

"Bullshit," Harmsway said. "That's fucking bullshit, and you know it. Just because you don't like thinking you're one of us, just because you and him"—his free hand swept out to indicate Lord Faro, who lifted an arrogant eyebrow in response—"have had the Baron's favor, you don't want to admit what you are. You could get us all killed, or you could save us. You're a vampire, damn you, and right now that could save all our lives."

Belfortune's good hand closed convulsively over the gun, and he brought it up in a single smooth motion, leveling it at Harmsway. Harmsway stared back at him unmoving, handsome face set in his mask of habitual contempt. Avellar stirred, but said nothing after all.

"I'm not a vampire," Belfortune said after a moment, and the gun's muzzle wavered and fell. "Yes, I'm psi, I've never denied it—"

"Like hell," Harmsway said.

Belfortune swept on as though he hadn't spoken. "—but I'm only an interference maker. All I can do is fuck up somebody trying to use their psi. I can't stop them. I can't take their power away."

"But you can." Lyall's voice was very soft, but they all heard her. "The tests were conclusive, I was there, I ran them. When you want to, you can stop all psi use cold."

"And then what?" Belfortune asked. He smiled bitterly, without a trace of humor. "That's the part no one ever asks about, do they, Mijja? Because what happens is they die. I take their power, and they die without it.''

"Bel." Faro's voice was gentle, as though there was no one else near them, and all the time in the world.

"You know what happens." Belfortune's voice scaled upward, toward hysteria. "You know how they die. Oh, God, the taste of it in my mind—''

Faro reached out to him, but Harmsway cut him off. "Jesus Christ. It's a hunter. And if you don't kill him, we're dead.''

"Shut up, Desir," Avellar said. He looked at Belfortune. "Bel—''

Belfortune shook his head. "I can't, Avellar. Not won't. I can't do it.''

"Let it be," Faro said, with unexpected authority. He and Avellar locked stares for a moment, and then Avellar turned away.

"Ready," Africa said, and held out the laser. Hazard took it warily, slipped his pistol and its spare clip back onto his belt.

"What do we do now, Avellar?" he said.

"Without Belfortune—'' Lyall began, and broke off with a gasp.

Avellar took a deep breath. "We have to get on board the ship. And if the Baron's brought in a hunter, they'll know where we are any minute now. We'll have to fight.''

"What a wonderful plan," Harmsway jeered. "And how typical of your planning. Damn you, Royal, why didn't you leave me here?''

Avellar looked at him, face absolutely without emotion. "I told you once, I need you, need your talent. I can't take the throne without your help.''

Africa looked up as though he'd been stung, and Hazard spoke quickly, cutting off anything the technician might have said. "But to fight, Royal?''

Jack Blue said, "He's right, Avellar. The odds aren't in our favor.''

Avellar looked at Belfortune. "You hear them, Belfortune. It's your choice.''

"I can't," Belfortune said, his voice little louder than a whisper. "I can't."

"He's found us," Lyall said. Her eyes were closed, face furrowed with concentration as she brought her minimal telepathy to bear on the problem. "He's at the east entrance, and the chase squads are joining him."

"Oh, shit," Harmsway said. "Shit, shit, shit." He flung himself out from under the shelter of the shelves, started down the corridor toward the eastern entrance. Overhead, a light fixture exploded in a shower of sparks; to his left, a cargo robot spun awkwardly on its treads, and started toward the entrance as well. Fat sparks gathered around him, snapped from his fingers and flickered away from him across the metal shelves and the walkways overhead as he tapped into and overloaded the cargo bay's electrical systems. He turned down the first side corridor, and vanished.

"Desir—!" Avellar began, closed his mouth over whatever he would have said. "Hazard, get after him, get him back if you can."

Hazard nodded. "But not for you, Royal," he said, and started after the electrokinetic, the laser still gripped in his hands.

Avellar looked down at Belfortune, who still crouched against the cases. "Damn you to hell, Belfortune," he whispered. "Give me a reason I shouldn't kill you now."

Belfortune did not answer, did not even seem to hear, and Faro said, "You pushed him too hard, Avellar, you and Harmsway. If you'd given me time—"

Avellar stared at him for an instant, but then nodded, acknowledging the rebuke. "All right," he said, "get moving, all of you. Head for the hatch."

"We can still back him up," Africa said.

Blue shook his head, said, in a voice suddenly as old and tired as he looked, "He's dead, man. They're both dead. They'll be on him in a minute."

As if to underscore his words, the whine of laser fire sounded from somewhere near the east entrance, followed a moment later by the distinctive crack as an electrokinetically induced overload destroyed a laser's powerpack.

Avellar winced. ''All we can do now,'' he said, ''is get to
the ship.''

''He's right,'' Blue said, and hauled himself to his feet,
steadied by Lyall and Africa. ''Let's go.''

Game/varRebel.2.04/subPsi.1.22/ver22.1/ses1.27

Harmsway moved through the corridors in a hailstorm of
electricity, glorying in a strength and skill he hadn't known
he possessed. Lights exploded overhead, spilled streamers
of fire from the open circuits; he caught and shaped that in-
choate power into bolts, and flung them in the faces of the
Baron's troops as they moved to engage him. Outside the
sphere of his influence, lights flickered, control panels flashing yellow and red as he overloaded the system. He felt it,
reached out to compensate, groping for access to the main
power grid.

The first laser bolt spun him sideways into a stack of
crates. He caught himself against their metal sides, electricity crackling unheeded from his hands, turned to point at the
soldier, using his finger as focus and guide for his power.
Stored electricity leaped from the nearest output node,
flashed along his arm and across the intervening meters to
strike the laser's powerpack. It blew in a sheet of flame, and
the soldier fell, screaming. Harmsway caught his breath,
aware of a new pain in his chest, tried to flex his shoulder
and failed, and shrugged the other shoulder and kept walking, back toward the east entrance where the hunter had been
waiting.

There were more of the Baron's guard waiting around the
next corner, crouched behind the shield of a heavy gatling.
Harmsway took a deep breath that burned in his lungs, concentrated, and reached out for the gun's control circuits. The
guards fired in the same instant, a brief hail of lead before
Harmsway found the gatling's electronics and destroyed the
system. They had barely had time to aim, but two of the bul-
lets struck his hip and leg. He staggered against the nearest
stack of crates, tried to take a step, and fell, sliding against
the bare metal until he was barely sitting, propped up against

the crates. The first of the two surviving soldiers leveled his laser. Harmsway fought back the pain, and reached for the nearest output node. He drew power from it, but his side and leg burned and throbbed, and the electricity streamed out uncontrolled, writhed across the intervening metal of the floor like a fiery snake. The soldiers fell back for a moment, but then the second man, better protected by the gatling's smoking carcass, raised his laser again. There were more soldiers coming up the corridor behind him, and an airsled rode in their midst: the Baron himself was coming to see the end of the hunt. Harmsway braced himself to die.

Hazard rounded the last corner at that moment, and the soldiers swung instinctively to cover him. He took in the situation at a glance—Harmsway down, blood and burned flesh everywhere, the soldiers with leveled lasers and the rest of the troop coming up behind them—and started to raise his heavy laser for the last time.

"Don't shoot," a whispering voice said from the airsled's closed cabin, and Hazard froze. Harmsway made a small, painful sound, but the voice went on anyway, as though no one had spoken. "Hazard, you're not a fool. Put down your gun, and I'm sure we can come to some agreement."

Hazard hesitated, the muzzle of the gun wavering slightly—to fire was suicide, his and Harmsway's, but the speaker was Baron Vortex, and his word could never be trusted.

"Your friend is badly hurt, maybe dying," the voice went on. "But he could be saved. Put down your gun, Gallio Hazard, and I'll see that he lives."

"And me?" Hazard asked, with a short laugh.

"And you," the voice agreed. "Both of you will live."

"Why?"

"You're running short of time," the voice murmured, with a note like amusement, and Hazard shook his head.

"Why?" he said again.

"I need telepaths," the voice said. "Electrokinetics of Harmsway's talent are rare, to say the least; he may even be unique. You were not badly treated here, and if you cooperate, you can live quite well—you both can live quite well. Is Avellar's rebellion worth that much to you?"

Hazard hesitated for a moment longer, then, very slowly, laid his laser on the tiles, slid it hard toward the waiting soldiers. "All right," he said. "We surrender."

"Excellent," the voice purred, and changed instantly to a snap of command. "Medics, see to that man. You, guard, search this one properly."

Hazard lifted his hands, and submitted to the search, watching over the soldiers' shoulders as a medical team swarmed over Harmsway's unconscious body, loaded it into a medsled, and sped away. The nearest soldier prodded him, and he forced himself to move, walking back toward the entrance and the long trek back to the prison complex.

Game/verRebel.2.04/subPsi.1.22/ver22.1/ses1.28

There were only two guards by the cargo door, both staring nervously toward the sound of Harmsway's attack. They were sheltered by the hatchway, not an easy shot at all, and Avellar paused in the shelter of the final rack of crates, considering them cautiously. After a moment, he beckoned to Africa. The man frowned, but slipped forward to join the rebel leader.

"You're the best shot of all of us," Avellar said, leaning close, his voice an almost soundless whisper. "Can you take them?"

Africa frowned. "Not with a pistol."

Avellar made a face, but eased back into the shelter of the crates. After a moment, Africa followed, still frowning.

"Let me," Faro said.

Avellar shook his head. Before he could say anything, Jack Blue interrupted.

"I can draw them out, Avellar. Leave it to me."

Avellar looked uncertainly at him for a moment—a fat man, wheezing, leaning awkwardly on Lyall's shoulder—but slowly nodded. "If you can lure them out here . . ."

"We can take them," Africa said. "Can't we, Faro?"

Lord Faro nodded, snapped the last power cell into the butt of his pistol.

"Do it," Avellar said.

Blue closed his eyes, frowned, and let himself sink cross-legged onto the tiled floor. Slowly, the frown eased away from his heavy features, and his hands lay lax on his thighs. A few moments later, something stirred in the corridor to their right: it sounded like someone walking, the heavy, uncertain footsteps of a wounded man.

Lyall said, almost in the same moment, "They're buying it."

The first of the guards peered out of the hatchway, put up his faceplate to listen more closely. Africa leveled his pistol, but Lord Faro laid a restraining hand on his arm.

"Wait for the other one," he said, very softly.

Africa nodded, lowered the pistol again.

Blue was sweating lightly now, forehead furrowed in concentration. In the corridor, the footsteps faltered, something metal fell with a clatter, and then the footsteps picked up again, more slowly. The guard cocked his head to one side, listening, then pulled the faceplate down again. Avellar held his breath, afraid to move. Very slowly, Lyall crossed her fingers, closed her eyes, and played out her minimal power the way a fisherman plays a line, easing out a tendril of curiosity to draw the guard toward the strange noises. The guard held up his hand at last, and beckoned to his partner. The second guard came up the edge of the hatch, but stopped just inside the heavy frame. Africa breathed a curse: the hatchway still blocked their shot.

"Wait for it," Faro murmured, the words almost a mantra. "Wait for it."

The guards stood still for a moment longer, visibly conferring via the helmet links. Then the first guard started toward the sound of the footsteps, and the second man moved out of the hatchway to cover him.

"Now!" Avellar said.

The others fired almost as he spoke. The second guard fell without a sound, crumpling back into the hatchway. The first guard spun around, staggered by the shot, but fought to keep his feet and bring his laser to bear. Africa fired again, and this time he went down.

"Did he warn the main party?" Avellar demanded, looking at Lyall.

The telepath shook her head. "I don't think so."

"Then let's go," Avellar said. He looked down at Blue, who was slowly opening his eyes, extended a hand to help him to his feet. Faro did the same, and together they pulled the telekinetic upright. Belfortune stepped forward without a word, took Avellar's place. He winced when his share of Blue's weight hit him, but made no sound.

"Let's go," Avellar said again, and started across the open corridor toward the hatch. The others followed, Africa still with his laser at the ready, but nothing moved to stop them.

They crowded into the narrow space, and Avellar laid his hand against the sensor panel that regulated access to the freighter's cargo lock. There was a soft click, and then a high-pitched tone.

"Royal Avellar," he said distinctly, and waited. A heartbeat later, the cargo lock creaked open. Familiar people, familiar faces, were waiting inside the lock, and Avellar allowed himself to relax for the first time since they had left the prison complex.

"Thank God you made it," a well-remembered voice said, and Avellar grimaced, relief and chagrin equally mingled in his face.

"Danile. I didn't get him."

"I know." The man—greying, thin, a long, heavily embroidered coat thrown over expensively plain shirt and trousers—looked back at him gravely. "But you're safe, and alive, and well out of this place. And the rest of you, too." His eyes swept over the others, stopped when he saw Faro. "So." The word was little more than a hiss. "You found something you wanted more than your lands, Faro?"

Faro glared back at him, then deliberately reached out to touch Belfortune's wounded shoulder. "Yes. And I've paid, Danile. I can't go back to the Baron now."

There was a little silence, broken by one of the crew saying urgently, "Sirs . . ."

Danile nodded. "All right, Faro. All of you, we have to hurry. We're cleared for departure, let's go while we can."

There was a ragged murmur of agreement, and the group began to move further into the ship, following Danile and Avellar. The cargo door slid shut behind them, closing off their last view of Ixion's Wheel.

EVENING, DAY 30

There was a little silence after the session ended, the images fading slowly from the VDIRT table, and then a murmur of satisfaction, of pleasure, before the applause began. Ransome joined with the rest, but long before they'd finished, he was pushing his way through the crowd to Medard-Yasinë's side. "I want to meet her, Davvi."

Medard-Yasinë looked blank for a moment, then visibly pulled himself out of the Game universe. "So long as you're not planning to kill her, I-Jay. I want her working here."

Ransome gave his crooked smile. "No, I wasn't planning on it. She did a pretty good job with that scenario." *Better than pretty good; it was her players who held her back. God, wouldn't I love to play a session, show them all how it should be done . . .* It had been a long time since he had felt that way about any of the Game versions, and his smile widened for an instant.

"Can I quote you?" Medard-Yasinë said.

"Maybe. Once I've met her."

Medard-Yasinë laughed. "Come on, then."

The players were gathering in one of the larger lounges, where food and drink were already set out for the players—on the house, Gueremei said loudly. Medard-Yasinë nodded his agreement, and moved off with only a quick word of apology to supervise the house staff. Ransome stood just inside the door, content to watch from a distance for now, matching names and real faces to voices that had become oddly familiar. Savian and Beledin he had recognized instantly, despite the new implants glimmering in Beledin's eyes, and seeing them standing with their arms around each other, he guessed that their old affair might rekindle for the night. A thin, olive-skinned young man in a steward's jacket stood blinking for a moment in the doorway, the mark of his shades prominent on his nose, and Beledin detached himself from Savian's hold to embrace the newcomer. *Jack Blue?* Ransome wondered, and the steward's voice confirmed it. Huard he knew also, admitted grudgingly that the man had done a good job within conventional limits, as had Mariche. He searched the crowd for an instant before he found her, was not surprised to find her hooked up to another terminal, waiting to see if her ratings had changed. Imbertine—*who did better than I expected, given the others' conventional play*—floated in his chair at her side, rubbing his wrists as though the bracelets chafed him. Ransome allowed himself another quick smile—Mariche had always been overly concerned with rankings. That left Roscha—*Galan Africa*—and Lioe. He looked again, and realized that the stunning redhead talking to Huard must be one of the players. *Roscha, then—and it's a shame her mouth is that hair too big, or she'd be perfect. So where's Lioe?*

Even as he thought it, the door from the session room opened again, and a tall, lanky woman came into the room. She was dark, her skin the color of old bronze, and her face was made up of stark planes, a severe and sculptural beauty. A pilot's hat, a small one, just a narrow toque with a knot of spangled fabric wound around it, hugged her close-cut hair. Then someone called to her, a voice out of the crowd congratulating her on the session, and she turned to face him, her expression breaking into a smile that shattered the stony beauty and gave her instead a vivid plainness. Ransome caught his breath—he hadn't expected that, had expected a woman with looks like that to use them, to stay always grave and expressionless, to fear the sudden change—and in that moment someone spoke his name.

"Having fun, I-Jay?"

He looked down and down again, to the upturned face and half-bared breasts of a tiny, perfect woman. She smiled up at him, well aware of and comfortable with his regard, and Ransome was unable to keep his own smile in return from twisting slightly out of true. "Oh, enormously," he said. "Are you here professionally, Cella, or are you here to play?"

If the barb touched her, she gave no sign of it. "To play— or to watch, rather. It was nice of you to drop in, I-Jay, after all this time. But then, somebody was playing with your toys."

She kept her tone light, masking the insult, but Ransome was not deceived. "Why do you care if I'm out of the Game?"

Cella laughed at him, a lovely, practiced sound. "We've missed you, I-Jay, missed Ambidexter. Though with this Lioe around, that may be less of a problem. She does very well with your templates, don't you think?"

"Well enough," Ransome said. *But I'm better.* He controlled the impulse to boast, said instead, "Have you been playing much lately, Cella?" He knew perfectly well that she had been, that her most recent session had been panned by most of the nets as too political, and that the one before that had gotten an A rating on- and off-world—*and did she deliberately blow a session, set it up so you couldn't miss the politics, just to try to lure me back on line?* It didn't seem likely—one did not waste a session that way, not if one was serious about the Game—but he couldn't shake the sudden suspicion.

"Oh, I've been running a session or two," Cella said. "But we've all missed your input."

"I'll have to see if I can remedy that," Ransome said slowly, and was not reassured by Cella's blinding smile. *I'm doing what you want, Chauvelin, but I'm not at all happy about it. At least I've got an excuse. Except that Lioe's good, good the way I was, and I don't think I'd've missed her play.*

"I'll look forward to it." Cella touched his arm lightly, and slipped away into the crowd. Ransome watched her make her way between the groups of much taller men and women, a tiny, opulent shape in rich violet silk, her blue-black hair piled in braids interwoven with strands of the same clear color. She paused to speak briefly with one of the other Gamers, and then vanished among the crowd. Ransome stared a moment longer, wondering what she and

Damian Chrestil were up to this time, then resolutely looked away.

"I-Jay!" Beledin was waving to him from across the room. "I should've known you'd come."

Ransome made his way to join the other, allowed himself one genuinely mischievous smile before he smoothed his expression. "Hello, Bel. It was a good session."

Beledin nodded. "It was."

"That's what I always liked about you, Bel," Ransome murmured. "No false modesty."

Beledin ignored him, gestured to the two men standing with him. "You know Peter, but I don't know if you've met Vere?"

Ransome started to shake his head, looking at the steward's jacket, then frowned, a vague memory teasing him.

"Audovero Caminesi, *dit* Vere," the young man said with prompt courtesy.

"Illario Ransome." Ransome held out his hand, still frowning. "Have we met?"

"I played a tenth-run session of yours a few years ago, back when you—when Ambidexter was still working out of Two-Dragons," Vere answered, and took the other's hand.

Ransome nodded, unable to sort him out from the hundreds of other players, and took refuge in present truths. "It was a good session, quality play, tonight. I liked what you did with Jack Blue—did you set the weight, or was it a given?"

"Player's choice," Vere answered. He shrugged, trying for nonchalance. "I figured he'd need all the help he could get, playing with Grand Types, and the heavier he was the more powerful he was."

"Makes sense," Ransome said. In spite of himself, in spite of everything he'd ever said about the Game, it was too easy to get caught up in the old interests. He shrugged one shoulder, annoyed at himself for no reason, and looked away.

The servers had already been around with the drinks tray. Savian drained the last of his glass, and lifted a hand to wave to someone in the crowd. "Na Lioe! There's someone here you should meet."

"Peter." Beledin frowned quickly at him, at the emptied glass, and looked at Ransome. "I-Jay. She's good—"

"Trust me," Ransome said, and turned to face the woman as she emerged from the crowd.

Lioe looked warily from Savian to the stranger, aware of undercurrents but uncertain of their meanings. The stranger smiled back at her—a gaunt, white-faced man with deep lines that bracketed his mouth, turning his expression crooked—and said, "I'm pleased to meet you, Na Lioe."

Lioe nodded, waiting for the name, and the stranger's smile broadened.

"I'm Illario Ransome."

"Na Ransome." Lioe held out her hand, and the stranger took it, his grip neither testing nor condescendingly weak, still with that crooked smile.

"He's Ambidexter," Vere said, and for an instant sounded all of twelve years old. Ransome gave him a fleeting, amused glance, and the younger man flushed to the roots of his hair.

"You left some good characters," Lioe said, mildly annoyed by his treatment of her player. "It's a shame you quit the Game."

There was a sudden silence, spreading from her words, and she was aware of Savian's open grin, daring her to say more. Beledin kicked his friend just above the ankle, not gently, but the Republican ignored him. Ransome stared back at her for a long moment, and then, slowly, the crooked smile widened, became real and unexpectedly appealing. The whole shape of his face changed, gaining sudden lines and hollows; his coarse grey-streaked hair fell untidily into his eyes. He pushed it back impatiently, as though he were no longer conscious of the movement, said, "I mightn't've done, if there'd been sessions like this to play in. I enjoyed watching."

"Thanks," Lioe said. *I will not apologize for playing your characters.*

"I'll be looking forward to seeing more of your work," Ransome said.

"That's high praise, from Ambidexter," Savian murmured.

Ransome cocked an eyebrow at him, but did not answer. Lioe said, with deliberate nonchalance, aiming for exactly the tone she would have used with anyone, "Thanks. You should come and play sometime."

The expressive eyebrows rose even higher. Lioe met the stare blandly, and, quite suddenly, Ransome laughed. "I might, at that. It was a pleasure to meet you, Na Lioe."

"And you," Lioe said, and couldn't keep a hint of irony out of her voice. She was already speaking to his back, however; she was sure he heard, but he made no response. "I think," she added, mostly under her breath, and was rewarded by a rather nervous giggle from Vere.

"Would you like some *methode?*" Beledin said hastily, and Lioe nodded.

"So that's Ambidexter," she said, and accepted the glass that Beledin held out to her. The liquor was thick and fizzy, and cheaply sweet. She took a careful swallow, waiting for their answers.

"Indeed it is," Savian said.

"He's a good player," Beledin said. "Nobody's matched his Court templates, outside the Grand Game."

"Harmsway's a great character," Vere agreed.

Once diverted into the Game, they could go on for hours. Lioe glanced away from the conversation, searching for Ambidexter—Ransome—among the crowding bodies. He was not a tall man, and it took her a minute to find him. He was standing with Gueremei and the man who had been pointed out to her as Davvi Medard-Yasinë, Shadows' primary owner—standing between the two of them, so that he seemed to be holding court, the other two dancing attendance. *Does he do that on purpose?* she wondered. *It's obnoxious—but he does do it well.* "Why did he quit gaming?" she asked, and the others looked at her in surprise.

"Ransome, you mean?" Beledin asked, and Lioe nodded.

"Sheer pique," Savian said, with a wicked grin.

"Give it a fucking rest," Beledin said. He looked back at Lioe, shrugged one shoulder. "He said he was bored. And he's got his story eggs to keep him busy."

There was a note of constraint in his voice, the faintest hint of something unspoken. Lioe cocked her head, wondering how to ask, and Savian said, "They're easier than real people."

Beledin scowled, opened his mouth to say something, and Savian held up both hands. "I'm not being bitchy, that's the truth. I think he got tired of trying to bully his players into doing what he wanted." There was something in his voice—a certainty, maybe—that silenced Beledin.

"So what did Ambidexter want?" That was Roscha, emerging from the crowd like the avenging angel in a popular film. Lioe caught her breath, impressed in spite of herself—in spite of being all too familiar with the type, of having written the template for the type—by the streetwise swagger and the striking figure.

"He said he enjoyed the session," Vere said.

Roscha whistled softly. "From him, that's a compliment and a half."

"So what does he do?" Lioe asked. "Now that he doesn't play."

Roscha shrugged—clearly, the world outside the Game meant nothing to her, Lioe thought, not sure if she admired or was annoyed by the attitude—and Beledin said, "He's an artist, an imagist, actually. He makes story eggs."

"What are those?" The others looked rather oddly at her, and Lioe smiled broadly to hide her embarrassment. "I don't know them." *And I dare you to comment, either.*

Beledin gestured, shaping a sphere, an ovoid, about twenty centimeters long, miming a size and weight that would be reasonably comfortable in the hand. "It's . . . they have these pictures in them, like a holofilm loop, that tells a story—suggests it, more like. You look through a lens at one end to see the display. They're really neat, the ones I've seen, very stylized, so you do a lot of guessing." He stopped, shrugged. "I'm just a musician, though. I don't know much about it." There was frustration in his voice, as though he was still looking for the words to describe what he'd seen.

Savian said, all trace of malice or mischief gone from his tone, "They really are spectacular, some—most of them. I saw one, it was just a plain, black metal case, smaller than usual, something you could put in your pocket, but when you looked into it, it was as though you were looking into a Five Points palazze. It was all golden lights, and carved furniture, and jewels, and velvets, and you could just see two figures moving through that setting, in and out of the clutter of things. You could turn the egg, rotate it, I mean, and you could see more bits and pieces of the scene, but you could never be quite sure what the two were doing, whether it was courtship, seduction, or one of them trying to escape. And you never could see the end of the scene, either, no matter how hard you tried.'' He shook his head. ''It was very— well, sensual, more than sexy, but ambiguous, too, so you couldn't be comfortable with it.'' He paused, tried a smile that carried at least some of his former detachment. ''I don't think Ransome likes you to be comfortable.''

I can believe that, Lioe thought, glanced again through the crowd. Ransome had moved away from Gueremei and Medard-Yasinë, was standing for that moment a little apart from all the rest, a glass of *methode* in one hand, the other deep in the pocket of his plain black trousers. For just an instant, his face was without expression, held nothing but its lines and a bone-deep exhaustion. Then someone spoke to him, and Lioe saw his face change, take on a mask of detached amusement. *So that's where Savian got it,* she thought, and had to hide a grin, deliberately turning her back to Ransome.

''That was a great session, Na Lioe.''

Lioe turned to face the speaker, a stocky, dark-haired man with a horus-eye tattoo on one cheek, half concealing the delicate data socket.

''Thanks,'' she said, and Gueremei, coming up behind the man, cleared her throat gently.

''I don't think you've met Davvi—Davvi Medard-Yasinë, our main owner.''

Lioe murmured something, and Medard-Yasinë grinned, rather sheepishly.

''Sorry, Na Lioe, I've seen enough of your work on the intersystems nets that I feel as though I know you. But it was a great session tonight.''

''I enjoyed it,'' Lioe said, and waited.

''I wonder,'' Medard-Yasinë began, and turned a shoulder to the other players, deftly easing her away from the others, "if you'd consider coming to a temporary agreement with us here at Shadows. I understand from Lia that you're only on planet for half a week?"

"Five days at minimum," Lioe said, and then remembered that Burning Bright kept a ten-day week. "The ship I'm crewing for is in dock for recalibration of the sail projectors, so I'm dependent on the dockyards. They told my boss it would take five to eight days."

Medard-Yasinë nodded. "Would it be presumptuous to assume you meant to spend most of that time gaming?"

"This is Burning Bright," Lioe said, with a smile to take the sting out of her words. "I'd call that a reasonable assumption. Yes, I was hoping to get in as many sessions as possible."

"After tonight's session," Medard-Yasinë said, "we'd be interested in anything else you might have ready to run. We'd be willing to offer twenty-five percent of the fees, and free machine time to prepare any new ideas."

"That's very generous," Lioe said, and meant it. Most Gaming clubs made a good proportion of their income from the fees they charged for use of the club's equipment. A session could be outlined easily enough on a Gameboard, but fine-tuning the details took the raw power—and often the more extensive libraries—available through the clubs. It had cost her over a hundred credits to complete just the prison segments of Ixion's Wheel.

"We're very interested," Medard-Yasinë said.

Lioe grinned. "Would this be an exclusive deal?"

"We'd want it that way," Medard-Yasinë agreed.

"I see." She hadn't really meant much by that, was just buying time, but Medard-Yasinë's thick brows drew together slightly.

"We'd also be prepared to pay an exclusive-use fee, for Ixion's Wheel, on a time-limited basis."

"You are serious," Lioe said, smiling, and Medard-Yasinë nodded. His face was completely without expression, and Lioe realized for the first time that he meant to buy her—her presence at the club, as a session leader—and her scenario, whatever it cost him. It was an unfamiliar feeling, and somewhat unsettling; she wondered if she had been selling herself short, back on Callixte. That was an unpleasant thought, and unproductive: she dragged herself back to the business at hand. "What kind of a time period?"

"The length of your stay," Medard-Yasinë said promptly. "Or, since you're not sure how long that will be, a week—ten days. We're prepared to offer you five hundred *real*, over and above your cut of the session fees, and of course the free machine time, on a second-priority basis, if you'll let us have an exclusive license on Ixion's Wheel for the next ten days. And, of course, if you'll run at least five sessions for us."

Lioe hesitated, juggling numbers in her head. She could expect to clear about fifty *real* per session, if Shadows' fees were in line with the rest of the club system's; that plus the five hundred would pay all her bills at the transients' hostel, and the machine time would let her explore some ideas that had been nagging at her for most of the trip, ideas that sprang directly from Ixion's Wheel. . . . She curbed her enthusiasm. It also meant that someone else would be running her scenario several times a day, without her having any control at all over how it was handled. But then, most of those players would be household Gamers anyway, people who couldn't handle the scenario without a highly interventionist session leader, not at all the kind of players she wanted to be bothered with anymore. "What if it turns out that people want to play more than five sessions, and my schedule lets me handle it?" she asked, still playing for time.

Medard-Yasinë said, "From what you've told me, I don't know how likely that is." He grinned, and looked suddenly years younger. "With Storm coming—the Carnival, that is—I'd expect you to want to see some of the celebration. Frankly, I don't expect my full-timers to do much work, this time of year." Gueremei gave a short bark of laughter, and Medard-Yasinë gave her a conspiratorial glance. "But if you do find time to give us some extra sessions, I'll match whatever you make from fees."

Lioe nodded. "All right," she said. "It sounds like a good deal. I'm willing to try it."

"Excellent," Medard-Yasinë said, and smiled again.

"I'll draw up a contract, and you can drop by anytime tomorrow—"

"Anytime?" Gueremei said, and Medard-Yasinë grimaced.

"All right, anytime after noon. I'll have a voucher for the fees waiting then, too."

"It sounds good," Lioe said. "I'll see you then."

"It's good to have you in the house," Medard-Yasinë said. "Even if it's only for a few days." They clasped hands again, and then he and Gueremei moved away.

Left to herself, Lioe took a careful step backward, away from the crowd of Gamers. She was flattered by Medard-Yasinë's praise, flattered and startled and suspicious in about equal measures, and she wanted time to think. It wasn't that she disliked the noise and the babble and the flying cross-talk that surrounded her, compliment and critique and commentary filling the air around her, but it distracted her, made her feel almost too much at home. Her decision wasn't irrevocable—she could always refuse to sign the contract the next morning—but she felt the sudden need to sit down somewhere quiet and work out what she'd done. Nothing but good, seemingly: a damn good session, a contract, even a compliment from Ambidexter, which, after she'd used his character without permission, was an accomplishment indeed. From what the others had said, Ambidexter had a reputation for being possessive—*and I probably wouldn't've done it if I'd realized he was still around.*

She scanned the groups of players, looking again for Ambidexter—*Ransome,* she corrected herself, *Illario Ransome*—but the thin figure had vanished. *Out of sight, or gone?* she wondered, and the stab of disappointment was unexpectedly keen. *Why the hell should I care? Except that he was—is?—Ambidexter, and he complimented my play. That's reason enough for any Gamer. But . . . I want to talk to him again.*

"So."

That was Africa's voice, at her elbow, and Lioe turned, was vaguely startled to see Roscha's striking face instead of the session's icon. Roscha went on, apparently unaware of the other's surprise, or so used to it as to be immune to the effect.

"Did he make you a decent offer?" She held out a glass of *methode* as she spoke, added, "I saw you weren't drinking."

"Thanks," Lioe said, and accepted the tall glass. The wine was comfortingly familiar, and she drank with pleasure.

"So will you be working here?" Roscha asked.

Lioe lifted an eyebrow, and the other woman stared back, unimpressed and still curious. "We're—negotiating," Lioe said after a moment, and Roscha grinned, not the least abashed.

"Shadows is a good club, and the play's quality. You ought to think about it."

"I am thinking about it," Lioe said, and laid the lightest of stresses on *thinking*. The party was winding down around her, session participants and observers alike edging toward the door. She glanced sideways to call up the implanted chronometer's display—one of the minor conveniences that came with a pilot's job—and saw without surprise that it was past local midnight. Savian and Beledin stood close together near the far wall; even as she watched, Beledin smiled, and touched the other man's shoulder, easing him toward the door. He caught her eye, and the smile widened to a grin, and then they were gone. Vere was nowhere in sight, nor Imbertine; Mariche was deep in conversation with a handsome, grey-haired man, who leaned close, resting a tentative hand on her waist. Huard stood next to a full-bodied woman with gold flowers painted on her dark skin and hsaii ribbons woven in her hair. Even as Lioe watched, the woman reached up to touch Huard's face, the flowers glittering in the cold light.

She looked away politely, feeling vaguely jealous—why should she be the only one going home alone?—and Roscha said, "If you're interested, I know a good after-hours bar. After that session, I owe you a drink."

Lioe glanced curiously at her, wondering if she really had heard a double invitation, and what she would do about it if she had. Roscha was a striking woman, there was no doubt

about it, the strong sexy curves well displayed by the plain
workcloth trousers and the thin knit shirt beneath the worn
jerkin. More than that, though, she was something familiar, a
kind of Gamer Lioe knew and understood, and all of a sudden she was hungry for just that familiarity. "Thanks," she
said. "I'll take you up on that."

Roscha's smile in return was dazzling. "It's the least I can
do. You gave me a great character."

I didn't choose you, unfortunately, Lioe thought, *and
Africa's pretty conventional.* She mumbled something in answer, and looked around for Aliar Gueremei. The older
woman was standing with a group of Gamers on the far side
of the room. Lioe lifted a hand to catch her eye, and started
toward her, but Gueremei waved her away, her expression at
once amused and approving. Lioe waved back, and turned
toward the door. Roscha followed her from the room.

The hallways were less crowded than they had been, but
players still clustered in the courtyard, busy at the food bars
and in the lobby. A few of them called congratulations; Lioe
nodded back, called polite responses, and felt the sense of
satisfaction growing in her. She had done well, and she de-
served the praise. Outside Shadows, the street was quiet,
only dimly lit by the cool spheres at each intersection, and
Lioe checked in spite of herself. The food shop seemed all
but deserted, the orange light behind its open door like the
glow of a banked fire. Music no longer spilled into the street,
and even the bouncers had disappeared.

"The club's down toward the Straight," Roscha said, and
Lioe jumped a little.

"How are the streets, this late?" she asked.

Roscha shrugged, looking rather surprised at the question.
"Not bad—not in this quarter, anyway." She tossed her
head to send her thick hair tumbling back over her shoulders.
"Come Storm, of course, everybody will be out all night,
but I don't know if that makes you any safer."

True enough, Lioe thought, *true on any planet. But I wonder if your definition of "safe" matches mine.* "That's the
Carnival, right?" *Keep her talking, and see what it is she
wants. Since I think I could want her too.*

"Yeah. The winds have already shifted, you can feel it,

but the weather people aren't predicting anything yet. There'll be fireworks tomorrow night—the Syncretist Congregations are sponsoring that—and a big display on Storm One, that's day after tomorrow. There's a lot going on—people have scheduled stuff for the whole three weeks.''

There was an amusement in her voice that Lioe couldn't translate. Was it because the city had scheduled events for the whole period, as though there was a chance that nothing would happen? Or was it just that she thought Storm was funny? Vaguely, she remembered reading stories of floods and damage, docks and whole waterfront neighborhoods washed away. Burning Bright City nestled inside the circling islands as if it lay in the bottom of a bowl; let a storm into that confined space, and wind and water would wreak havoc. She shivered, thinking of Callixte's summer storms, the blue-black clouds marching along the horizon, lightning striking fires to scour the central plains. She couldn't quite imagine that force unleashed on a city—a crowded city—or with the force of the sea behind it. *Maybe all you can do is laugh.*

''The Syndics parade is tomorrow night,'' Roscha went on, and Lioe dragged her attention back to the conversation. ''That's on the Water.''

''Parade?'' Lioe asked.

''Yeah. They run barges—the big, flat-bodied ones, set up pageants on them.'' She grinned again, a look of pure mischief, and Lioe wondered just how young she was. ''They do all the fittings outside of Mainwarden Island—that's the big island, sits astride the southern end of the Water?''

Lioe nodded.

''They try to keep the presentations a big secret,'' Roscha said. ''When I was a kid, we used to sneak out there, try and see them ahead of time. It's Beauties and Beasts this year—that's the theme. You should get yourself a costume, if you go.''

''I'm not much one for dressing up,'' Lioe said doubtfully, and Roscha sounded a little subdued when she answered.

''I could recommend a good costumer.''

Lioe looked sideways at her, and Roscha looked away, as

though she'd said something wrong. "Thanks," Lioe said, but the other didn't answer. Lioe sighed slightly. She wasn't much one for costume, had never really learned how to play those games: Carnival wasn't part of Callixte's heritage, and Foster Services hadn't wanted to offend the Neo-pagans by encouraging its client-children to mask at Samhain.

They walked on in silence, through the dimly lit streets, passing from the pool of light that marked each intersection to the brief edge of almost-dark where the first light ended and the next did not quite reach, then into the light again. The neighborhood was not very different from the one where Shadows lay, the same flat-fronted, oddly decorated, anonymous buildings that could be shops or houses or factories; the same tiny parks and gardens, half hidden behind grillwork and brick walls; the same sudden bridges arching over an all-but-invisible canal. Lioe found herself concentrating on them anyway, trying to drown her sudden awareness of Roscha walking next to her. The cold, blank walls with their cryptic patterns, bands of lighter stone against the dark main body, were no help at all; she imagined she could feel the heat of the other woman's body, a subtle radiance in the night air. She looked up, looking for the stars, for that distraction, but the star field was drowned in the city lights. A moon showed briefly over her right shoulder, an imperfect oval just past or not quite full; ahead—to the north, beyond the Straight and the Junction Pools—a shuttle rose like a firework from Newfields, a familiar and comforting flare of light and almost invisible cloud. She was not surprised when Roscha's hand brushed her own.

She closed her hand around Roscha's fingers, felt calluses under her touch, calluses across Roscha's palm and on three of the fingertips, all sensed in a single rush of sensation, and then she slipped her hand, still awkwardly twined with Roscha's, into the pocket of her trousers. Roscha's knuckles rested against her thigh; the sudden movement pulled Roscha sideways a little, so that she stumbled, and made a small noise like a laugh, and their shoulders touched. Lioe smiled, said nothing, too aware of the warmth and weight of the other's touch to speak. Then Roscha's hand wriggled in hers, loosened and shifted its grip to shape a familiar code.

Sex? the shifting fingers asked, and Lioe moved her own hand to answer, *Yes.*

Plain or fancy?

Either.

Latex?

Nothing oral without it. Lioe felt Roscha pull away slightly, knew her own answer had come too quickly, and looked sideways to see Roscha looking at her with an expression that hovered between amusement and irritation. "Well, you don't know where I've been, either," she said aloud, and Roscha's anger dissolved in a shout of laughter. She flung her head back, the light from the intersection gleaming in her hair, and Lioe couldn't help laughing with her.

"Your place or mine?" Roscha asked, after a moment, and Lioe shrugged.

"I'm staying in a hostel in the Ghetto," she said. "You're welcome, but it's a long way."

Roscha laughed again, more quietly. "I live on my boat. I drive a john-boat for C/B Cie., deliveries and stuff. The tie-up's not far—as long as you don't mind a boat."

"Your place, then," Lioe said, and they walked on. Roscha freed her hand from Lioe's pocket, slipped it around the other woman's waist; a heartbeat later, Lioe did the same. She was very aware of the gentle pressure of Roscha's hand against her skin, and at the same time the texture of Roscha's stiff jerkin under her hand. It felt a little like thick leather, but the surface was oddly patterned, like scales. She squeezed Roscha's waist, trying to feel her body under the jerkin, and felt Roscha's fingers tighten in answer against her shirt. It was not satisfactory, to be touched, and to feel so little in return: she squeezed Roscha's waist again, and then released her, sliding her hand and arm up under the skirts of the jerkin so that her hand now rested directly against the thin shirt. Its weave was loose; she prodded experimentally at it, working one finger into the fabric so that she could feel warm skin, and Roscha jerked and gave a stifled giggle.

"That tickles."

"Sorry," Lioe said, and stopped poking, but she did not take her hand away.

They reached the edge of the Straight at last, a broad stretch of road, quiet now, only a few bicycles and a single flatbed carrier visible along its length. The Old Dike loomed in the distance, towering over the housetops. The noise of the carrier's engine echoed oddly between the housefronts and the water; a bicycle whispered past, tires singing against the pavement. Lioe caught a glimpse of the rider's face stern with concentration as he flashed under the nearest street-lamp. They crossed the trafficway cautiously, mindful of bicycles, and Roscha stepped up onto the wide poured-stone ledge that edged the river. Lioe copied her, more cautiously, and looked down to see the water black beneath her, shadowed from any glint of light by the stone wall that was its bank. Bollards, low iron things with rounded tops like fantastic mushrooms, sprang up at regular intervals along the wall, one or two with a coil of bright yellow safety line looped around them. Roscha led the way along the ledge, Lioe following a little more slowly—the wall was broad, but the black emptiness beside and beneath her, and the low rush of the water, were enough to encourage caution—and stopped beside a bollard that carried a double loop of safety line around its base.

"Here we are," Roscha said, and nodded at a rope ladder that was hooked into two of the holes drilled into the bank. Lioe looked down rather dubiously, was reassured to see the soft glow of a steering lamp. In its dim light, she could see most of Roscha's boat, a long, narrow shape, blunt at both ends, with an arched section at the bow that vanished into the shadows. The deck glowed gold directly under the lamp, and a solar strip glittered softly. Roscha frowned absently down at the boat, one hand buried in a pocket, and a few seconds later Lioe heard the faint double chime of a security system disarming itself. "I'll go first," Roscha said, and let herself down the ladder without waiting for Lioe to agree.

Lioe lifted an eyebrow at that, but waited until the other woman had reached the deck before easing herself onto the unsteady ladder. It took her a moment to find her balance, but then she had it, and lowered herself cautiously onto the deck. Roscha was waiting to steady her, and Lioe accepted the support for a few seconds, until she caught the rhythm of the boat in her feet and legs. She nodded to Roscha—the boat moved less than she had expected, but it was a jerky movement, unpredictable—and Roscha released her, moved forward to the shelter and crouched on the deck to release a hidden latch. A section of the deck came up in her hand, revealing a short ladder and a dim, red-toned light. Lioe grinned, even though she knew perfectly well why any boat-man—*or pilot, for that matter*—kept red lights in the sleeping quarters, and came forward to join her. Roscha smiled and said, "After you."

The cabin space was mostly bed, a thin mattress on top of a good-sized platform that probably concealed storage space. Lioe sat on the edge of the mattress—there was no room for two to stand in the narrow stairwell, and the arched ceiling kept her from standing upright except in the very center of the cabin—while Roscha secured the double-doored hatch behind them, and turned at last to face her. One hand was in her pocket still: the security system chimed again, resetting itself, and the red light strengthened slightly. In the comparative brightness, Lioe could see more details, the crumpled blankets and the cases of disks, Rulebooks and session supplements, mounted on the bulkhead just above the bed. Roscha slipped out of her jerkin, hung it on a hook mounted beside the hatch, and seated herself on the mattress beside the other woman. Lioe smiled and reached for her, and Roscha reached back. They kissed, lips meeting and parting, slow and awkward until they'd settled on who would lead. Lioe leaned into Roscha's strong embrace, let herself be held and touched, Roscha's callused fingers fumbling under her clothes to free her breasts, pinching her nipples into stiffness. And then they were scrambling with clasps and zippers and catchtape, struggling to get all the way onto the bed without letting go, either one of the other, until they were lying nearly face to face, legs tangled, thigh to crotch. Lioe leaned back a little to let Roscha's hand between her legs, to let the deft fingers slide between her labia, circling and searching and teasing in the thick wetness until she found the right stroke. Lioe buried her face against the other woman's shoulder, riding her hand and the rhythm of the boat until she came. Roscha came a few minutes later, driving her crotch against Lioe's thigh, and they lay tangled, breathing hard, until finally Lioe shifted her shoulders so that she could lie flat, displacing most of Roscha's weight sideways onto the mattress. Roscha mumbled something, already half asleep. Lioe craned her neck awkwardly to look at her, caught between amusement and chagrin—*no particular sense of prowess, I didn't* do *anything*—but it was late, and there was no place she needed to be. She shifted again, freeing herself from the uncomfortable parts of Roscha's embrace, and let herself relax toward sleep.

PART THREE

EARLY MORNING, DAY 31

It was very late by the time Damian Chrestil came home to
bed, a bored helio pilot lifting him from the Junction Pool
helipad up and over the light-streaked mass of the Old Dike
to the Chrestil-Brisch compound on the headland that was
the third of the original Five Points. Most of the lights were
out in the narrow buildings, only faint security lights glowing behind the arches of the first floor. The second and third
stories, solid walls of dark stone broken by unlit slit windows, looked ungainly, top-heavy, without light to give
them balance. Only the ring-and-cross of the landing pad
glowed blue through the darkness, and the helio pilot landed
them with the rotors barely moving, balancing the weight of
the passenger pod against the gas in the lifting cells. Damian
nodded his approval—*no need to wake everyone in the
house*—and let himself in through the security ring, raising
his hand in greeting to the single human being sitting sleep-
ily at the center of the glowing banks of controls. Like all the
Five Points families, and most of the other groups that dominated Burning Bright's commerce, the Chrestil-Brisch had
good reason to employ a private police force. It was a matter
of pride that theirs was smaller than many. The guard nodded back, and said, "Na Damian, there's a visitor waiting in
your suite. She's on your admit list."

Damian lifted an eyebrow at him. The only woman the
guard would describe as a visitor whom he would let into his
rooms was Cella, and he couldn't imagine what she would
be doing here. Her regular nights were the fourth, fourteenth,
and twenty-fourth. "Is there a message?" he asked, and the
guard shook his head.

"No, sir. She just asked to be let in."

"How charming."

Damian turned away, made his way down the echoing corridors toward his own suite of rooms. The palazze's floors were seamarble, quarried from the uninhabited, and uninhabitable, Midseas Islands; his footsteps sounded hollow on the green-veined stone, and he found himself stepping lightly, trying not to wake the distant echoes. The automatic lamps lit at his approach, fretted globes held in fantastic sconces, and closed down again after he had passed, so that he walked in the center of a moving tunnel of light. His private rooms were at the northwestern corner of the palazze, where short domed towers sprouted like mushrooms, looking out over the old city toward the rising mass of the Landing Isle and Newfields. As he approached them, the security board outside the main door lit, and chimed softly for his attention. The lights glowed green and yellow among the wide leaves and thick clustered fruit of the frieze of sea grape carved around the doorway, spelling out a familiar pattern. Even so, Damian Chrestil slid his hand into his pocket, curled his fingers around the familiar shape of his household remote, feeling for the control points by instinct. He trusted Cella as much as he trusted anyone, but it was as well to be prepared. He palmed the device, cutting off the system's programmed announcement of his presence, and let himself into the suite.

Cella was waiting in the reception room, as he'd known she would be, in the corner of the room under the arches that held up the main tower. Moonlight poured in through the window on her left, draping her with the shadow of the fretwork tracery outside the window, drawing blue fire from the seabrights scatter-sewn across her fractal-lace overskirt. Behind her, the Old City was spread like a faded carpet, the regular lights of square and street broken by the darkness of the distant reservoirs and the unlit lines of the Straight and the Crooked rivers and the velvet texture of the parklands. She was wearing a violet bodice above the lavender and silver lace, dyed raw silk cut close to her full breasts, rising and sweeping outward to expose her shoulders; braids of the same clear violet were woven into the glossy black of her

hair. The double light, the moonlight and the city lights behind her, rounded even further the lavish curves of her body.
Damian Chrestil caught his breath as she turned to smile at
him, and saw the faint pulsing light of an orbiter rising over
her shoulder from the pens at Newfields. It was perfectly
timed, it had to have been timed, and he knew he should
laugh, tease her for it, but the effect was too perfect, good
enough to convince even him. Then she took a step forward,
and he saw from the look on her face, the uncalculated,
crooked grin so different from her usual cool smile, that effect was the last thing on her mind. He blinked, but touched
the remote to light the wall lamps and opaque the windows,
and said aloud, "What brings you here, Cella?"

Her grin widened. "You told me," she said, "you told me
you wanted Ransome back on the nets, and by the very God,
he's back."

"So?" Damian was suddenly very tired, not in the mood
for games or the Game. "So you're good. I knew that, it's
what I pay you for."

Cella tilted her head at him, still smiling, but turned away
toward the sideboard bar. She ran her hands across the
carved border of lions and deer, fingers working deftly on
the disguised controls, and then extracted bottles and two
ice-lined tumblers. She poured two drinks, *ardente* cut with
the sweet-and-sour syrup distilled from sugarwort, and
brought one across to him. The ice in the tumblers cracked
sharply as the warmed *ardente* hit it. She said, over the random noises, "But I didn't do it, Damiano. He came back on
his own."

Damian lifted an eyebrow at her, and settled himself on
the long, low chaise, deliberately stretching out his legs to
keep her from sitting beside him. Cella smiled, not the least
put out, and seated herself demurely in a willow-work chair
opposite him. She might, from her expression, have been the
perfect salarywife greeting her corporate husband.

"I've been trying to lure him in, get him interested—I
even botched a scenario on his account—but he's been too
damn careful." She grinned suddenly, lopsidedly, an expression as unexpected as her attempts at respectability. "Or

at least too busy with those story eggs of his. I was beginning
to think you'd do better to commission one, Damiano.''

"But he came back," Damian said. "Do stick to the
point, Cella, I'm tired.''

One eyebrow flickered up in mute but pointed question,
but Cella said only, "That's right. He came back because
there's a new notable in town, and she had the temerity to
play one of his Grand Types. And she did it well, too. So I
think Na Ransome will have his mind on the Game for at
least a week—that's how long this woman is going to be
here. Or maybe longer. When I left, he was buying Rulebooks, and I haven't heard of him doing that in years.''

"So." Damian sipped at his drink, considering her news,
and slowly allowed himself to smile. The Game, or at least
the new notable, would keep Ransome busy in the Game
nets, and he could slip the lachesi quietly into the system,
and ship without interference from the Republic, local Customs, or Chauvelin. It seemed that ji-Imbaoa's interference
hadn't roused anyone's suspicions after all. "Tell me about
this new notable.''

Cella shrugged, a calculated indifference. "I don't know
much. She's a Republican, union pilot—from Callixte, or at
least she plays out of Callixte's nets. Her ship's supposed to
be in dock-orbit for repairs, and she's planning to spend the
time gaming. Decent-looking woman, if you like them thin
and stern. And a damn good session leader.''

"Find out about her," Damian said. "Politics, background—whatever.''

Cella nodded. "Ransome was really interested," she said.
"I haven't seen him in a club in years, he won't let it rest at
just one session. He'll be busy with this scenario for the rest
of Storm, at least.''

"Not bad," Damian Chrestil said, and allowed his approval to color his voice. He considered the invitation that he
knew was waiting in his files, added, "Are you working tomorrow—I mean, tonight?''

Cella frowned slightly, slipped a hand into the folds of her
skirt to consult a scheduler hidden somewhere out of sight.
"Tonight, no. Why?''

"Chauvelin is having his annual night-before-Storm party," Damian said. "I'd like you to accompany me."

Cella paused, shrugged slightly. "All right. Our usual arrangement, I assume?"

"Of course."

"All right, then."

"Excellent," Damian said.

"Not bad," Cella answered, "not bad at all." She set her now-empty tumbler aside, and came to sit next to him, pushing his legs out of her way. "All things considered, I think I have every right to be pleased."

"For whatever it was you did," Damian said. He eyed her almost warily, recognizing the mood. It was neither drink nor drugs, but the solid high of an unexpected success, and he would reap the benefits of it, whether he liked it or not. She smiled down at him, well aware of her own excitement and his lack of immediate response, and ran two fingers up the inside of his thigh. It was a touch that rarely failed to rouse him; he laid one hand flat against her breast, and felt her nipple already stiff against the palm of his hand, easily discernible through the rough silk. She had done the job he wanted, however she'd done it, and her choice of coin was sex: sex of her choice, for her pleasure, at her whim. He caught his breath as her hand moved higher, brushed past his groin, and came to rest flat against his lower belly, a steady, urgent pressure. Not that it was a difficult payback—*a hard one, maybe*—but it was unavoidable, if he wanted to keep their tacit agreement. Cella's smile widened, as though she'd read his thoughts, and she slid an expert hand under his clothes, ending all possibility of protest.

He woke in his own bed the next morning, to sunlight and the steady shrilling of an alarm. He swore, wondering for a bleary instant why Cella let it sound, then reached across the empty bed for the remote. The time was flashing on the far wall, the red numbers almost drowned by the bright sunlight: almost the ninth hour. He had slept through at least two earlier wake-ups. *No wonder Cella hadn't waited.* He sat up, wincing—he wasn't hung over, but he functioned badly on fewer than six hours' sleep—and touched the remote again. His fingers slid clumsily over the rounded surface. It was a

pretty thing, shaped like a wide-web node with a single
broad leaf wrapped around it, carved from a brown stone so
dark that it looked almost black except in direct sunlight, but
this morning the carving distracted him. He found the proper
control points at last, launched the program that displayed
his schedule on the far wall below the chronometer's numbers. The ninth hour was given over to the weekly breakfast
meeting with his siblings.

He swore again, checked the time—less than a quarter
hour, barely enough time to shower and shave and dress,
much less find a wake-up pill—and forced himself out of
bed. Neither the shower nor the pill Cella had kindly left for
him helped much, but he managed to dress with reasonable
care, and made his way to join the others. He was not the last
to arrive, and Chrestillio—Altagracian Chrestil-Brisch, the
family pensionary and titular head of the family by virtue of
being firstborn—nodded at him from his place at the head of
the long table. Bettisa Chrestil-Brisch, known as Bettis
Chrestil, the family's representative to the Five Points Bank,
did not look up from the workboard where the night's downloaded trade figures were playing.

"Good morning," Damian Chrestil said, keeping his
voice suitably subdued, and crossed to the sideboard to pour
himself a cup of coffee from the intricate silver brewer. The
coffee was cut half-and-half with milk from the Homestead
Island farms—even the Chrestil-Brisch couldn't afford to
import coffee in bulk—and he added a toffee-colored crystal
the size of his little fingernail from the sugar bowl. Sugar
was expensive, too—most of the sugarwort crop went to the
distilleries—but there was no point in being stingy this
morning. He collected breakfast as well, a wedge of soft,
mild cheese, a few thin, chewy slabs of docker's bread, and a
spoonful of sour preserved fruit. There was fish sausage as
well, and a bowl filled with half a dozen hard-boiled eggs,
their shells painted with swirls of dye, but he ignored them
both, and seated himself opposite Bettis Chrestil. The sunlight, mercifully, was behind him; it streamed into the room,
casting shadows across the polished and inlaid tabletop and
onto the olive-and-gold paneling. The carnival scenes that

filled the central medallion of each panel looked bleached in the strong light.

"Has anyone seen the weather?" Damian asked.

Bettis looked up from her board. "About what you'd expect, this time of year. There's a depression to the southeast, but there's no saying if it'll strengthen, or come this way."

Chrestillio said, "The street bookmakers are saying it's at forty-to-one to hit at all, at any strength, but I hear that's dropping."

And the street bookies would know, Damian thought. *They know as much and more than the weathermen, but then, they have more to lose.* The canalli bet on the weather with the same passion that he himself played politics.

"I'm sorry I'm late," a new voice said, and Damian looked up to see the last of his siblings standing in the doorway. She came fully into the room, a broad-shouldered, broad-hipped woman in the grey-green coveralls that anyone wore to visit the distillery, and a whiff of the mash came with her, a sour odor almost thick enough to taste. Damian winced, and Calligenia Chrestil-Brisch finished stripping out of the heavy coveralls and dropped them in the hallway outside the door. She closed the door behind her, leaving the clothes for a household cleaner, said, "I got caught up in some stuff at the plant."

"Problems?" Chrestillio said, and Calligan Brisch shook her head.

"Not really. We were doing preliminary slow-down for Storm, and there was a minor hassle with one of the big vats. About what you'd expect, this time of year."

Chrestillio nodded, satisfied, and Damian took a cautious sip of his coffee, trying to drown the last of the smell.

"Did you get that shipment in, Damiano?" Calligan went on, and turned to the sideboard. She filled a plate—a little of everything, cheese, sausage, bread, a couple of the eggs, a healthy spoonful of the preserved fruits—and came to take the final place at the table. Looking at her, at all of them, Damian was struck again by the resemblances between them. Not that they precisely looked alike, beyond a general similarity of coloring—Chrestillio and Calligan Brisch had both gotten their mother's build, big, broad-shouldered peo-

ple, while he and Bettis Chrestil took more after their slimmer, fine-boned father—but there was a certain something,
the shape of the long nose and the quirk of the wide mouth,
that marked them unmistakably as siblings. He shook himself out of the reverie, and made himself answer her question.

"Yes. There was some minor spoilage in one of the batches of red-carpet—TMN again."

"I think we ought to cut ties with them," Calligan Brisch
said, and reached for a saltcellar. Bettis Chrestil slid one
across to her, still not taking her eyes from the workboard.

"We probably should," Damian agreed. "Unless they
give us a real break on the next few batches." *And anyway,*
he added silently, *they've served their purpose. I've got
enough information on their codes to fake a shipment from
them, and that will help the lachesi get through.*

"What I'd like to know," Chrestillio said, "is why the
Republicans have been sniffing around our warehouses
again."

"Not here, surely," Bettis said.

"No," Chrestillio said.

"On Demeter, right?" Damian said, with all the innocence he could muster. "I think it was TMN they were
after—another reason to drop them, I guess."

"You heard about it, then?" Chrestillio asked.

"I got your message yesterday," Damian said. "I'm
sorry I didn't get back to you, but I did have time to look into
the matter, and from what our factor tells me, they were
looking for something in the TMN shipment that came
through yesterday." *Was it only yesterday? It feels as if it
were years ago.* He shook the thought away. Republican
Customs-and-Intelligence had certainly been tipped off to
the lachesi that had traveled with the red-carpet; the only real
question was, by whom, and the factor would deal with that.
But C-and-I had no proof; it would be safe enough to begin
the next stage of the transfer. In fact, the sooner the better.

"As you say," Bettis murmured, "another good reason to
sever ties with TMN. I've never understood why you dealt
with them in the first place, Damiano. They've got a reputa-

tion for shady dealing, buying smuggled goods and the like.''

That was why I started dealing with them. Damian curbed his tongue, said mildly, ''They were cheap, and they're brokers for a growers' union that—until last year, anyway—was reliable, gave us a quality product. I agree, I think they've outlived their usefulness.''

Chrestillio said, ''I'm still concerned that C-and-I was down on one of our houses, Damiano.''

''It wasn't us they were after, but I agree,'' Damian said. ''I'll make sure it doesn't happen again.''

Chrestillio shook his head. ''Not good enough. Are you running shadow cargoes, Damiano?''

Damian hesitated, not sure how he wanted to answer this—*of course I am, but I'm not sure you want to hear that*—and Chrestillio went on, ''We do a lot of business with the Republic. I don't want to screw up our good relations there.''

''We do a lot of business in Hsaioi-An, too,'' Damian said, sure of his ground in this well-worn argument. ''We need to keep on good terms with them, too.''

''But I don't want to do it at the expense of our Republican connections,'' Chrestillio said.

''They could make it pretty difficult to get the red-carpet if they wanted to,'' Calligan Brisch said. ''We have stockpiles, of course, and they will get us through Storm, but they won't last long after that. And the distillery will need a few weeks to get back up to speed.''

''To put it bluntly,'' Chrestillio said, ''what do we get out of this, in return for this risk?''

''What risk?'' Damian asked, and suddenly realized that his siblings knew, or guessed, more than he'd intended. *Not that it should surprise me. But I didn't expect them to challenge me quite so soon.* ''What I'm hoping to get is permission to trade directly with Highhopes and the human settlement on Nan-pianmar. I'm doing a favor for certain persons, and those worlds lie within his sphere of influence.''

''It would be nice not to go through the Jericho brokers,'' Bettis said, ''but do you really think they'll allow it?''

Damian grinned. "Frankly, I think it's a long shot, but the—the main person with whom I'm dealing has invested status in the question, and it'll be worth his while to buy us off. And ours, too. And he will be indebted to us."

"Well?" Chrestillio looked at the others.

"As long as it doesn't screw up my production schedules," Calligan Brisch said. "Otherwise, it sounds like a chance worth taking."

Bettis nodded. "I agree. Our investments in the Republic can stand a little scandal."

Chrestillio nodded. "All right. But I don't want trouble on Demeter."

"There won't be," Damian answered, and kept himself from crossing his fingers under the tabletop, as though he were a child again. *And there shouldn't be any trouble, not if ji-Imbaoa gets me the codes he's promised. With Ransome off the nets, or at least busy with the Game, there's no one else on the hsai side who can spot what's happening, and I know there aren't any traces on Demeter that will lead to me. TMN can fend for itself. And if I win—never mind the trading rights, there will be people on both sides deep in debt to me.* He smiled to himself, and reached for the dish of preserves.

DAY 31

Lioe settled herself at a console in one of the club's work-rooms, her fingers moving easily over the controls, probing the club's extensive libraries for ideas for a new scenario. It would be nice to pursue some of the ideas from Ixion's Wheel—particularly Avellar's bid for the throne, dependent as it was on the same psionics that had been banned through-out the Imperium. Avellar, tied to his surviving clone-sib-lings by a telepathic link, was potentially a fascinating character, though she would have to find a player who could be relied on to avoid Gamer angst. *Ambidexter could do it,* she thought, *if he was still playing.* She shook that thought away. Ambidexter was no longer a player; there was no use pining over what might have been. Avellar's bid for the throne would provide the most interesting resolution to the unstable political and emotional balance within the Game it-self; his plot had ties to all the other versions and variants of the Game, could pull it all together into one final, complete scenario that would take years to run. She could see how it could be structured, how to use Avellar to bring in each strand of the Game, all the plots that had evolved and mutated from the original scenario—they were linked any-way, so intermingled that a schematic of the Game looked more like a snarled web of string than a normal variant tree. But Avellar, or, more precisely, Avellar's bid to take the throne, could untangle it all, and bring the situation to a final resolution.

And that, of course, was the problem, and the main reason she would never float that grand scenario. To follow that line would mean coming dangerously close to the end of the Game. About the only convention that was held sacrosanct by every Gamer was that no scenario could be allowed to tip the balance between Rebellion and Imperium: to change that would be to change the Game itself. *It wouldn't be the end, not really,* a voice whispered, *just the start of a new Game,* but that was almost as unacceptable. She had been told, years ago, when she was just starting out in the Game, that she had too much of a taste for endings. She sighed, and touched the key sequence that would load another file into her Gameboard—Shadows had given her unlimited copy privileges—and got the double beep that warned her that the datasphere was reaching capacity. She sighed again, released it from the read/write slot, and fumbled in her carryall until she found the case of disks she had bought that morning. She fitted a new one into place, touched keys again, and saw the monitor screen shift to the familiar transmission pattern.

She leaned back in her chair, watching the patterns change, and wondered what she would do for another scenario. Ixion's Wheel was fun, but neither last night's session nor any of the off-line test sessions back on Callixte had been quite what she wanted. There was always somebody who wouldn't play the templates the way they were written, or something to throw off the balance she had imagined. Maybe a different set of players would do better, or maybe a different scenario—something in the Court Life variant, say, secret rebels working at court—would give her what she was looking for, would give her the perfect session that no one would ever want to rewrite.

She turned her thoughts away from that impossibility—the point of the Game was that everything could be rewritten, that the main points of the evolving story could only be arrived at by concensus, the acceptance of large numbers of one's peers—and flipped a secondary screen to the in-house narrowcast. One of the house notables was running Ixion's Wheel already, and she paused for a moment, touched keys to bring up the audio feed.

"—but can you be trusted to support the Rebellion, my lord?" a voice said, and she winced, and flipped the screen away. She hadn't expected the players to be very good, playing in a low-level session like this one, but that was the kind of Gamer dialogue that she particularly disliked.

She called up another set of menus, but let them sit untouched, staring at the complex symbol strings. Just at the moment, none of them were terribly interesting. She sighed again, and touched keys to move out of the Game systems and into the regular communications net. It was probably past time to check her temporary mailbox; it would be just like Kerestel to call to see how she was doing, and to worry if he received no answer. She touched codes, frowned for a moment at the mailbox prompt, and then searched her bag until she found the slip of foil with the account numbers printed on it. She typed them in, followed it with her password, and the screen went blank for an instant before obediently presenting her with a list of messages. As expected, Kerestel had called—twice—but at least the second message confirmed that they would be staying on Burning Bright for a full ten days. She dispatched a quick acknowledgment—*at least he'll know I'm all right, and checking my mail*—and called up the third message. The sender's code was unfamiliar. She wondered for an instant if Roscha had sent some kind of note—that sort of gesture didn't seem to be at all her style—and then the screen windowed again on the short printed message:

I ENJOYED YOUR SCENARIO, AND WOULD LIKE TO TALK MORE ABOUT IT. WOULD YOU BE INTERESTED IN COMING TO A PARTY TONIGHT AT THE HSAI AMBASSADOR'S WITH ME? I THINK YOU MIGHT FIND IT INSTRUCTIVE. RANSOME.

Lioe studied the note for a moment, trying to work out the implications. It was flattering that Ransome/Ambidexter had thought enough of the scenario to extend this invitation, and if sex was intended, she wasn't entirely sure she'd say no—*but I really don't think I like the word "instructive." And why is the hsai ambassador inviting him to parties, anyway?* She left the message hanging on that screen, touched her keyboard to move onto a general data net. A chime sounded and glyphs flashed, warning her that any charges from this node were her personal responsibility. She sighed, and hit the accept button, though she touched a second series of keys to post a running total at the base of the screen. The screen went dark for a moment, then presented her with another series of menus.

Burning Bright's datastore was indexed according to an unfamiliar system. She wasted perhaps five minutes and ten *real* learning how to phrase her questions, but at last found the hsai ambassador's public file. He was human—*and I probably oughtn't be surprised at that; the hsai do tend to staff their embassies with adopted members of the local species*—but not jericho-human, not born inside the borders of Hsaioi-An. What was unusual was that he had been born on Burning Bright, one of the select few who had been coopted for adoption into the hsai kinship system. Lioe stared at that information for a moment, wondering how it must feel to come back to your homeworld after all this time—over thirty years, if his age was correct, and he had been coopted in his twenties, like most *chaoi-mon*. She shook herself then, seeing the list of honors that followed his name: membership in the imperial family, half a dozen different awards for merit, including a personal letter from the Father-Emperor himself. Whatever he had felt about cooption at the time, Tal Chauvelin had adapted, and flourished. And there were reasons to accept cooption, after all. Lioe frowned slightly, remembering the last big series of hsai cooption raids. She had just begun piloting then, and the risk had been real enough, even on the fringes of the Republic, that she had had to consider what she would do if she were faced with that choice. The hsai wanted to join the entire galaxy in kinship, according to their own phrase, and, however you felt about it personally, they did live up to their side of that philosophy. *Chaoi-mon* were, by law and custom, full members of hsai society, fully part of the elaborate system. Given a choice between that and death, or at best a few years in a holding pen while the metagovernments squabbled over repatriation, becoming *chaoi-mon* was not that bad an option. And if you came from a poor world, either in the Free Zone or on the fringes of the Republic, or even from a poor sector of a good world, it was a definite step forward.

However, Chauvelin's background didn't tell her why Ransome was invited to his party, or why Ransome would invite her. She skimmed through the rest of the file, and found nothing useful. Ransome's public file was short, and heavily edited: it made no mention of his Gaming career, and concentrated on a list of the awards he had won for his story eggs and other image installations. He had been born on Burning Bright, held Burning Bright citizenship, but the only remotely personal piece of information in the file was the note that his parents had been Syncretist Observants, minister/administrators of Burning Bright's peculiar religion. She hesitated, wondering if it was worth her while to try to hack the system—there had to be other records available somewhere—but then smiled, slowly. There was, of course, an even simpler way to answer her question: ask him directly.

She flipped herself out of the datastore—the charges read fifty *real,* and she made a face at the total—and back onto the main communications net, transferring Ransome's mailcode from the message that still waited on the secondary screen. There was another brief pause, and then the communications screen lit and windowed.

"Na Lioe. I see you got my message."

Lioe leaned back in her chair to look at the face in the screen. Ransome was looking even paler than he had the night before, and a hectic flush stained his high cheekbones. *But then, I probably don't look so great myself, after last night.* She had not slept well on Roscha's boat. She put that thought aside, said aloud, "I did. I was wondering why."

There was a little pause, and Ransome said, "Why what?"

"Why you invited me," Lioe answered. *And why you were invited in the first place.*

Ransome grinned. "I told you, I like your play, and I think you might find hsai politics amusing—maybe even useful. Are you committed to a session tonight?"

"No." Lioe hesitated, unsure of the right move. *But I want to go, she realized abruptly. I've never seen real hsai society, just the jericho-humans who broker for them. And most of all, I want to find out more about Ransome.* "Yes," she said slowly. "Yes, I'd like to come. How do I get there—and how formal is this, anyway?"

"Moderately," Ransome said. "I'll meet you at the Governor's Point lift station at eighteen-thirty, and we can ride together—if that's agreeable to you."

"Thanks," Lioe said. "I'll be there."

"Until tonight, then," Ransome said, and cut the connection.

Lioe stared at the empty screen for a moment longer, then made herself begin closing down the systems. From what she had seen of Burning Bright, "moderately formal" here should probably be translated as "strictly formal" in Republican terms. Nothing in her carryall—nothing in the storage cells back on the ship, or indeed left behind in her one-room flat on Callixte—fit that description; she would have to find the local shop district, and hope she could pick up something appropriate. She hesitated then, her fingers poised for the final sequence. The cab driver had said something about Warden Street, the street that ran along the top of the Old Dike, being a center for fashion. Why not go there, especially when she had money to spend? Less than she had before she'd gone into the datastores, but still enough to afford a few more indulgences. She smiled to herself, and finished closing down the system.

She paid her fee at the main desk in the lobby, and found her way to the nearest waterbus stop. Roscha had tried to explain the local transit system before she'd dropped Lioe off on the canalside south of Shadows, and so far the hurried explanation seemed to make sense. She bought a regular ticket—she didn't want to indulge in express buses, not when she was planning to buy clothing—and when the bus arrived, seated herself in the stern, under the faded brick-red awning. The bus was crowded, and slow, stopping every two hundred meters or so to take on more passengers or to drop someone off, and for once Lioe let herself enjoy the scenery.

The canal was filled with traffic, from covered barges half again as long as the waterbus to the narrow, high-tailed passenger boats that Roscha had called gondas, to one- and two-person skids. Most of the people riding skids were young, standing barefoot on the platform, skimming in and out of the traffic trailing a plume of spray. One bright-red craft cut close enough to the bus to send water spraying across the open passenger compartment, and Lioe joined in the general shout of anger. A woman at the head of the bus pitched a piece of fruit after the skid's driver, hitting him neatly in the back of the head, and the other passengers applauded. The woman stood and bowed, like an actor, and Lioe saw the mask sitting on the bench beside her, a grinning devil-face, the gold and black vivid against the faded grey of the seats.

At the next stop, a gaggle of children in school uniforms, black high-collared smocks open over a variety of shirts and trousers, climbed aboard; they vanished one by one as the bus wound its way up the canal toward the Crooked River. At last the bus turned onto a much broader canal, this one paralleling the Old Dike, so that they moved between a narrow embankment, and the houses shouldering each other for place beyond it, and the immense bulk of the Dike itself. Even in the daylight, with the sunlight to soften it, it was an impressive sight, towering over the traffic, bicycles and three-wheeled carts and denki-bikes and the occasional heavy carrier, that moved along the embankment at its foot. The stone of its face had faded from its original near-black, and the salt stains had all but vanished, replaced by the softer faded lavender and grey-green of rock-rust. Lioe leaned back, trying to see Warden Street at the top of the wall, but she could only hear it, the traffic moving in counterpoint to the noise of the street at its base.

The canal widened perceptibly, and the banks were crowded with low-slung barges, their open decks piled high with crates and boxes. Shoppers, men and women alike in loose shirts and trousers, many of them barefoot on the sun-warmed stones, moved along the banks with string sacks balanced on each shoulder, calling to each other and to the merchants on the barges. The barge tenders seemed to sell anything, Lioe saw with amazement. There was one stocked with food, set up like any land-bound store with neat aisles and display cases; tied to its stern was a much smaller boat that seemed to be filled with rags. A couple of adolescents were pawing through the piles. As Lioe watched, one of them straightened with a crow of delight, and slung a salvaged cape around his thin shoulders, striking a dramatic attitude. Farther on, a closed barge sold custom masks, a white, unpainted face peering from each of the tiny portholes. It was an unsettling effect, and Lioe looked away quickly.

The bus stopped three times in the market basin—Warden Mecomber's Market, the signs read, in Burning Bright's old-fashioned, legible script—and the passengers climbed out in droves, calling to the driver as they went. As the bus pulled away from the final stop, only Lioe and a trio of musicians, two towheaded young men who looked like siblings and a stocky, flat-faced woman, remained. The musicians huddled together, talking in low voices, their cased instruments tucked between their feet. The woman, sketching phrasing and tempo in the air, had beautiful hands.

The bus moved more slowly now, and the tone of its engine deepened, as though it were fighting a new current. Lioe glanced over the side, curious, but the oily water slid past, apparently unchanged. Then she heard a new rushing noise—not so new, she realized; she had been hearing it since the market, but the babble of voices had kept her from realizing what it was. The bus slanted in toward the left-hand bank, the embankment side, and the driver's voice crackled in the speakers.

"Crooked Underpass, people. End of the line."

Lioe followed the musicians up onto the bank, and stopped short, staring at the Dike. Directly ahead of her, the embankment ended in a woven iron railing; beyond that, water spurted from a hole in the Dike, a short, meter-long fall to the river below—not a hole, she realized instantly, but a tunnel. The Crooked River had to pass through the Dike— she had known that, but it hadn't quite sunk in to her consciousness—and this was the mouth of the tunnel that carried it. *The tunnel probably has hydro generators in it, too,* she thought, striving for some kind of perspective. *Burning Brighters don't seem to waste power.* Beyond the railing, the water roared, and a segment of the spectrum danced in the spray. She stared for a moment longer, then made herself look away.

She rode the elevator up the face of the Dike—it was a

closed car, and she wasn't entirely sure if she was glad or
sorry—and passed through the elevator station and into a
blaze of noise and color. She blinked, startled, checked instinctively, and nearly ran into someone. Warden Street was
mobbed, people jostling shoulder to shoulder along the
walkways and spilling out into the street, so that the trolley
sounded its two-toned whistle almost continually, and still
barely moved more than a few meters at a time. A group of
musicians—not the trio from the bus—were playing on a
wooden platform that looked temporary, the stinging sound
of steel strings ringing over the crowd, but the singer's
words were lost in the general uproar. Lioe blinked again,
realized that she was becoming a traffic hazard, and made
herself start walking.

The crowds here were better dressed than they had been
on the streets below. Here most of the people, men and
women, wore either the full-skirted, nip-waisted coats or
loose, unshaped wraps of some silky fabric that seemed to
float in the air around them, trailing strange perfumes. Quite
a few wore strands of bells, silver or gold or enameled in
many colors, slung from shoulder to hip, and Lioe found herself eyeing them curiously, wondering if the style would suit
her. The shop windows were enticing, holograms revolving
in the thick display glass, showing off clothes more improb-
able even than the Republic's highest fashion, the prices
flickering discreetly just below the items. A few of the older
buildings had real windows, with real goods in the boxes behind them. Lioe slowed her step to stare, not caring if that
betrayed her as a foreigner—the neat hat would do that anyway, marked her as a pilot and a Republican on any human-
settled world—and realized that the prices in these windows
were sandwiched in the glass itself, faint opalescent numbers visible only from a certain angle. She couldn't begin to
guess how much such a display would cost, but she suspected the shops made more than enough to cover their expenses. Still, one of them was bound to have what she
needed.

She found what she was looking for at last, in a smaller
store toward the center of the Dike, a place crammed with
racks of the full-skirted coats and the silky wraps, and a pile

of skirts made of reembroidered lace, each pattern in the lace itself redefined by an overlay of colored shapes cut from sequensa shells. She fingered that fabric cautiously, admiring its elaborate beauty, but knew better than to buy. She wouldn't know how to wear a skirt, how to make herself look good in it, but even so, she sighed for the lost possibility. She bought a coat instead, this one straight-bodied, a rich gold-on-gold brocade embroidered at the neck and shoulders with gold beads and leaf-shaped paillettes of gold-dyed sequensas. It looked good, she had to admit as she looked at herself in the shop mirror, the counterwoman hovering in the background, good enough to make her reckless. She bought a shirt as well, a loose tunic of the floating silk dyed a darker mustard color, and a thin scarf bordered with more sequensas and gold embroidery. It took everything that was left of the voucher from Shadows to pay for it all, but she shrugged away the thought that she was doing it to impress Ransome. This was easy money, easy come and easy go, to be spent on indulgences like this. *And if I want to impress somebody with it, well, I'll just call Roscha. I might do that anyway.* She passed the last of the vouchers over the countertop, watched the woman feed them one by one into the bank machine. *I think I'll do just that—and if I need money, there's always Republican C-and-I. Kichi Desjourdy's station chief here, and she always paid well for information. There's bound to be enough stuff going on here that would interest her.* She watched the counterwoman wrap the clothes into a tidy bundle, accepted it with thanks. Certainly there should be enough happening at this party of Ransome's. She tucked the bundle under her arm, and stepped out of the shop to catch the trolley back toward Governor's Point and her hostel in the Ghetto beyond.

EVENING, DAY 31

It was evening in Chauvelin's garden, and Damian Chrestil stood with his back to the terrace wall, looking inward toward the house. It was almost as large as a midsize palazze, the sort that cousins of Five Points families built in the districts below the Five Points cliffs. The white stone glowed in the twilight, very bright against the purpling haze of the sky; the open windows were filled with golden light, spilling a distant music into the cooling air. In the gap between the southern wing and the main house, he could just see a blue-black expanse of ocean, reflecting a rising moon in a scattering of light like foam. He looked away from that, made uneasy by the sight of open water—the sea should be viewed from the security of the barrier hills, or from an open deck, not glimpsed like this across a garden—and found the lesser moon, just rising, riding low beneath a bank of cloud. The larger moon was well up, and all but invisible, just a faint glow of pewter light behind the thickening clouds. The street brokers were saying it was thirty-to-one that the storm that was building to the south would hit the city, but no one was taking odds on strength.

The distant rumble of an orbiter, lifting from Newfields, caught his attention, drew his eyes west just in time to see the spark of light dwindle into a pinpoint no brighter than a star, and vanish in the twilight. The sky behind it was streaked with cloud and layered with the orange and reds of the sunset, the distant housetops outlined against it as though against a sheet of flame. The sound of the takeoff hung in the air, undercutting the drifting music. It was nothing special,

and he looked away, back toward the crowd of people filling
the terrace. One of them—a woman, tall, face thin and sculp-
turally beautiful, the lines of her bones drawn hard and pure
under skin like old honey—had heard the orbiter too, was
still staring upward as though she could pick out the light of
its passage from among the scudding clouds. There was
some expression behind that still face, knowledge, perhaps,
that was no longer hunger, and Damian caught his breath in
spite of himself, watching her watch the orbiter's flight.
Then there was a movement in the crowd beside her, and she
turned away, her face breaking into movement, the stone-
hard beauty shattering into a sort of vivid ugliness. Ransome
smiled crookedly at her—they were of a height—and drew
her away with him toward the house. As she turned, Damian
saw the hat slung over her shoulder, dangling from a spangled scarf that from this distance looked as though it had
been woven from the sunset sky. A short grey plume flowed
like a cloud from the hat's crown. *So that's the pilot,* he
thought. *She'll certainly bear watching.*

"I see you've spotted her. That's Lioe."

Damian looked down and down again, smiled in spite of
himself at Cella's delicate face turned up to him. She was a
tiny woman, barely tall enough to reach his shoulder; even
her eight-centimeter heels did not bring her chin above his
armpit. She was beautifully dressed, as always, this time in a
sleeveless bodice the color of bitter chocolate that hugged
breasts and hips and gave way to a swirling skirt embroidered at the hem with a band of pale copper apples. The al-
most-sheer fabric emphasized perfect calves and elegant
ankles. Her breasts swelled distractingly above the jerkin's
square neckline.

"Have you found out anything more?" Damian asked.

Cella smiled. She had painted her lips and cheeks and
nails to match the new-copper apples on her skirt, a cool me-
tallic pink barely paler than her skin. "Not much. She's from
Callixte—born there, apparently, not just works from there.
She's a notable by anyone's reckoning, and the people on
the intersystems nets like her a lot. If she's political, she's a
Republican, but that's a big if. Between piloting and the
Game, I can't see that she's had much time for politics. She

did know Kichi Desjourdy when Desjourdy was on Falcons-reach, but I can't trace anything more than just knowing each other. Desjourdy's a Gamer, after all, and a class-four arbiter.''

Damian nodded thoughtfully. Kichi Desjourdy was the new Customs-and-Intelligence representative to Burning Bright, a clever woman, and therefore dangerous. And that made any connection between her and this Lioe a dangerous one. ''Do you think this—this whole thing, meeting with Ransome and all—could be some kind of setup?''

Cella shook her head. ''Not with his consent, anyway. I'm quite certain they met at the club—that that was their first meeting, and that it wasn't staged in any way.'' She paused then, and her smile took on a new edge. ''I did find out one thing interesting, though. She spent last night with one of yours, Damiano. A john-boat girl called Roscha.''

''Did she, now?'' Damian said, softly. *Trust Roscha to be more trouble.* ''Why didn't I hear about it?''

''No one knew you were interested,'' Cella said. ''I didn't know you were interested, until last night.''

''They sleeping together?''

''I would say so.'' Cella shrugged. ''I would.''

''Charming.'' Damian stared out into the crowd, did not find the pilot, turned slowly so that he faced back toward the cliff and the Old City spread out beyond the lower terrace. Most of the lights were on now, the sky faded to a thick and dusty purple, and the pattern of the lights in the lower garden echoed the play of light from the city below, disrupted only by the figures moving along the silvered stones of the pathways. Neither Ransome nor Lioe was anywhere to be seen.

''I could introduce you,'' Cella said. ''I've met her.''

Damian glanced down at her, surprised less by the offer than by its timing, and she nodded to the window above them. A woman stood silhouetted in the golden light, a newly familiar, broad-shouldered shape with a hat slung across her back. She was looking in at the party, standing quite still, and Damian hesitated, tempted. *It would be interesting to speak to her directly, get some feel for what she was like*— He shook his head, not without regret. It was much safer to keep his distance, just in case she did turn out to have some connection with C-and-I. "No, not right now, I think. But keep an eye on her, Cella. I want to know exactly what she's doing."

"All right," Cella said, and sounded faintly surprised.

Damian looked away from her curiosity, back toward the lower terrace, and his eyes were caught again by the grey-and-silver stones that covered the paths. The more distant paths seemed to glow in the last of the light, and the nearer ones, closer to the cool standard-lamps, caught the blue-toned light and held it, odd shadows playing over their surfaces. He frowned, curious now, and walked away, down the steps to the graveled paths of the lower terrace. Cella followed a few steps behind, but he ignored her, stooped to examine the stones. A dozen, a hundred tiny faces looked back at him, all smiling slightly, as if they were amused by his surprise. He caught his breath, controlled his instinctive revulsion—*how could anyone stand to walk here, if they saw those looking back at them?*—and said, "Ransome's work, I take it?" His voice sounded strange to him, strained and taut, but Cella didn't seem to notice.

"I would say so."

"They are," Damian said, with precision, "very strange men, he and Chauvelin." He paused, and shook his head. "I suppose I had better pay my respects to the ambassador." He did not wait for her response, but started back across the terraces toward the ambassador's house.

Chauvelin greeted his guests in the main hall. The long room was lit as though by a thousand candles, light like melted butter, like curry, pouring from the edges of the ceiling across the polished bronzewood floor, gilding everything it touched. It turned the ice statue on the buffet—a sleek needle-ship poised on the points of its sailfields—to topaz, set deeper red-gold lights dancing in its heart like the glow of invisible reactors. Chauvelin smiled, seeing it, and made a mental note to thank his staff. They had done well in other things, too: the heavy bunches of red-streaked flowers that flamed against the ochre walls, the food, the junior staff—jericho-human, *chaoi-mon* and hsai alike—circulating among the guests to diffuse tension and keep the conversation and the wine flowing with equal ease. Je-Sou'tsian had the unenviable task of keeping an eye on ji-Imbaoa, but she seemed to be handling it without undue strain. She had chosen to wear her full honors, and the clusters of ribbon flowed from her shoulders almost to the floor. Perhaps it was not the most tactful of gestures, Chauvelin conceded—*ji-Imbaoa has fewer hereditary honors than she*—but he couldn't bring himself to reprove her. In any case, ji-Imbaoa seemed unaccountably sober, and in control of himself. There should be no trouble until later, if at all.

Satisfied that everything was at least temporarily secure in that quarter, Chauvelin looked away, searching the crowd for Ransome. He owed him thanks, as well as money, for the stones that paved the garden paths, and he was more than a little surprised that the imagist hadn't already collected. He found him at last, standing by the arched hallway that led in from the garden, and lifted a hand to beckon him over. Ransome raised a hand in answer, but glanced back over his shoulder, toward the tall woman who followed at his heels. Chauvelin lifted an eyebrow—he had thought that he knew most of Ransome's friends and protégés—but made no comment as the two made their way across the crowded room. The woman was striking, not at all in Ransome's usual line—his taste in women, such as it was, ran to flamboyant Amazons like LaChacalle—and she wore her clothes, Burning Brighter clothes, by the familiar cut and fabric, with the bravado born of unfamiliarity. Then he saw the way Ransome was watching her—she was even with him now, moving shoulder to shoulder with him through the room—and felt the touch of an unfamiliar pain. That intensity of gaze should be for him, not this stranger, and he resented the shift in Ransome's attention. He put that thought aside, frowning slightly at himself, as Ransome approached.

"Sia Chauvelin."

The tone even more than the choice of title was a warning that Ransome was in one of his more playful moods, capable of almost any mischief. Chauvelin nodded warily, said, "Good evening, I-Jay."

"I'd like to introduce someone to you," Ransome went on, still in the light tone that Chauvelin had learned to distrust, and motioned to the woman at his side, not quite touching her shoulder. "This is Quinn Lioe, one of the better Gamers I've seen in years. I'm enjoying my return to the Game much more than I'd expected."

"Na Lioe," Chauvelin murmured, and the woman answered, "Ambassador Chauvelin." Her voice was deep, soft, and rather pleasant, the clipped Republican vowels adding a tang to her words.

Ransome smiled, but it did not quite match the expression in his eyes. *Anger?* Chauvelin wondered. *Or triumph?* "I'm very grateful to you, Sia," the imagist went on. *Look what I found in the Game,* his expression implied.

Chauvelin made himself keep his expression neutral, though his mouth wanted to twist as though he'd bitten something sour. The woman Lioe—*the pilot Lioe,* he realized abruptly, seeing the hat hanging at her shoulder—recognized that there was some undertone of passion here; she was watchful, but uninvolved, her face set in a serene and stony calm. *Whatever Ransome thinks he's doing,* Chauvelin thought, *Lioe will have her own ideas.* The recognition steadied him; he said, "I still owe you part of your fee."

Lioe lifted an eyebrow in mute question, glancing from one to the other, and Chauvelin said, "I-Jay was good enough to hurry a commission for me—the stones on the paths in the lower gardens." He took a petty pleasure in emphasizing Ransome's subordinate position.

"Was that your work?" Lioe said, and Ransome nodded, still grinning. Lioe nodded back, her expression still serene. "Yes, I can see you don't like people to be comfortable."

There was a little silence, and Chauvelin wanted suddenly to cheer. Ransome said, "Why should they be? I'm not." He paused again, and added, striving for the earlier lightness, "Who have you been talking to, anyway?"

Lioe smiled slightly. "Other Gamers."

"I should've expected that," Ransome murmured.

"I still owe you money, I-Jay," Chauvelin said, riding over whatever else either one of them might have said. "You must have had workshop fees."

Ransome nodded. "Oh, I've submitted the bills, have no fear. But I think the result was worth it."

"It is spectacular," Chauvelin agreed, and, to his surprise, Lioe nodded.

"The faces are very beautiful," she said. "It must have changed your garden completely, Ambassador."

"It did," Chauvelin said.

"For the better, surely," Ransome said.

"I think so," Chauvelin said, and smiled. "Certainly it was a change."

His eye was caught by a sudden movement, a subtle gesture from across the room. He looked toward it, past Ransome's shoulder, and saw je-Sou'tsian standing a little apart, one hand lifted in mute appeal. Ransome saw his eyes move, controlled the impulse to look, said instead, "I don't want to monopolize you, sia."

"Not at all," Chauvelin said. "But something seems to have come up." He nodded toward je-Sou'tsian, and Ransome glanced over his shoulder.

"Ah, the Visiting Speaker's arrived?"

"My honored guest the Speaker has been here since the first arrivals," Chauvelin said, not without irony. "Na Lioe, it was a pleasure to meet you. I hope I'll have the pleasure again."

She murmured something inaudible in response, but there was an amusement lurking in her gold-flecked eyes. Chauvelin bowed over his clasped hands, hsai fashion, and moved away.

Je-Sou'tsian bowed slightly at his approach, but her hands were still, suppressing whatever she was feeling.

"What is it, Iameis?" Chauvelin said, and kept a smile on his face with an effort of will.

The steward's hands moved slightly, shaping anger and apology. Her fingerclaws, gilded for the occasion, glowed in the buttery light. "I'm sorry to have troubled you," she said, her tradetalk even more precise than usual, "and indeed I wouldn't have if it hadn't been Sia Ransome you were speaking with, but several members of the Visiting Speaker's household have asked permission to use the intersystems link. They've also asked that our technicians not oversee the linkage."

Chauvelin bit back his first response, knowing he was on

firm ground here. "I'm hurt that the Speaker's people should imply distrust of my household, knowing as I do the Speaker's respect and friendship. You may tell them that, word for word."

Je-Sou'tsian bowed again. "I will do so, with pleasure."

She started to back away, but Chauvelin said, "Iameis. Is there anything else?"

The steward hesitated for a heartbeat, then gestured negation, the movement solid and decisive. "No, sia. But I thought that should be nipped in the bud."

Chauvelin nodded. "I agree. Keep an eye on them, Iameis."

"Of course, sia." Je-Sou'tsian bowed again, and backed away.

Chauvelin stared after her, furious at ji-Imbaoa for trying such an obvious and infantile trick. *What can he think he'll gain from that? And why in all hells does he have to do it now, when I can't do anything about it?* The answer was too obvious to be considered, and he made himself put it out of his mind, turning away to greet a stocky man who served on the board of the Five Points Bank. He answered mechanically, his mind on ji-Imbaoa, and on Ransome and his new friend, and was not sorry when the banker excused himself, heading for the buffet. He stood alone for a moment, found himself scanning the crowd for Ransome. The imagist was standing near one of the windows that overlooked the garden, Lioe beside him, tall against the glass. Her coat blended with the golden light caught in the mirrorlike panes, drawing her into the reflections like a ghost; in contrast, Ransome was looking pale and interesting. It was hard to tell, these days, if it was deliberate or inevitable. Chauvelin suppressed the worry, reminding himself that he could always query the medsystems records if he really wanted to know. But whatever the cause, the look worked: Ransome had dressed with millimetrically calculated disorder, plain-slashed jerkin hanging open over equally plain shirt and narrow trousers, his unbrushed boots a well-planned disgrace. He made a perfect foil for Lioe's severe elegance, and Chauvelin felt again a stab of jealousy. *Who in all hells is she, that Ransome should behave like this?*

"Good evening, Chauvelin," a familiar voice said, and Chauvelin turned without haste to bow to Burning Bright's governor.

"A good evening to you, Governor."

Kasiel Berengaria nodded back, the gesture as much of a concession as she would ever make to hsai etiquette. She was a stocky, broad-bodied woman, comfortable in a heavily embroidered coat and trousers; a massive necklace of Homestead Island pearls made a collar around her neck, and held a seabright pendant suspended just at the divide of her full breasts. The skin exposed there was weathered, like her coarse, salt-and-pepper hair, and the short hands with their broken nails. "I haven't seen the Visiting Speaker tonight, Chauvelin."

Chauvelin picked his words carefully, well aware of the amusement in her mismatched eyes. One was almost blue, the other green-flecked brown: a disconcerting effect, and one he was certain she enjoyed. "The Visiting Speaker has been holding court in the inner room, Governor. I'm sure he'd be glad to see you."

Berengaria made a face. "I doubt it. Or at best, no happier to see me than I am to see him."

Chauvelin smiled in spite of himself. "Quite possibly."

"You have had an interesting time of it, with him in your household."

"Interesting is a good word," Chauvelin said. He and Berengaria were old adversaries, almost friends by now; she preferred the Republic to Hsaioi-An, but Burning Bright before both of them. It was a position he understood perfectly, and he had always admired her skill.

"One hears that the je Tsinra-an are rising in favor at court," Berengaria went on.

"One of them made a decent profit for the All-Father on Hazuhonë," Chauvelin said. She would already know at least that much; there was no point in denying it. He shrugged, carefully casual. "I must say, I doubt it will last."

"One hopes not," Berengaria said. "And not just for your sake."

She didn't have to say more, and Chauvelin nodded in agreement. The je Tsinra-an, having been out of favor for years, were attempting to rally other groups who had stood aloof from court politics by advocating a return to the old, hard-line, imperialistic policies of two generations ago. Unfortunately, now that Hsaioi-An and the Republic were trading freely, or at least relatively freely, through the merchants on entrepôt worlds like Burning Bright, both sides would suffer from a change in attitude. And Burning Bright and her fellow entrepôts would suffer most of all.

"The All-Father knows perfectly well where his bread is baked," Chauvelin said aloud, and hoped it was true.

"I hope so," Berengaria said, in unpleasant, unintended echo. "Whatever else happens, Chauvelin, I'd be very sorry if you were a casualty."

"I don't intend to be," Chauvelin answered. His mouth was dry, and he smiled to hide the sudden fear.

"Good," Berengaria said. She smiled back, but the expression did not touch the lines around her mismatched eyes. "It would be very dull without you." She nodded, and turned away into the crowd.

Chauvelin watched her go, turning her words over in his mind. It was not a good sign that Berengaria had heard rumors of power shifts between the factions in Hsaioi-An, and even less good that she was expressing concern for his future. *And I wonder, did I hear a hint that she might offer sanctuary, if things get bad?* There would be a price, of course—*and probably a high one*—but it was an option to keep in mind. At least Ransome was, for once, doing what he was told: that might buy enough time to deal with ji-Imbaoa. They said, on Burning Bright, that Storm brought a change in luck—he could remember, dimly, his mother buying lottery chances on the first day of Storm, hoping to bring money into the household. *I have to hope that's true.*

Ransome made his way through the maze of smaller rooms off the main hall. Chauvelin's household had thrown them open as well, knowing the space would be needed. Ji-Imbaoa was holding court in the largest of these, and Ransome paused at the door for a brief moment, glancing in past the crowding guests. He had lost Lioe some while back, to a conversation with the novelist LaChacalle, and hoped to find her—*though probably not here.* The Visiting Speaker was popular with certain groups on Burning Bright, most notably and most obviously the ones who traded heavily with Hsaioi-An, and he was surrounded by their representatives, but Ransome hardly thought that a Republican pilot would be likely to join them. The members of ji-Imbaoa's own household stood watchfully at the Speaker's shoulder, and at the edges of the room. Their ribbons, short strands of red that fell barely to their waists, were vivid against the sea-green panels. It was an elegant display, and one that deliberately overshadowed Chauvelin's less formal presence.

He had looked too long. Across the room, the Visiting Speaker lifted his hand in acknowledgment, and beckoned for Ransome to approach. It was not a request. Ransome hid a scowl, and started toward ji-Imbaoa. The crowd made way for him, a few people murmuring his name. Overhead, false lightning flickered through holographic clouds, and Ransome couldn't resist a quick look to see how the installation was doing. He had made the image canopy for Chauvelin a few years before; so far, he thought, it seemed to be holding up well.

"Tso-eh, Ransome,'' the Visiting Speaker said, granting the courtesy of a formal greeting. He continued in tradetalk, however, lifting his voice a little to be sure that the fringes of the group could hear. Conversations faded at that signal, and Ransome was suddenly aware of all eyes intent on him. Ji-Imbaoa was making this a matter of prestige, and for Chauvelin's sake—*and my pride, too*—he could not afford to make mistakes.

"I'm told you made this display?'' Ji-Imbaoa gestured to the image in the dome overhead, where half-hawk, half-human figures now swirled through the gaps in the clouds, riding the illusory lightning.

"That's right,'' Ransome answered, and forced himself not to mimic the hissing accent, the heavy emphasis on terminal sibilants.

"It's very striking,'' ji-Imbaoa said, without looking up. "But when will you come back to Hsaioi-An and show your talents there?''

Ransome pretended to glance up at the dome, not really seeing the roiling clouds, controlled his anger with an effort.

Ji-Imbaoa had threatened him with prosecution if he returned to Hsaioi-An; this was a particularly clumsy maneuver. He looked back at the Visiting Speaker, said politely enough, "Probably when such a generous commission is offered me. Do you think your *t'üanao* would be interested, Na Speaker?" He deliberately used the word that meant more than just family or household unit, that carried connotations of political rank and power as well, and saw from the sudden convulsive clenching of ji-Imbaoa's hand that the implications had struck home. Chauvelin was still a member of the tzu line; Ransome carried some of the same prestige by virtue of his patronage.

Ji-Imbaoa mastered his annoyance instantly, though the fingers of his free hand were still crooked slightly, and the red-painted fingerclaws rapped gently against his thigh. "Perhaps we shall," he said. "I am sure such a—thing— would please my dependents. You would come if we asked?"

Ransome bowed slightly, perfectly aware of where this game could lead if not precisely judged. He could not let himself be trapped into a commission, even if it meant seeming to back down. "If the price were right, and the time were convenient, and I were committed to no other business, yes, of course, Speaker." He paused, then added, "And, of course, assuming that all issues of freedom could be resolved. Some people take offense at images when none is intended; it seems—safer—to settle that ahead of time, than risk displeasing anyone."

Ji-Imbaoa showed teeth in an approximation of a human smile. The expression was delicately close to the bared teeth of insult, but not quite; Ransome admired his control even as he bit back anger. "I'm sure we could work out appropriate compensation," the Visiting Speaker said, and looked away, lifting a hand to beckon another guest. The woman turned toward him at once, and ji-Imbaoa took a few steps to meet her, bringing the group's attention with him. Ransome hesitated for a moment longer, tempted to protest this dismissal, but made himself turn away.

Lioe was standing just inside the doorway. "Were you having fun?" she asked, and Ransome made a face.

"How much of that did you hear?" He touched her shoulder lightly, easing her out into the more dimly lit hallway. The walls here were painted a deep red, the rich color of wine held up to a light. Golden vines coiled along the ceiling just below the hidden lights.

"Most of it, I think. I gather he doesn't like you."

"Not much," Ransome agreed. Lioe kept looking at him, one thin eyebrow lifted in an expression that reminded him suddenly of Chauvelin, and he touched her shoulder again, steering her toward one of the side rooms. It was little more than an alcove, pillared walls painted in a coppery brown, the pillars themselves painted with more delicate vines, the lighting concealed in thick clusters of sea grapes that dangled from the heads of the pillars. Bench-seats had been built into the side walls, and the space between the central set of pillars on the rear wall had been turned into a display recess. The shelves were filled with odd objects, and Ransome was startled to recognize one of his own story eggs among them.

"All right," Lioe said, "why doesn't this Visiting Speaker like you?"

Ransome hesitated again, then grimaced. "I'm not trying to put you off, I just don't know where to begin."

Lioe laughed. "You make friends easily, I see."

Ransome smiled back. "All right. For one thing, he and Chauvelin are from opposite factions, and Chauvelin has been my patron for years. For another—" He stopped, took a breath. "When I was younger, I worked for a local company, worked in Hsaioi-An, on Jericho, and I got into trouble there. I offended some people as well as breaking a few laws, but because I was only *houta* then they couldn't do anything about it—the insults, I mean. They enforced the laws. Now that I'm *min-hao,* though, they can take notice of those insults, and ji-Imbaoa—aside from being personally stupid and therefore an irresistible target—is closely related to someone with a serious grudge against me."

"That does explain a lot," Lioe said, after a moment. She cocked her head to one side, clearly reviewing his conversation with the Visiting Speaker. "Given all that, though, was it wise to antagonize him?"

"Probably not," Ransome admitted. "But he really is irresistible."

Lioe shook her head, but she was smiling. "I hope you and your patron get along."

Ransome winced, remembering their earlier conversation. "I'm sorry about earlier," he said. *It was because Chauvelin's been pushing me, pushing me back into the Game when that's the last thing I want to waste my time with—* But that was not something he could say aloud. "Do you do your own backgrounds, for the Game?"

Lioe nodded, obviously glad to accept the change of subject. "Yes. I carry a recorder when I go planetside. A lot of times I stumble into places that I can use later. When I can get time on the club machines, I do some manipulations, of course, but most of the time I can't afford it. That's the good part about this deal with Shadows. I've got all the time I want, and the run of their libraries."

"For ten days," Ransome said. That wasn't nearly enough time, not for any real work.

Lioe shrugged. "I have a contract with Kerestel."

Ransome stared at her with a certain frustration, wondering how she could stand to work part-time, only when there was time available on club machines, only when she wasn't piloting—how she could stand to stay confined, stuck inside the boundaries of the Game, where the ultimate rule was, *never change anything?* He opened his mouth, searching for the right words, and saw her pick up the story egg, hold its lens to her eye. He remembered that one well—an early work, filled with flames and a figure made of flame that shifted from male to female and back again with the fire's dance—and closed his mouth again, wondering what she would say.

"Is this yours?" Lioe asked, after a moment. She set the egg carefully aside, as though she thought the mechanism was something delicate. Her voice was without emotion, without inflection, polite and unreadable.

"Yes," Ransome said, "it's one of mine."

"How do you do that?" Abruptly, Lioe's voice thawed into enthusiasm. "How do you pull it all together?"

"Do you mean mechanically, or how I structure the images?" Ransome asked.

"Yes—both, I mean." Lioe grinned again, looked slightly embarrassed. "Sorry, I don't mean to hassle you."

"No!" Ransome had spoken more sharply than he had intended, shook his head to erase the word. "No, you're not hassling me. I like to talk about my work." *And anything to get her away from the Game.* "It's a lot like finding settings for Game sessions," he said, and heard himself painfully casual. "I spend a lot of time on the nets. I've got a pretty complete tie-in in my loft, and a good display structure. I pull clips off the nets, break down the images, then rebuild them into the loops for the eggs."

"That must take a lot of storage," Lioe said.

"But only linear, that's cheap enough," Ransome answered. "Look, it's easier to show you what I do than it is to talk about it. Would you like to go back to my loft, look at the system? I've got some things in progress, you could see how everything fits together—you could even play with the machines, if you'd like."

Lioe gave him a measuring look, and Ransome felt himself flush. "No strings attached. This is not an unsubtle way of getting you into bed."

Lioe smiled. "I wasn't really worried about it." She laid the lightest of stresses on "worried."

"Will you do it, then?" Ransome asked, and did his best to hide his sudden elation at her nod. Maybe, just maybe he could show her what was so wrong with the Game, why it was a waste of any decent talent—she was good at the Game, good enough that she should have a try at something else, something that would last beyond the ephemeral quasi-memory of the Game nets. He shook those thoughts away. Time enough for that if she was interested, if she cared about anything beyond the Game. "I was wondering," he said aloud, and Lioe glanced curiously at him. "You've got a great reputation on the Game nets. Why haven't you gone into it full-time, become a club notable? You could make a living at it, easily."

Lioe looked at him for a long moment, obviously choosing her words with care, and Ransome found himself, irra-

tionally, holding his breath. "Two reasons," she said at last.
"One, piloting's a better living. Two—the second reason is,
I can't see making it my life." She shrugged and looked
away, embarrassed. "It's a game. It's only as good as all its
players."

Yes, and that's most of what's wrong with it, Ransome
thought. *But there's so much else out there, besides the
Game. What the hell were your parents thinking of, to send
you into piloting?* There was no answer to that, and he
curbed his enthusiasm sharply. "Let me show you my
setup," he said, and started out of the room.

The second moon was setting over Chauvelin's garden,
throwing long shadows. Beyond the garden, fireworks flared
in silent splendor over the Inland Water, great sprays of colored light that rivaled the moon. Damian Chrestil stood in a
darkened embrasure, one of the archways that looked out
onto the upper terrace, idly tugging the curtain aside to
watch the departing guests, filing by ones and twos along the
path that led to the street. His eye was caught by a familiar
figure: Ransome, and the pilot was with him. That was a
good sign—Ransome should stay preoccupied with the nets,
with the Game, with Lioe to distract him—and he smiled
briefly.

"So you see it's going well." Ji-Imbaoa slipped into the
embrasure beside him, gestured to one of his household,
who bowed and backed away.

Damian let the heavy curtain fall back into place, effectively cutting off any view from the garden. He was blind in
the sudden darkness, heard ji-Imbaoa's claws chime against
a crystal glass, a faint, unnerving music. "So far," he said.

"Chauvelin has accepted that it is important, and Ransome will do what he tells him," the Visiting Speaker went
on. "I should think that conditions would be ideal."

Damian's eyes were beginning to adjust to the dimness.
He could see ji-Imbaoa outlined against the faint light from
the hallway; he shifted slightly, his shoulder brushing the
curtains, and a thin beam of moonlight cut across the space,
drawing faint grey lights from the Visiting Speaker's skin.
"Conditions will be ideal," Damian said, "once I have the
codes."

Ji-Imbaoa gestured unreadably, only the fact of the movement visible in shadow behind the moonlight. "It takes time to get those, time and a certain amount of privacy. I will have them for you tomorrow, I am certain of that."

I was expecting them tonight. Ransome won't be distracted forever, and C-and-I is sniffing around on Demeter. I don't have time to waste on this, I need to move the cargo now. . . . Damian bit back his irritation, said, "I hope so, Na Speaker. The longer I have to wait for them, the more risk to all of us."

"Tomorrow," ji-Imbaoa said again, and there was a note in his voice that warned Damian not to push further.

"All right," he said, but couldn't resist adding, "Tonight was such a good chance. I'm just sorry we missed it."

Ji-Imbaoa made a hissing sound, but said nothing.

"Until tomorrow, then," Damian said, cheerfully, and slipped out of the embrasure before the Visiting Speaker could think to stop him.

PART FOUR

DAY 1

Lioe woke slowly, blinking in the light that seeped in through the filtered windows. She lay still for a moment, remembering where she was, then cautiously pushed herself upright. The door to Ransome's bedroom was still closed, but the light was on in the little kitchen, and she could hear the last gasps as an automatic coffee maker completed its cycle. She glanced sideways, checking the time, and made a face as the numbers flashed red against the stark white wall. Almost noon, and she was committed to a midafternoon meeting at Shadows, reviewing her scenario for a group of club session leaders.

She reached for her shirt and trousers, the loose silky tunic incongruous at this hour of the morning, and dressed quickly, then went into the kitchen alcove. The coffee maker was obviously on a standard program: the tiny pot held barely enough for a single mug. She hesitated for an instant, but poured herself some anyway. That emptied the pot, and she searched cabinets, the little room as compulsively ordered as a ship's galley, until she found the box of makings and set another pot on to brew. She folded up the bed as well, but could not remember where Ransome had kept it; she left it sitting against the wall, and went back to the computer setup that dominated the working space. She touched one of the secondary keyboards lightly, but did not bring up the system, remembering instead what she had done the night before. It had been like the best parts of the Game, the preparation, hunting through the nets and libraries and her own collection of filmed scenes until she found just the right image—*or the image that can be adjusted, manipulated, until it has exactly the impact you wanted, that will conjure up just the right responses from your players, and they can take that knowledge and run with it. . . .* Except, of course, that Ransome's work stopped there, before the others, any others, entered the picture. He set up the image, calculated the effect, but didn't stay to finish the job. Or else he assumed he had finished his job, that the effect would be what he intended. She shook her head, not sure if she even really believed in that sort of confidence—*or is it arrogance?*—and turned away from the computers, touched the window controls to clear the treated glass.

The city stretched out below her, a breathtaking view over the housetops toward the Inland Water. The sky above the city was milky white, sunlight filtered by clouds, but light still glinted from the solar panels and on the murky water of the Junction Pool at her feet. It was busy, barges and lighters of all sizes snugged up to the multiple docking points that lined the Pool's edges. One of the largest ships, broad-beamed, its deck piled high with the familiar scarred-silver shapes of drop capsules, was moored at the foot of a cargo elevator. As she watched, fascinated—pilots rarely got to see where their cargoes ended up—a crane swooped down, delicately picked up two of the capsules, and added them to the neat pile growing in the elevator's open car.

She finished the coffee before the crane operator finished loading the elevator, and looked sideways again, checking the time. Past noon, and it would take almost an hour to reach Shadows—more, if she understood right, and the Storm celebrations had already begun. She looked again toward Ransome's door, blinking away the chronometer's numbers, wondering what she should do. It seemed rude just to leave, but it might well be worse to wake him. Of course, she could always leave a note. She looked around, searching for a notepad/printer or pen and paper, and the door to the bedroom opened.

"Good morning," Ransome said. He looked tired, Lioe thought, more tired than she would have expected. "I see you found the coffee."

"Yes, thanks," Lioe answered. "I made a second pot."

"Thank you," Ransome said, and stepped into the kitchen. "I'm glad you found the makings, most people I know drink tea." He came back out into the loft's main room, mug of coffee in one hand, a polished spherical remote in the other. His hand moved easily over the steel-bright surface, and the display space in the center of the room flashed into life. Lioe looked away, vaguely embarrassed, from the loop she had compiled the night before.

"That's really quite good," Ransome said.

"Beginner's work," Lioe said, more roughly than she had intended. In the display space, a metal-skinned woman transformed herself into a bird, the fingers elongating into feathers, hair into the crest of a hawk, body melting and shrinking into a compact and vicious form, rose and turned and swooped on something invisible, then landed, body beginning to turn again into a woman's even as she fell the last few meters, until the silver-skinned woman sat again on a bench in the sun, inspecting her long, bony feet. Even in the light from the window, the forms were clear and vivid.

"Certainly," Ransome said. "Everybody starts off with this kind of thing. But it's got promise. You could do something with it."

Lioe looked suspiciously at him, but he was staring at the images, watching the loop run its course one more time. It wasn't often one heard judgment and praise so neatly balanced; there was something in his tone that let her believe his words. "Thanks," she said. She sounded stilted, even to herself, and added, "And thanks for letting me play with your equipment. I really enjoyed it."

Ransome touched the remote again, and glyphs flashed in the air around him. From where she stood, Lioe could only see enough to recognize the drop-to-storage sequence. "You should try it again. I'm serious, you have a knack."

"Thanks." Lioe looked at the chair, the wire gloves discarded on the stand beside it, but made herself look away. "I've got to be at Shadows, though. I'm committed to a training group for their session leaders."

"For Ixion's Wheel?" Ransome asked, and Lioe nodded.

"They're paying me," she said, and didn't know quite why she felt so defensive.

Ransome grinned. "Well, that's a good reason, there. But don't you ever get sick of the Game?"

"No," Lioe said, automatically, and then, because Ransome had been honest with her, added, "It's not like I do it for a living."

"You could," Ransome murmured.

Lioe made a face. "I suppose. But I like piloting, which is a steady income, unlike Gaming, and—" She stopped abruptly, acknowledging what he had said. "And, yes, I think I'd be bored—well, not bored, exactly, but the Game, the scenarios never seem to resolve anything."

Ransome nodded. "Ixion's Wheel comes pretty close, from what I saw."

Lioe smiled, and didn't bother to deny it. "It could be the start of something. I think Avellar could pull the whole Game together into one really big scenario, but I know damn well no one's going to want to play that."

She stopped then, knowing how she sounded, but Ransome nodded again, more slowly, his expression remote. "A scenario that concentrated on Avellar's bid for the throne—you're right, that would pull everything in, wouldn't it? Rebellion, Psionics, Court Life . . . it would be worth playing. And Ixion's Wheel really sets it up. Have you started work on it?"

"No one wants to change the Game," Lioe repeated. "Not that drastically, anyway."

Ransome sighed. "You're probably right, which is why I stopped playing. It's a pity, though."

It's the nature of the Game. Lioe said instead, "I suppose. But, listen, I do have to leave, if I'm going to make this meeting on time. Thanks again."

"My pleasure," Ransome said, automatically. "You know where the helipad is?"

"I know where the tourist-trolley stops," Lioe answered. "I can't afford helicabs."

"All right," Ransome said. "Are you running any sessions yourself today?"

"Tonight," Lioe answered. She looked back, her hand on the main latch. "Why?"

"I thought—" Ransome paused, then gave a wry smile.

"I thought I might see if there were any places left. Like I said the other night, it's been a long time since I've seen a scenario that made me want to play."

"Shall I hold Harmsway for you?" Lioe asked.

"Why not?" Ransome's smile changed, became openly mischievous. "I don't think that part was played to its potential."

Lioe smiled back, flattered and apprehensive at the same time. Ambidexter in the scenario, playing his own template: it was a thought to conjure with, and to strike terror into the souls of lesser players. It was also a challenge, and she did not turn down a challenge. "I'll do that. And thank you again for a fascinating evening." She let herself out into the hallway, not quite hearing his murmured reply.

Left to himself, Ransome went back into the narrow kitchen, rummaged in the cold storage until he found a package that promised to cook in three minutes. He fitted it into the wall-mounted cooker, and made himself open the container once the timer sounded. The spicy pastry smelled good, but his appetite did not return; he forced himself to finish it anyway, standing at the counter, and turned his attention back to the main room and the empty display space. Lioe's hat was sitting on the folded bed, forgotten in her hurry. He sighed, and hoped he would remember to return it that night.

The hawk-woman had been a good image, for someone who'd never worked with more than the Game's more limited editors, and Lioe had been quick to sense the difference in form between the Game images and the image loops that filled a story egg. It was just too bad she was so caught up in the Game. . . . He crossed to the windows, staring down on the city. It would be Carnival already in the Wet Districts, the streets and canals busy with costumed figures. It would be Carnival on the nets as well, and that might be the best time to look into just why Damian Chrestil wanted him back in the Game.

He turned back to the display space, spun his chair into place at its center, but hesitated, slipping on the wire-bound gloves. It would be Carnival, all right, but that didn't mean that his usual net projection wouldn't be recognized. He

crossed to the shelves where he kept the shells of the unfin-
ished eggs, searched among the clutter until he found the
mask he had bought two years before, for a party he could no
longer clearly remember. It was a plain white mask, of the
three-quarters size that left only mouth and chin free, a standard form, eyebrows and cheekbones and nose all coarsely
modeled from the dead white plastic. He contemplated it for
a moment—it had always been an affectation of his not to
mask, to walk the streets and nets at Carnival as himself—
but this was not the time for that. He set the mask carefully
on one of the imaging tables, and switched on the cameras.
Lights flared, crisscrossed, catching the mask in a web of
stark white beams. He turned back to the display space, and
saw the mask's image floating in the air above his chair,
waiting to be remade.

He fingered the remote to dim the windows, and the
image grew correspondingly stronger as the competing daylight faded. He set the remote aside, pulled on the remaining
glove, and settled himself in his chair. The servos whirred
softly, tilting it and him to the most comfortable position; the
image moved with him, floating in the air within easy reach.
He studied it for a moment longer, then reached tentatively
into another image bank to pull out a series of other faces.
He found one with a mouth he liked, bleached that image to
match the mask's absolute lack of color, then patched the
two together, bringing the mouth and chin from the new
image to cover the missing parts of the original mask. He
studied the result for a moment, then ran his hand over the
compound image, deepening the modeling of mouth and
chin so that it matched the mask. He cocked his head to one
side, then drew the corners of the mouth down into a parody
of tragedy's mask. He tilted the eyes down as well, filled the
empty holes with absolute black, and dumped the resulting
image to main memory. It was not at all his usual style: no
one on the nets should recognize it as him.

He reached into control space to change modes, rewriting
his usual identification-and-projection package to display
the newly created mask, and flipped the whole system to
Carnival mode. Now all identification inquiries would automatically be ignored—this was the only time of year when

that routine would not get one dumped from the nets in short order—and a secondary program would deflect any attempt to trace the point of origin. He smiled then—he was going to enjoy this after all—and flipped himself out onto the nets.

The nets were crowded with ghostly shapes, a cheerful anarchy overriding the narrowcast lines and filling the unreal echo of the city with light and sound and sheets of brilliant color. Scenes like the loops of a story egg filled a number of nodes: rather than simply projecting an image, many of the maskers had chosen to create a brief repeating scene, and let that represent them to the world. Ransome let himself drift for a while, slipping from one system to the next with the ebb and flow of the crowds. A few groups and systems still tried to keep to business-as-usual, pale geometrics and strings of symbols competing with the gaudy loop-displays of the revelers, but they were easily overwhelmed. Some of the Carnival displays were elaborate, a sphere of scenery enclosing a character or two—often Grand Types from the Game—so that Ransome had either to bypass that particular node or move through the ongoing scenario. Near the Game nets, it was easier to go through than to try to find a way around the miniature worlds; he let himself slide through like a ghost, ignoring the spray of words and images that greeted any stranger, idly tracking the Grand Types that appeared. There were quite a few Avellars, as well as the inevitable Barons and Ladies: *Lioe should be pleased,* he thought, and turned his attention toward the port systems.

If Damian Chrestil wanted him back in the Game, it was all but certain that the Game was not really important, was only a blind—and certainly he'd found nothing during his time on the Game nets to indicate otherwise—which made it well worth his time to see what was happening on the various nets that served the port and the traders who depended on the port for their living. He dimmed his own image further, so that he saw his mask floating ghostly through a Bower of Love that currently filled a transfer node. It was a striking image, the death-white mask drifting expressionless, incurious, through the flower-draped temple where an improbably well-endowed man and woman were locked in vigorous and detailed sex, and he touched the capture sequence to record the moment. It would make an interesting story egg, someday, but he made himself turn away once the capture was complete and follow the multiple channels into the port systems.

There were fewer Carnival images here: more off-worlders used the port nets, and there weren't many Burning Brighters who dealt with them who could afford to give up a day's trade. Still, an Avellar walked through a segment of corridor, striding hard as though it was work to keep up with the moving tiles; another Grand Type, the Viverina, braided tiny human skulls into her long hair. Ransome frowned, trying to remember the scenario that had spawned the image, but couldn't place it. The Judge Directing presided over a node that gave entrance to a merchant bank. The serene face was semitransparent, and Ransome recognized familiar features behind the cloaking Carnival image. He adjusted his own projection, allowing his familiar on-line presence to show behind the floating mask, and slipped into the node.

The Judge Directing turned to face him, the stern serenity melting to a more familiar grin, and codes flashed through the display space, weaving a private link-in-realtime. "Ransome. I didn't expect to see you masking."

"Neither did I," Ransome answered, truthfully. Guyonet Merede was a Gamer as well as a banker, and a former patron who owned several of his earlier story eggs. "But it seems to have worked out well."

"It's a nice image," Merede said. He was older than he looked behind the Judge's face: the projection's stony beauty reminded Ransome for an instant of Lioe's face in repose.

"Thanks," he said. "I wonder if you could do me a favor, Guy. I need access to the raw feed from the port computers—the unsorted line, the one that carries the general traffic." If Damian Chrestil wanted him on the Game nets, it could only be to keep him away from some other part of the greater system. C/B Cie. was an import/export firm, and that most likely meant smuggling. And the best way to track that down was to sift the day-to-day chatter and hope that, despite the sheer volume, he could find some hint of an irregular shipment, something that didn't match the more public records. *And if I can't find it, well, there are other places to look, political games he could be playing, and I won't have wasted much time. But I'm betting it's a doctored cargo.*

Merede was silent for an instant, his face gone very still, and then he said, cautiously, "You know I can't do that, I-Jay."

You've done it before. Ransome said aloud, "I just need to pull some numbers for a piece I'm working on. It's a commission for the MIS, and I need some strings for background. I thought I'd tie part of the loop to the trade balance."

It was an easy lie, and plausible, but to his surprise Merede shook his head. "I'm sorry, I-Jay. If it weren't Carnival—but we've had some complaints recently, people saying stuff's been pulled out of the raw feed that should've stayed confidential. I just can't do it."

Ransome nodded. "I can see that. I guess I can rig what I need some other way." He did his best to look thoughtful, glad of the mask that screened his features. "Who's been complaining, anyway?"

Merede glanced down at something out of camera range. "The Five Points Bank's merchant division—you know, the exchange-rate people?—and a couple of importers, Ionel Factor and C/B Cie., and one of the private captains."

Who I just bet is connected to the Chrestil-Brisch, too. Ionel Factor was closely tied to the Chrestil-Brisch—Ionel dealt in off-world spirits, and therefore, inevitably, was tied to the Chrestil-Brisch distillery and their various wholesalers—and Bettis Chrestil was head of the merchant division's steering group. "You think there's anything in it?" he said aloud, and Merede shrugged.

"We haven't seen anything on our screens, and we tap pretty carefully. I suppose it could be a very directed probe, but—between you and me only, Ransome—I think they're overreacting."

"I'll keep it quiet," Ransome said. "Thanks anyway." He touched the key sequence that released the private linkage, and let himself drift deeper into the port nets. He adjusted his presence, making the mask opaque again, so that his identity was completely hidden except to the most deter-

mined probe, and shifted the scale slightly. To a cursory
scan, he should look like a bounce-echo from the chaos on
the public nets, a common enough phenomenon at this time
of year. Satisfied, he let himself slide further into the system,
looking for an interface of commercial and customs data.

It took him over an hour to find that node—it shifted, as
did the codes that guarded it—and another hour to prove to
himself that it was unusually well guarded. None of the
usual sources would provide a key, and that left Selasa Arduinidi, who was one of the better security consultants in the
business and, on the shadow nets, a reliable data fence. She
had a name as a netwalker, too, prided herself on knowing
how to access any part of the net, but when he finally tracked
her down, she shook her head in disgust.

"I've been fighting with that one for two days now, I-Jay.
I haven't cracked it yet. You'll have to get legit codes for
that one, I'm afraid."

"Nobody's telling—or selling," Ransome answered. He
stared at her icon floating in the air in front of him, a huge-
eyed owl perched in a glowing tree branch that seemed to
grow directly out of the lines of the net itself. "What's going
on, Selasa?"

"I don't know," Arduinidi answered, but there was
something in her voice, a subtle admiration that belied her
words. "Somebody's up to something, that's for sure." She
broke the connection before he could ask anything more.

Somebody like Damian Chrestil, Ransome thought,
sourly. The deeper he tried to probe, the more likely it
seemed that the Game was just a blind, and that Damian
Chrestil was hiding something. From the way his own
probes were being blocked, it seemed to have something to
do with run cargoes. *But if that's all, why is ji-Imbaoa involved?* Politics and smuggling: the two did not often overlap, but when they did, it was a particularly volatile mix.
Which is what I will tell Chauvelin myself, he thought, and
began to extricate himself from the maze of the port's multi-
net. It would be easy enough simply to shut down his system, but then the automatics would take over the shutdown
procedures and leave a clear trail back to his loft. Better to
do things slowly, and make sure he wasn't followed.

DAY 1

Chauvelin sat in his office at the top of the ambassador's residence, staring into the desktop displays without really seeing the multiple screens. The hazy sunlight poured in through the slightly curved windows, dulling the displays; he hit the key that brought the glyphs and numbers and the harsh strokes of hsai demiscript to their greatest brightness, but did not dim the window glass. He could see the first signs of the approaching storm on the horizon beyond Plug Island, a thicker bank of clouds like fog or a distant landfall. The weather service still said that bank was only an outrider, and the real storm behind it would not arrive for days, but Chauvelin could feel it waiting, a brooding, distant presence. The street brokers had it at twenty-to-one to hit within the next five days, though the pessimists were hedging their bets by excluding lower-category storms. Chauvelin sighed, and leaned back in his chair. If nothing else, the storm was already starting to interfere with the connection to the jump transmitter orbiting the planet, the one that carried the communications link with Hsaioi-An. On the one hand, the erratic reception was a good excuse to keep ji-Imbaoa from using the house transmitters without one of Chauvelin's own household present, ostensibly to monitor the machinery. On the other, he was under no illusion that this would keep ji-Imbaoa from finding some way to contact his patrons in Hsaioi-An, nor would it prevent the Visiting Speaker from dealing with someone on planet. And it annoyed the Visiting Speaker. Chauvelin allowed himself a quick, private smile. That also had disadvantages, but it did give him a certain sense of satisfaction.

A chime sounded in his desktop, a discreet, two-toned noise, and Chauvelin glanced down in some surprise. He had left instructions that he was not to be disturbed, and je-Sou'-tsian was usually scrupulous about obeying him. He touched the icon, and the tiny projector hidden in a disk of carved and lacquered iaon wood lit, forming a cylindrical image. Je-Sou'tsian bowed to him from the center of that column of light.

"I'm very sorry to interrupt you, Sia, but Na Ransome is here, and says he needs urgently to speak with you."

Chauvelin lifted his eyebrows, but nodded. "All right, show him into—no, bring him up here. Without any of the Visiting Speaker's people seeing him, if you can." If Ransome had come in person, and not on the nets, it was bound to be something important.

"Yes, sia," je-Sou'tsian said. "I'm sorry, but I'm not sure that some of the Speaker's household didn't meet him as he came in." Her voice trailed off, and she gestured apology.

"That's all right, it can't be helped," Chauvelin said. "But bring him up here."

"At once, sia," je-Sou'tsian said, and her image vanished from the cylinder. The empty rod of light retreated into its base, and a string of lights played across a secondary screen: the steward and Ransome were on their way. Chauvelin ran his hands across the shadowscreen, closing down some programs and putting others to sleep, watched as the multiple screens beneath the desktop copied his movements. A few moments later, the door slid open, and je-Sou'tsian appeared in the arched opening.

"Sia, Na Ransome is here."

"Thanks," Chauvelin said, and gestured for the other man to come in. Ransome did as he was told, settled himself comfortably on the corner of the desk. Chauvelin smiled slightly, but said nothing: the seat would prove its own punishment.

"What is it?" he asked, and Ransome smiled back at him.

"You've been suckered," he said bluntly—*and with entirely too much enjoyment,* Chauvelin thought. But that was his own fear speaking, not his intellect.

"How so?"

"I did exactly what you wanted," Ransome said. "I've gone back into the Game, I've trawled the Game nets, every one of them at least twice, and there's nothing going on— except Lioe's scenario, of course. But nothing, absolutely nothing, that involves Damian Chrestil. But when I went onto the port nets, into the commercial systems, I found a lot of blocks that didn't used to be there."

"Such as?" Chauvelin kept his tone strictly neutral, buying time. He had been half expecting something like this, some new revelation of wheels within wheels, but not from the port district. He frowned slightly, readjusting his thoughts to add money and shipping to the already volatile political mix. It didn't make sense, not yet—the Chrestil-Brisch were supposed to favor the Republic, not Hsaioi-An—but if Ransome was being shut out of the port computers, then there had to be an economic motive.

"For one thing—" Ransome paused, laughed shortly. "This is at best unethical, by the way, if not actively illegal."

"I'm not surprised," Chauvelin murmured.

Ransome nodded again, conceding the point. "It's not usually very hard to get someone to give you an address and an access code for the raw datafeed from the port computers—you know, the ones that control the warehouse records for individual firms, scheduling, all that sort of thing." He shrugged. "Too many people know about it, and there are always plausible reasons to want access. And of course, a lot of people owe me favors."

"Of course."

"But today, when I tried to get those codes, first of all no one was selling them—and I've never seen that happen, somebody's put the fear of Retribution into the shadow-walkers like I've never seen—and then no one I know would give me anything. Now, that's happened before, especially after someone's scored a coup, but no one has, that I've heard, and I hear these things." Ransome paused, all the humor gone from his voice. "What I did find out was that some companies complained that information had been copied from those feeds, and used against them. And when I got names, they were all tied to Damian Chrestil.''

"Who were they?'' Chauvelin asked.

"C/B Cie. itself, Ionel Factor—they import wines and spirits, and they've got ties to the Chrestil-Brisch distillery business—and one of the FPB's steering groups.''

"Let me guess,'' Chauvelin said. "The merchant division, the one that Bettis Chrestil heads?''

"Got it in one.'' Ransome smiled sourly. "But what exactly it all means is beyond me.''

And me, Chauvelin thought. *At least for the moment.* He looked down at the empty screens under the surface of the desktop, debating whom to query—*Eriki Haas, certainly, once we're in phase and if the transmitter is reliable enough, just to see what connections ji-Imbaoa has with Damian Chrestil or C/B Cie.* The chime sounded again beneath the desktop. He frowned, more deeply this time, and touched the icon flashing in the shadowscreen. The projector lit, and je-Sou'tsian bowed from within the cylinder of light.

"I apologize again for disturbing you, sia, but the Visiting Speaker is on his way to your office.''

That's all I need. Chauvelin said, "All right, Iameis, thank you.''

"Wonderful,'' Ransome murmured, a crooked smile on his face.

"Quite.'' Chauvelin leaned back in his chair, deliberately closed the last of the sleeping files. There was nothing he could do to stop ji-Imbaoa—the Visiting Speaker was technically head of the ambassadorial household during his visit, and no doors could be shut to him—but he did not have to welcome him. The shutdown codes were still flickering across the screens when the door slid back and ji-Imbaoa strode into the room.

"So, Chauvelin,'' he said, "your agent's here. I want to talk to him.''

"As you wish,'' Chauvelin said, spread his hands in a deliberate gesture of innocence. "I didn't want to trouble you until I was sure it was worth your time.''

Ji-Imbaoa's fingers twitched—*annoyance?* Chauvelin thought, *or fear?* He did not move, but felt himself suddenly,

painfully tense, waiting for the Visiting Speaker's next
move.

"What have you found? Have you gone back to the
Game?"

Ransome hesitated, visibly choosing his words with care,
and Chauvelin wondered for a moment if the other might
have learned discretion. He need not have worried, however.
Ransome said, "Yes, Na Speaker, I've been back to the
Game, and found very little of interest."

"Then surely you haven't looked very hard, or very
long," ji-Imbaoa snapped. "Particularly since you have
only been looking for two days."

"I don't need any more than that to tell you there's nothing there," Ransome said.

Chauvelin said, "If Na Ransome says he's found nothing
in the Game, then there's nothing to be found."

Ji-Imbaoa glanced back at him, fingers still twitching with
unreadable emotion. "Then why should Damian Chrestil go
to so much trouble to get him back into those nets? It must
have to do with the Game."

"Na Ransome thinks it's a distraction," Chauvelin said.
"That Damian Chrestil's real interests lie elsewhere."

"Don't you think you're being overelaborate?" ji-Imbaoa interrupted rudely.

"Perhaps the Visiting Speaker is being underelaborate,"
Ransome murmured. "After all, he isn't used to the complex
dishonesties of our local politics."

He had used the hsai word that linked dishonesty and fo-
reignness, so that the statement hovered delicately between
compliment and insult. Chauvelin said, "I think Na Ransome's assessment is plausible, sia."

"And I tell you it is unlikely," ji-Imbaoa said. "I tell you,
on my name and my fathers', this must be pursued, and pursued through the Game."

Chauvelin kept his face impassive with an effort, torn between anger and elation. Ji-Imbaoa had made it a direct
order, one that Chauvelin could not directly disobey, but at
the same time he'd made it equally clear that there was
something important at stake. "Very well, sia," he said

aloud. "Na Ransome will remain with the Game a little while longer."

"Until he finds what Damian Chrestil wants," ji-Imbaoa said.

"So be it," Chauvelin said. Behind ji-Imbaoa's shoulder, Ransome rolled his eyes.

"You must do more," ji-Imbaoa said, and turned to face the imagist.

"I do my poor best," Ransome murmured, and bowed, too deeply for sincerity.

Ji-Imbaoa ignored that, and glanced back at Chauvelin. "I expect to be kept informed."

"As you wish," Chauvelin said, and the Visiting Speaker lifted a clawed hand to signal the door. It slid open obediently, and ji-Imbaoa stalked out, his ribbons flurrying behind him.

Ransome said, even before the door had fully closed again, "Pity everything else isn't so docile."

"You'd better have meant the door," Chauvelin said, without heat.

"What else?" Ransome darted him a suddenly mischievous glance, said, "Am I to keep on with the Game, then? Or would you rather know about the larger nets?"

"Both," Chauvelin said. "You heard him. I need you to be visible on the Game nets, to be sure he knows you're doing what he ordered."

"That won't be too difficult," Ransome said.

"You've changed your tune." In spite of himself, Chauvelin felt a stab of jealousy, remembering the way the other had looked at the pilot, Lioe, the night before.

Ransome gave him a rueful smile. "She's good," he said. "And she's wasted in the Game."

Chauvelin said, more abruptly than he'd intended, "Whatever. But I do need you to be seen in the Game."

"I've said I would," Ransome said. He pushed himself off the corner of the desk. "But, damn it, Damian Chrestil is up to something that has nothing at all to do with the Game."

"I believe you," Chauvelin said. "I'm doing what I can to find out what."

"That would make sense," Ransome said. He lifted his hand to open the door, paused with the gesture half completed. "Do you want me to keep on the port nets?"

Chauvelin nodded. "If you can, yes, but the main thing's the Game. I think you're right, but ji-Imbaoa's forced my hand."

Ransome nodded abruptly. "I know, I'm sorry. I'll do what I can." He finished his gesture, and the door slid open.

Chauvelin watched him leave, watched the door slide shut again behind him. *As long as you stay on the Game nets, as long as you're conspicuously doing what ji-Imbaoa wants, then I've got a little time.* He reached for the shadowscreen, recalling one of the chronometers, and checked the transmission pattern between Burning Bright and maiHu'an. He had just missed a window: the two planets would not be in phase for another twenty hours. *Not until tomorrow, then,* he thought, *and tomorrow afternoon at that.* For a moment, he considered using the more complicated—and expensive— emergency channels, but rejected the thought almost at once. The Remembrancer-Duke would never sanction the expense. But tomorrow he would send a message to Eriki Haas, and find out if, and how, the je Tsinra-an were connected to the Chrestil-Brisch. He leaned back in his chair, staring at the ocean and the distant cloud bank without really seeing them. There were too many possible connections right now, but with any luck Haas would be able to narrow them down, and then . . . He smiled slowly. Then ji-Imbaoa would have to regret the way he had behaved. *Maybe,* he thought, *maybe the old superstitions are right, and my luck will change with Storm.* He glanced down at the shadowscreen again, and touched icons to shift to another mode. It was time to start asking questions of his own.

DAY 1

Lioe blinked even in the filtered sunlight that filled the inner courtyard, set her workboard down beside an unoccupied datanode, and turned her attention toward the food bars in the corner. She fed one the last of her free cash, and chose a box of thick rice and seacake from the cheaper half of the menu. She chose a bottle of medium-priced water as well, and carried the food back to her table. It had been a long session, and a rewarding one; the session leaders had been excited by the scenario, eager to follow her suggestions, and genuinely interested in preserving her intentions for the session. It was a new experience, being taken that seriously: *on the whole,* she thought, *I think I like it.*

She triggered the self-heating unit, waited the required thirty seconds while the little charge cycled, and opened the box. The steam that rose from the mix of rice and onions and chunks of palmweed and the flower-shaped seacakes was thick and appetizing, smelling of salt broth and the smoky oil that preserved the fish. There was a tiny dish of sweet mustard as well, but she had learned that it was far more mustard than sweet and should be approached with caution. She spread a pinpoint of the condiment over the first of the seacakes, and tasted warily. It was spicy, cutting the oil, but not so hot that it brought tears to her eyes. She hadn't realized quite how hungry she had become, caught up in the intricacies of the Game, and she ate with relish, pursuing the last grains of rice around the bottom of the box. Both rice and seacakes were ubiquitous on Burning Bright, the staple of everyone's diet—the rice grown in the tidal shallows, the seacakes processed at sea from the bits and pieces left over after the more expensive fillets and chunks were set aside— but she had not been on planet long enough to get tired of the salt-and-smoke flavors.

She reached for the datacord then, plugged her workboard into the unoccupied node, touched keys to activate the unit and call up the night's schedule. Somewhat to her surprise, the session hadn't filled yet, but then she remembered that it was the first night of Storm, the first night of the Carnival. It wasn't that surprising, after all, but it was a shame that she wouldn't be making as much money from the session fees as she had hoped. Unless, of course, she could fill the session herself. . . . She tilted her head to one side, considering. She had reserved Harmsway for Ransome, as he'd asked, and Savian and Beledin had signed up to play Lord Faro and Belfortune again—*I'd like a second chance at him,* Beledin had said, when she had met him in the hall on her way to the session leaders' meeting—and a couple of unfamiliar names filled other slots, but no one had signed up for Jack Blue, or Mijja Lyall, or Avellar. Lioe frowned, seeing that. She had expected the unfamiliar names to fill last—and neither Jack Blue nor Lyall was a well-known template—but she would have assumed that Avellar would go quickly. An inexpert Avellar would throw off the balance of the entire scenario; she needed someone good in that spot, if the session was to work at all.

"Quinn. I've been looking for you."

The voice was familiar, but Lioe couldn't quite place it. She looked up, still frowning, and felt the frown dissolve as she looked up at Roscha. "I've been around," she said. "Are you playing tonight?"

Roscha's wide mouth widened further in a grin that showed perfect teeth and heightened the impossible cheekbones. "I hope so. I just got off work, and they told me there were still places left for tonight's session."

Lioe looked down at the little screen, juggling choices. Roscha was good, all right, but volatile; there had been moments in the first session when she'd amply justified Gueremei's description of her as "difficult." On the other hand, that volatility might make for a very interesting key character. "How would you feel about playing Avellar?" she said slowly. "The other real option is Jack Blue—Lyall's open, too, but that doesn't strike me as your style."

"Avellar." Roscha's voice caressed the name. "Hell, yes, I'd like to play him—or her, if you'll let me play the she-clone."

Avellar, by Game convention, was actually a four-person clone, the survivors of a larger clone that had been partially destroyed some years before, in the clone's childhood. It provided an explanation for the character's limited telepathy; it also gave players who didn't like crossing gender lines further options. Lioe shrugged. It made no difference in the context of the scenario; she was just a little surprised that Roscha, of all people, would choose not to cross gender. "If you want, sure," she said. "I don't have any problem with that." She touched keys, and watched the program add Roscha's name to the list of players.

"Great." Roscha ran a hand through her hair, dislodging the strip of indigo silk that confined it, and impatiently re-wrapped it, tossing the red curls out of her eyes. "I was wondering. I see you've eaten, but you've got some time before the session starts. Would you like to go down to the Water, and see the Beauties and Beasts?"

Lioe frowned, knowing she'd heard the term before, and Roscha said, "The Syndics' parade, I mean. It's well worth seeing."

Lioe looked back down at the screen, at the two slots that remained. Both of them were important—she prided herself on never having written a scenario that included unnecessary characters—and she hated to think she would have to run them from a distance. On Callixte, of course, she had a list of people she could call at short notice, fellow players and session leaders who were glad to fill in in exchange for a rebate on session fees, but here she would have to rely on the club's resources. She hesitated then, and touched keys on the workboard to find an outgoing communications channel. "I'd like that," she said, "but there's one thing I have to do first."

"Sure," Roscha said easily, and seated herself in the

chair opposite, where the unfolded screen blocked her view of the other woman's hands on the keys and controls.

Lioe nodded her thanks, her attention already back on the Game. When Kichi Desjourdy had been Customs-and-Intelligence's representative on Falconsreach, she'd been known to sit in on Game sessions on a fairly regular basis. Lioe herself had relied on her as a player as well as an arbiter. *Maybe, just maybe,* Lioe thought, *she could help me out now.* Desjourdy was good; she'd be an excellent choice either for Jack Blue or Lyall. She touched the final sequence, one of Desjourdy's private code-strings, letting her know it wasn't business, and dispatched the package into the communications system.

Carnival had not taken over ordinary communications yet. A few thin images, a masked face, a dancing, six-armed figure, drifted across her screen, while the connect codes blinked behind them, and then the screen lit fully, driving out the last of the Carnival ghosts. Kichi Desjourdy looked out of the little screen, the office wall behind her distorted by its limited projection. Desjourdy herself looked normal enough, Lioe thought, but with Desjourdy it was sometimes hard to tell. The Customs-and-Intelligence representative had a round, rather ordinary face, with only the silvery disks of two triple datasockets set into the bone at the corner of each eye to set her apart from most net workers. At the moment, none of the sockets were in use, and Lioe, who had seen Desjourdy bristling with cords, was oddly grateful.

"Quinn," Desjourdy said. "It's good to see you. I've been hearing a lot of talk about you on the Game nets." Her voice was clear and true, an elegant soprano, and Lioe was struck again by the mismatch of voice and face.

"Thanks," she said. "That was sort of what I was calling you about."

"Oh, yes?"

"I've got a session going tonight," Lioe said, "and I'm short. I need a player I can rely on. Are you free?"

Desjourdy laughed. "I never know whether I should be flattered or not when somebody asks me like this. Is this for Ixion's Wheel?"

"Yes."

Desjourdy's smile widened. "Well, that one I can't turn down. Who is it, anyway?"

"There are two slots still open," Lioe answered. "Jack Blue, the telekinetic, leader of the prison population, and Mijja Lyall, who's a secret telepath and a member of the research staff at the prison."

"Put me down for Jack Blue," Desjourdy answered promptly. "He—is it he?—sounds interesting. Can you flip me a copy of the template?"

"Sure." Lioe touched keys to call the file from storage and duplicate it for transmission. "Are you ready?"

"Line's open and ready."

"Sending," Lioe said, and waited while icons formed and shifted at the bottom of the screen.

"All set," Desjourdy said, and in the same instant the icons vanished. "What time does the session start?"

Lioe glanced at her reminders list. "At twenty hours."

"I'll be there," Desjourdy said. "And thanks, Quinn. I owe you for this."

"I think I owe you," Lioe answered and closed down the connection.

"Who was that?" Roscha asked.

Lioe glanced at her warily, wondering if she had heard a possessive note in the other woman's voice, but Roscha's expression was merely curious. "A woman I know from Falconsreach, a Gamer. I told you I was short a couple of people." *And I'm still short one player, for Lyall.* She touched keys again to call up the list, to add Desjourdy's name, and was startled to see that someone had already signed up for Lyall. It was not a name she knew, but at least it solved the problem. She added Desjourdy's name to the list, and closed down the system.

"Are you still interested in going down to the Water?" Roscha asked, and Lioe shrugged.

"Why not?" She knew she sounded less than enthusiastic, and added, "I would like to see the procession."

"Leave your board," Roscha said, pushing herself back from the little table. Lioe glanced at her curiously, and Roscha made an embarrassed face. "If there's going to be any trouble, it'll be tonight, kids steaming—you know, a gang of

them runs through the crowd, grabs at whatever people're carrying? That doesn't often happen down here, it's more something they do up in Dry Cut, or over on Homestead, but you don't want to take chances.''

''Right,'' Lioe said, allowing the skepticism to color her voice, but she left her Gameboard and most of her credit and cash with Gueremei.

The streets were already crowded, the sun low on the horizon, so that the buildings cast long shadows and only the open plazas were still bathed in amber light. Nearly everyone was masked, faces obscured by strips or full stiffened ovals of beaded lace, or completely hidden by fantastic, beak-nosed half-masks painted in every color of the rainbow. A few men and women in seemingly equal numbers, simply painted their faces, the aged-ivory complexion that was common on Burning Bright making a perfect backdrop for the delicate sprays of color. Gold flowers climbed one woman's neck and cheek, appeared again at her bare shoulder, a golden vine winding languidly down to her wrist and a hand that bloomed like a bouquet, each knuckle sprouting a tiny, perfect rose. Her clothes were otherwise ordinary, a sleeveless vest and docker's trousers, and Lioe caught herself staring at the brilliant contrast, wishing she had her recorder with her. In one of the plazas, a trio of drummers in black, shapeless robes and grotesque masks like the skulls of birds beat a complex almost-tune, the high-pitched hand drum weaving a stuttering, offbeat counterpoint to the steadier, full-toned notes of the larger drums. A slim man in black—*in Avellar's black and gold,* Lioe realized, and felt a thrill of absolute delight run up her spine, *Avellar's black and gold and Avellar's face for a mask*—paused to listen, and then pushed the mask back on his head, reaching for something inside his jacket. He pulled out a slim silvered pipe, began improvising against the beat of the drum. The hand-drummer nodded to him, beckoned him with a movement of head and chin, and the group—a quartet now, for as long as the spirit seized them—played on. A pair of women, their blank silver masks topped with fantastic turbans, flowers and leaves dripping from braided coils of iridescent fabric, danced with them for a moment, then darted away, the

metal and glass that weighted the hems of their enormous
skirts flashing in the last of the sunlight.

"You should mask," Roscha said. "I want to mask."

Lioe hesitated, uncertain, and Roscha caught her arm.

"Come on, Gelsomina was tied up in the public cut not
more than an hour ago. If we hurry, she might still be there."

"I don't know," Lioe said, but let herself be towed
through the busy streets. Roscha paused at the first canal
bridge, looking right and left as though searching for a scent,
then started left along the bank. This was a narrow water-
way, barely wide enough for two gondas to ride side by side,
and the embankment was equally narrow, so that she had to
step carefully to keep up with Roscha. She dodged another
Avellar—a woman this time, but with the same familiar features shaping the hard-faced mask, the corners of this one's
mouth drawn down in a frown that was almost tragedy—and
nearly ran into a street vendor, his cart folded to its minimum width. She murmured an apology, and saw Roscha
beckoning from the bend in the bank ahead of them.

The streetlights were starting to come on—the sun must
be down by now, Lioe realized, though it hardly seemed to
make much difference in the shadowed streets—and their
light fell into the canal's dark water. A boat, a small barge
with its mast unstepped and laid from bow to stern, lay at the
center of one pool of light, and a woman looked up at them
from the boat's low deck. She was dressed as the Viverina,
rich purple robe embroidered with dragons, sleek black wig
that fell almost to her knees, skulls with bright red eyes
braided into that mass, and she was laughing at them from
behind the painted mask. Dozens, a hundred masks and piled
cloth that must be costumes filled every available centimeter
of the deck; masks hung from the horizontal mast, crowded
cheek to cheek along its length, and still others dangled from
the crossbar of the Viverina's spear.

"Gelsomina," Roscha said. "Are you still selling?"

"Since you're here, I suppose so," the Viverina answered. She was older than Lioe had guessed at first, about
sixty, but straight as the spear she carried. "What will it be,
something from the Game?"

''Yes, if you have it,'' Roscha answered, and the woman beckoned to her.

''Well, come aboard, then.'' She looked up at Lioe, tilting her head inside the painted mask. ''And you too. Are you here for a mask?''

''I don't know,'' Lioe began, and Roscha answered for her.

''Yes, probably.'' She dropped down onto the deck—not a long drop, not much more than a meter—and the boat rocked under her. Gelsomina kept her balance effortlessly, and beckoned for Lioe to follow. Lioe hesitated, but lowered herself more carefully onto the unsteady planks. The boat rocked anyway, and she steadied herself against the mast. It shifted under her hand, and the faces danced, seeming almost alive in the streetlight's glow.

''These are beautiful,'' she said, and didn't quite realize she'd spoken aloud until Gelsomina bowed to her.

''Thank you. But then, I enjoy my work.''

''Do you have any Avellars left, Na Mina?'' Roscha asked, and Gelsomina shook her head.

''No, child, not a one. There's some off-worlder doing a scenario with him at the heart of it; I sold my last one before noon.''

''Damn,'' Roscha said, and then, belatedly remembering her manners, ''Na Mina, this is a friend of mine, Quinn Lioe. She's the one who wrote that scenario.''

''I've heard a lot about you,'' Gelsomina said. She tilted her head to one side, studying Lioe from behind the mask. ''What were you looking for, do you know?''

''Thanks,'' Lioe said, and heard her own uncertainty in her voice. ''I didn't really have anything in mind. I've never been on Burning Bright during Storm.'' She scanned the rows of masks in the hopes of finding something, and, to her surprise, one face seemed to leap out at her from the row crowded on the mast. It was a full mask, with a heavy, elaborately braided wig covering the back of the head. One half of the face was plain, smooth, a bland collection of planes and angles, pleasing enough, but nothing out of the ordinary; the other was deformed and distorted like the carvings on a ritual mask, the cheek eaten to the bone, the mouth drawn

down by a scar like a sneer, the eye hidden by a painted
patch. And the rest of the scars were decorated, too, layered
with color so that they became almost an abstract painting of
a face. Lioe reached out to touch it, drawn and repelled at the
same time, and Gelsomina nodded.

"That's from one of LaChacalle's novels—Helike, from
The Witch-Vizier. Do you know it?"

"I'm afraid I don't," Lioe answered, and didn't know if
she was glad or sorry. The new name, the last name on the
session list, had been LaChacalle. "Is LaChacalle a
Gamer?"

Gelsomina shrugged one shoulder. "She used to be. I
haven't seen her much lately—she quit about when Ambidexter did. They were old friends."

"She's playing tonight, I think," Lioe said. "Or someone
with that name is, anyway."

"There's only one of her," Gelsomina said.

"What about Hazard?" Roscha asked, and Gelsomina
shook her head.

"No, but I do have Cor-Clar Sensmerce. I remember you
used to play her."

"Thanks," Roscha said, and Gelsomina turned to the
lines of masks, running her staff idly along the rows until she
found the one she wanted.

"There you are. It's twenty *real.* Or we can make a
trade."

Roscha stopped, her hand on the purse inside her belt.
"What trade?"

"You needn't sound so suspicious," Gelsomina said.
"Are you going to watch the parade?"

"We were, yes," Roscha answered, and despite Gelsomina's words still sounded wary. Lioe grinned, and then
wondered if she should be more cautious.

"I'd rather watch it from the Water, myself, with all the
stock aboard," Gelsomina went on, "and I wouldn't mind
having some younger bodies to help me get this cow down to
the canal mouth. I'll trade you each a mask, and bring you
back to your club—is it Shadows you're playing at? as close
as I can get, then—before the session starts."

Roscha relaxed visibly. "That would make life easier."

Lioe shrugged. "Can we get back in time?"

"When is the session?" Gelsomina asked.

"Twentieth hour," Roscha said, and looked at Lioe. "It shouldn't be a problem. The parade starts at dark—seventeenth hour."

Lioe glanced sideways, checking the time, and shrugged again, willing to let herself be overruled. "If you're sure, why not? It should be worth seeing."

"It always is," Gelsomina answered. "There's nothing quite like our Carnival, not anywhere in human space."

Or anywhere at all, Lioe thought. Under Gelsomina's instructions, she and Roscha stowed most of the masks and costumes that cluttered the decking in the storage cells that ran along the gunwales, but left the ones that lined the mast. Then Roscha freed the mooring lines while Gelsomina took her place in the steering well. Lioe, knowing nothing of boats, crouched beside the mast and waited to be told what to do. The motor coughed and caught, settled almost instantly to a steady purr. Roscha shoved them free of the embankment, and the barge swung out into the channel, heading toward the Inland Water.

The people on the banks were moving toward the Water, too, knots and groups of them in bright matching costumes, a few who walked alone, families with strings of children going hand in hand under an elder's watchful eye. There were more boats on the canal, too, some smaller than Lioe had seen before, little more than a shell with a racketing motor slung over the stern, and, of course, the inevitable mob of gondas. A Lockwardens patrol boat moved silently through the crowd, its flashing light sending blue shadows across the water and along its own black hull. The civilian craft all carried bright lights at stern and bow—the littlest shells had handlights rigged to the motors—and even as Lioe noticed that, lights blossomed along the sides of Gelsomina's barge. They were directed outward, shielded from the boat's occupants, but Lioe could see their brilliance reflected in the water. It was a beautiful effect, the shape of the barge outlined in light, but she guessed it was as much precaution as decoration. There would be a lot of traffic on the canals tonight: it was a good time to be visible.

Horns sounded as they came up on the wide feeder channel that carried local traffic down to the Water, and Lioe
jumped as Gelsomina sounded their own horn in answer.
The barge swung over, stately, Roscha standing ready in the
bow, boatpole in hand to fend off any unwary craft, and then
Gelsomina had tucked them neatly into the line of traffic.
The canal was jammed with barges and gondas, and here and
there a bigger commercial boat—heavy barges and seiners
in about equal numbers—loomed above the crowd, their
sides dripping with strings of chaser lights. A heavy barge
swayed past, set Gelsomina's boat rocking in its wake, the
strings of lights dipping into the water as it heeled over
slightly to avoid a passing gonda. Its open deck was crowded
with people of all ages, from babies in flotation suits to old
men and women in support chairs. *Families of the regular
crews?* Lioe wondered, but it was too noisy to ask.

Blatting one-note trumpets sounded from the walkways
that lined the shore—children, mostly, carrying the brightly
colored horns that were a full meter long, taller than some of
the children who sounded them—and were answered by another clutch of children on the heavy barge's deck. Other
boats took up the sound, and Lioe covered her ears, wincing,
until the boats had passed and the shore children had admitted defeat. People called to each other, their words drowned
in the general din, and a man dressed all in bells danced on a
bollard, the clanging all but inaudible as Gelsomina's barge
slipped past only a few meters from the wall. A disk of light
swept across the crowd, and Lioe looked up to see the familiar shape of a hovering security drone scanning the crowd.
The Lockwardens' insignia was picked out in lights on its
stubby wings. A cheer, ironic but not hostile, rose from the
crowd as the light touched them.

Farther up the canal, there were whoops, and then a
splash, the sound distinct and chilling even in the uproar.
Lioe turned her head sharply, even though it had been too
loud to have been a child, saw Roscha's body a tense shadow
against the shore lights. Then, as suddenly, she saw her relax
as two drones flung their lights onto the source of the sound.
Caught in that double disk of light, a dripping boy hauled
himself back onto a fingerling dock, shaking water from the

ruined feathers that decorated his mask. He shook his fist at
another boy, but a third grabbed his shoulders, and hustled
him away. One of the drones followed the group for a moment longer, then turned away, taking the light with it. As
the bright circle swung briefly aimless along the buildings
that fronted the canal, it hit a doorway where a man and a
woman were locked in blind embrace, her skirt rucked up to
her waist, and flashed away again. Lioe blinked, not sure if
she'd seen the woman reaching not for her partner but for his
wallet, but there was nothing she could do about it if she had.

The feeder widened suddenly as it opened onto the Water.
Gondas were clustered in flotillas along either bank, filled
and overfilled with masked and costumed figures, standing
shapes balanced precariously against the chop where the two
currents met. The Water itself was black and empty, except
for a few speeders that carried the blue lights of the Lockwardens; another Lockwardens speeder, throttled back so far
that it barely made headway against the chop, moved along
the line of gondas, a tall man calling instructions from the
pilot's well.

"Which way?" Gelsomina called from her place in the
stern, and Lioe saw Roscha look right and left before she
answered.

"It looks clearer down toward the Warden's Channel."

"Right." The boat swung left as Gelsomina answered,
pulling out around the mob of smaller boats, and Lioe felt
rather than heard the beat of the engine strengthen as they
picked up speed.

"Do you see a buoy?" Gelsomina called.

"No, not yet—wait." Roscha leaned precariously out
over the bow, one hand clinging tight to the mast. "Wait,
yes, past that seiner there's a free point."

Gelsomina did not answer, but Lioe felt the boat surge
again, as though she'd opened a throttle. The barge passed
two more ships—another barge filled with people costumed
from the Game, several Avellars among them, and then a
seiner, its nets spread to let a horde of children climb to a
better view—and then started to slow. They were almost on
top of it before Lioe saw the mooring point. Roscha had had
it in view long before, however, and caught it easily with the

boatpole's hooked end. Gelsomina saw the movement, the swoop and jerk of the pole against the shore lights, and reversed the engines. The barge slid neatly up to the orange-painted buoy, coming to an almost perfect stop against its scarred sides. Roscha looped a cable into place, tugged twice to snug it home. Flares blossomed in the distance, toward the entrance to the channel.

"They're coming," Roscha called, and Gelsomina pulled herself up out of the steering well, came to sit on the unstepped mast. Lioe seated herself beside the older woman, careful of the masks and the barge's unpredictable roll, and Roscha joined them a moment later, tucking the boatpole neatly under their feet. A larger Lockwardens boat, a slim needle of a ship twice as long as a gonda, slid past down the center of the channel, a tail of spray gleaming behind it.

"In that compartment there," Gelsomina said, "you'll find a bottle of raki."

Roscha grinned, and rummaged in the shallow space until she had found the bottle and three small, unmatching cups. She poured a cup for each of them, and came back to sit beside Lioe. "Health," she said, and the three touched cups.

They did not have to wait long for the parade to appear. Lioe sipped cautiously at the bitter drink—it tasted of anise, a flavor she didn't like—and looked south again just as another flare blossomed in the darkness over the Warden's Channel. A trio of speeders, all with Lockwardens lights and markings, swept into view, and another group of three followed more slowly, peeling off to take up stations just inside the line of spectators.

"Soon now," Gelsomina said, and Roscha said, "Mommy . . ." She caught a five-year-old's whine so perfectly that Lioe laughed aloud.

"Five more minutes," Gelsomina said.

Lioe looked south again, still smiling, toward the light at the point of Mainwarden Island, and saw a dark shape eclipse the light. *The parade?* she thought, and Roscha whooped beside her.

"There they are!"

Gelsomina fumbled in the folds of her costume, and produced a slim set of night glasses. She laid her staff aside and used both hands to work the focusing buttons. Lioe narrowed her eyes at the dark platform, wondering how anyone would be able to see anything on that distant deck. And then a giant figure unfolded itself from the barge, a woman in a full skirt and low-cut bodice, a giantess with a crown of blue-white stars, and more stars draped and scattered across her dress. She stood for a moment, a sketch in light and shadows, and then spotlights came on, revealing her full glories. There was a gasp from the crowds on the banks and on the boats to either side, and then shrill applause. It had to be some kind of puppet, Lioe knew, an enormous automaton that swept into an astonishingly graceful curtsy as the sound of the cheers reached it, but the illusion was nearly perfect. The face was serenely beautiful, elegantly proportioned; as Lioe watched, the features shifted, rearranging themselves into a gentle smile.

"Oh, they're not going to like that," Gelsomina said. "Half the crowd will miss the lighting."

"No, look," Roscha answered, pointing as the spotlights faded again, leaving the giantess wreathed in her own lights. "Oh, very nice."

Gelsomina nodded, fumbling again with her glasses.

"It must be, what, ten meters tall," Lioe said, and Roscha nodded.

"Between ten and twelve. Whose is it, Na Mina?"

"Who pays for them all?" Lioe asked.

"Civic groups," Gelsomina answered, not taking her glasses from her eyes. "That's Estens there—one of the Five Points families, Na Lioe. They, the Five Points Families, I mean, and the Merchant Investors Syndicate, the Five Points Bank, cartels like Yardmasters and Fishers Co-op, and the Lockwardens, of course, each one sponsors a barge. Once a group's bought the framework, it's just a matter of dressing it each year."

"It's a way of proving your importance," Roscha said.

Gelsomina went on as though she hadn't spoken, lowering the glasses into her lap. "I used to dress for Yardmasters, a long time ago, and then for the MIS. Before it got so political."

Lioe nodded, not really understanding, and a second barge

swept into view. This one carried a massively muscled male shape, naked except for a blue-and-gold loincloth and heavy golden bracelets running from its wrists almost to its elbows. Its head was the head of a bull, the horns tipped with gold as well, and its body glittered in the spotlight, as though its skin were sheathed in some kind of faintly mottled coating, a gold iridescence like tiny scales. It threw back its head as the crowd's noise reached it, massive mouth opening in a silent roar, and beat the air with its fists.

"Five Points Bank?" Roscha said, and Gelsomina nodded.

"More money than sense. But that's always been their problem."

"It looks," Roscha said slowly, frowning, "you know, it looks almost hsaia, with that skin. I wonder if they meant it?"

"I doubt it," Gelsomina said. "I heard talk about this. They hired Marrin Artisans to come up with a new way to make the sheathing, out of sequensas—rejects and scrap, mind you, but still. You can imagine what that cost." She stared at the figure for a long moment, and added, grudgingly, "Still, it does look pretty good from here."

"It still looks hsaia to me," Roscha said. "And the FPB does a lot of business with Hsaioi-An."

"And that," Gelsomina said, "is what's wrong with the parade these days. Remember the year the Five Points Families each did one of the Four Judges? That started it, once their candidate got elected that year. Everything's got a political angle, some kind of message—even when you don't mean it to, somebody's going to see it. The old days were a lot better."

Roscha looked away, her expression at once embarrassed and mulish in the dim light, and Lioe said hastily, "Who's that coming?"

Gelsomina adjusted her glasses again, focusing on the third barge that was just coming into view its deck still empty of its puppet. "MIS."

Merchant Investors' Syndicate, Lioe translated, and leaned forward a little. On the distant deck, a dark figure lifted its head, rose forward as though to its knees, and hung

there for a moment, an indistinct shadow against the thin
bank of light that was the far bank of the Water. Lioe caught
her breath, heard a shocked murmur from the people filling
the seiner to her right, and the same questioning noises from
the crowd on the bank behind her. Gelsomina smiled faintly,
said nothing. Then the figure straightened fully, and the
lights came on, revealing a shape in a nip-waisted coat and
the blood-red shoulder-cape-and-hood of Captain Rider. She
was a familiar template in the Game, one of the heroic al-
most-pirates who defended the Scattered Worlds against the
Imperium, and Lioe waited eagerly for her to lower her
hood. The puppet lifted both hands—light glinted from the
ring, Captain Rider's seal, worn on its right forefinger, and
Lioe smiled at the careful detail—and slipped the hood back.
There was something not quite right about the face, though,
something unfamiliar, added or taken away from the template. Lioe frowned, puzzled, and realized that the puppet's
eyes didn't match, one blue, one brown. Behind her, the
crowd cheered.

"Holy shit," Roscha said, "that's Berengaria."

"More politics," Gelsomina said, but did not sound particularly displeased this time.

"The governor?" Lioe said.

Roscha nodded, grinning, and raised her voice to carry
over the cheers and shrill whistles from the crowd. "She's
one of theirs, the MIS's, I mean. And they're proud of her."

"She's favored them enough, you mean," Gelsomina
said.

For all she hates politics, Lioe thought, *she knows a lot
about what's going on.* Still, it was a clever move, associat-
ing Governor Berengaria—who from all accounts supported
Burning Bright's freedom from both the metagovernments,
and leaned to the Republic, her friends said, only because
they were less of a threat than the Hsaioi-An—with Captain
Rider, protector of the Scattered Worlds. *Not subtle, admit-
tedly, but clever.*

"And Rider's not what you'd call a Beauty," Gelsomina
went on, her voice rising, querulous.

"She's surely not a Beast," Roscha answered, and Lioe
intervened again.

"What is the rule?"

"There isn't really a rule," Gelsomina said, grudgingly. "Not written down, anyway. But the tradition is to alternate the pageant barges, a Beauty and a Beast, and the figures are usually taken from mythology. Not from the Game."

"The Game's a kind of mythology," Lioe said mildly, overriding something Roscha started to say, and after a moment the john-boat pilot subsided.

"Oh, I know," Gelsomina answered. "It's just—oh, very God, I hate getting old. You always end up sounding like your own mother."

Lioe grinned and saw Roscha relax even further. "Who designs the puppets?" she asked at random, hoping to turn the conversation even further, and saw a fourth barge pull into view.

"Who's that?" Roscha demanded.

Gelsomina worked her glasses, shook her head. "Can't tell yet."

On the distant deck, a figure unfolded, barely rising out of a crouch before the spotlights struck it. A dancing satyr leered back at the crowd, goat-legged, rude horns jutting from its forehead and implied beneath its gilded fig leaf; it was crowned with oak and ivy, golden acorns—*they must be the size of melons,* Lioe realized, *too big to span in my cupped hands*—and carried a double flute. The cheers were less than enthusiastic, to her surprise, and she looked at Roscha.

"It's been done before," Roscha said, and Gelsomina shook her head.

"It's Soresin, too. I expected better, after what I heard they spent this year."

Then, quite suddenly, the satyr began to move. As though it had heard the comments, it thumbed its nose to each bank in turn, still grinning, then lifted its flute to its thick lips. It began to play, and, seconds later, the sound reached the watching crowd, a thin, seductive melody that carried the urge to dance and weep in the same quick, minor-keyed strain. A moment later, the puppet began to dance to its own piping, the movements timed so perfectly that for a long moment Lioe forgot the barge, forgot that it was a puppet, and saw only the ghost of an abandoned god dancing against the horizon.

"Now that's more like it," Gelsomina said, and her words were nearly drowned by the cheering from the shore. On the seiner next to them, some of the people were dancing, sketching the same quick steps to the satyr's music. Lioe glanced toward them, saw a young man clasp a woman's hands and swing her in a sweeping circle. She leaned back, eyes closed, bright skirt flying, her long hair tumbling loose from a Carnival crown of braids, brushing the decks. She came upright laughing, and Lioe looked away from the wild abandon in her face.

"If that doesn't take all the awards," Roscha began, and her voice trailed off into nothing.

Gelsomina nodded, but her expression was less certain. "Everything for puppetry, certainly."

The barge that followed Soresin's dancing satyr carried another female puppet, this one tall and very slim, dressed in a short, one-shouldered tunic and carrying a spear nearly as tall as the puppet itself. Light flared from the fingers of her free hand; she touched the spear's point, and fire ran up and down the shaft. It was impressive, but after the dancing satyr anything would have been an anticlimax.

The next barge carried a stooped and cloaked figure, red lights glowing like eyes from the shadows within its hood— "Imbriac," Gelsomina said, "one of the Five Points Families"—that received no more than polite applause, and the next was a crowned man, very handsome, sponsored by a fishing cooperative called Tcheirin Sibs. The next barge slid into view, its puppet already outlined against the lights of the distant shore, a stooped and crooked figure, one shoulder higher than the rest. The lights came on, revealing the twisted body, the sneering scowl of one of the Game's grand villains, the Baron's henchman Ettanin Hasse. The puppet stood for a long moment, only its head moving as it looked from side to side, mouth still twisted in contemptuous amusement, and then, quite slowly, it lifted a mask to its face. The mask was perfect, ordinary, a man's face without deformity; the puppet set it into place, and straightened fully, the crooked shoulder and twisted body easing away.

There was a murmur, approving and uneasy all at once, before the applause. The puppet lowered the mask again, and sank back into its first character.

"That," Gelsomina said, "was Chrestil-Brisch."

"That takes guts," Roscha said. "Considering that's what most people think of them anyway."

Lioe glanced at her, and Roscha shrugged. "They've got a reputation for being, well, chancy. You're never really sure where you stand with them—or so they say."

Lioe looked back toward the line of barges to watch the next group of puppets mime their reactions against the starless sky. There were only three more—a female shape with a fan, from a popular video series; something with the head and shoulders of a dragon, beautiful but incomprehensible; and, last and best, neither Beauty nor Beast, a shape that seemed to be made of glass and mirrors, each curve of its body turned to facets and angles. It barely moved—"too fragile to move much," Gelsomina said—but it threw back the spotlights in a storm of white fire. It was all too much, and Lioe found herself strangely glad when the last of them slid past. Gelsomina sighed, and motioned for Roscha to release the mooring.

They made their way back to Shadows by the quickest route, up the Crooked River to the turnoff below the Old Dike, then back through the maze of canals to the Liander canal just south of Shadows. The streets were quieter here—most people were still on the Water, or in the streets and plazas along its banks—and Lioe was not sure if she was relieved or worried to see a security drone sail past overhead.

"I appreciate your help," Gelsomina said. "It's nice to see the parade from a decent viewpoint." She had pushed the Viverina's mask back onto her forehead to see while she steered, but the wig was still in place, the skulls clattering against each other.

"Thank you," Lioe said. "I didn't—I don't know what I was expecting, but that was just incredible."

Gelsomina smiled. "And I owe you masks, too. Roscha, do you want Cor-Clar?"

"Yes, and thank you," Roscha answered, and reached with unerring speed for the rich brown-skinned mask.

"And you, Na Lioe?" Gelsomina asked.

Lioe shook her head. "I can't decide. They're all gorgeous, and I don't know who I want to be."

"Well, you're not leaving empty-handed," Gelsomina declared. "We had a bargain." She turned slowly, leaning on the Viverina's stick, running her gaze along the masks still hanging from the unstepped mast. They looked back at her, their colors mellowed in the amber light from the embankment. She smiled then, and reached out with her staff. "Take that one."

"If you're sure, Na Gelsomina," Lioe began, and the woman nodded.

"Take it. I insist."

"Thank you," Lioe said, helplessly, and loosened the mask from the clips that held it. It was made of stiffened lace, roughly formed to the shape of a human face, with a single six-millimeter stone of clear faceted glass set above the mouth like a beauty mark. The web of lace, black and faintly metallic, looked almost transparent in the light. "Thanks," she said again, and let Roscha pull her up onto the embankment. She looked back once, to see Gelsomina— the Viverina again, her mask pulled down into place and staff in hand—standing beside the row of masks that looked almost alive in the amber light.

"We've got some time," Roscha said. "Do you want to stop for coffee, or something?"

Lioe looked sideways, found a patch of grey stone that would let her see the chronometer's numbers. In a little more than an hour she would have to start the night's session, and she shook her head decisively. "No. I want to get back to Shadows." She was aware suddenly that Roscha was frowning, added a belated, "Thanks anyway."

Roscha shrugged one shoulder. "Suit yourself."

"Some other time," Lioe said, and got no answer. They kept walking through the patches of light and shadow that filled the streets, pools of light puddling in the intersections, shadow creeping back at the middle of the blocks, where the streetlights did not overlap. Distant music wound through the darkness, fits and snatches that she could almost weave into a tune. She tilted her head to one side to listen—she didn't even quite recognize the instruments, except for the heavy bass and the thin whine of metal strings from a violo—and started when Roscha's hand brushed her own.

"Hey, I'm sorry," Roscha said, in an affronted voice and Lioe shook her head.

"I'm sorry, you just startled me. That's all."

There was a moment of silence, and then Roscha looked away. "I'm sorry," she said again, in an entirely different tone.

"It's all right," Lioe said, and did not move away when Roscha reached for her hand again. They walked on hand in hand, their footsteps echoing on the paving, and then Roscha pulled away again. Lioe bit back annoyance—she didn't need this, not before a session—but said nothing. *Whatever's wrong with her, she'll have to get over it on her own: I don't have the time to nursemaid her.* Then, in spite of herself, she gave a rueful smile. *Why are my one-night stands always more complicated than they should be?*

EVENING, DAY 1

Damian Chrestil stood on the wide balcony that ran along the base of the palazze's roof, watching the fireworks that bloomed over the Wet Districts and the Inland Water. Each burst drew a murmur of appreciation from the other guests, watching from the open doorways farther down the roof, but he enjoyed the annual display too much to share it. The bursts of red and gold flared like flowers, drowning the stars and the starlike lights of the distant buildings. He would rather have been watching from the Water itself, where the sky rained golden fire with each explosion, but Chrestillio had asked—*and we all agreed, in some perverse fit of compliance*—that they all attend the family's party as a show of solidarity. Customs-and-Intelligence was still asking questions about the Demeter shipment, and it was important that they look as though they trusted each other, and weren't worrying about anything. The fireworks slackened, the breathing space before the finale, and Damian glanced over his shoulder toward the guests who lined the balcony. About half of them were masked, all from the Five Points families: the Old City did not mask, preferred more refined pastimes, but the real power had never needed refinement. Damian smiled at the thought, nodded to a thin woman—*she was something in the bank,* he thought—who lifted her glass to him, and looked away.

The finale caught them all by surprise, and there was a collective gasp as the first burst flowered into an enormous spray of red that turned to gold and then fell in streamers of light toward the distant Water. Another shell burst into a flare of purple brightening to pink, and then another, and another, so that the balls of light hung for a moment on a trail of gold fire like flowers on a stem. Even as they fell, dissolving into a shower of sparks, four more shells flew up, trailing thin lines of flame, exploded into flat sheets of light. From the Water, Damian knew, it would be as though the world were frozen for an instant by that crack of light, and he sighed for what he was missing.

In his pocket, the house remote buzzed softly, a tingling vibration against his thigh. He swore under his breath, and reached for it, cupping his fingers over the control points. The message vibrated against his hand: *urgent message, come at once.* He swore again, but the code was his highest priority. He glanced over his shoulder again, saw no one watching, and turned the remote to touch the control combination that released the gate to the outside stair. It was in shadow, and everyone's attention would be on the finale for at least half an hour. He looked again toward the Water—red and green halos flared around a golden center—and made himself turn away.

The staircase spiraled down the outside of the palazze, with only a single entrance before the ground level. He twisted the remote again to release that lock, and let himself in past impassive human security to the third floor's secondary hall. The corridor connected with his own rooms; he made his way there, the lights growing brighter at his approach, dimming as he moved away, let himself into the suite. Lights were blinking on the communications console, but he paused long enough to clear the windows completely before he crossed to the control board and entered the security codes. The little screen sprang to life, but Damian ignored it, tilted the boxy display so that he could see at least some of the fireworks through the window beyond it.

In the screen, ji-Imbaoa glared at him, claws tapping somewhere out of sight. "Your plans are starting to unravel," he said, without preamble.

Damian Chrestil lifted an eyebrow at him—*how did I come to join forces with him?*—said aloud, "Weren't you able to get the codes?"

Ji-Imbaoa waved away that question. "They are coming.

There has been some trouble with the transmitter; I've had to go through the commercial links. But that is not the issue.''

"Forgive me, Na Speaker, but I thought precisely that was the cause of this delay," Damian said.

"The codes are on their way," ji-Imbaoa said again. "Do you doubt me?''

Damian bit back his anger, waved a hand in apology. "No. I don't doubt they'll get here." *Eventually.*

"I accept the apology.''

It was only a formal phrase, effectively meaningless, but Damian felt his hackles rise. He controlled his temper with an effort, and said, "Then, Na Speaker, what's happened to upset you?''

"Ransome," ji-Imbaoa said. "He has concluded that the Game is a blind, and he is encouraging Chauvelin to look elsewhere.''

Damian frowned at the screen, a cold knot forming in the pit of his stomach. If that was true, if Ransome was back on the port nets, and with Customs-and-Intelligence still asking questions about the shipment from Demeter, it would be only too easy to track down what was really going on. *Easy for Ransome, anyway.* He took a deep breath, trying to banish fear, and ji-Imbaoa went on.

"I have taken steps to forestall him, but I don't know how long it will last.''

"Good," Damian said, and then considered. "What did you do?''

"The only thing I could do," ji-Imbaoa answered. "I have made it a matter of honor and prestige that Ransome continue with the Game—I have wagered my name and my fathers' that there will be something there for him to find. I trust that it's so.''

Do I care about your fathers' names? Damian ran his hand through his hair, tried to consider things calmly. "There are things for him to worry about, yes," he said, "and I can arrange for him to find some more political material." *I think. If Cella can get time.* "But under these circumstances, Na Speaker—let me put it plainly, if you don't get me those codes, tonight or tomorrow, this deal will fall through. At a high cost to both of us, money and prestige alike.''

"Let me remind you," ji-Imbaoa said, his hands suddenly as still as Damian had ever seen them, "that you have significantly more to lose than I.''

"I've done all that I promised," Damian answered, and left the rest unsaid.

"I'll get you the codes," ji-Imbaoa said. "But you will have to keep Ransome busier." He cut the connection before Damian could reply.

Damian swore at the blank screen, slapped the controls with more force than was really necessary. But ji-Imbaoa was lord and master of Highhopes, and if the jericho-human colony there was going to trade with Burning Bright without the interference of the brokers backed by the tzu Tsinra-an, they had to work through ji-Imbaoa. And ji-Imbaoa had to get his share of the profits. The system shut itself off, and he stood for a moment staring at the sky beyond the long windows. The last shells made a curtain of fire, sheets of gold and red that frayed to long streamers against the invisible stars, but he barely saw it, lost in calculations. If Ransome wasn't distracted by the Game, his own security was probably inadequate: he paid well, employed the best experts, but Ransome was a superb netwalker in his own right, and he knew too many people within the systems. If he couldn't crack the security wall himself, he would know someone who could give or sell him the keys. Damian tapped his fingers against the case, winced at the echo of ji-Imbaoa's gesture. He'd increase security—*it's a good thing I thought to organize a blockade of the port feed already, but I'll have to do something more. And I can't transfer the lachesi to the transshipment group without those codes.* Still, it would be better if Ransome stayed in the Game.

The door chime sounded then, and the remote buzzed gently against his thigh. He frowned—*no one should know I'm here*—and touched the code that threw the security feed onto the small display. Cella was waiting in the hall, demure in a sheer overdress. Damian's frown deepened, and he touched the controls that released the lock.

"They're starting to wonder where you are," Cella said, without preamble.

"Damn them," Damian said, and then, "Which them, anyway?"

"Your siblings, mostly," Cella answered, and Damian made a face.

"I'd better go up, then."

"I do need to talk to you," Cella said.

Damian Chrestil looked at her. "I hope it's good news. I've not been having a pleasant evening."

Cella smiled wryly. "I'm afraid not."

Damian sighed. "Well?"

"I suppose it's good and bad, at that. I stopped in at Shadows before I came here. Lioe—Ransome's pilot—is running a session tonight, and I wanted to look over the play list. The good news is that Ambidexter himself is back in the Game—he's even playing Harmsway—but the bad news is that Kichi Desjourdy's also part of the session. And as best I can discover, it was Lioe herself who asked her to play."

Damian's hand closed convulsively on the pocket remote, and there was a squeal of protest from the mechanism. He released it hastily, and Cella went on.

"Desjourdy is known as a Gamer, but I thought you ought to know."

"Damn," Damian said softly, as much to himself as to Cella, and he stared into space for a long moment, trying to order his thoughts. The sky beyond the windows was very black, the fireworks over: *no inspiration there*, he thought, and turned his eyes away. "This Lioe," he began, "is she still seeing Roscha, or was it a one-night affair?"

Cella shrugged. "I don't know. Roscha was slated to play Avellar, but Lioe seems very taken with Ransome. And he with her, for that matter."

"So." Damian shoved his hands into his pockets again, running his fingers over the remote's smoothly indented surface as though it were a talisman. *If I can get Roscha to watch Lioe—Roscha's done that kind of job before, she can certainly handle it—then I can be sure to find out if she contacts Desjourdy again.* He touched the remote's control points again, and the image in the display screens shifted, became a memo board. He leaned over the keyboard, typed a quick message into the wharfingers' computers—CONTACT JAFIERA ROSCHA 2 STORM AM, SEND HER TO MY OFFICE AS SOON AS SHE ARRIVES—and set it loose on the main systems. *And if all else fails, she can deal with Lioe, and I can get Ransome out of the way.* "Can you get a transcript of this session for me?"

Cella blinked, startled. "Yes, of course. It'll be on all the Game nets by three this morning if not before. Why?"

"I just want to see how they behave," Damian said vaguely. *I want to see if Roscha thinks she's competing with Ransome, and I want to see how good she is at it. Because if she has any grudge against him, I can make good use of it.* "Dump it to my private system as soon as you can get a copy, please."

"I'll do that," Cella said.

Damian Chrestil smiled crookedly. "Then let's rejoin the party."

INTERLUDE

They crouched in the uncertain shelter of the cargo bay, hearing the clatter of boots recede along the walkways to either side. The overhanging shelves, piled high with crates, gave some cover, but they all knew that if the baron's guards came back out onto the center catwalk it would take a miracle to keep from being seen. Galan Africa/ALEMO TOMSEY frowned over the power pack of their only heavy laser, working methodically to mate a salvaged blaster cell into the nonstandard housing. Jack Blue/KICHI DESJOURDY sprawled gasping against the nearest stack of crates, hand against his chest as though it pained him. Mijja Lyall/LACHACALLE crouched at his side, one hand on his wrist, as though somehow knowing his pulse rate could help. Blue's great bulk had displaced the lower crates slightly, and Gallio Hazard/HALLY VENTURA edged out of its line of fall, his pistol drawn and ready. He knelt cautiously in the shelter of a second stack of crates, laid a fresh clip on the floor beside him, and settled to wait. Lord Faro/PETER SAVIAN and Ibelin Belfortune/KAZIO BELEDIN crouched as always a little apart from the rest, Faro a little ahead of the wild-eyed Belfortune, as though he could protect him.

"We're still waiting for this contact," Desir of Harmsway/AMBIDEXTER said. "Well, Avellar? What happened this time?"

"How can I know?" Avellar/JAFIERA ROSCHA answered. "Something's gone wrong, obviously." She smiled suddenly. "I say we press on, Desir, unless you want to go back."

Harmsway looked away, made a face of disgust. Avellar's grin faded, and she went to kneel on the warped flooring beside Jack Blue. "How is it?"

"Not so good." Blue's voice was thin and wheezing, and, behind his back, Lyall shook her head. She reached into her much-depleted kit, came out with a slim injector, but hesitated, and did not lay it against the telekinetic's arm.

"If you weren't so damn fat, you wouldn't be in this bad shape," Harmsway snapped. "Christ, what a waste."

Blue frowned, his eyes losing their focus for a moment. A cracked piece of the floor tiling snapped loose and flung itself at Harmsway's face. He ducked away from it, but too late, and the tile's sharp edge drew a thin line of blood along one cheekbone. Avellar snatched the tile out of the air before it could strike anything else.

"A waste to bring me," Blue said, mimicking Harmsway's precise voice. "You didn't bring me, little man—"

"Shut up," Avellar said, and was obeyed. "Save your strength," she added, and looked at Harmsway. "The ship's right there, Desir, just waiting for us. Go right ahead."

Harmsway looked longingly at the cargo door, only forty meters away across the width of the warehouse. It was even open, the ship's hatch gleaming in the loading lights, and he could feel that the last barrier was sealed only with a palm lock, the kind of thing he could open in his sleep . . . if he could reach it. His lips thinned, and he looked away.

"Avellar." Lyall's voice was suddenly sharp with fear, and Avellar swung to face her.

"I think—" Lyall began, then shook her head. "No, I'm sure. They've brought in one of the hunters."

Harmsway swore, and Hazard looked back over his shoulder at them all.

Africa did not look up from his work, his hands still busy with the laser. "Hunter?"

"Another telepath," Blue said. "The kind that specializes in hunting down his own kind."

"How close?" Harmsway demanded, and Lyall shook her head again.

"I can't tell. He-she-it's shielded."

"All right," Avellar said. "No one use anything, telekinesis, telepathy, electrokinesis, anything at all, unless there's no other choice.'' There were murmurs of agreement from the others, and she looked at Africa. ''Galan?''

The technician shrugged, his hands never slowing on the balky connection. ''I don't know. Even if I get it hooked up, I can't make any guarantees.''

Avellar grimaced, and for the first time looked at Belfortune. ''Bel.''

Faro shifted his position slightly, putting himself between Avellar and Belfortune. ''Let him be.''

''Bel,'' Avellar said again.

''I can't do it,'' Belfortune said flatly, without lifting his eyes from the floor.

''Oh, that's a lie,'' Harmsway said, soft and deadly, ''a lie and you know it, Belfortune. That's what bought the Baron's favor, bought you a lover and almost anything you wanted, just as long as you learned to use your power. Tell me, is it true the Baron liked to watch while you killed them?''

''Jesus, Desir,'' Hazard said, and was ignored.

Belfortune looked up slowly, met Harmsway's glare for the first time unflinching. ''Yes. It's true.''

''Then you can stop the hunter,'' Avellar said.

''It won't do any good,'' Belfortune said. ''Where else could we be, but in one of the cargo bays? All it'll do is buy you time.''

''That'll be enough,'' Avellar said.

''But if it isn't—'' Lyall began, and closed her mouth over what she would have said.

Avellar answered her anyway. ''If it's not enough, then we fight.''

''Brilliant,'' Harmsway jeered. ''How clever of you, Royal.''

''Shut up, Desir,'' Hazard said. ''Avellar. Belfortune's right, much as I hate to admit it.''

Avellar nodded. ''We need a diversion, I agree. But to make it work, we have to get rid of the hunter.'' She looked back at Belfortune. ''Well? Will you do it?''

Belfortune closed his eyes for a moment, pain etched deep in his face, then nodded. ''Oh, yes. What's one more?'' Lord Faro reached out to touch his shoulder.

"Then we'll need to distract the rest of the searchers," Avellar said.

"No, really?" Harmsway murmured.

"Yes, and you're just the man to do it," Avellar answered. She smiled briefly, daring him. "This bay is right next to the main computer nexus, Desir. Think what you can do with that."

Harmsway said, "But why should I, Royal? Give me one reason, after everything you tried to do."

There was a little silence, and then Avellar looked at him, her face absolutely without emotion. "I told you then. I'm telling you now. I need you, need your talent, to make up for what I lost when my sibs—my twins, the rest of the clone, the rest of me—were killed. I can't take the throne without you."

"To hell with you," Harmsway said, and there was an odd, gloating note in his voice.

"I need you," Avellar said again. "I came here for you, didn't I? I did what you couldn't do, I broke you out of the Baron's prison because I need you. Isn't that enough?"

"Maybe if you went down on your knees," Harmsway said, "but not before."

"For God's sake," Hazard said. He pushed himself to his feet, grabbed Harmsway roughly by the shoulder, and swung him to face the others. "If you don't do it, Desir, we're going to die."

Harmsway lifted an eyebrow at him. "I'm surprised at you—"

"I want out of here," Hazard said. "We can sort out the rest of it once we're free, but right now, getting off planet is a hell of a lot more important than Avellar or the goddamn throne."

"I won't work with her again," Harmsway said.

"So what?" That was Jack Blue, hoisting himself to his feet. "It won't be as good, Avellar, but maybe I can do something if this shit won't."

Avellar nodded her thanks, still watching Harmsway, who smiled bitterly.

"All right. I'll do it—if only to spare your talents, Jack."

"Too kind," Blue said, and achieved a passable imitation of Harmsway's sneer.

"There's only one thing," Faro said. "How close do you need to be to a—a subject, Bel?"

"I don't really know," Belfortune said. "A few meters, probably closer." He looked at Lyall. "Any ideas, Doctor?"

Lyall shook her head. "I wasn't involved in that part of the project. I would think within two meters."

Belfortune laughed softly to himself. "Do you know who it is? Which hunter?"

"No," Lyall answered. "I told you, it's shielded."

"You'll need support," Avellar said.

Belfortune shook his head, and Faro said, "I'll go with him. One's enough."

Avellar nodded. "Good luck, then, both of you."

Lyall said, "The hunter's coming closer. Moving along the east wall, toward the entrance there."

"Careful," Africa said. "You don't want to tip him off."

Lyall shook her head, and Blue said impatiently, "She's not strong enough. Nobody can hear her, not unless they're right on top of her."

"Let's go, Bel," Faro said gently, and Belfortune nodded. Faro reached down and pulled the other man to his feet.

"Take an extra power pack," Hazard said, and handed his last spare to Faro.

"Thanks," Faro said, and he and Belfortune stepped out into the corridor. They turned left at the first cross corridor, heading east, toward the entrance and the searching hunter.

Avellar looked at the others. "Dr. Lyall, tell me when the hunter's dead."

Lyall winced, but nodded.

"And the rest of us?" Harmsway demanded.

"We wait," Avellar answered, grimly. "Be ready to act when Lyall gives the word."

Game/varRebel.2.04/subPsi.1.22/ver22.1/ses4.25

Faro and Belfortune moved warily through the corridors,
ready to duck under the shelter of the cargo racks at the first
sign of patrolling guards. To their surprise, however, the
racks and catwalks were empty, and they reached the eastern
wall without incident.

"What now, Bel?" Faro began, stopped abruptly at the
look on Belfortune's face.

Belfortune was staring into the middle distance, pale eyes
vague, unfixed, pupils dilating. He ran a hand delicately
along the bare metal skin of the cargo bay's exterior wall, a
gesture unnervingly like a caress, and began to walk, slowly,
a faint smile curving his lips. Faro, who had seen this before,
this stalking hunger, shivered convulsively, but kept his
place at Belfortune's shoulder, gun drawn and ready, the
spare power pack ready to hand.

"Come to me," Belfortune whispered. "Come here, you,
I feel you walking there, come to me now. . . ." The words
trailed off into a hissing murmur, rising and falling with his
slow breath. He could feel the hunter's presence, a vague
warmth beyond the cold wall, allowed his own hunger to rise
to match that warmth, played out his desire as a fisherman
plays a line, a thread of appetite disguised as curiosity. He
could feel the hunter's presence more clearly now, and recognized the man, had considered him a friend, but his unleashed hunger accepted that knowledge only as a way to
make the bait more attractive. He leaned against the thin
metal of the wall, flattening himself against the cool surface
as though he could feel the hunter's body against his own,
and let the tendril of thought unfold. He felt the hunter take
the bait, felt him turn his attention toward the faint, stray
presence, the oddity that must be investigated, and kept tight
control of his own power, letting the hunter's own curiosity
draw him nearer. Belfortune could almost see the slight
frown, the familiar lines of his face; he pressed himself
harder against the wall, willing the hunter closer. And then,
at last, he was close enough. Belfortune smiled, let himself
go at last, and felt the hunter's whole body jerk convulsively

as he realized he was no longer free. Belfortune felt him struggle and tightened his grip, felt the sudden terrified release as the hunter's shields failed, and tasted the hunter's power, his strength and his cunning and the delicate flavor of his mind. He drained him, not bothering to savor it—there was no time for such niceties, and it had been too long since the last one, anyway—and saw/felt, in the last moment of double vision, the hunter's body slumping to the ground just on the other side of the wall. He slid down the wall with it, sucking the last dregs of life, and crouched there for a moment, breathing hard.

Faro looked away, swallowing bile, unwilling to watch the sated hunger turn to disgust in Belfortune's eyes. "Tell them it's done," he said, and a whispering voice said, from the end of the corridor, "Tell who what, Faro?"

Faro spun, gun leveled, even as he knew it was useless, and felt as much as heard the snap of a laser bolt. He ducked instinctively, but the shot had been meant as a warning only.

"Hold your fire," the voice said. It came from the closed cabin of an airsled that blocked the corridor behind them. Soldiers—soldiers in the black uniforms of Baron Vortex's elite troops—flanked it, their lasers lowered and ready. Belfortune shook his head, trying to drive away the cloying satisfaction, made a small, pained noise of despair. The voice went on, as though no one had spoken. "Faro, you're not a fool. I think we can come to some agreement."

Faro hesitated, the muzzle of his gun wavering slightly—to fire was suicide, his and Belfortune's, but the speaker was Baron Vortex, and the Baron could never be trusted.

"I find you useful," the voice went on, "just useful enough to salvage from this mess. Put down your gun, and I'll let you live."

Faro dredged a laugh from somewhere. "To what end?"

"I told you, I find you useful," the voice said. "You can return to your previous employment."

"Not much better off than the prisoners," Faro muttered, said more loudly, "What about Bel?"

"Ah." There was a note like amusement in the Baron's voice. "For him, there is a price."

"Well?" Faro said.

"I asked you before, tell who what," the voice said. "But I think I know that. Where are they, Faro? Where are Avellar and the rest?"

"Faro," Belfortune said, and the word was ambiguous appeal.

Faro glanced down at him, at the renewed sanity in the pale eyes, saw him start to pull himself to his feet, clinging to the wall of the cargo bay, looked back at the Baron's airsled and the flanking soldiers. He let the gun fall to his side.

"Your lands and your lover," the voice whispered. "You can still have them both. Is Avellar's rebellion worth that much to you?"

"I don't know for sure," Faro said. "She—they were back toward the middle of the bay, heading for a ship."

He paused, hoping that would be enough, a large enough betrayal, saw the nearest soldier raise his laser, and waited for the baron to pronounce the sentence.

"Put down your gun, Faro," the baron said at last, and Faro laid the pistol on the floor tiles, kicked it toward the line of soldiers. Two of them came forward, slinging their rifles, and Faro let them drag him forward, stood quite still as they ran their hands roughly over his body, then locked his wrists together behind his back. Another pair dragged Belfortune to his feet, and did the same to him.

Flame flared overhead, bursting from the shattering light fixtures, and raw electricity leaped like lightning from the power nodes. One of the soldiers fired reflexively at the snapping currents, and screamed as the laser's power pack exploded in a sheet of flame.

"Harmsway," Belfortune said, and the pale eyes were suddenly alive again.

"Get them out of here," the Baron ordered. "The rest of you, come with me."

Game/varRebel.2.04/subPsi.1.22/ver22.1/ses4.28

"The hunter's dead," Lyall said, and in spite of her best efforts the disgust showed in her voice.

Avellar nodded, hiding the same repulsion. "Then let's get on with it." She looked at Harmsway. "It's your show now, Desir."

Harmsway nodded, allowed himself a smile of pure pleasure. "So we need a diversion," he said aloud. "And the computer center is right behind these walls." He turned in a full circle, scanning the racks until he found a power node, and went to crouch beside it, laying one long-fingered hand gently over the input jack. There was a faint crackling, and then he had matched the current precisely. He closed his eyes, and let his consciousness wander out into the bay's power grid. There was a faint humming, and a haze of blue light, all but invisible, formed around his hand. He could feel the pattern of the electrical systems, and of the computers and other instruments that fed off it, could almost see their regularity like lines against his eyes. He felt his way into the grid, merging himself with the flow of power until he was all but invisible, a faint surge of current that was still within the tolerances of the port computers. He found the access port, and teased it open, then slipped cautiously into the alien space within the network.

He had the electron's view, current flashing on or off, and he hung for a moment, disoriented, trying to match that image with what he knew must be hidden in the computers. The lights blinked on and off, too fast to follow even in his heightened state, tuned perfectly to the flow of the currents; he stared a little longer, still trying to analyze the workings, and heard, very distant, Lyall's cry.

"My God, it's the Baron. He's found them."

At the same moment, someone touched his shoulder, and he opened his eyes to see Hazard bending over him.

"Desir. Blow the system, we've got trouble."

Harmsway was already moving within the distant system, calling power from various nodes. Throughout the building, terminals flickered and died; across the complex, screens wavered, the sudden drain triggering backup power supplies. Harmsway kept pulling, drawing power to himself, letting the minuscule energies collect and build, feeding on themselves.

"Hurry, Desir," a voice said—Avellar's voice, he thought, but he could not be sure.

The process could not be hurried, not if he was to do it right. He blocked all thoughts of the Baron, all fear, concentrating on the energy around him, tracing an escape route in his mind. He felt it cross the threshold at last, and released it, let the surge blast through every circuit in the system, and let the same wave of power carry him back into the grid that fed the cargo bay. He felt overloaded systems crash, felt the surging power flare at every node, and in a heartbeat redirected that power, away from the local nodes into everything electrical near the eastern entrance. He opened his eyes, and heard the flat, hard crack of explosions from the far side of the bay.

"The port computers are down," he said. "They shouldn't be able to stop lift-off."

"And it should give them something else to worry about," Avellar said. Fire sirens whooped in the next building, underscoring her words. "Let's go."

They made their way quickly through the last corridors, dodging between the half-full cargo racks. At each exposed power node, Harmsway paused to send another wave of power through the building's systems. He could feel the network overloading under his manipulations, knew that he was literally burning out their defenses as he used them, but the explosions behind them seemed to mean that it was working.

There were still two guards at the door that gave access to the ship's hatch, both staring nervously toward the sounds of Harmsway's attack. They were sheltered by the hatchway, not an easy shot at all, and Avellar paused in the shelter of the final stacks of crates, considering them cautiously. After a moment, she beckoned to Hazard. He frowned, but slipped forward to join her.

"You're our best shot," Avellar said, her voice an almost soundless whisper. "Can you do it?"

Hazard shook his head. "They're too well covered. Why the hell didn't they run for the fighting?"

"Be glad they didn't just close the access door," Avellar said with a grin, and eased back into the shelter of the crates.

"You're going to have to do something quick," Harmsway said. He was sweating, breathing hard, as though he'd been lifting heavy weights. "I'm draining the grid, and the wiring isn't going to take this abuse much longer."

"The Baron's still back by the door," Lyall said. Her eyes were closed, and Jack Blue steadied her, guiding her with a hand on her shoulder. "But you've only delayed him."

"I can draw the guards out," Blue said. "Leave it to me."

Avellar considered him for a moment—a fat man, still wheezing a little, but no longer leaning on the others—and nodded. "If you can get them out into gunshot, we can take them."

Hazard nodded, snapped the power pack out of his pistol, checked the power remaining, and snapped it in again. "I've got about a dozen shots left. That should be enough."

"It ought to be," Harmsway said, and managed a grin.

"It'll have to be," Avellar said. She looked at Blue. "Do it."

Blue closed his eyes, frowning slightly, and a moment later they all heard something stir in the corridor to their right. It was a faint noise, as though someone trying to be careful had brushed against an imperfectly balanced crate, but one of the guards heard it and looked up warily. Blue's frown deepened, and there was a quick patter of footsteps, as though someone had darted across a corridor into cover. The guard peered out of the doorway, put up his faceplate to listen more closely.

"They're buying it," Africa said, and leveled his pistol.

Hazard laid a restraining hand on his arm. "Wait for the other one."

Africa nodded, lowered the pistol again.

Blue was sweating lightly now, his forehead furrowed in concentration. In the corridor, there was another stirring, and then the distinctive click of a power pack snapping home into a pistol butt. The guard cocked his head to one side, listening, then pulled his faceplate slowly down again. Avellar held her breath, her own pistol ready at her side. There were no more noises from the corridor, a silence that seemed somehow ominous, more dangerous than the sounds had been. The guard held up his hand, and beckoned to his partner. The second guard came up to the edge of the hatch, but stopped just inside the heavy frame. Africa swore under his breath: the hatchway still blocked his shot.

"Come on," Hazard muttered. "Come on, now."

The guards stood still for a moment longer, obviously conferring via the helmet links. Then the first guard started toward the sound of the footsteps, and the second man moved out of the hatchway to cover him.

"Now!" Avellar said.

The others fired almost as she spoke. The first guard fell without a sound, sprawling on the warped floor tiles, but the second guard fired back blindly, dodged back toward the access door. Africa and Hazard fired at the same moment, and the guard went down.

"Did he get out a warning?" Hazard demanded, looking at Lyall.

"It doesn't matter," Avellar said, impatiently. "Let's go." She started across the open space without looking back.

Hazard glanced over his shoulder, saw Harmsway reaching across to steady Jack Blue, and smiled in spite of himself. They crowded into the narrow space between the doorway and the ship's hatch, and Africa fiddled with the controls to bring the door down behind them. Avellar nodded her approval, and laid her hand against the sensor panel that controlled access to the freighter's cargo lock. There was a soft click, and then a high-pitched tone.

"Royal Avellar," she said, and waited. A heartbeat later, the cargo lock creaked open. Familiar people, familiar faces, were waiting inside the lock, and Avellar relaxed for the first time since they had left the prison complex.

"Thank God you made it," a well-remembered voice said, and Avellar sighed.

"Danile." She smiled then, careful not to look back at the others, particularly Harmsway. She had risked everything to get him back, and she had at least freed him from the Baron's prison. The rest—his return to her rebellion, his proper place at her side—would come, in time. He owed her that, and he would eventually pay.

"We have to hurry," Danile went on, "so everybody, get inboard now." The hatch sealed itself as he spoke, closing off their view of the cargo bay. "It's chaos back there, there's nothing they can do to stop us. But we have to go now."

There was a ragged murmur of agreement, and the group began to move farther into the ship, following Danile and Avellar. Underfoot, the ship's main power plant trembled, building toward blast-off and freedom from Ixion's Wheel.

PART FIVE

DAY 2

Lioe woke to the noise of distant traffic and the easy motion
of the boat against the sluggish current. She turned her head
away from the bars of sunlight that crept in through the gaps
in the shutters, lay still for a moment, remembering where
she was. She was meanly glad that Roscha was nowhere in
sight. Not that it hadn't been fun—and after Roscha's performance in the session, especially; it was one of the best
character readings Lioe had seen—but in the cold light of
morning, she found herself wondering exactly why she'd
done it. She shook the thought away—it was a little late for
regrets, and anyway, it *had* been fun—and crawled out of
the low bunk. The bathroom was tiny, and smelled of aggressive cleaning; she washed quickly, the water tasting
flatly of chemicals, and found her clothes hanging on the
bulkhead beside the low stairs that led up onto the deck. She
pulled on shirt and trousers and the loose vest, slung the
mask that Gelsomina had given her around her neck, and
pushed open the double doors. She had left her hat somewhere, she realized, either at Shadows or at Ransome's loft,
and she made a mental note to look for it later.

The sunlight on the deck had an odd cast to it, a sickly,
uncertain tone, and Lioe glanced toward the sky. It was almost white, hazed with clouds as it had been for the past two
days, but when she looked south, toward the mouth of the
Inland Water, darker clouds showed between the housetops.
An erratic little wind was blowing fitfully, sending bits of
trash skittering along the embankment above the boat, and
Lioe felt the hairs rising on the back of her neck.

"Oh, there you are," Roscha said. She made her way forward, stepping easily over the solar panels set into the decking. "I was just coming to wake you. It looks like that storm's going to hit us after all, and I've got a call from the wharfinger to report at once to the main dock."

"That's too bad," Lioe said.

"I don't see why I couldn't make it to Roche'Ambroise for the puppet shows," Roscha went on. "That is, if you still want to go."

One of the local artists' cooperatives was giving its annual free show that afternoon. It was supposed to be a spectacular event, a combination of athletics, mime, and robotics, and Lioe had said she would like to see it. "I don't want you to go to any trouble," she began, and Roscha frowned.

"Look, if you don't want to go, no problem." Her tone implied the opposite.

"It's not that," Lioe said, impatiently. "Yes, I want to see the show, but you've got this call—"

"It shouldn't be anything serious," Roscha said, and gave a fleeting grin. "I haven't done anything. They probably just need help securing the barges. I should be able to make the show."

"Fine," Lioe said. *If you don't, I can enjoy it by myself.* "Where do you want to meet?"

"They do the show in Betani Square, right off the Hartzer Canal," Roscha answered. "Why don't we just meet there, mid-afternoon? By the fountain."

"Fine," Lioe said again. The sunlight faded, and she glanced up, to see a thicker strand of cloud turning the sun to a disk of bronze. "How bad is this storm going to be?"

Roscha shrugged. "Not bad, I'd say. The street brokers are saying a category two at most. That's not anything to worry about."

By whose standards? Lioe wondered, squinting again at the sky. The sun was back, but the clouds looked darker than before. Still, Roscha was the native; if she said it wasn't that bad, it shouldn't be. "I'll see you at the fountain in Betani Square at fifteenth hour," she said aloud, and reached for the rope ladder that led up to the embankment.

Roscha nodded. "Will you help me cast off?"

"Sure." Lioe climbed easily up onto the broad stones, unhooked the ladder, and let it drop. Roscha caught it as it fell, folded it neatly into a well on the deck.

"Ready for the cables?" Lioe asked, and Roscha nodded again.

"I've already switched over."

Lioe unhooked the double-headed cables from the power nodes at the base of the bollard. Roscha caught those as well, guiding them back into their housings, and took her place in the steering well. Lioe released the bow and stern lines, tossed them onto the deck, and stood watching while Roscha shoved the boat away from the embankment, and fed power to the engine. She was out of earshot before Lioe realized she hadn't asked how to get to Roche'Ambroise. She laughed, and started back toward Shadows, where food and her mail would be waiting.

The streets were still busy with costumed figures, despite the impending storm. A cloaked trio was visible in the window of a restaurant, masks set aside to let them eat; a bedraggled pair—male and female? no, two women—were obviously on their way home after a long night of revelry, the skirts of their straight gowns hiked up to make walking easier, their feathers drooping. Yet another indistinct shape wrapped in a cloak lay sound asleep under a bench in one of the little parks, mask tucked under its head for a pillow. Others were just starting the day—another Avellar, a striding Baron Vortex, an odd shape like an egg with trousers that everyone else seemed to recognize—and Lioe was suddenly glad of Gelsomina's mask. It made her feel less alien, among the bright maskers, more as though she belonged on Burning Bright. *And I want to belong here,* she realized suddenly. *I'd like to be a part of this.* She shook the thought away as impractical, left her mask hanging around her neck where it couldn't tempt her, and kept walking.

As she came up on the Underface helipad, she saw the lights flashing to warn of an incoming flight, and then recognized the figure sitting on the bench at the edge of the pad. *At least I can ask him about my hat.* "Good morning, Ransome," she called, and the man on the bench lifted a hand in answer. He did not speak, and Lioe wondered if she'd offended him. He looked up as she approached, met her eyes fully, and she was shocked by his pale face and the brown shadows like ugly bruises under his eyes.

"Jesus, you look awful," she said, and bit her tongue as he managed a wry grin.

"Tactful."

There was something wrong with Ransome's voice; even the one word came thin and breathless, as though he had been running. "Are you all right?" she began, and realized in the same instant what it had to be. White-sickness was most common in Hsaioi-An, among jericho-humans, but it was not unknown in the nonaligned worlds, or in the Republic. And this was white-sickness, no question about it: like all pilots, she'd had enough basic medical training to recognize the symptoms.

Ransome read that recognition in her face, and his grin skewed even more. "I have what I need at home," he said, and Lioe had to lean closer to catch the strangled words. "The doctors changed the medication; I'm not as stable as I used to be. So I got caught short again."

Lioe nodded, wordlessly, hearing the voice of the school's medical trainer droning in her mind. *White-sickness—pneumatic histopathy, also known as lung-rot or uhanjao, drown-yourself, in Hsaioi-An—is classified as a dangerous condition less because it is fatal, which it is, than because it is contagious until treated. Once proper treatment is begun, the danger of infection is over, but the damage to the victim is irreversible. Most planets require a certificate of treatment before customs will admit an infected person; pilots are advised to adopt the same precaution.* There had been more—details of how death occurred, how and why simple organ transplants inevitably failed, the mechanisms by which the disease altered the lung tissue, slowly dissolving it into a thick white mucus, so that the patient drowned in body fluids even as the lungs themselves stopped working—but she did her best to push that aside. "Do you want me to come with you?" she said cautiously, and did her best to keep her voice normal.

Ransome looked for a moment as though he would refuse,

but then made a face. "Yes," he said, and then, with an effort, "Thank you."

"No problem," Lioe said, and seated herself on the bench beside him. But it was a problem, it was a hell of a problem, and she found herself filled with an irrational fury. *How could he be sick—how dare he?—just when she'd found—* She stopped abruptly, closed off that line of thought. *Found what? You barely know him, except through the Game. Just because he showed you the imaging system he uses doesn't mean that he'd want to teach you—or that you could learn, or even that you want to.*

The sound of rotors overhead was a welcome relief, and she squinted up into the hazy clouds. The helicab dropped easily toward the pad, balancing the weight of the machine against the lift of the rotors and the gas in the envelope. The two pods were fully inflated, one to each side of the passenger compartment, so that the cab looked rather like a rodent, both cheeks filled with scavenged food. The unseen pilot brought it down carefully, setting it precisely in the center of the bright-blue guidelines, and the passenger door opened. Lioe stood, uncertain whether to offer her hand, and Ransome pushed himself to his feet. He climbed into the cab, and Lioe followed him, pulling the door closed behind them.

"You're going to Warehouse?" the pilot said, and Ransome nodded.

"That's right," Lioe said aloud, and wasn't sure she'd done the right thing until she saw Ransome's fleeting smile.

The helicab rose slowly, rotors whining, and the whole machine shivered suddenly in a gust of wind. The pilot corrected it instantly, adjusting power and lift, glanced apologetically over his shoulder.

"Sorry, people. It's going to be a rough ride."

" 'S all right," Ransome murmured.

"The storm?" Lioe asked, as much to distract the pilot as anything, and was not surprised when he nodded. The braided wires that connected him to the cab bobbed against his neck.

"Yeah. The dispatcher's saying we'll probably have to shut down this afternoon."

Lioe leaned back in her seat. Through the transparent door

panel she could see the Dock Road District spread out beneath her, buildings clustered around tiny spots of green that were the open plazas, and crowding shoulder to shoulder along the banks of the myriad canals. ''I think this is the first time I've seen this in daylight,'' she said, in some surprise, and saw Ransome smile again.

As they rose above the cliff edge, approaching Newfields and the Warehouse helipad, the wind caught them, jolting the cab sideways before the pilot caught it. Lioe braced herself against the safety webbing, watching the muscles of the pilot's arms tense and relax as his hands moved inside the sheaths of the on-line controls. His lips were moving, too, and she guessed he was talking to his dispatcher, warning other pilots about the winds. He took the approach to Warehouse very carefully, and Lioe was grateful for it: the helicab shuddered and bounced, but finally dropped the last meter or so onto the hard paving. The credit reader unfolded from the cab wall, beeping for payment.

Ransome reached for his card, but Lioe got there first. ''Pay me back,'' she said, and ran her own card through the slot. She managed not to wince at the total—about twice what she had expected—and hit the key that confirmed the payment. The pilot opened the passenger door, and they climbed out onto the pad. The helicab started to lift as they crossed the low barrier, and Lioe flinched as grit stung her face and bare arms. Ransome turned away from it, one hand cupped over his mouth and nose, did not move until the cab had lifted out of range.

''Do you want a velocab?'' Lioe asked, tentatively, more to make sure he was all right than to get an answer to her question, and was relieved when he shook his head.

''No. It's not far to the loft.'' He sounded a little better, and Lioe let herself relax.

The streets were all but empty of pedestrians here, and only a few heavy carriers rumbled past, stirring the drifted dirt and sand. A fickle wind was blowing, a warm wind that carried an occasional hint of a chill at its heart. Lioe shivered at its touch, glanced again to the sky, but saw only the same hazy clouds, the sun a hot white disk behind them. It felt like the afternoon winds on Callixte, the summer wind that brought the big storms down onto the plains, and she found herself walking warily, as though too quick a movement would trigger lurking thunder. Ransome glanced curiously at her, then looked away.

They turned the last corner onto a street shadowed by the buildings to either side, and Ransome led her past a tangle of denki-bikes, their security fields humming at an annoying pitch, to the access stair that ran along the side of the building.

"Isn't there a lift?" Lioe asked involuntarily, but Ransome didn't seem offended.

"There is, but it's in use." He nodded to the main doorway, where a red flag drooped, moving only sluggishly in the breeze.

"Oh." Lioe followed him up the stairway, past the Carnival debris, broken bottles, a cluster of stained and ragged ribbons at the base of the stairs, another bottle on the landing; the crumpled papers and stained foils from a packet of Oblivion lay on the landing outside Ransome's door. He stepped over them without looking, and Lioe did her best to follow his example.

The loft was pretty much as it had been when she'd left it, nothing changed except the pile of clothes on the floor outside the bedroom door. Her hat was sitting on the folded bed. *Was it only yesterday that I left it?* she thought, said aloud, "Can I get you anything?"

Ransome was already heading for the tiny bedroom, said over his shoulder, "Coffee?"

"Right." Lioe went into the kitchen. She filled the machine and set it running, came back out into the main room just as Ransome emerged from the bedroom. His eyes looked slightly unfocused, and there were two spots of red on his cheeks that spread as she watched, as though he were blushing deeply.

"I appreciate your coming back with me," Ransome said. His voice already sounded better, less choked. "I wasn't sure I'd be able to talk the pilot out of taking me to a clinic."

"Should you have gone to a clinic?" Lioe asked. "Should you go to a clinic?"

Ransome grinned. "No, I told you, I had what I needed here. They couldn't've given me anything different."

Lioe nodded, watching him. "Are you all right?" she said slowly, and Ransome looked away.

"For the moment." He sighed, turned back to face her. "As you probably already figured out, I have white-sickness —it's under treatment, so you don't need to worry—but I've had it for a while, and the system's slipping out of equilibrium."

Which translates as, you're starting to die. Lioe said, "I'm sorry," and cringed at the inadequacy of the words.

Ransome went on as if he hadn't heard, his tone so matter-of-fact that she winced at the unvoiced pain. "I have five to seven years, or so they tell me, so it's not an emergency."

Except that you can't be much more than forty, and you ought to live another forty years. Lioe said again, "I'm sorry."

"So am I." There was a little pause, and then Ransome achieved a kind of smile. "Do you want some coffee?"

"Sure, thanks," Lioe said, glad of the change of subject, and Ransome disappeared into the kitchen. He returned a moment later with two steaming mugs. Lioe took hers with a murmur of thanks, sipped cautiously at the bitter liquid.

"There's something I've been wanting to ask you," Ransome said, and his voice was carefully casual, so that Lioe glanced back at him warily. "Especially since last night's session."

"Oh?" Lioe paused, and then shrugged. "Go ahead, I guess."

"What the hell were your parents thinking of, to let you become a pilot?"

Lioe blinked, completely taken aback by the question. It was not at all what she'd been expecting—*though what I was expecting I don't know*—and she didn't quite know how to answer. She opened her mouth, stopped, closed it again. "I was good at it," she said at last, and heard the annoyance in her voice.

Ransome spread his hands, almost spilling his coffee. "I didn't mean to pry. It's just that you've got an artistic sense, a talent for the Game, and for imaging. I'm surprised you didn't get a chance to pursue it—I'm surprised nobody picked up on it.''

"No, it's all right," Lioe said. *And after what you've told me, I'm not sure I have the right not to answer.* She ordered her thoughts with an effort. "I was raised by Foster Services, on Callixte. They steered me toward the union certificate program, and when I won one of the scholarships—well, you know how hard they are to get. I wanted to take it, at least to prove I was as smart as the docents had always said.''

Ransome nodded. "Your parents died?"

Lioe shrugged. "I don't know. I don't remember much about it—I pretty much don't remember anything before the Service crèche—but what they told me was, a couple of people found me in an abandoned house near the port district, Mont'eranza, it's called. I was undernourished, but otherwise unhurt, and about six years old, as best the medical people could tell. So I ended up with Foster Services.''

"And the Game," Ransome said. "Your scenario's good, near brilliant, in fact.''

"Thanks." Lioe grinned. "I'd still like to take this situation a little further, though, pull it all together. Can you imagine what that would do to the Game?"

Ransome nodded, his tone quite serious. "It would be enormous fun while it lasted, though, wouldn't it?"

"I'm not eager to be lynched afterwards," Lioe said. "Besides, I'd have to set it up now, change this scenario a little.''

"Do it," Ransome said. Lioe looked at him, startled, and he said again, "Do it. And let me play Avellar."

"Not Harmsway?"

Ransome shook his head. "Avellar."

God, Lioe thought, *that would be a brilliant bit of casting, and if anybody could pull it off, give me the setup I need for Avellar's Rebellion—* She smiled, realizing that she had already given the scenario a title. "When I run it again," she said, slowly, "you can have Avellar, if you want him. But I'm not sure about making the changes."

"If you won't," Ransome said, "I will."

She lifted an eyebrow at him, not sure she believed him, and his smile widened. "I'll do it, you know," he said.

"I believe you," Lioe answered.

"You needn't sound quite so worried," Ransome said. He paused, looked back toward the windows. The clouds had thickened a little since they had come in, turning the sky the color of milk, and the shadows had vanished. Lioe moved to join him, staring down into the Junction Pool. It was even more crowded than it had been, seemingly hundreds of barges tied up two deep at the piers, and smaller craft darted like beetles among them. She wondered briefly if Roscha were somewhere among them.

"There was something else I wanted to ask you," Ransome said. "How did you happen to pick Harmsway for the scenario? Did Cella Minter—or anyone—mention him to you?"

Lioe blinked again, startled, and shook her head. "No. I'd worked up the scenario before I got here. We didn't expect to spend any time on planet; we lost calibration in one of the sail projectors en route from Demeter, and had to lay over to reset it. I'd kind of forgotten that they were local Types when I showed the scenario." Ransome nodded, still looking out the window, and Lioe frowned. *My turn to ask questions, I think.* "Why? Who's—Cella, did you say?"

"Cella Minter." Ransome paused. "You may have seen her at Chauvelin's party the other night, a tiny woman, absolutely a perfect beauty. She's Damian Chrestil's mistress, when he isn't chasing something else."

Lioe paused, trying to remember, could vaguely recall a tiny woman with copper-colored braids woven into sleek, jet-black hair. She had been startlingly beautiful, seen from across the room, and more than a little intimidating. "So who's Damian Chrestil? Any connection to C/B Cie.?"

There was a little silence, and Ransome looked at her. "He *is* C/B Cie. Decidamio Chrestil-Brisch is his full name, he's head of C/B Cie. Did you, your ship, bring in a cargo for him?"

"It was a C/B Cie. cargo, yes," Lioe said. "Why?"

"Because Damian Chrestil has been trying to keep me out of the port nets for two days now," Ransome said, anger and glee mixed in equal measures in his voice. "And maybe, just maybe, you can help me figure out why."

"I don't quite see the connection," Lioe began, and Ransome cut in.

"What were you carrying?"

"I don't want to be overly delicate about this," Lioe said, "but why do you want to know? We're supposed to keep our mouths shut about what we carry. General union rules."

Ransome nodded. "Sorry." He took a deep breath, gestured, spilling coffee, and set the mug aside, scowling. "Look, it's like this. Chauvelin's my patron. We've known each other for years—"

"I remember," Lioe said. She could still see the little room in Chauvelin's monumental residence, light gleaming off the story egg, the first one she'd seen. *Chauvelin is your patron, and Chauvelin's rival the Visiting Speaker hates you, quite personally.*

"I've done various kinds of work for him," Ransome went on, and there was a distinct note of pride in his voice. "I'm good on the nets, very good, and I occasionally do some research for him."

"The charge is usually common netwalking," Lioe murmured, and remembered, too late, that Ransome had been in jail. To her surprise, he laughed.

"True. Anyway, I've been—walking the nets for him lately, because the damn Visiting Speaker got it into his head that Damian Chrestil was up to something in the Game. When I checked it out, sure, he wanted me back in the Game, back involved, but there wasn't anything really happening. It was all just a blind. So I started wondering what Damian Chrestil really wanted, and I haven't been able to get into the port nets at all. So you see why I'd really like to know what you were carrying."

Lioe shrugged. "Red-carpet, according to the manifest. En route to a distillery here. We had a couple of bungee-gars on board."

"Is that normal?"

"Depends," Lioe said. "I wouldn't think red-carpet was quite that valuable, but it's close enough, I guess."

"Who was the shipper?"

Lioe frowned, pulling names from her mental files. "A company called TMN, I think. They weren't much."

"I bet it's smuggling," Ransome muttered, as much to himself as to her. "There's no other reason to keep me out of the port nets, except that he hasn't rechristened the cargo yet. Damn it, if I could just get in!"

Lioe eyed him warily. It seemed overelaborate to her, a lot more complicated than simple smuggling would need to be—*and I've seen enough smuggling combines at work to know that simple's the way to go.* "So why should the Visiting Speaker be worried about it?" she asked aloud.

"I wish I knew," Ransome answered. He stopped suddenly, eyes wild. "But I do know, I just had it backward. Ji-Imbaoa doesn't want to know what Damian Chrestil's up to, he already knows that because he's involved in it. What he wants is me out of the way, me and Chauvelin, so that he can gain favor with whatever it is they're smuggling."

"That sounds a little complicated," Lioe said when it became clear that some answer was expected of her.

"But that's it," Ransome said. "I'm sure of it. Ji-Imbaoa's a je Tsinra-an, and they need to consolidate their position with the All-Father. Chauvelin's a tzu Tsinra-an, he'd stop him on principle, regardless of what the cargo is. And Damian Chrestil's an ambitious little bastard; he's got lots of friends in the Republic, but not many in Hsaioi-An. But if the je Tsinra-an owed him a favor, that would give him some substance over the border, and that kind of connection there translates to power here, on Burning Bright. It makes good sense."

"If you say so," Lioe said, and didn't bother to hide her own uncertainty.

"Trust me," Ransome said. "Look, this has to be what's going on—Christ, won't Chauvelin be pleased, it's the perfect excuse to get rid of ji-Imbaoa—but I have to talk to some people."

"Netwalking?"

Ransome shook his head. "I've tried that already. But there are some people up at the port who still owe me favors, and I think it's time I called them in."

"How are you feeling?" Lioe asked, pointedly. Ransome looked blank for a moment, then laughed.

"Fine. Look, I need to do this now, before it's too late, but I wanted to know, were you serious about this scenario?"

Lioe hesitated for an instant—it would mean the end of the Game as she knew it—but then nodded firmly. "I'd like to work it out."

"Do you want to use my systems?" Ransome asked. "It's a little more private than Shadows would be, and I've got most of the library disks you'd need. We could talk about it when I got back, you could show me what you need to have happen to set up the new scenario."

Lioe thought for a moment. It would be easier, working here—more privacy, fewer interruptions from players and would-be session leaders who had questions about Ixion's Wheel—but she'd already made plans for the day. "I'm supposed to meet Roscha. We're going to see a puppet show in Betani Square."

"So work here anyway; if I'm not back by the time you have to leave, come back when you've finished. I can give you a key, just in case I'm not back by then—though God knows I should be—but if I'm not, let yourself in and make free with the systems." Ransome grinned. "You should know where things are by now."

"All right," Lioe said. "We'll do this."

"Great." Ransome rummaged in a drawer without result, then stood scanning his shelves before he came up with a flat black rectangle about the size of a dice box. He handed it to her, and Lioe took it cautiously, feeling for the almost invisible indentations.

"Upper left is for the stairs," Ransome said, "upper right is the main entrance, center is the loft door, lower right calls the lift—when it's free."

Lioe nodded.

"Then I'm off," Ransome said. "I probably won't be back before you have to leave, but I'll see you after the show, all right?"

"I'll be here," Lioe said, and shook her head slowly as the main door slapped shut behind him. *How do I get into these situations?* she wondered, then grinned. Maybe Burning Bright was the home of the Game precisely because its own politics were as baroque as those of the imaginary Imperium. *Let's see if I can come up with something as complex for Avellar.* She found the room remote, and touched its gleaming surface, darkening the windows and bringing up the display space. She pulled on the wire-bound gloves and settled herself in the massive chair, wriggling a little as the cushions shifted beneath her, accommodating her weight. She reached into control space, touching virtual icons, and found a copy of her scenario waiting in storage. She defined a space, called it into those new confines, and sat for a moment, staring at the tree of symbols. Then she touched the first icon, and began to work.

DAY 2

Damian Chrestil stood at the back of the plotting shed at the end of Isard's Wharf, watching the display table. A model of Burning Bright's oceans, spread to scale on a virtual globe, floated above the tabletop; the shapes that represented C/B Cie.'s various ships ghosted through the mirrorlike surface, the codes that represented their cargoes and destinations flickering to life at a gesture from some one of the attendants. The coiled shapes of the blossoming storms, a grand procession of them sweeping up the trade winds from the shallows below the equator, marched over the surface, interdicting great sweeps of sea. Most of the company's ships were already in port, or within a day's journey, but a few were still well out to sea, and the wharfingers studied them carefully, murmuring to each other. They and their assistants each carried a smaller plotting tablet and a delicate, gold-tipped wand. As they gestured at the model, circling it like acolytes to adjust symbols and times and weather forecasts in search of the most economical arrangement, they reminded Damian of some mysterious and primitive cult. Behind him, the windows rattled in the rising wind, and one of the assistants glanced nervously toward the cloud-white sky. On the model, a tight spiral of cloud was poised south and east of the entrance to the Inland Water.

"Have they made any guesses as to when the storm barriers will go up?" Damian asked, and the senior wharfinger, Rosaurin, shook her head.

"They're hedging."

"So what else is new?" Damian murmured. He glared at

the model as though it could provide answers on its own, then shook his head. "I think we're cutting it too close with the short-haul boats. Have them ride it out south of the storm track." He gestured with his own control wand, highlighted a grid mark on the model.

Rosaurin nodded slowly. "I'd rather get them home, but you're right, we can't risk it. Not when they can't give me an estimate of when they'll raise the barriers."

Damian nodded back. The triple line of barriers lay at the bottom of the channel, were raised as the storm approached. They would hold back the worst of the storm surge, and protect the city, but once they were in place, no ships could enter the channel. They had all agreed, himself, the wharfingers, and the short-haul captains, that it was worth taking one more trip to the seining grounds before Storm set in. Now the captains, at least, would have to live with the consequences. Still, they were experienced people, with good crews, and the boats were solid, well equipped. *They should be all right,* he thought, and turned his mind away.

"Na Damian?"

He turned, to find one of the younger dockers in the doorway, a thin young man with close-cut blond hair that almost disappeared against his scalp. "Well?"

"You wanted to be told," the docker said warily. "Roscha's called in. She'll be in the channel in about ten minutes."

"Right," Damian said, and couldn't keep the satisfaction from his voice. "Can you take care of the rest of this, Rosaurin?"

The wharfinger nodded. "I'll put together a final plot for your approval."

"Do that," Damian said, and left the shed.

Because of the approaching storm, there were perhaps twice as many ships tied up to the mooring points as usual, and the dock was littered with lines and spare gear. Damian stepped carefully through the clutter, and let himself into the outer office. The secretary pillar was, for once, clear of messages. He smiled rather bitterly—*this once, I would have liked to have something waiting, preferably from ji-Imbaoa* —and went on into the inner room, seated himself behind his desk. The workscreen lit obediently, sensing his presence, but he ignored the flickering prompts, debating whether or not he should call the Visiting Speaker himself. *Not just now,* he thought, and touched keys to call up his security files. The check files were all in place—*or not quite all.* He frowned, studying the origination codes that the security programs had preserved for him: *Ransome, almost certainly, and that means I'll have to do something about him. Or about ji-Imbaoa.* He put that thought aside with regret—he'd gone too far to back out now—and the secretary chimed discreetly.

"Na Damian, Roscha is here."

Damian touched the shadowscreen to hide the security programs. "Send her in."

Roscha appeared in the doorway almost at once, her perfect figure obscured by a loose jacket knotted at her waist. "You wanted to see me, Na Damian?"

"Yes." Damian paused for an instant, assessing how best to approach the question. "I hear you've been sleeping with this new notable, Lioe."

Roscha blinked—whatever else she had on her conscience, she hadn't expected this—and said, cautiously, "We've seen each other a couple of times, and I played in a couple of her sessions. I only met her three days ago."

"You played a session with her last night," Damian went on.

Roscha nodded.

"The C-and-I rep was part of that Game, too, am I right?"

"Yes," Roscha said again, and waited.

"I gather they knew each other, Lioe and Desjourdy?"

"Yes." Roscha drew the word out to two syllables, frowning now. "Look, Na Damian—"

"Are they just old friends, fellow Gamers, what?" Damian interrupted her. "Or has Lioe worked for her?"

"Jesus." For the first time, Roscha looked worried. "I don't think so, Na Damian. I was there when she—when Quinn invited Na Desjourdy to play this session. Quinn said she was short a player, and all they talked about was the Game. Desjourdy's on the Game nets a lot, she's a rated arbiter."

"And she works for Customs-and-Intelligence," Damian said, but more gently. He paused, studied her from under his lashes. "I'm a little worried, Roscha. This Lioe's been hanging around with Ransome, too, and Ransome's no friend of mine." He saw from the quick, involuntary grimace that Roscha had noticed that attraction, too, and was less than comfortable with it. "Lioe and Desjourdy, Lioe and Ransome—it just doesn't add up well."

"I guess not," Roscha said, slowly.

Damian hid his sudden pleasure. *It's working, she's starting to think just the way I want her to, to think that maybe Lioe is a C-and-I agent.* "So what I'm asking is, did you notice anything after the session? Any conversations, anything that might mean she was passing information to Desjourdy?"

Roscha shook her head. "No. They just talked about the session afterwards, and then—then Lioe came back to the boat with me. I dropped her off this morning when I got your message." She stopped suddenly. "Boss, I ran into Tamia Nikolind on the docks coming in. She said she saw Lioe going off with Ransome this morning, taking a helicab out of Underface."

"Damn." Damian scowled, realizing he'd spoken aloud. That was the last unfortunate coincidence—in fact, it was too perfect to be a coincidence. One way or another, the two of them, Lioe and Ransome, had too many pieces of the puzzle to be allowed to go to either Chauvelin or Desjourdy. *In fact, that's probably the only thing I've got going for me right now: they'll have to decide which one to alert first.* He touched the shadowscreen to distract himself, making meaningless patterns on its surface. *I'll have to get them out of circulation, one way or another, and it's too late for niceties. Lioe's not important enough; security can find me plenty of "friends" who can dump her in a canal, and no one will think twice about it, but Ransome . . . Ransome's another matter. But I can deal with that later.* "Were you planning to see Lioe again?" he asked.

"Yes. We were going to the puppet shows, over on Roche'Ambroise. I was planning to meet her there."

Damian took a deep breath, put on his most sincere face.

"I need you to do something for me," he said. "I need—I want you to break your date. I know I've no right to ask you to do it, but I need to keep an eye on her. And I don't want to get you into any trouble." That was true enough, even if the trouble was bigger than Roscha would think. "But I want some people of mine to watch her, and the puppet show is a good place for them to find her. Can you—will you do this?"

"Ransome and Desjourdy," Roscha said. She smiled, without humor. "Hells, I told her I might not be able to make it. All right, Na Damian. I told her we'd meet by the fountain, there in Betani Square. She's been wearing one of Gelsomina's lace masks. I thought you should know."

"Thanks, Roscha," Damian said. *Thank you more than I ever intend to tell you.* Instinct kept him from offering to pay her fines after all. "I want you to stay here, at the docks—there's enough work, God knows—but I want you visible the rest of the day. I don't want you out of call until"—he paused, calculating—"until after midnight."

Roscha frowned, hesitating over her next question. "You're not—she won't be hurt?"

Damian managed a tolerant smile. "This isn't the Game, Roscha. No, I just don't want you to be vulnerable if she—or Desjourdy, really—gets pissy about my keeping an eye on her. Because my security is going to be pretty obtrusive this time. You don't need any extra hassle."

"Thanks, Na Damian," Roscha said, low-voiced, and Damian nodded.

"Get on back out there, and try to stay visible for the next eight or nine hours."

Roscha nodded, visibly reassured, and backed out of the little office. Left to himself, Damian stared for few moments longer at the empty screens glowing in the desktop, then touched keys to summon his security files. *Lioe and Ransome* . . . On balance, it wasn't very likely that Lioe was actually an agent for Republican Customs-and-Intelligence; she was too active a Gamer, and too busy a pilot, too, according to the records he'd obtained from the Pilots' Union, to be employed by C-and-I as well. But she did know Desjourdy rather well, by everyone's reckoning, and she had gone home this morning with Ransome. It wasn't a risk he could afford to take.

He had more options in dealing with her than with Ransome. The imagist would have to be handled with care, because he himself couldn't afford to antagonize Chauvelin—*not yet, anyway, but if ji-Imbaoa does even half of what he's promised . . .* He made himself concentrate on the immediate problem. Ransome would have to be taken out of circulation temporarily, but couldn't be killed, or even too badly damaged: that meant kidnapping, and then the question of where to keep him. Damian ran his fingers over the shadowscreen, slaving it temporarily to the household systems in Five Points. The palazze was closing down for the storm, topping up the batteries, workmen ordered to bring the shutters in over the massive windows; the summer house, out in the Barrier Hills behind the Five Points, was shut down completely, all systems on standby, doors and windows sealed against the storm. Damian considered it for a moment, then nodded. The house was reasonably well sheltered, tucked into the side of a hill well above the water, and clear of the stand of trees that topped the ridge. It had stood through worse storms: *an ideal place to keep Ransome,* he thought. *And Lioe, too, I suppose. If nothing else, once the storm starts, they'll be stuck there until it passes.* He nodded to himself, and touched the shadowscreen, detaching himself from the house systems and recalling his security programs. He culled a picture of Ransome—a publicity photo, a recent one, that showed all the lines in the imagist's thin face—from the main systems, and then used his C/B Cie. ID numbers to gain access to the union files. It was a little galling to think that Ransome could probably get the same information without codes, either netwalking or through one of his friends, but at least he could get Lioe's photo. He dumped both of the images into a minidisk, the kind that would fit either a pocket system or an implanted reader, and after a moment's thought added the security codes that would unlock the summer house. He tucked them into his pocket, and went looking for Almarin Ivie.

He found the security chief in his office, a big man who dwarfed his desk and the constantly changing displays on

the walls behind him. The tiny space was dark, lit mainly by
the blue-toned flicker of the displays, but Ivie touched controls as the door opened, focusing a faint halo of warmer
light on the space before the door.

"Na Damian," he said, and rose hastily to his feet.
"What's up?"

Damian waved for him to be seated again, found the
guest's chair, and spun it into position opposite the desk. "I
need you to do something for me."

"Whatever," Ivie said, with a sincerity that Damian always found slightly unsettling. He killed that uncertainty—
this was the time to appreciate his subordinates' fervor—put
the thought aside and slid the minidisk across the desk. Ivie
caught it easily, the button of plastic disappearing in his
thick fingers, and said, "For me?"

Damian nodded, and waited while Ivie slipped the disk
into the reader tucked at the base of his left wrist spur. "I
need these people taken out of circulation for a while," he
said. "The woman—her name's Lioe, Quinn Lioe—I don't
really care how you do it as long as we're not connected with
it in any way. Ransome has to be handled with care: I don't
want him killed, or damaged too badly, but I want him out of
circulation for at least the next half-week. The summer
house is empty, and I've given you the system codes. Can
you do it?"

Ivie looked almost offended for an instant, but the expression passed across his flat face almost as fast as it had appeared. His heavy hands moved over a shadowscreen with
surprising delicacy, and he said, "It looks as though Ransome is up in Newfields now, talking to people. I don't find
the woman. At least not at first look." His fingers danced
over another set of controls, and he went on, "I've got a
trace going through the Game nets—she's the Gamer,
right?"

Does everyone know her reputation? Damian wondered,
irritably. "That's right."

"I've got some people in Newfields now, and I'll put
them on him," Ivie went on, fingers still working. "I'll send
them to the summer house once they've secured him." He

stopped then, looked impassively at Damian. "I'd like a little more guidance with Lioe, Na Damian."

Damian sighed. He had been hoping to avoid this decision, had hoped, even knowing better, that Ivie would make it for him. "If you can secure her without killing her, I'd prefer it. Murder's messy, even at Carnival. But if you can't get her to come quietly, I'd rather have her dead."

Ivie nodded calmly. "All right."

"There's one other thing that may help you," Damian said. "One of my people was supposed to meet Lioe at the puppet show in Betani Square, over on Roche'Ambroise. They were to meet at the fountain, half an hour before the show."

Ivie nodded again. "Good. That is a help. If we don't get her before that, we'll get her there."

"I leave it in your capable hands," Damian Chrestil said.

DAY 2

Chauvelin waited in the transmission room, leaning over the technician's shoulder to study the hissing screens. The technician, jericho-human, small and square-built, looked back at him reproachfully.

"I'm doing the best I can, sia."

Chauvelin nodded, gestured an apology. "I'll leave you to it, then." He stepped backward, but couldn't bring himself to leave the little room, stood instead still staring at the static that coursed across the screens. It was awkward enough at the best of times, contacting the Remembrancer-Duke's household on maiHu'an, given the time corrections between the two planets; during Storm, when the first link of the long connection, the transmission between the planet and the relay satellite, was notoriously unreliable, it was all but impossible. *But I really don't have much choice. Whatever ji-Imbaoa is up to, it has roots in Hsaioi-An.*

"Got it," the technician said, and hastily corrected himself. "Sia, I've established the link. The Speaker Haas will be on-line directly."

"How stable is the connection?" Chauvelin asked.

The technician shrugged. "About what you'd expect this time of year, sia. But I can patch it through to the reception room. That won't make any difference."

Chauvelin nodded. "Do that, then. And thank you."

The technician ducked his head in acknowledgment, not moving from his position in front of the multiple control boards. Chauvelin nodded back, and went on past him into the reception room. There had not been time to make the formal preparations, but then, this was not a formal call. Nonetheless, he laid the thin cushions, black-on-black embroidery, the geometric patterns dictated by a thousand years of tradition, in front of the low table, and poured two cups of the harsh snow-wine. The warning chime sounded as he set the cups on the table, and he knelt on the cushions, settling himself so that he faced the massive screen. The grey static faded as the last of the check characters crossed its surface, and Eriki Haas tzu Tsinra-an looked out at him. She knelt on identical cushions in front of an identical table; only the cups that held the wine were different, marked with the *n-jao* characters of her name. The fan that marked her rank was folded in her hand, and Chauvelin wished for a brief instant that he had changed into hsai dress for this meeting. But it was too late for those regrets, and he bowed his head politely.

"Tal je-Chauvelin," Haas said, acknowledging his presence, and Chauvelin looked up.

"Sia Speaker. It's good of you to speak with me on such short notice."

Haas gestured quickly, the fluttering of the fingers that meant a hsaii wished to be informal. "I accept that things have gotten complicated. Let's dispense with ceremony."

Chauvelin allowed himself a soundless sigh of relief, and went on in tradetalk. "Complicated is a good word. I need your help, sia—I need information."

"If I can get it, of course," Haas said. "What can I do?"

"I want to know what kind of connections there are between ji-Imbaoa and Damian Chrestil—Decidamio Chrestil-Brisch, head of the import/export company C/B Cie.," Chauvelin said bluntly. "Or any connections between the je Tsinra-an and C/B Cie., particularly if any of C/B Cie.'s clients are also *houta* dependents of the je Tsinra-an."

Haas paused, one hand busy with the notepad fastened to her belt, out of sight beneath the loose, semiformal coat. "This could be difficult to do discreetly, Tal. What does it matter?"

"I don't care about discretion," Chauvelin began, and bit back the rest of his words. He said, more carefully, "There isn't time for discretion. I have reason to think that the Visiting Speaker and Damian Chrestil are working together here on Burning Bright, not as enemies, and I think that their real connection is something in Hsaioi-An. The last thing my lord would want is to see Damian Chrestil elected governor of Burning Bright.''

"Do you think that's likely?'' Haas asked, but her hand was busy again, transferring notes to the household computers.

"I wouldn't bother you if I didn't,'' Chauvelin said, and Haas waved her free hand in apology.

"I'm sorry, Tal. It's just—the je Tsinra-an have been making real inroads at court in the last week, and my lord is eager not to antagonize them.''

"My lord's existence annoys them,'' Chauvelin said dryly. "I don't think he would care to do much about it.''

Haas grinned in spite of herself. "I know.'' She looked down at the tabletop, and Chauvelin guessed that there was a screen concealed in its surface. "I'll see what I can find out for you. C/B Cie. does a lot of business on the jericho-human worlds, and on Jericho itself, for that matter.''

"Which worlds?'' Chauvelin asked.

"I know,'' Haas said, with a touch of impatience, "over half of them are client-bound to the je Tsinra-an. I'll find out.'' She looked down again, ran her hand over a control bar hidden in the table's carved edge. "I'm glad you called me, Tal. This could be something important.''

Certainly it's important to me, Chauvelin thought. He said, "I'd appreciate an answer as soon as possible.''

"I'll do what I can,'' Haas answered. "Between your weather and my ignorant staff—well, I'll do my best.''

No one of lesser rank than yours is allowed to blame her staff for failures. Chauvelin bowed again, more deeply. "Thank you for your help, Sia Speaker.''

"Thanks for the information, Tal,'' Haas answered, and signaled for her system to break contact.

Chauvelin touched his own remote to close down his end of the transmission, leaned back on his heels to watch the characters cascade across the screen. If there was a connection between the je Tsinra-an and the Chrestil-Brisch—more specifically, between ji-Imbaoa and Damian Chrestil—and if he could prove it, then it should be possible to parry ji-Imbaoa's threats. And if the connection went deep enough, it might be sufficient to discredit the entire je Tsinra-an. That was probably too much to hope for, he knew, and he sighed as he pushed himself up off the low cushions. *A nice thought, but not to be counted on.*

A chime sounded gently from the speaker set into the wall beside the door, the red pinlight flicking on as well, and Chauvelin touched the remote again to establish the connection. "Yes?"

"I beg your pardon, sia," je-Sou'tsian said, "but there's something that needs your urgent attention."

Chauvelin lifted his eyebrows at the blank space, but answered the tone as much as the words. "I'll be in the breakfast room in three minutes."

"Thank you, sia," je-Sou'tsian answered, and the pinlight faded. Chauvelin sighed—*I wonder what new disaster I'll have to deal with*—and let himself out of the reception room.

Je-Sou'tsian was ahead of him in the breakfast room, the curtains half-drawn across the long windows. Beyond them, beyond her shoulder, Chauvelin could see the distant wall of cloud, a little higher on the horizon now, dark against the milk-white sky. The garden looked subdued in the dimmed light, only the stone faces in the paths still reflecting the minimal sunlight.

"Your pardon, sia," je-Sou'tsian said again, and Chauvelin dragged his eyes away from the approaching storm.

"It's all right," he said. "What's happened?"

"The Visiting Speaker has not come home today." There was a tension in the set of je-Sou'tsian's hands and arms that made Chauvelin frown even more deeply.

"It's later than he usually stays away, certainly, but is it important?"

"Sia, I don't think his household knows for certain where he's gone. At least none of the ones left here. And they are worried, if only because they don't know what's happening."

Have I left things too late? Chauvelin suppressed the stabbing fear, said, "So what happened, do you know?"

Je-Sou'tsian made a quick gesture, one-handed, the equivalent of a shrug. "As best I can tell—and I'm reading between the lines for much of this, sia—the Visiting Speaker left the house last night just after dark, saying he wanted to experience the Carnival. His household expected him back sometime this morning, but he hasn't arrived, and they haven't had word from him. By midday, his chief of household was worried enough to ask me if I had heard anything."

"Who does he have with him?" Chauvelin asked.

"That's what worries me," je-Sou'tsian answered. "Only two people, ji-Mao'ana and that jericho-human, Magill."

The Speaker's secretary and his head-of-security. Chauvelin sighed. "And that's all you know?" It was unfair, he knew, and je-Sou'tsian gave him a brief, reproachful glance.

"Sia, I've only just found this out. The chief of household only just spoke to me. And naturally I was reluctant to pursue things any further without knowing what you wanted me to do."

Chauvelin gestured an apology. "I'm sorry, Iameis, you were right." He paused for a moment, fingers tapping nervously against his thigh. "Still, it's Carnival. Things happen during Carnival. I think you should make discreet inquiries, Iameis, just to make sure nothing's happened to him. Check his usual haunts, and the Lockwardens. No need to inquire at the clinics and hospitals yet, they'd've notified me if a stray hsaia was brought in."

"The Lockwardens?" je-Sou'tsian said.

Chauvelin nodded. "Ask—with discretion, mind you—if there have been any complaints or queries. I just want them to be aware that we are looking for him." *And that way, if I've miscalculated, if he's not working with Damian Chrestil, I'll have been seen to do my duty in protecting him.*

"Very well, sia, I'll get on it at once." Je-Sou'tsian bowed again, and backed toward the door.

"Thank you, Iameis," Chauvelin said. "You've done

well." There was no formal way to respond, but he saw from
the sudden movement of her hands, quickly suppressed, that
she had heard, and was pleased.

Chauvelin made his way back through the corridors and
coiling stairs to his office at the top of the house. The light
that streamed in through the curved windows was as milky
as the clouds, heavy with the promise of the coming storm.
He ignored it, locking the door behind him, touched the shadowscreen to bring up his communications system even
before he'd seated himself at the desk, resolutely turning his
back on the clouds to the south. A screen lit beneath the
desktop; he touched the shadowscreen again, calling the
codes that would connect him with Ransome's loft, and
waited for the screen to clear. If anyone could track ji-Imbaoa, it would be Ransome.

The screen stayed blank, the call codes scrolling repeat-
edly across the base of the screen. Chauvelin let them cycle,
waiting, long after he was sure Ransome would not answer.
Of all the times for Ransome to be away from his loft . . .
Chauvelin killed that thought, burying his fear with it, and
tied his system into the Game nets. Half a dozen Harmsways
were playing, but none of them was Ransome. Chauvelin
swore again, freed himself from the Game, and touched keys
to set up a new program. The communications system would
access Ransome's loft every half hour—he hesitated, then
changed the numbers, making it every quarter hour—until
someone answered. *And that is all I can do. I've done everything; now I have to wait.* It was not a pleasant thought, and,
after a moment, he flipped part of his system back to the
Game nets. If nothing else, he could distract himself in their
baroque conventions.

DAY 2

Ransome waited in the narrow reception room, lit by the long windows that ran like stripes from floor to ceiling and by the thin blue glow of the secretary system. Beyond the windows he could see the cliff face, and the cold grey-green sea beneath it, the strands of foam bright against its choppy surface; he shivered once, and turned his back on the hypnotic waters. The office was on the north side of the building, away from the approaching storm; as he'd come in, a horde of workers had been drawing shutters across the southern windows. It was not like Arduinidi to make him wait. *It just proves how hot I am—if I weren't, Selasa wouldn't make me wait here like this, while she decides if she can afford to see me. Or,* he realized suddenly, *while she finds out if I've been seen, coming here.* That was not a pleasant thought, and he reached into his pocket to touch the datablock that nestled there. It was not a good habit to get into and he took his hand away, fingers tingling. *Maybe, just maybe I should've quit after I talked to the factors at Bonduri Warehouse, they told me enough to be able to tell Chauvelin what's going on—* He put the thought aside as unprofitable. He was here; it was too late to turn back.

The secretary chirped discreetly on its pedestal, the blue light strengthening slightly. The affected mechanical voice said, ''N'Arduinidi will see you now.''

In the same instant the inner door slid open, a soft chime drawing his attention. Ransome rose to his feet, and stepped through the doorway into Arduinidi's office. It was as if he had stepped from Storm into High Summer, and he stood blinking for a moment, disoriented. Light, the hot sunlight of full summer, poured through the windows, falling from a clear and brassy sky; a faint breeze stirred, bringing with it the smell of the summerweed that choked the cliffs in warm weather and the acrid undertone of the port. Very distantly, he could hear the slow slap of the waves against the cliff face and the screech of metal from the port. It was an illusion, of course—holoimages inside the false frames of the windows, carefully controlled ventilation and a scent mixer, subtle sound effects—but even knowing that, Ransome found himself relaxing in the summer warmth.

"It's very good," he said, and Arduinidi smiled at him from behind her desk. She was a big woman, tall and broad-shouldered, short hair further restrained by a band of metal disks. A single wire fell from it, running down her forehead to the socket at the corner of her left eye; her earrings were in the shape of an owl, her on-line icon.

"Thanks," she answered, but her tone was less than enthusiastic. "You're a very chancy item right now, did you know that?"

Ransome managed a smile, did his best to hide the sudden chill that ran up his spine. "I'd kind of gathered that, yes."

Arduinidi glanced down at her desktop. "You were followed here, and there's talk just coming in about a disturbance at the Bonduri Warehouse—somebody beat up a factor, it looks like. That wasn't you, was it?"

Ransome shook his head. "Not my style." *Not my style at all. It sounds like someone's getting desperate.*

"But I'll bet it had something to do with you," Arduinidi said.

Ransome hesitated, but there was little point in lying to her. Arduinidi was not only one of the better network security consultants on planet, she was also one of the more reliable data fences, and a superb netwalker in her own right. Nothing happened on the nets that she didn't know about. "Something," he said aloud. "More to do with Damian Chrestil."

"I told you before," Arduinidi said. "I don't know anything about it."

Meaning he's put the fear of Retribution into all of you,

Ransome thought. "Selasa," he said, and managed to make his tone faintly teasing. Arduinidi lifted an eyebrow, but said nothing. "I know you," Ransome went on. "You're worse than I am about a blocked access. It wouldn't be like you not to get into the port feeds, especially after someone warned you off. I want that data."

Arduinidi looked at him. "I'm not that stupid," she said. "You may do this for fun, I-Jay, but half my business comes from my reputation. Even if I had the information—if—I wouldn't sell it. And doubly not to you."

"I know what it is," Ransome said, "what it has to be. If I tell you what you found, will you give me a yes or no?"

Arduinidi shook her head. "No dice. How would you know whether to believe me, anyway?"

"Because, as you say, your reputation is your business." Ransome looked at her, weighing his next words. His only choices were money or a threat, and he would never have enough money to make it worth her while. "I'm prepared to make sure that your legitimate clients find out about your second job, Selasa. If it comes to that."

"You're fucking crazy," Arduinidi said.

Ransome shook his head. "I want that data."

"You push it, and I won't deal with you," Arduinidi said flatly. "I'll make damn sure you don't walk my nets again, make sure no one buys from you, make sure no one deals with you at all. Do you really want to risk it?"

Stalemate, Ransome thought, *because she can do it.* He hid his despair, said, "Can you afford to risk word getting out that you're the best data fence on planet?"

Arduinidi sat silent, nothing moving on a face gone suddenly like stone.

"I'm willing to settle for a yes or no," Ransome said again. "That's all I need, Selasa. That's all Chauvelin needs."

"Hah." Arduinidi's mouth twisted, as though she'd tasted something sour. "I should've guessed he'd be behind this." She sighed. "All right. What is it you think you know?"

Ransome took a deep breath, felt congestion drag at the bottom of his lungs. *Not now,* he thought, and knew he should have expected it. He put that fear aside, knowing he could wait a little longer to breathe the Mist, said, "Damian Chrestil is smuggling something—Oblivion, I think—into Hsaioi-An, to receivers on Jericho and Highhopes, and he's doing it for ji-Imbaoa and the rest of the je Tsinra-an, who have the receivers for clients."

Arduinidi paused for a moment, then, reluctantly, nodded. "Yes. So far as the smuggling goes, that is. I don't deal in hsai politics." She gave a short, humorless bark of laughter. "And it's lachesi, not Oblivion."

"What's the difference?" Ransome said.

Arduinidi shook her head. "Lachesi is—mostly—legal, it's just the spite laws that keep the Republic from exporting it to Hsaioi-An. Oblivion is restricted. So Damian Chrestil stays on the good side of general opinion, if not the law." There was a sneaking note of admiration in her voice.

"I see," Ransome said, and heard the same note in his own voice. *And it would work, too: a lot of the Republican merchants have been lobbying for years to dissolve the spite laws, and wouldn't feel too bad seeing them broken.* "Thanks," he said, and heard the congestion tightening his voice. "There's just one more thing—" He pointed to the datanode, eyebrows lifted in question, and was not surprised when Arduinidi shook her head.

"Not from my nodes. I've done a lot more than I like, I-Jay, don't push it."

Ransome nodded, gave her a rueful smile. "It was worth a try."

"I hope you think so tomorrow," Arduinidi said. Ransome looked sharply at her, and she gave him her sweetest smile. "I'm pissed at you, Ransome. Remember that."

"I expect I'll be in no danger of forgetting," Ransome said, and Arduinidi nodded.

"I'd be careful, if I were you."

"Thanks a lot," Ransome said. Behind him, the door slid open; he turned and left the office, aware of her eyes on his back the whole while. He paused for a second in the outer office, glancing wistfully at the secretary pillar, but red lights glowed all around the base of the data drives, warning him from trying to make contact. He made a face, even though he'd expected it, and the outer door swung open, ushering him out of the office.

He made his way back through the hallways toward the main stairs—not the elevator today, not if Damian Chrestil's people were feeling desperate enough to risk attacking a warehouse factor in broad daylight; there was too much chance of being caught in a closed space, with no room left to run. *Which really brings up the next question,* he thought. *What do I do now?* The main thing now was to get the information, his own reconstruction of Damian Chrestil's plan, to Chauvelin; once that was done, Chauvelin could be counted on to deal with Damian Chrestil. It sounded simple enough, and he paused in a corner to chord the last bit of information, Arduinidi's confirmation, into his datablock. The little machine chirped softly, confirming the record, and he smiled wryly. However, contacting Chauvelin could prove difficult.

He took the side stairs down to the second floor, paused on the balcony to look down into the building's open lobby. As he'd feared, a pair of men in docker's clothes were standing by the main entrance; a woman whom he recognized as belonging to C/B Cie. warehouse security was standing beside the main information kiosk, one hand cupped loosely over the controls. He frowned, narrowed his eyes, but couldn't see if she was using a tap. *All the more reason to hurry,* he thought, and turned left, walking along the short end of the building, staying close to the wall where he was less likely to be seen from the lobby floor. There were no public terminals here, and a quick scan of the directories showed no names he knew. That left the general mail system, with its kiosks on every floor at each corner of the building. He lengthened his stride, found the nearest kiosk, luckily unoccupied. It was set into a small alcove, partly screened by a sculpture of panels of sequensa-covered fabric, and he began to hope that he might have time to contact Chauvelin after all.

He glanced over his shoulder, saw no one except a secretary at the far end of the corridor, and quickly fed cash slips into the system. This was no time to use his money cards: it would be like shouting his presence to everyone who might be watching. He had just enough; the system lit and win-

dowed, and he slid the datablock out of his pocket. The jacks
and cords were standard, and he plugged the thin wire into
the mail system's receivers. It wasn't perfect—for one thing,
he had far less control over who would ultimately receive the
information than he would if he were able to use the regular
networks—but it would have to do. He touched the codes
that would connect him with the ambassador's house, and
the system flashed back at him: CONNECTION NOT POSSIBLE,
PLEASE TRY AGAIN.

"Fuck it." Ransome stared for a fraction of a second at
the little screen, hit the codes again. The screen went blank,
and then the same message flickered into view. He'd been
suckered: the woman at the main kiosk wasn't bothering to
tap the mail system; instead, she was interrupting it, blocking any transmission that he tried to make, and she was
bound to be tracing his location at the same time. He stared
at the screen, feeling the seconds slip away. It was too late to
get away, his own mistake had seen to that; the only thing he
could hope for was to dump the information somewhere
where Chauvelin could find it. Maybe his home systems, if
he couldn't reach Chauvelin himself in time. He killed that
sense of panic, forcing himself to think clearly, dredged the
emergency codes out of his memory. He had bartered for
them almost two weeks ago, eons on the nets, but they were
Lockwardens codes, and the Lockwardens were notoriously
conservative. He typed them in, making himself work carefully: he would only get one chance, if that. The screen went
blank again, then lit, presented him with an open channel.
He suppressed a cheer, and hit the codes that would dump
the entire contents of the datablock to a holding node, one of
a thousand secure datastores that laced the nets. The block
whined softly to itself, the seconds ticking past, and then the
screen cleared. He started to type a mailcode, allowing the
datastore itself to transfer the information to Chauvelin, but
heard footsteps on the stone floor behind him. *Too late.* He
touched a second series of illegal codes, saw the screen fill
with trash, effectively destroying his trail. Lights flickered
across the datablock, warning him that its contents had been
permanently erased. He sighed, and heard a woman's voice
behind him.

"Na Ransome."

He turned slowly, not wanting to provoke anything, and found himself facing a wiry woman—not the one who had been working at the kiosk in the lobby. She had a palmgun out and ready, half hidden by her hand and body, invisible to anyone working in the offices along the corridor. A much bigger man stood just behind and to her left, screening her still further from the offices. He wore a bulky coat that could hide a dozen weapons. Ransome looked to his own left in spite of himself, in spite of knowing better, and saw another pair—dockers, this time—moving toward him along the cross corridor.

"Someone wants to talk to you," the woman went on, her voice low and even.

"Someone like Damian Chrestil?" Ransome asked, but she didn't flinch.

"Someone." She beckoned to him with her free hand, the palmgun still leveled. "Someone who prefers to keep this tidy. If you'll step this way."

Ransome hesitated, but there was no real choice. *I'm too old—and not sick enough yet—for a suicide leap, and I was never good at fighting.* He spread his hands, showing empty palms, and stepped carefully away from the mail kiosk.

"Search him," the woman said to one of the dockers, and Ransome submitted to the rough and efficient search. She stepped past him then, unplugged the datablock, and stood studying the kiosk screen for a moment. Ransome saw her frown over the hash of random characters and touch a few keycodes before she shook her head and pocketed the datablock. *At least she wasn't able to trace the destination codes,* he thought, and felt a flicker of hope revive.

"Nothing here," the docker said, and she nodded.

"I hope you'll come quietly, Na Ransome."

"I'm not stupid," Ransome answered. *This is how the game is played; you cut your losses, and hope for your connections to save you. Please God, Chauvelin will try to contact me, will sort through the net stores when he can't—*He pushed that thought aside, pushing away panic with it. But this had happened before; he'd done his best, and sacrificed himself, and ended up abandoned. *That was Bettis Chrestil,* *twenty years ago. Chauvelin is different. I can rely on him. I have to rely on him.* The fear was a taste of metal in his throat.

"Walk with him," the woman said to the big man, who nodded unsmiling and took Ransome's arm. Ransome felt the muzzle of a palmgun touch his side briefly, felt the plastic warm against the inside of his elbow. The big man had a grip like iron; there was no hope of pulling free. *All I can do now is wait,* Ransome thought, and let them walk him slowly down the stairs and across the lobby. No one looked twice at them, and a part of Ransome's mind had to admire their efficiency.

"I hope Damian Chrestil pays you what you're worth," he said, experimentally, and the big man's hand closed painfully on his arm, grinding the palmgun into his elbow.

"Do stay quiet," the woman said, conversationally, and turned her head to murmur something into a hand-held comunit. As they passed through the main doors, a heavy passenger carrier, its rear pod sealed tight, windows darkened, pulled up in front of them. The door of the sealed compartment sighed open, and the woman said, "In there, please."

There was no point in a struggle, and no chance even if he'd wanted to. The big man leaned into him, putting him off balance, and as Ransome stumbled, the woman tripped him neatly, so that he practically fell into the darkened pod. He righted himself instantly, steadying himself with both hands against the padded seats, but the big man pushed in after him, palmgun now displayed, forcing him back against the pod's wall. The door closed behind the big man almost as soon as he'd cleared the frame, and the carrier slid away from the curb.

Ransome leaned back against the cushions, knowing better than to move too quickly. The big man settled himself opposite him, moving with the rocking of the carrier, sat comfortably, with the palmgun resting on his knee. Ransome eyed it for a moment, but knew better than to think of attack. He could hear the rasp of his breathing even over the purr of the carrier's motor, felt the familiar pain tugging at his lungs. "Hey," he said, and his voice cracked even on the single word. He made a face, hating the weakness, hating to have to ask, said again, "Hey. I need to take some medicine. It's in my pocket."

The big man looked at him for a long moment, his face utterly without expression. "All right," he said at last. "Which pocket?"

"Jacket. Left-hand side."

"Go ahead."

Ransome reached for the cylinder of Mist, making himself move at half the speed he wanted, slid the squat cylinder from his pocket, and started to hold it up even with the big man's eyes. The man leaned forward instantly, caught Ransome's wrist before he could finish the movement.

"Don't make trouble."

Ransome shook his head, did his best to suppress the cough that threatened to choke him. The big man eyed him warily, then released him, leaned back against his cushion. Ransome unfolded the mask, set it against his mouth and nose, and touched the trigger. The cold mist enfolded him, drove away even the fear for a brief second; he leaned back, eyes closed, and let the drug fill his lungs. He'd betrayed another weakness, he knew, something that they could use against him, and for a moment the fear rose with the thick mucus to choke him. He made himself breathe slowly, until the worst of the fear passed and he was left with the lethargy of the drug. He let himself fall into it, repeating his thoughts like a mantra. He would wait: there was nothing else he could do, and the situation might change. And in the meantime, he would wait.

DAY 2

Lioe made her way through the fringes of the crowd that filled one end of Betani Square, pressed as close as possible to the stage where the puppeteers would be performing. It was less crowded by the fountain, but not by much; a dozen or more children in varying degrees of costume were playing on the edges of the three-lobed basin, and several more were splashing in the shallow water, parents—or at least parental-looking figures—watching from the sidelines. There was no sign of Roscha. Lioe scowled—*I knew she wouldn't be able to get away*—but walked around the fountain's edge until she was certain the other woman had not arrived. She looked sideways, poising the chronometer's numbers against one of the bands of darker stone that crisscrossed the square's paving, dividing it into diamonds. There were still a few minutes until the show was supposed to start. She sighed, and resigned herself to wait.

A line of bollards marked the square's legal limits, twenty or thirty of the low mushroom shapes running along a line of dark paving that seemed to mark the top of the short flight of stairs that led down to the canal. A handful of people were sitting there, mostly in ones and twos, some staring toward the distant stage, more looking out toward the water or toward the smaller canal that formed part of the square's southern edge. Lioe glanced around again, and seated herself on the bollard nearest the fountain. She could see well enough, could see all the likely approaches, from the water-bus stops on the canals or from the nearest helipad, and at least she could be relatively comfortable. *Besides, I don't think she's coming.*

Lioe tugged her jacket closed against the wind. It wasn't cold, but it had picked up even in the half hour since she'd left Ransome's loft, was blowing steadily now, from the south and east. The air smelled odd, of salt and thunder, and the children's shouts fell flat in the heavy air. She glanced over her shoulder toward the mouth of the Inland Water, saw only the housetops on the far side of the canal. The last forecast she had seen had predicted the storm would strike around midnight, and she looked around again for a street broker. To her surprise—the brokers had seemed to be everywhere for a while—there were none of the bright red-and-white umbrellas in sight.

Music sounded from under the stage, distorted by distance and wind and the thick air. Lioe rose to her feet with the others, and saw the first of the puppets move out onto the platform. It was a massive construct, maybe two and a half meters tall, and nearly as broad; fans unfurled from what should have been the shoulders, and a crest of bronze feathers rose from the stylized head. More of the feathers appeared below the fans, and wings parted to reveal several small, white-painted faces. They were set slightly askew, Lioe saw, and jagged cracks ran down their centers, detouring around the long noses. As she watched, the first of them split open, revealing an animal shape too small to recognize. Intrigued, Lioe moved toward the platform, circling south toward the smaller canal, where the crowd was thinner, to try to get a better view. It was a bird, or something with delicate, arching wings and a glittering, peacock-blue body. She edged farther into the crowd as the second face split, revealing what seemed to be a model of the local solar system, and the entire assemblage leaned sideways, elevating the fans and turning the feathered crest into an almost architectural arch. There was a person inside that structure, Lioe realized suddenly, a single human being at the center of the spines and wings and the delicately made creatures; each precisely controlled movement set changes flowing through the puppet's outer layers. But what did it mean? It was not like any puppet she'd ever seen, or even imagined, and she stood staring, trying to puzzle out a story, some purpose, from the complex metamorphosis.

"Na Lioe?"

The voice was unfamiliar, but polite. She turned to face a thin, plainly dressed man with a plain, unmemorable face.

"It is Na Lioe, isn't it?"

Lioe nodded. "Yes." She kept her voice and face discouraging, but the man nodded anyway.

"I thought it must be you. Roscha said you'd be here. She asked me to tell you, she's running late." He gestured toward the street that led away from the square, running along the edge of the smaller canal. "She said she'd meet you at the Mad Monkey, instead of here."

Lioe glanced down the street—the sign was there, all right, a grinning, contorted holoimage dancing above a doorway at the far end of the street, where the canal turned left, away from the street itself—and looked back at the stranger. He was dressed like a docker, all right—dressed much like Roscha herself, for that matter, dockers' trousers and a plain vest under a loose, unbelted jacket. "When?"

The man shrugged, looked sideways as though to call up his chronometer. "She said she'd be there at fifteen-thirty— by the sixteenth hour at the latest."

Lioe glanced sideways herself, saw the numbers flash into existence against the dark paving: *almost sixteen hundred already.* "Thanks a lot," she said, and the man nodded.

"No problem." He turned away, already looking for a better vantage point among the crowd.

Lioe watched him go, wondering just who he was. He looked vaguely familiar—*maybe someone from Shadows,* she thought, and looked back at the stage. The puppet seemed to be melting into the platform, dozens of indistinguishable little mechanisms churning frantically around its edges. The operator was doing the splits within the confining mechanism. The crowd murmured, sounding both awed and approving. *I must have missed something,* Lioe thought. *I don't understand at all.* She looked again toward the Mad Monkey, wondering if Roscha was there yet, and if she could get food and/or drink. The sign looked like a bar's, the monkey dancing in the air, very bright in the shadowed street. *And even if it isn't, it might be more fun than watching the puppets. Mechanical perfection palls after a few min-*

utes, in my opinion. She eased her way out of the crowd, and started down the narrow street.

She had not traveled more than a dozen meters before she realized that she was being followed by a nondescript man who looked like another docker. She glanced back, wondering if she could turn back toward the square, slip between the back of the stage platform and the storefronts that defined the square, and saw a second person detach himself from the knot of people beside the curtain that screened the back of the stage, effectively cutting off her escape. She swore under her breath, wishing that she were armed—wishing that she'd carried even a pilot's tool-knife—and with an effort kept herself from looking around wildly. They were between her and the fringes of the crowd; she could shout, but none of the people watching the puppet show could reach her before the two men did. *I'll pretend I haven't seen them,* she decided, *keep walking and hope I can get to the Monkey before them—if that's safe. The man who said he was from Roscha, he must've been one of them, set this up.* . . . She shoved her hand into her pocket, closed her fist over thin air so that it made what she hoped would look like a dangerous bulge, and kept walking. *I'll try the Mad Monkey, and then the cross street, and if it comes to it, I'm not carrying much cash and it's not a good place for rape—*

A third man stepped out of a doorway ahead of her, hands deep in the pockets of his jacket. Lioe stopped, took an instinctive step sideways and back, toward the edge of the canal.

"Na Lioe," the third man said. "There's someone who wants to see you."

"Like hell," Lioe answered. She drew breath to scream, and the man freed his hand from his jacket, displayed a palmgun.

"Yell and I'll shoot."

Lioe released her breath cautiously, glanced back toward the square. Sure enough, the two strangers—and a third, the man who had spoken to her about Roscha—were coming toward her, blocking her escape in that direction. She took another step toward the canal, turning so that she could see all of them. "What do you want?"

"There's someone who wants to talk to you," the leader said again. "If you come quietly, no one will get hurt."

Lioe took another slow step backward, toward the canal edge, so that she stood barely half a meter from the bank. She could swim, that had been bullied into her in Foster Services, but the current was fast, and the far bank was not distant enough to offer an escape. "Not likely," she said aloud, fighting for time. "Come any closer, and I'll scream—and if you shoot me, nobody's going to be talking to me."

There was a little silence, and a quick exchange of glances, and then the leader raised his palmgun. "Last chance. Come quietly, or I will shoot."

Shit. Lioe froze for a second, frantically weighing her options. If she screamed, the leader would shoot—she had no doubt about it, and at this distance, he could hardly miss. He was too far away to try to jump him, get the gun away from him, and even if he weren't, there were the others to consider—probably armed, too. That left the canal, her only— and not very good—choice. *Unless I want to go with them.* She rejected that thought even before it was fully formed. *I don't even know why they want me, who this mysterious someone could be—unless this is Ransome's doing, his weird intrigue rebounding on me?* She pushed that thought aside as irrelevant, said carefully, "Wait a minute, now."

The leader relaxed slightly, the palmgun's muzzle wavering just a little. It was all the chance she was going to get. Lioe flung herself blindly backward, into the canal's murky water. Fleetingly she heard one of the men shout, and she hit the water hard, shoulder and hip, throwing a great plume of spray. She righted herself under the cold surface, risked opening her eyes for just an instant. The water, salt and oil and chemicals, stung miserably, but she saw light above her, and oriented herself against it. The current was strong, as she'd hoped and feared, and she let it take her, sweeping her down toward the junction where the canal turned south, away from the street. Already her lungs hurt her; she let out a little of her air, exerting herself only to keep herself parallel with the surface, and risked another glance into the dirty water. The surface glimmered just above her, tempting her with air and light, but she made herself stay down, trying to put a meter or so of water between her and the palmgun's projectiles. She let out a little more air, darkness gathering at the edge of her vision, and could hold her breath no longer. Gasping, she broke the surface, flinging her hair out of her eyes, and heard the flat crack of the palmgun from the nearer bank. Someone shouted, but she dove again, striking out strongly across the canal. The current clutched at her, rolling her sideways and down, then back in toward the canal bank. She floundered in momentary panic, eyes opening in spite of the pain, and clawed her way back to the surface. She was at the corner, where the canal narrowed and the water ran the fastest, rolling and folding over itself. She forgot about the gunmen in her struggle to free herself from the current's pull. For a terrified moment she thought she'd failed, that she would be pulled under and drowned, and then the water flung her with bruising force against the first of a set of pilings. She cried out in spite of herself, choked on a mouthful of the salty water, and struck the pilings again. This time, she grabbed for them, her hands sliding in the slimy mess of waterweeds, and then she worked her fingers into the dripping mat and clung, head above water, the current still dragging at her clothes and body. Her face burned where she had struck the piling, pain like long lines of fire running from cheek to jaw, and the corner of her mouth stung painfully. Her shoulder hurt, too—it was the same shoulder each time, she thought, with a crazy feeling of injustice. She'd fallen hard on her left shoulder when she went into the canal, and now it was her left shoulder that had hit the piling. She caught her breath, flailed her feet against the piling until she found something—it felt like a metal band, or an old mooring ring—and braced herself against it. It had all happened so fast, she hadn't had time to kick off her shoes.

She looked back down the canalside, saw the four men huddled together, staring along the canal in her direction. She froze for a second, new fear shooting through her, and realized that they couldn't see her after all. The bend in the bank protected her, at least a little bit, and at this distance she would be no more than a dark dot against the dark water. That was reassuring; she tightened her grip on the piling, and began to look for a way out of the water. This was a one-bank canal, with a single pedestrian embankment on the opposite side. Above her stretched blank formestone walls, banded with darker blocks of stone; the nearest window was a good ten meters above her head. The current swept past her, tugging her body away from the piling: *not a place to try and swim,* she thought, and turned her attention to the wall. The pilings stretched the length of the house row, and there seemed to be a break in the walls beyond that. *Maybe if I can work my way down to that break, I can just climb out,* Lioe thought, *or even just get out of the worst of the current, and swim to the embankment. If it weren't for the current, I could do it, no problem.*

She looked back down the canal, ready to duck out of sight if the would-be kidnappers were looking in her direction, but they were standing close together, one of them with his hand cupped to his head as though he held a portable com-unit. They seemed to be distracted, or as distracted as they were likely to get, looking back toward the stage. Lioe leaned out cautiously into the current, reached for the coat of waterweed that fringed the next piling. There wasn't much above the water, and she leaned out a little farther, reaching beneath the surface to grope for the matted weeds. She found them, dug her hand into the slimy surface, the individual strands slipping slack between her fingers. They were covered with a gelatinous coating that made her shiver even as she tightened her grip, pulling back as hard as she could. The weeds stayed fast to the piling. She took a deep breath and released her grip on the first piling, reaching for the second, letting the current toss her against it. She tightened her hold, breathing hard, ignored the new pain where her knee had scraped the formestone wall, and reached for the next piling to try again.

She inched her way down the canal wall, groping from piling to piling, her hands slimed and green from clutching the weeds. Their air sacs burst and oozed a sticky ichor, staining her hands despite the running water; her face burned where the salt hit the cuts, and her waterlogged clothes dragged heavy on her limbs. She hesitated for a moment, wondering if she should finally get rid of her shoes, but she would have to walk once she made the bank, and she was

getting close to the open space between the buildings. She
started to smile, but winced as the expression jarred her
scraped face, and reached for the next piling. She grasped
the ring of waterweed—it seemed thinner than the others,
but solidly attached—and let go. The waterweed came away
in her hand as the current caught her, whirling her away from
the bank. She flailed for a moment in panic, then got herself
under control. The current was not as strong here on the
straight of the canal. She brought herself abreast of it, angled
in slowly toward the bank.

The space she had been aiming for turned out to be one of
the tiny canalside parks, neatly paved, with low umbrella-
shaped trees growing in tubs and a wide strip of open ground
filled with extravagant white flowers. There was a gonda
landing as well, three steps leading up out of the water, and a
mooring ring on the wall, and Lioe clung to that for a moment, grateful to feel solid land under her feet, before she
dragged herself up onto the bank.

A woman was sitting under the nearest umbrella-tree, on
the edge of the tub, a paper parcel open beside her, the re-
mains of a meat pie strewn on the ground for the local cats.
Her head came up sharply as Lioe staggered up onto the
bank, and Lioe hastily lifted her hands to show them empty
of weapons.

"It's all right, I'm not going to hurt you. Somebody tried
to mug me."

The woman swallowed whatever she was going to say,
swept the last crumbs off her lap. She was a big woman, tall
and heavy-set, dressed in the dark robe that belonged to the
Four Judges. Lioe saw the tall headdress and mask of the
Prospering Judge set aside on the tub's edge beside her.
"Are you hurt?" the woman asked, and came forward
briskly.

Lioe shook her head, was suddenly grateful for the other's
steadying arm. "Not really, just cuts and bruises." She
looked down, saw her knee raw and scraped through the
ripped trousers. "I went into the canal, back toward Betani
Square."

"Jesus," the woman said. "The current's murder there.
You were lucky." She shifted her grip, taking more of

Lioe's weight, said firmly, "Come on. You'll want to talk to the Lockwardens."

"Lockwardens?" Lioe echoed, and then remembered. They were the local police, responsible for the locks and storm barriers as well as the usual laws.

"Our police," the woman answered. "You're an off-worlder, then?"

Lioe nodded.

"The bastards will pick on strangers," the woman said, with a kind of dour satisfaction. "Come on, it's not far."

Lioe let the stranger half lead, half carry her across the courtyard, suddenly too tired, too drained to care if she were part of the group. The woman paused by her tree, stooped with surprising grace to collect her mask, and Lioe realized with a sudden pang that she had lost the mask Gelsomina had given her. It was a strange thing to bother her, but her eyes filled with tears, and she stood shivering for a moment, mouth trembling painfully.

"Easy now," the big woman said. "Not far."

The nearest Lockwardens station wasn't far, barely forty meters along a narrow side street. It occupied the corner of one of the larger buildings, and all its windows blazed with light. The door stood open, men and women in uniforms that Lioe didn't recognize hurrying in and out, clutching work-boards and datablocks and even sheafs of paper. Someone exclaimed, seeing their approach, but Lioe was too tired and too cold to care. She let herself be led into the station, and then into a side room, unable to focus on the questioning voices that surrounded her. Someone eased her into a chair—a warm, well-padded chair—and then wrapped her hands around something warm, held it to her lips. She sipped obediently, and recognized the flat, bitter taste of antishock drugs beneath the sweet tea. In the distance, she heard the soft chirping of a medical scanner, and looked up in confusion.

"Finish the tea," a new voice said, and she did as she was told. Someone else—she was aware of him only as a pair of long-fingered, rather beautiful hands—wrapped the edges of a heated cocoon blanket closed around her. She had been sitting in it, she realized, and she huddled into its stiff embrace, letting its creeping warmth seep into her, drying her clothes. The tea was starting to work; she looked up, feeling more alert than she had before, and saw a spare, grey-haired woman sitting on the edge of a table opposite her. She herself was sitting in the only chair.

Even as she realized that, a male voice said, "Let me take a look at your face."

She turned her head obediently, winced as the long fingers probed the cuts on her cheek and jaw. The man—he wore a medic's snake-and-staff earring—winced in sympathy, and reached for the supply box that lay open at his feet.

"Close your eyes," he said, and laid a delicate mist of disinfectant over the entire side of her face. The stuff stung for a moment, and then a sensation of coolness seemed to spread across her jaw. She felt an applicator dab quickly at each of the cuts—it hurt, but remotely, the pain reaching her from a distance—and then the medic said, "All right, you can look now."

Lioe opened her eyes, to see that the woman was still staring at her. Lioe's identification disks and the contents of her belt purse were spread out on the tabletop beside her.

"So, can you tell me what happened, Na Lioe?" The hard-boned face was not unfriendly, but Lioe found herself choosing her words with care.

"A bunch of guys tried to kidnap me, pulled a gun on me—this was on the little street that runs away from Betani Square, where the Mad Monkey is. I ended up jumping into the canal to escape, and I got kind of banged up."

"Kidnap?" The woman's voice sharpened. "The woman who brought you in said you'd been mugged. Why would someone want to kidnap you?"

"Because—" Lioe stopped abruptly. *I'm not fully sure why, but it's bound to have something to do with Ransome, and Damian Chrestil and the cargo that I helped bring in, and the hsai, or at least hsai politics. And even if I did know what was going on, I don't know how much I can afford to tell you: Ransome's in this up to his neck, and he's a Burning Brighter working for the hsai.* She shrugged, feeling more bruises on her arm and shoulder. "I don't know. It was what they said—"

"Why don't you tell me about this from the beginning?" the woman said, not ungently. "My name's Telanin. I'm the chief of the station." She looked at the medic, who nodded.

"Let me just get you another cup of tea," he said. "And then I want to look at your knee."

"Thanks," Lioe said. Her clothes were drying nicely in the cocoon's steady warmth; only her shoes stayed cold, squishing slightly when she moved her toes, and she loosened the cocoon's lower edges to kick them off. She took the mug the medic held out to her, sipped cautiously, and wasn't surprised to taste more of the bitter restoratives beneath the minty tea. It wasn't as sweet as the first mug. The medic set her shoes aside to dry under the orange-red glow of a drying rack, and pulled the cocoon aside to begin working on her leg.

"About what happened?" Telanin said, and Lioe dragged her attention back to the other woman.

"Sorry." She pulled the cocoon closer around her body, buying time. "I was supposed to meet someone in Betani Square to watch the puppet show, but she didn't show up. She had to work this morning; I had a feeling she wouldn't be able to make it. So I stayed to watch the show anyway, and this man came up to me, said he had a message from Roscha—that's the woman I was supposed to meet. He said she wanted to meet me at the place called the Mad Monkey, and went off. I waited a little bit, but I was getting bored with the show, so I decided to see if she was there, at the Monkey, I mean. A couple of guys followed me away from the square, and there was a third man waiting in the street—he was the one with a gun." *And he said "someone" wanted to talk to me. But if I mention that, she'll want to know why this mysterious someone would go to this much trouble over me.*

"Did any of them say anything, say what they wanted?" Telanin asked. Her hand was resting on the control pad of an ordinary-looking noteblock, Lioe saw, and she chose her words very carefully.

"Something about coming quietly, I think. It happened pretty quickly."

Telanin's fingers shifted almost imperceptibly, recording

the answer. "So they didn't say anything else, nothing about kidnapping?"

Lioe shook her head, contrived to look sheepish. "I guess I overstated it."

Telanin nodded. "What about this woman you were meeting, this Roscha? Did you see her?"

Lioe shook her head again.

"How well do you know her—what's her full name?"

"Jafiera Roscha." Lioe paused. "We met at one of the Game clubs, Shadows, a couple of days ago. I'm only on planet for few days while my ship is in for repairs, but I'm a Gamer, and I've been spending my time in the clubs."

"So you don't know her well?" Telanin persisted.

"She's a Gamer," Lioe said again, and was suddenly aware of how ridiculous she must sound. *We've played together, I've seen her play my characters—yes, I know her very well, and not at all. About like I know Ransome.* She shrugged, helplessly, and the other woman nodded.

"Jafiera Roscha's known to us, though she's never been involved in the bash-and-grab gangs. But it's worth checking out, see if she set you up. She hasn't been asking you about your movements, whether you carry cash, anything like that, has she?"

Lioe shook her head.

Telanin nodded again. "We'll check her out, though. It seems odd they'd use her name, otherwise. How many people knew you were meeting Roscha today?"

"I don't know," Lioe said. "We talked about it in the club last night. We weren't making any secret of it, so probably a lot of people heard."

"Probably." Telanin gave a rather sour smile. "Look, I have to say I don't think this was a kidnap attempt. I hate to admit it, but this kind of bash-and-grab isn't uncommon during Carnival, especially when off-worlders are involved. A couple of canalli manage to lure a stranger into a dark alley, demand money and movables at gunpoint, and run. We'll check it out, see if Roscha's involved, and I'll ask you to look at our files, see if you can pick anyone out of the visual database—" She smiled again, more genuinely this time. "It's set up a lot like the *Face/Body* books. You shouldn't have any trouble finding them if they're in there. But I don't know how much chance we have of finding them. You were lucky.''

There was a little murmur of agreement from the medic, who had finished spreading a film of selfheal over the cuts on her knee. "Lucky twice," he said aloud. "The current's dangerous at that corner.''

Telanin nodded in agreement. "We'll do what we can," she said again, "but with this storm coming in, frankly, we've got to concentrate on that. Our investigation won't get started properly until it's past, and by then, the trails will be pretty cold.''

"I understand," Lioe said. "Hell, I wouldn't mind seeing these guys in jail, but, as you say, I was lucky. They didn't get anything, and I'm not hurt." She managed a quick grin. "I don't want to push my luck.''

Telanin smiled back, and Lioe thought she looked faintly relieved. "I'll have you look through our database, then, and sign a complaint, and then I'll have one of my people fly you back to your hotel. Are you up in the Ghetto?''

"Yes," Lioe said, "but that's not necessary—''

Telanin held up a hand, cutting off any further protest. "Just in case I'm wrong, and your first feeling was right," she said. "Besides, a lot of the helicab companies are going to be shutting down soon, and you don't want to be taking the buses. Not the way you're going to be feeling.''

"I'm all right," Lioe said, but it was only a token protest. She freed herself from the cocoon. Her clothes were all but dry, only a few damp spots remaining, but she was faintly sorry to give up the warm embrace. She followed Telanin out of the little room, the medic close on her heels. The public parts of the station were crowded and noisy, half a dozen men and women leaning over a single console and its harried operator, another group clustered around a display table. Lioe couldn't see all of the image that floated above the polished surface, but she could see enough to guess that it was a model of the neighborhood. Telanin touched her arm, turning her over to another woman, this one darkly elegant even in the Lockwardens' bulky uniform, and Lioe let herself be led away to the database.

She looked through the files under the dark woman's tute-
lage, and, as she had expected, found nothing. About halfway through, a young man appeared with the complaint
form. Lioe skimmed through it—she was mildly surprised to
see that it was real paper, not a noteboard and disk—and
signed her name in the necessary places. When she had finished, she followed the dark woman back again through the
chaos of the main rooms and out onto the helipad, where a
helicab stood waiting, the Lockwardens' markings muted.
She looked back once, from the doorway, to see Telanin
staring down at the tabletop display. By chance, one of the
Lockwardens stepped aside, so that for a brief moment Lioe
saw the full display. As she'd guessed, it was a model of the
area around the station, but that neighborhood transformed
by water and fire. Then another Lockwarden moved in front
of her, blocking her view. Lioe shivered—*if that's what
could happen, I'll be glad to be on high ground*—and
climbed meekly into the helicab. The pilot nodded a sympa-
thetic greeting, and the cab rose easily into the unsettled air.

DAY 2

Storm: C/B Cie. Offices, Isard's Wharf, Channel 9, Junction Pool 4

Damian Chrestil sat in the serene gold-tinged light of his office, the plans for a new long-haul carrier floating in the desktop screens in front of him. It was an elegant design, with ample cargo space, but surprisingly narrow-beamed, so that it would be half again as efficient as the larger long-haul craft in the current fleet. Even so, he had trouble forcing himself to concentrate, to keep his mind on the minutely detailed calculations sketched in the margins. Ivie—or at least his people—were somewhere out there, searching for Ransome and Lioe. *I should be hearing something soon,* he thought, and made himself look down again at the model that hung in the illusory space within the desktop, rotating slowly in response to a command he did not remember giving. He touched another key to stop it, called up the specifications for the power plant, and stared at the numbers for a long moment without really seeing them. Something—sand or gravel, it sounded like—rattled against the wall of the office, carried by the rising wind.

Enough of this, he thought, and touched keys to banish the gleaming images. They disappeared in a flurry of shutdown codes. He pushed himself away from the desk, and walked past the twin secretaries into the darkened warehouse. The large doors were shut, of course, but the side door was wedged open, letting in the rush and the smell of the wind. The door itself vibrated against its clips, jumping a little as each gust hit it. *Another two or three hours,* Damian thought, and stepped out onto the wharf.

The activity was less frantic than it had been earlier: the

barges and john-boats lay close to the docks, their heaviest fenders in place and double lines securing them to the piers. Damian nodded his approval, glanced up to see the power line that ran from the warehouse to the plotting shed swinging wildly in the wind. *Better see to that before it comes down on its own,* he thought, and looked around for the nearest docker. A blocky woman was crouched between bollards on the deck of the closest barge, tapline attached to a test node, workboard on her lap, and Damian lifted his hand to get her attention.

"Where's Rosaurin?" he shouted, raising his voice to be heard over the wind.

"I don't know, Na Damian," the woman called back. "In the shed, maybe?"

Damian waved in answer, turned away.

"Na Damian!" That was Rosaurin's voice, coming from the head of the dock, beyond the plotting shed. Damian waved to get her attention.

"Over here!"

Rosaurin came to join him, the wind whipping her short hair and flinging the skirts of her coat wildly so that they seemed in danger of tripping her. A smaller figure was visible behind her, a tiny woman in loose trousers and a fitted coat, posed so unobtrusively that for a moment he didn't recognize her. "It's that hsaia, Na Damian—I'm sorry, the Visiting Speaker. He's here, and he insists you promised him a tour of the facilities."

Ji-Imbaoa. What would he be doing here, except to bring me the codes? And Cella, too. Damian Chrestil suppressed his excitement and said, with what he hoped was convincing asperity, "And at a time like this. Tell him—I'll see him in my office, you can bring him in there." Rosaurin looked warily at him, and Damian smiled. "Don't worry, there won't be any tours. I'll deal with him. And secure that cable, will you?" ·

"Right, Na Damian. I'll bring him to your office."

Rosaurin turned away, balancing herself against the unsteady wind, made her way back down the wharf. Damian followed her, more slowly, doing his best to hide his elation. There was no other reason for ji-Imbaoa to visit the Junction

Pool docks, no reason except that he'd finally gotten the codes, and if he had, and Ransome was off-line, held in the summer house, there would be no one who could stop the transfer. Except—maybe—Lioe, and she was being dealt with, too. He smiled then, unable to stop himself, and Cella smiled back at him.

"He came to the palazze," she said. "He said it was important, so I brought him here. Your sibs don't know he was there." She paused then, still smiling. "Do you want me to wait with him?"

Damian nodded, knowing he did not need to wait for an answer. He ducked though the clamped-open door into the shadows of the warehouse, and stepped back into his office. He glanced quickly at his reflection—his hair was a mess, blown out of its ties by even that short an exposure to the wind, and he tidied it hurriedly—and then settled himself behind the desk. He lit the screens, calling up the plans he had been studying, and leaned back in his chair to wait, struggling to keep himself from grinning like a fool.

"Na Damian," the secretary said, after what seemed to be an interminable wait. "You have a visitor. The Visiting Speaker Kugüe ji-Imbaoa. And Na Cella." The expensive voice module did a fairly good job with the alien name.

"Show them in," Damian said, and this time couldn't keep the satisfaction out of his voice.

He rose to his feet as the Visiting Speaker entered, gesturing for him to take the guest's chair beneath the painted triptych. "Welcome, Na Speaker, it's good to see you again."

Ji-Imbaoa waved a hand, waving away the need for formality, and Damian did his best to swallow his excitement.

"Your woman was good enough to bring me here. Time is of the essence now," the Visiting Speaker said. "We can neither of us afford to waste any more time."

In the background, Cella lifted one precise eyebrow, and said nothing.

"I've not been wasting time," Damian said.

Ji-Imbaoa waved away the comment. "No matter."

"No," Damian Chrestil said. "It does matter." It was a risk, pushing him at this point, but he could not afford to let ji-Imbaoa treat him like an employee. "I have been ready to fulfill my part of the bargain. The delays come from your end."

There was a little silence, ji-Imbaoa's hands closing slowly on the arms of his chair. Damian waited, and, as slowly, the hsaia's hands relaxed.

"It is so," ji-Imbaoa said. "However, that delay has ended. I have the codes."

It's as much of an apology as I'm likely to get. "Excellent," Damian Chrestil said, and held out his hand.

Ji-Imbaoa ignored it. "I have gone to a great deal of trouble to get this information. I had to contact my friends through commercial linkages—at great expense—because Chauvelin refused to allow me the use of the ambassadorial channels. I think I should have some recompense for this."

Damian swallowed his first response, said, with careful moderation, "Na Speaker, surely that's one of the ordinary risks of doing business."

"I am not a business person," ji-Imbaoa said.

That's for certain. Damian said aloud, "You expect me to pay for your connect time to Hsaioi-An."

The fingers of ji-Imbaoa's hands curled slightly, a movement Damian had learned to interpret as embarrassment, but the Visiting Speaker nodded. "I think it would be fair."

Damian hesitated, looked down at his screens to cover his uncertainty. This was part of the hsai power games, one more attempt to jostle for status; he himself couldn't afford to lose, and so drop lower than ji-Imbaoa, but he wasn't sure he was good enough to win. The secretary chimed softly, signaling an incoming message, and he seized gratefully on the excuse. "I'm sorry, Na Speaker, I need to take that."

"Shall I go?" Cella asked softly, and Damian shook his head before the hsaia could take offense.

Ji-Imbaoa gestured acceptance, and Damian leaned back in his chair, touched the string of codes that activated the security filter, translating spoken words to a stream of letters across the bottom of the screen. A second set of codes flared, and he touched a second key to cut in the family's decryption routines. The screen lit at last, and Ivie's face looked up at him.

NA DAMIAN.

It was disorienting, watching Ivie's lips move without sound, while the words scrolled past on the bottom of the screen. Damian nodded. "I hope things went well? I'm with a visitor, so you'll have to make it fast."

Ivie nodded, in comprehension as well as agreement. I'M AT THE SUMMER HOUSE NOW, he said. THE FIRST GUEST IS WITH ME. WE'VE HAD A LITTLE TROUBLE WITH THE SECOND, BUT I HAVE HOPES THAT WE'LL BE ABLE TO FIND HER AGAIN SOON.

So he's got Ransome, but not Lioe. Damian said, "It's a start, anyway." He looked back at ji-Imbaoa, the germ of an idea forming in his mind. "I'm coming to join you myself, and I may be bringing a guest of my own—a colleague, rather. How's the weather?"

Ivie shrugged. DETERIORATING. IF YOU'RE GOING TO BE MORE THAN AN HOUR OR TWO, I WOULDN'T FLY, BUT THEY TELL ME THE ROADS SHOULD STAY OPEN UNTIL DARK.

"Good enough," Damian said. "I'll be there directly." He touched the sign-off key, and watched the picture dissolve, then looked back at ji-Imbaoa. "I've had to do some improvisations of my own," he said bluntly, "thanks to your delays. And suffer some inconveniences. Illario Ransome is off the nets right now, but only because I am holding him in my family's summer house. I think that is equal to your expenses in getting the codes."

Ji-Imbaoa nodded slowly. "Ransome is your prisoner."

"To put it bluntly, yes." Damian watched him, aware that something had changed, but not certain what it was. It was as though the rules had changed, or even the game itself. Cella was watching him with renewed intensity, as though she'd sensed the change, too.

"I would like to speak with him," ji-Imbaoa said. "I will give you the codes there, once we are at this house of yours."

Damian shrugged. There was no reason not to do it, as far as he could see; the nets were too well shielded for work to be interrupted by any but the worst storms, and he could access them from the summer house as well as anywhere. "All right," he said. "I'll call my flyer. I assume you have staff with you?"

Ji-Imbaoa gestured agreement. "My secretary, and one guard."

Damian looked at Cella, who was still watching him with that same unnerving fixity of purpose. "Do you want to come, too?" From the look in her eyes, it was a pointless question.

"Yes," she answered, gently. "If you don't mind."

"Fine." Damian Chrestil opened a working channel, typed in a quick series of commands, and waited half a second for the confirmation. "The flyer will be waiting for us at Commercial Street in ten minutes."

The wind had eased a bit by the time they reached the Commercial Street helipad, but the first fringes of rain had overspread the city. It fell in huge drops that left wet irregular circles the size of a man's hand on the dusty pavement. Damian ignored it as he shepherded the others into the heavy flyer, but ji-Imbaoa hissed irritably to himself, and the other hsaia, ji-Imbaoa's secretary, huddled himself into an incongruous plastic overcoat. The jericho-human Magill, who handled security, flipped up the hood of his coat, but made no comment. Cella followed demurely, moving through the rain as though she didn't feel it. The passenger compartment would seat only four in comfort, and Damian seized the excuse with some relief.

"I'll ride with the pilot," he said, raising his voice over the noise of the engines, and let the compartment's door fall closed without waiting for an answer.

The pilot didn't look up as he climbed into the control pod, already deep in her rapport with the machine, hands and feet encased by the controls, but one of Ivie's men was riding in the copilot's space. He scrambled to his feet as Damian opened the hatch, moved back to the jumpseat that folded down from the compartment wall.

"Thanks, Loreo," Damian said, and took his place beside the pilot. "How's it look, Cossi?"

The pilot shrugged one shoulder, her attention still on the displays that filled the air in front of her, visible only through her links. "Not too bad. The rain's fading, and on the screens it looks like we'll have some better air for the next forty minutes or so." She looked down at her controls again, and Damian hastily fastened himself into the safety webbing. "I have clearance from the tower," Cossi went on, "so I can lift whenever you're ready, Na Damian."

Damian touched the intercom button, opening the channel to the passenger compartment. "We're ready to lift, Na Speaker. Please be sure you're strapped in, this could be a rough ride." He took his hand off the button without waiting for an answer, looked at Cossi. "Ready when you are."

The flyer lifted easily, jets whining as it rose past the warehouse fronts and through the lower levels of sky traffic. As Cossi had predicted, the winds did not seem to be as strong as they had been, though the flyer dipped and shuddered. Damian clung to the edge of the hatchway, peered out the tiny window toward the Old Dike and the cliffs that marked the edge of Barrier Island. Even in the grey light, it was easy to make out the five projecting bits of cliff face that were the Five Points; he could even see the sparkle of lights behind the rows of windows. The Soresins' palazze looked busy, a swarm of servants and robohaulers clustered around an ungainly-looking cargo flyer, unloading supplies for the family's annual first-big-storm party. Behind him, Loreo laughed softly.

"Looks like the party's on."

Damian nodded. "Pity we can't make it."

The flyer lifted further, looking for a clearer path through the updrafts off the Barrier Hills, and for the first time Damian had a clear view of the sky to the south. Wedges of grey clouds piled over and on top of each other, steel-colored overhead, shading to purple at the horizon; their edges met and meshed, deforming under the pressure of the wind. The light that came in through the flyer's forward screen and windows was dull, lifeless, dim as twilight. The flyer banked sharply, heading south past the last of the hills, and Damian caught a quick glimpse of the mouth of the Inland Water. The storm barriers were up at last, three ranks of dark, wet metal closing off the channel, and the waves were starting to break against them, grey-green walls of water streaked with skeins of foam that were startlingly white in the dim light. Damian shivered, thinking of a childhood visit to Observation Point just before a storm. The low, hemispherical building, set on the southernmost point of Barrier Island, on a spur of land that curved out into the sea, had obviously been built to withstand the worst hurricanes, but he had never forgotten the sight of the surf pounding at the base of the cliffs, throwing spray and stones ten meters high. At the height of a bad storm, the man in charge had said, boasting a little but also stating simple fact, the waves broke completely over the station for hours at a time.

"We're going to have to land from the southeast," Cossi said, breaking into his train of thought. "Otherwise we'll be crosswise to the wind."

"Go ahead."

Damian braced himself as the flyer bucked, dropped several meters, but then Cossi had made the turn, and the flyer steadied slightly, riding with the wind instead of against it. They dropped lower, and Damian saw the scrubby trees bent even farther into the hillside by the wind. The family's landing strip gleamed ahead of them, the rain-darkened pavement outlined by double rows of tiny blue lights. The flyer fell the last few meters with a roar of jets, and then they were down, Cossi converting the drop smoothly to forward momentum. The braking fans rose to a scream, and died away as the flyer came to a stop, directly on the markers.

"Nicely done," Damian said, and meant it.

Cossi smiled, in genuine pleasure, then turned her attention to the difficult task of prying herself out of the control links. "Do you want me to wait for you, or do I head back to the city?" she asked, still working herself free of the controls.

"There's no point in your flying back," Damian said. "Put the flyer under cover—the hangar's rated to stand a class three—and then you can either wait it out here or take a groundcar."

"I'll wait," Cossi said.

Damian nodded, and swung himself out of the pilot's compartment. The others were already standing on the rain-spattered pavement, ji-Imbaoa still hissing to himself, his household clustered miserably at his back. Cella was standing a little apart, a little behind them, her eyes downcast, hiding that unnerving smile. Damian managed a smile in return,

wondering what she was up to, and waved them on toward
the house itself. He could see Ivie waiting in the doorway,
light blazing behind him. Shutters covered the windows; he
glanced hastily over his shoulder and saw Loreo by the door
of the domed hangar, guiding Cossi and the flyer inside.

"No word yet on the second guest," Ivie said softly as
Damian approached, and stood aside from the door.

"You can give me the details later," Damian answered,
and went past him into the house. He could feel the floor
trembling under his feet, and knew that the household generators were already at speed, ready to cut in when the power
grid went down.

The others were waiting in the main room, the glass that
formed the viewing wall now covered by heavy wood and
steel shutters. Damian paused at the top of the short stairs,
blinking in the unexpectedly warm light of a dozen hastily
placed standing lamps. He had never been in the house during Storm, had never seen the shutters from the inside, the
almost-black panels cutting off the view. It was an alien,
disorienting sight. One of Ivie's people had set up a pair of
service trays and activated a mobile bar, and most of the
group, four men and a pair of women, were clustered either
by the food or in front of the communications console. The
largest of the screens was tuned to the weather station, and
Damian caught a quick glimpse of a redscreen report before
one of the women moved, cutting off his view. Ransome sat
a little apart from the others in one of the large armchairs,
leaning back, a glass of deep amber wine on the table beside
him. He seemed very much at his ease, despite the third
woman who stood against the far wall, palmgun in hand, and
Damian hid a frown. Then he saw the slight, nervous movement of Ransome's hand, one finger slowly tracing the lines
of the carved-crystal glass, and the way his eyes roved from
point to point when he thought no one was looking.

"So," ji-Imbaoa said, too loudly. "Ransome is here. And
your prisoner?"

Ransome smiled, and lifted the glass of wine in ironic sa-
lute. "Not a guest, Na Damian?"

Damian came down the last two stairs, ignoring both of
them, snapped his fingers to summon the bar. It rolled over

to him, wheels digging into the carpet, and he poured himself a glass of raki. "Help yourself, Na Speaker, we're informal here. Will you see to him and his household, Cella?" He looked at Ransome, barely aware of Cella's politely murmured answer. "You were becoming an inconvenience, you know. This seemed a—reasonable—way to handle the situation."

Ransome's smile widened, became briefly and genuinely amused. "I suppose I should tell you that you won't get away with this."

"I don't see why not," Damian said, deliberately brutal. "This isn't the Game." He had the satisfaction of seeing Ransome flinch.

"Na Damian." Ji-Imbaoa turned away from the mobile bar, a tall cylinder in one hand. "I have the codes for you, but there is a favor you could do me in return."

A favor? Damian barely managed to keep himself from raising his eyebrows in sheer disbelief. *That is a change of tune, from the hsaia who was trying to bully me into a subordinate position not an hour ago. You only ask favors from your superiors.* "If I may," he said, carefully casual, and gestured toward the door behind him. Shall we talk in private?"

"That might be well," ji-Imbaoa said.

Damian led the way into the side room, fingering his remote to switch on the lights. Shutters covered the single window, but he could hear the sudden drumming of rain against the walls. He gestured toward the nearest chair—the room was set up as a communications space, with heavy, comfortable chairs and complex machinery lining the walls—and said, "What is this favor?"

Ji-Imbaoa suppressed a gesture, seated himself with a kind of heavy dignity. "Ransome, I would imagine, becomes a liability to you once this is over."

Damian shook his head. "Not necessarily. He's a known netwalker, I can prove he's been stealing information. If he tries to go to the Lockwardens, I can bring an equally strong complaint against him."

"Still, Chauvelin will know," ji-Imbaoa said.

"Chauvelin doesn't like me anyway," Damian Chrestil said. *I wish you'd come to the point.*

Ji-Imbaoa looked away, said, as though to empty air, "I might be able to help with the situation."

I don't need your help, thank you, Damian thought. He bit his tongue, and waited.

"And it would be doing me a favor." Ji-Imbaoa said the words reluctantly, almost as though they were being pulled out of him. "There is a matter of face between my family and this Ransome, the matter of an insult which could not be acknowledged then, but is lesser treason now. If you will give him into my custody, we—my kin and I—will be able to settle this. And I, and they, will be in your debt."

Damian made himself look down at his hands to hide his sudden elation. *To have ji-Imbaoa, and, more than that, his entire family, indebted to me—in exchange for Ransome. Not much of a trade, an arrogant netwalking imagist—or should that be an image-making netwalker?—for the friendship of an equally arrogant fool. But ji-Imbaoa has powerful relations, they could be very useful to me. I've no illusions, Ransome's no friend of mine, but can I afford to do it? He's Chauvelin's client, after all. . . . But if it means connections in Hsaioi-An, a deep connection to the je Tsinra-an, can I afford not to?* He said, slowly, "I can't give you an answer now. There are practical considerations involved—"

"Chauvelin will not be ambassador much longer," ji-Imbaoa said. "There is already pressure on the All-Father to remove him from this post."

And that would make an enormous difference, Damian thought, if it's true. If Chauvelin were no longer a factor, there'd be no reason not to do it. He had a sudden image of Ransome at Chauvelin's eve-of-Storm party, sitting on the wall of the garden he had designed, the paths paved with thousands of delicate faces spread out at his feet, a mocking half-smile playing on his lips as he watched the other guests recognize what they were walking on. Not a lovable man, certainly. *Brave enough—and I do respect that—but this is a risk you take when you play politics.* He nodded slowly, looked back at ji-Imbaoa. "If I can do you this favor," he said, "I will."

DAY 2

•

The Lockwarden pilot set the cab down on the helipad just beyond the lift complex that ran down the cliff face into the Old City, balancing the light machine against the gusting winds. He was obviously skilled, but the ride was rough, and Lioe was glad to be on the ground. The pilot insisted on escorting her to the door of the hostel. Lioe made only a token protest, grateful for his support, and did her best to ignore the concierge's smirk at her arrival, clothes torn and under Lockwarden escort. The smile turned to a frown of concern when he saw the white patches of selfheal on her face, and he came out from behind the counter to meet her.

"Na Lioe? Are you all right?"

"Na Lioe got mugged," the Lockwarden said, politely enough, but Lioe found herself wincing a little at the suggestion.

"I'm all right," she said. "I just need to change clothes."

"You look like death," the concierge—Laness, his name was—said, and shook his head. "You go on up to your room, and I'll send a supply cart. Do you need anything in particular?"

"Something to eat," Lioe said, and was surprised by the intensity of her hunger. She turned to the Lockwarden. "Thanks for getting me here."

"No problem," the pilot said easily, and let himself out.

"You go on up," Laness said again, "and I'll send a cart."

"I'd appreciate it," Lioe said. She rode the narrow lift up to the third floor—the first time she'd been back to her

rented room in three days; most of her spare clothes were at
Shadows—and let herself into the narrow room. It was
small, but comfortable, and it had its own temperature controls. She turned up the heat to drive away the lingering
damp of the canal, and stripped off her crumpled clothing. *I
need to call Ransome, find out what's going on,* she thought,
but I want to be in shape to cope with him. She showered,
not too quickly, letting the hot water wash away the fear and
stiffness and the last faint green stains from the waterweed.
The supply cart was waiting for her when she had finished,
one of the covers pushed back slightly to release the steam.
She dressed quickly, scrambling into her last spare pair of
trousers and a loose, Reannan-knit pullover, and pushed
back the lid of the cart. The food was good, standard local
fare, fish cakes and rice and a quick-fry of vegetables, and
Laness had included a bottle of the resinous local wine. She
poured herself a glass, and wolfed a couple of the fishcakes
straight from the cart, then turned her attention to the communications table. She seated herself in front of it, dragged
the supply cart into easy reach. There were three messages
from Kerestel waiting in storage. She hesitated, feeling
guilty, but none of them were marked urgent. She ignored
them, and called up the cheapest of the local communications nets. Its prompt flickered into view, and she punched in
Ransome's mailcode. There was a fractional hesitation, and
then the familiar message: TERMINAL IN USE, PLEASE TRY
LATER.

She smiled and reached for the cart again, one unacknowl-
edged worry assuaged. At least Ransome was all right, and
could probably explain what was going on, who had tried to
kidnap her and why. *And in the meantime,* she thought, *I
think I'll start carrying my work knife again.* She pushed
herself away from the terminal, went to rummage in her bag
for the knife. It was meant to be used as a survival tool, and
was classified as such when it passed through customs, but
the longer of the two blades made an effective weapon. She
slipped it into her pocket, turned back to the terminal. There
was a repeat function; she found it after a moment's search,
and hit the codes. This time, the screen stayed dark, codes
flickering across its base; after half a minute, a new message

appeared: INTENDED RECEIVER NOT RESPONDING, CANCEL YES/ NO. Lioe made a face, but hit YES. The screen flickered, and a moment later presented her with the list of charges. She ignored it, staring past the numbers. *Someone was on the circuit only a few minutes ago,* she thought, *so where the hell did he go? Unless it was someone calling him?* She hesitated, then tried again. There was no answer except the cancellation prompt.

She closed the system, wondering if she should wait and try again, or if she should go back to Ransome's loft and see if there were any messages waiting there. That made the most sense, especially since she had Ransome's key, but she had to admit that going back out on the streets didn't particularly appeal to her. *Which is silly. There's no reason to think that these people—whoever they are—will try anything in the port district; more to the point, and more likely, there's no reason to think the hostel is all that safe.* She stood frowning for a moment, and the communications table buzzed, the screen displaying the intercom symbol. Her frown deepened, but she reached across to touch the flashing icon.

"Yes?"

"Na Lioe." Laness sounded oddly hesitant. "There's a woman to see you. She says her name is Roscha. Shall I send her up?"

Roscha? What the hell is she doing here? "Is she alone?" Lioe asked. *And if she isn't,* she wondered suddenly, *are you in a position to warn me?*

"Yes, Na Lioe."

"I'll come down," Lioe said, and cut the connection before anyone could protest. She made her way down the side stairs rather than the lift, and paused just inside the doorway to scan the lobby. Roscha was standing by the concierge's counter, her beautiful face looking oddly forlorn as she watched the lift entrance. There was no one else in sight. Feeling rather foolish, Lioe took her hand off the button of the work knife, and stepped out into the lobby.

"Quinn!" Roscha turned at the sound of the other woman's footsteps, her eyes going instantly to the patches of selfheal. "Are you all right?"

"Yes, fine," Lioe said, irritably, and made herself stop. "It's just cuts and bruises," she said. "Listen, did you send someone to tell me you were at someplace called the Mad Monkey?"

"No." Roscha shook her head, sending the red hair flying. "No, I didn't, and the Lockwardens have been talking to me already. What happened?"

Lioe looked over her shoulder, saw Laness leaning against his counter, listening shamelessly. "Over here," she said, and drew Roscha away into the shelter of the pillars that defined the common entertainment center. No one was there, the VDIRT consoles empty, and she turned back to face Roscha. "Maybe you can tell me," she said. "This man came up to me, called me by name, and said you'd given him a message to be passed on, to meet you at this place called the Mad Monkey."

"I know it," Roscha muttered, and waved a hand in apology. "I'm sorry, go on."

"When I tried to go there," Lioe said, and heard her voice tight and angry, "I was followed, and someone stepped out of a doorway carrying a gun. He said somebody wanted to talk to me, and I was to come quietly. Do you have any idea who that somebody might be?"

"No." Roscha shook her head, stopped abruptly. "Do you work for C-and-I?"

"What?" Lioe blinked, irrationally offended by the question. "No, I'm a pilot. And I'm a Gamer. I don't need to work for Customs."

"Na Damian—Damian Chrestil thinks you do," Roscha said, slowly. "And you've been hanging out with Ransome, who's not exactly clean when it comes to politics." There was a fleeting note of malice in her voice that vanished almost as soon as Lioe recognized it. "And Na Damian went out of his way to make sure I had an alibi for this afternoon."

"So you think Damian Chrestil is behind this?" Lioe asked.

"You don't sound that surprised," Roscha answered, bitterly.

"I'm not, exactly. Ransome—" Lioe stopped abruptly.

How the hell do I know who to trust, if I can trust you, or anyone? You work for C/B Cie., which is the same thing as working for Damian Chrestil, and Ransome isn't answering his calls. What the hell am I supposed to do now? "Why should I tell you?"

Roscha made an angry sound that was almost laughter. "Because I don't like being jerked around. Because I don't like being used to set somebody up—especially you, somebody I've been sleeping with, somebody I like. Somebody as good as you are in the Game." Her voice cracked then, and she looked away, scowling. "Na Damian lied to me, and he used me, and he maybe would've murdered you, and it could've been my fault. I'll be damned if I'll let him do that to me."

There was something in her voice, the street kid's—*the canalli's*—ancient, bitter grievance that made Lioe nod in spite of herself. "All right," she said slowly, "I believe you."

Roscha nodded, silent, still scowling.

"I need your help," Lioe went on, more slowly still, a voice screaming reproaches inside her head. *Are you crazy? She still works for C/B Cie. Even someone as Game-addicted as Roscha isn't going to give up a good job for a total stranger. She could be setting you up again.* She shook the thoughts away. *I have to have help, and the only other person I can trust is Ransome. And he's not answering. I have to take a chance, and Roscha's my best shot. She's a good actor, but I don't think anyone's that good. I think she meant exactly what she said. I hope.* "I need to find Ransome, he's the one who really knows what's going on. Can you get me back to his loft? It's back at Newfields, where the cliffs overlook the Junction Pools."

"I know where it is," Roscha said. She nodded, her face grim. "Na Damian's going to be looking for both of us now—I was supposed to stay on the docks until midnight. I guess I don't need an alibi now." She smiled wryly, but shrugged the thought away. "I borrowed a denki-bike, we can take that."

"In this weather?" Lioe said. The thought of riding one of the unstable little two-wheeled vehicles in the same winds that had tossed the Lockwardens helicab across the sky was not appealing.

Roscha glanced toward the window beside the door, shrugged slightly. "It's not raining yet."

"Right," Lioe said. She looked toward the concierge's counter, where Laness was pretending to be absorbed in the tourist display-tapes. *No harm in providing a little insurance,* she thought, and walked over to join him. "Laness," she said, and the man looked up in an unconvincing flurry of surprise.

"What can I do for you, Na Lioe? Is everything all right?"

"Yes," Lioe answered. *So far.* "I need you to do me a favor," she went on. "I have to go out, but after what happened earlier, would you—if I'm not back here tonight, or if I don't call you, would you give the Lockwardens a call?"

"Of course, Na Lioe," Laness said. His eyes widened slightly, his whole being torn between enjoyment of the Game-like intrigue and concern for a guest. "But, Na Lioe, if there's any chance—what I mean is, with the storm predicted for tonight, if anything happens to you, the Lockwardens are going to have enough to do."

"That's all right," Lioe said. *Or at least it can't be helped.* "I'm not really worried, not really expecting anything. But if I'm not back, and you don't hear from me, I want you to call them."

Laness nodded. "I'll do that," he said, and added, awkwardly, "Good luck."

Roscha's denki-bike was parked outside, under the shelter of a news kiosk's awning instead of in the racks outside the hostel's door. The wind—a warm wind, unpleasantly warm—sent dust and a few errant pieces of trash whipping along the pavement; across the road, a pair of women struggled with a storefront banner, fighting to fold the heavy cloth. Up and down the street, wooden shutters had been clamped into place across the larger windows, and there was a line out the door of the single grocer's shop. "It looks bad," Lioe said, involuntarily, and Roscha shrugged.

"It's always like this when a storm's coming. They say it's only going to be a class two." She reached into the

bike's security field, expertly touching the release codes.
"Let's get going before the rain starts."

The streets were all but empty in the port district, most of
the workers already heading home to secure their own property. Shutters covered most of the upper-floor windows, and
there were storm bars across the warehouse doors. Lioe
leaned close against Roscha's back, felt the denki-bike shud-
der each time they turned a corner. A few drops of rain were
falling as they turned the last corner and pulled into the alley
beside Ransome's loft. Lioe winced as the first huge drops
hit her face, looked toward the building's entrance. The red
flag was still out, whipping frantically against its stays, and
she wondered if its owner had just forgotten to take it in.
Still, the stairs weren't difficult, and at least she knew where
they were. She reached into her pocket for the lockbox, and
closed her fingers gratefully over its smoothly dented surface. *At least I didn't lose it in the canal.* She started toward
the stairwell, motioning for Roscha to follow. The other
woman straightened from hooking her bike to the recharging
bollard, gave the connector a last tug, and came to join her.

"Where away?"

"Upstairs," Lioe answered, and laid the lockbox against
the stairway door. It clicked open, and she stepped into the
sudden darkness. It smelled odd, sour and rather yeasty, and
Roscha made a small noise of disgust.

"Better watch your step."

"What is it, anyway?" Lioe turned to secure the door behind them. A tiny light came on as she refastened the latch,
casting a sickly glow over the landing.

"Someone's been chewing strawn," Roscha answered.
"There'll be a cud around here somewhere."

"What's strawn?" Lioe started up the stairs, avoiding the
shadows.

"It comes out of hsai space, makes you feel very calm,"
Roscha answered. Lioe could hear the sudden smile in her
voice as she added, "Not something I indulge in much."

"I guess not." Lioe paused outside Ransome's door, fumbling with the lockbox until she found the depressions that
released the lock. The lights were out, just as she'd left it, the
big window open to the city view. Dark clouds, almost pur-

ple, filled the left side of the window; the sky to the right was
still only grey. "Ransome?"

There was no answer, and she hadn't really expected one,
but she called his name once more before crossing to the display space. Lights flashed along the base of the main console, signaling at least a dozen messages waiting. She
frowned, puzzled now as well as worried, and touched keys
to retrieve the latest. A secondary screen lit, displayed a
string of hsai *n-jao* characters. *Chauvelin?* she wondered,
and touched keys again to scroll back to the first message.

"He hasn't even gotten the shutters down," Roscha said,
and Lioe looked back at her. "If you were looking for Ransome," Roscha went on, "he hasn't been here. He'd've put
storm shutters up, the way that sky is looking."

"Damn." Lioe looked around, saw nothing that looked as
though it could cover the enormous window. Her hat was
still sitting on the folded bed, and she realized that she had
left it behind that morning as well. "Can you take care of it,
please?"

"Sure," Roscha said, sounding slightly surprised, and
crossed to the window. She ran her hand along the left-hand
side of the frame until she found an all-but-invisible panel.
She popped that open, studied the controls for a moment,
then turned a dial. There was a shriek from outside the window, unoiled metal reluctant to move, and then the shutters
began to lower themselves into place, creaking and groaning
along their track.

Lioe reached for the room remote, touched keys to bring
up the lights, and then turned her attention back to the messages. The first message in the queue was flashing on the
screen: *more n'jao characters,* she thought, but these looked
different from the first ones she'd seen. Frowning now, she
split the screen, recalled the last message. Sure enough, the
characters were different, forming an entirely different pattern. She knew only a few *n'jao* glyphs, mostly trade-rela-
ted—like most Republicans, her dealings with the hsai were
generally done through a jericho-human broker, and none of
these were familiar.

"Do you know any *n'jao?*" she asked, and Roscha came
to look over her shoulder at the screen.

"A little. I can't read that, though."

Lioe glanced back at her, saw the delicate eyebrows draw down into a thoughtful frown.

"Wait a minute, though." Roscha reached out to touch one tripart character in the first message. "I think that's the ambassador's name-sign. And I think these are repeats—message repeats." She indicated another set of symbols.

"Chauvelin?" Lioe asked.

"I saw it on a crate once, when we handled some diplomatic shipping out," Roscha answered. "I'm sure that's what it is."

"I'm not surprised," Lioe muttered. She touched more keys, searching for a main directory, and wished she had had more time to learn Ransome's idiosyncratic systems.

"Why not?" Roscha asked. "Look, what's going on?"

"I wish I knew," Lioe answered. She took a deep breath, made herself look away from the screens crowded with useless information. "What I think is happening—what Ransome said was happening—is that Damian Chrestil and the hsaia Visiting Speaker are probably smuggling something, mainly to get Damian Chrestil some political advantage in Hsaioi-An, which he could use here."

Roscha nodded. "That makes sense. He wants to be governor."

"Chauvelin and the Visiting Speaker are enemies," Lioe continued, "members of rival factions—and the Visiting Speaker doesn't much like Ransome, either—so there's a hsai dimension to this, too."

"*Sha-mai.*" Roscha shook her head. "It's a mess, but it does make sense."

"I'm glad it makes sense to someone," Lioe said. She fiddled with the shadowscreen again, found the main directory at last, and ran through it hastily, searching for translation programs. There was only one, and it was really only for transliteration. *Ransome certainly speaks tradetalk, and probably a couple of modes of hsai,* she thought, but copied the two screens to its working memory anyway. The prompt blinked for a few seconds, and spat strings of letters. She recognized Chauvelin's name, and, in the second message, a string of numbers that looked like routing codes. She studied

those numbers, cocking her head to one side. They were certainly routing codes; in fact, they looked like the kind of
codes that gave access to commercial data storage. *I wonder
what Ransome keeps in that kind of safe space,* she thought,
and copied the codes to a separate working board.

"I think," Roscha said slowly, "I think that means that
Chauvelin's been looking for him." She pointed to the first
message, her fingertip hovering just above the screen. "And
it looks like it's been repeated—what's the time check, anyway?"

Lioe touched keys. "That message has been repeated
every quarter hour for four hours. The last one arrived about
forty minutes ago." *Does that mean he got the message and
is with Chauvelin?* she wondered. *Or did Chauvelin just give
up?*

"Do you think he got the message?" Roscha said.

Lioe shook her head. "There's only one way to find out."
Roscha looked at her, and she smiled wryly. "Call Chauvelin and ask."

"Yeah, but do you think he'd answer?"

Lioe shrugged. "I've no idea." She reached for the workboard, typed in a string of codes, an inquiry first, to Ransome's own directories, and then into his storage. To her
surprise, the codes to contact the hsai ambassador were held
in open storage; she copied them to the communications system, but hesitated, wondering if she should send them. *What
do I say, anyway? "I'm so sorry to bother you, Ambassador,
but is Ransome with you?" How do I explain why I'm calling, if he's there, without getting him into trouble? More important, what do I say if he's not?* She touched the final key
before she could change her mind. *I can always just say he
told me he might be there. I don't have to tell a jericho-human—no, not even a jericho-human, a conscript, chaoi-
mon—anything of what's going on.* The handset chimed
softly, from beside the working chair, and at the same time
the secondary screen displayed connect symbols.

"What the hell?" Roscha said.

"I'm calling the ambassador," Lioe answered, and
crossed to pick up the handset. The green telltale was lit at
the base of the set, indicating a machine on the other end of

the connection. "I want to know if Ransome's there." She
touched the connect button before Roscha could say anything, heard a delicate mechanical voice in her ear.

"Hsaie house. May I help you?" A moment later, the
voice repeated the same message in tradetalk.

"I'm trying to contact Illario Ransome," Lioe said.

"Who may I say is calling?"

So he is there. Lioe felt a sudden surge of relief, a kind of
deflation, and said, "Quinn Lioe." She heard her voice flat
and irritable in the handset's reflection.

"One moment, please."

"He's there?" Roscha demanded, and Lioe shrugged.

"He seems to be—" She broke off as the handset clicked,
flipping over to the new connection.

"Chauvelin."

The voice was familiar from the ambassador's party, low
and crisp, with only a hint of the hsai accent. Lioe froze, not
knowing what to say, what she should do, and Chauvelin
said, "Na Lioe?"

"I'm sorry to have bothered you, Ambassador," she said.
"I—I was looking for Ransome, he said he might be with
you." *Maybe that wasn't the best phrasing,* she thought, *but
it's the best I could do on short notice. Things must be bad, if
Chauvelin himself is talking to me.*

"I've been looking for Ransome myself," Chauvelin
said. "Are you at his loft?"

There was a certainty in his voice that made Lioe think the
call had been traced. "Yes." *No point in lying: even if he
hasn't traced it yet, he will.*

"Has he been there, do you know?"

"I don't know," Lioe said. It was a safe answer; better
still, it was the truth. "Is there anything wrong?"

There was a little pause, just enough to make her sure he
was lying. "No, not at all. But I would like to talk to him as
soon as he returns."

"I'll tell him that," Lioe said, and waited.

"It's important," Chauvelin said. There was another
pause, barely more than a hesitation, and then the ambassador went on, "I was expecting a message from him. Did he
leave anything for me?"

Lioe shook her head, then remembered it was a voice-only line. "Not that I've seen." She glanced quickly at the console, double-checking the messages displayed on the screen. "No, nothing." She hesitated herself, wondering how much she could say, then said, "I was expecting to find him here. I'm a little—concerned."

"So am I." She could almost hear a kind of wry smile in Chauvelin's voice. "If you hear from him, please tell him to contact me."

"I'll do that," Lioe said, and broke the connection.

"So what happened?" Roscha asked.

Lioe shrugged, looked back at the massive console, at the symbols and code-strings filling the screens. "Ransome isn't there, as you heard, and Chauvelin badly wants to talk to him."

"That doesn't sound good," Roscha said. "What about hospitals, or the Lockwardens?"

"I bet Chauvelin's already done that," Lioe said, "but it couldn't hurt to check again." *Or could it? What if he wants to keep this quiet?* She shoved the thought away. "How are you on the nets?"

Roscha shrugged. "Good enough to find that out, anyway."

In spite of everything, Lioe grinned. "Can you take care of it? There's something I want to check."

Roscha reached for the handset. "All right."

One screen winked out, slaved to the handset; Lioe ignored its absence, stared at the routing codes displayed on her workboard. She was still learning her way around Burning Bright's nets, but this sequence looked straightforward enough. The header codes indicated a secure node, but the numbers following should be the owner's own codes. She ran her hands over the shadowscreen, recalling the main directory, and set the system scanning for a node that matched the header codes. She could hear Roscha's voice in the background, rising in inquiry, flattening out with each inaudible answer, but she ignored it, her eyes fixed on the screen. If this didn't work, she would have to try netwalking, personally checking the likely nodes. Then the screen lit, displaying a gaudy logo, a shield banded in blue and gold, with a scarlet dragon coiling over it, and presented her with a list of options: ADD, SUBTRACT, RETRIEVE, NEW FILE, CHARGES. She hit RETRIEVE, and her screen filled with symbols, scrolling past too fast for her to read. She touched the shadowscreen to dump the information to Ransome's local system—somewhat to her surprise, there was no request for a further password—and waited until the key bar flickered green again. She banished the connection, and turned her attention to the workscreen, scrolling back to the beginning of the file.

"Nothing at any of the hospitals," Roscha said, and came to peer over her shoulder. "But a friend of mine at C/B Cie. says Na Damian's gone off with a hsaia—it was somebody important, he said, so it could be the Visiting Speaker—and Almarin Ivie, he's head of security, has been sent off to look at something at the family's summer house."

"Look at this," Lioe said. She gestured to the screen, heard the repressed excitement in her own voice. "Damn it, how did he get all of this?" The outline was complete— *maybe a little iffy in courtroom eyes, especially when so much of it was gathered netwalking, but certainly enough to use. Enough to blackmail Damian Chrestil with, and enough to make Damian Chrestil willing to do—what? Kill him?* She pushed the thought away. *That seemed the least likely result, if only because a well-known body would be hard to explain, and Chauvelin would be likely to ask awkward questions. But certainly to keep him out of action for a few days. Especially since Damian seemed to be ready to transfer the lachesi to its new "owners."*

"So Na Damian was smuggling lachesi for clients of ji-Imbaoa's," Roscha said, slowly. "I think I worked that pickup."

"I brought it in," Lioe said. "Damn, that's why we had bungee-gars on board. I didn't think red-carpet was worth that much trouble."

Roscha laughed softly. "What a fucking mess. Na Damian is going to be really pissed when he realizes we know what's going on."

"I think he already is," Lioe said, and touched the patches of selfheal starring her face. "That has to be what this was all about." *He was willing to kill me, too—not*

eager, so I suppose I should be grateful, but willing. She
shivered, looked over her shoulder in spite of herself toward
the shuttered window and the locked door. *Which means we
need some kind of a defense, and not just physical.* "You
said Damian Chrestil went off with the Visiting Speaker?"

"It looks like it," Roscha said. "And if N'Ivie's at the
family summer house, then I bet that's where Ransome is.
It's remote enough to keep somebody out of circulation for a
while. Especially with the storm."

Lioe nodded, aware for the first time of the steady slap of
rain against the shutters. Every so often, a stronger gust
smacked against them, a sharp sound like a handful of nails
thrown against the metal plates. "All right," she said.
"How safe are we here?"

Roscha shrugged. "Na Damian has plenty of people in the
port," she said. "If he wants—well, if he doesn't care about
publicity, we're not safe at all."

"How much do you think he cares about publicity?"

"I don't know." Roscha looked back at the screen, at the
careful outline. "If that's what's been going on, it could
mean the governorship. I wouldn't care a whole lot, in his
shoes."

Lioe nodded at the answer she had expected. "Do me a
favor, make sure everything's locked, as secure as you can
make it. And see if Ransome owns any weaponry."

"All right," Roscha said, and sounded faintly dubious.
"But—"

Lioe looked back at the chair, Ransome's working space
inert, invisible around it. "I've got an idea," she said. "And
if it works, we shouldn't need guns."

DAY 2

Ransome waited in the sunken main room, staring at the glass of wine that stood untouched on the table beside him. His back ached with the effort of holding himself relaxed and easy against the chair's thick cushions; he was aware, painfully aware, of the rising noise of the rain and the murmuring conversations among the Chrestil-Brisch thugs standing by the display console. He was equally aware of the woman who held her palmgun with the comfortable stance of the expert, but kept his eyes away from her. The wind howled outside the shutters, and he wondered when the storm would hit its peak. Not that the storm was much of an advantage, but at least it limited their actions as much as his. *And I bet I know what favor ji-Imbaoa wants. Chauvelin warned me I shouldn't push him. The only question is, will Damian Chrestil sell me out?* Ransome smiled then, put the glass to his lips to cover the expression. *And why shouldn't he? If he wins—and he's winning so far—he has nothing to lose.*

"Na Ransome."

It was Damian Chrestil's voice: the younger man moved so quietly that Ransome hadn't heard him approach. He turned, setting the glass aside, contents untasted, forced a calm smile of greeting. "Na Damian."

Damian Chrestil snapped his fingers, and one of the heavy chairs trundled over to join them. At another gesture, the woman with the palmgun withdrew a little, resting her back against the shutters that covered the enormous window. Ji-Imbaoa made a slight, impatient movement of his fingers, but moved away toward the display console and the twin serving carts. Ransome, watching with what he hoped was a convincing show of incurious distaste, saw the other hsaia, ji-Imbaoa's secretary, present a plate of food. Cella said something to him, turned him away toward the shuttered windows. She glanced over her shoulder, and met Ransome's look with a quick, triumphant smile. It was gone almost as soon as he'd seen it, but Ransome felt the chill of it down his spine.

"There are a couple of things we need to get settled," Damian Chrestil said, and Ransome looked back at him a little too quickly.

"If you let me go, give me a ride back to the city and an apology," Ransome said, trying to cover his nervousness, "I suppose I'd be willing to ignore all of this." He gestured with all the grace he could muster to the woman with the gun.

Damian smiled. "That really wasn't what I had in mind."

Somehow I didn't think so. Ransome smiled back, the muscles of his face stiff and unresponsive, felt congestion tugging at his lungs again. He ignored that—*maybe it will go away, ease off on its own the way it sometimes does*—and said aloud, "It's a generous offer."

"So's mine," Damian answered, and the smile vanished abruptly. "I understand from my people that you dumped the contents of a datablock into the nets, into storage somewhere. I want that material."

Ransome spread his hands. "I don't hear an offer."

"Ji-Imbaoa tells me there are still some charges pending in Hsaioi-An," Damian Chrestil said. "He wants you back, to face them. I don't care either way, but I want that data."

Ransome froze, felt himself go rigid, as though he'd been turned to stone. He remembered the hsai courts, the hsaia judge—*"insults from houta are as the barking of dogs; it's fortunate you are of no status"*—most of all the dreary grey padding, walls and floors and ceiling, that was the hsai prison, months and months of grey cells and grey clothes and grey men, and finally the numbing grey fog of the first bout of white-sickness. *That's twice the Chrestil-Brisch have done this to me,* he thought, and could see the same fine shape, Bettis Chrestil's face imposed for an instant on her brother's features. *I can't go back. I don't want to die there, in that grey place.* . . . "If I give you the data," he said slowly, despising himself for the concession, "you won't turn me over to ji-Imbaoa."

Damian nodded.

"What, then? You'll just let me go?" Ransome let his disbelief fill his voice, and caught his breath sharply, just averting a coughing fit. He tasted metal, the tang of it at the back of his throat, and swallowed hard, willing the sickness away.

"Why not?" Damian shrugged with deliberate contempt. "Once the—product—is transferred, there's nothing you can do."

"The lachesi, you mean," Ransome said, and, after a moment, Damian nodded.

"That's right."

"Chauvelin won't be pleased," Ransome said, and Damian shrugged again.

"Chauvelin won't be in a position to do anything about his displeasure for very much longer. The tzu Tsinra-an are losing face by the day, they won't be in power much longer. And then Chauvelin won't be able to do a damn thing to help you."

Ransome sat very still, kept his face expressionless with an effort. It was true; if the tzu Tsinra-an lost their dominant position at the court on Hsiamai, then Chauvelin would go down—*and I'll go with him. I can't go back to Hsaioi-An. I don't want to die there, I know what that would be like, I saw it happen.* He controlled his fear with an effort, made himself reach for the wine. He sipped carefully, but did not really taste the faint sweetness. "So if I tell you where the data is, you won't turn me over to him." He nodded to the Visiting Speaker, still standing by the food carts. "What guarantee do I have that you won't get the data and still hand me over?"

"You don't. But you don't have another choice," Damian Chrestil answered. "I tell you—I'll give you my word—that if you give me the data, you can go free."

"Your word," Ransome said, in spite of himself, remem-

bering Bettis Chrestil. She had given her word, too, and it
had been less than useless. Damian Chrestil gave his sister's
humorless smile.

"I don't care if you believe me or not," he said. "This is
the only deal you've got. Tell me where you stashed the
data, or I'll give you to ji-Imbaoa, now."

It is the only deal, and worse than no choice at all. Ransome stared at him for a long moment, unable to come up
with any alternatives. *Whatever I do, I lose, because I don't
believe him for a second when he says he'll let me go. I'm
only prolonging it, and losing any bargaining power I might
have—but I can't give up without some fight.* "All right," he
said slowly. "I'll retrieve it for you." He hadn't expected
that attempt to work, and was not surprised when Damian
shook his head, refusing the gambit.

"Tell me the codes."

"They're in my loft, in the mail systems there," Ransome
said. "You'll find a message in *n'jao* there, a string of
codes. That accesses the secure storage." Damian frowned,
started to say something, and Ransome held up his hand.
"The program I used, I don't know the access numbers myself, or even where the data ended up. It's a random dump, to
whoever had space open at the time. But the retrieval codes
are in my mailbox."

Damian nodded then, beckoned to one of his people, a
thin woman with a pilot's calluses on her wrists. "Cossi,
you've done this before. I need to get some information out
of his mailbox."

Cossi shrugged. "Can you give me a key?"

"Well?" Damian said.

Ransome hesitated, then reeled off the string of numbers.

"Right, Na Damian," Cossi said, and turned away. Ransome watched her walk to the nearest netlink and settle herself at the workstation. For a crazy moment, he hoped that
she didn't know what she was doing—she was a pilot, after
all—but then he saw the way her hands moved across the
shadowscreens, and that hope died.

He looked away, not wanting to watch, but could still hear
the steady click of the machines as Cossi worked her way
onto the nets. This was it: there was no hope left, and he

could expect to choke to death in a hsai prison. . . . He heard his breath whistling in his lungs, and this time reached for the cylinder of Mist. There was no point in pretending anymore, no point in trying to hide his weakness. He'd played his best hand, and he'd lost. He laid the mask against his face, inhaled the cool vapor. Damian Chrestil watched him, his thin face expressionless. Ransom refolded the mask with deliberate care, and slipped the cylinder back into his pocket.

"Na Damian," Cossi said. "I'm being blocked."

"What?" Damian looked up sharply, frowning.

"I'm being blocked," Cossi said again. "Somebody's pulled that system off-line. There's no way I can access it."

Damian looked back at Ransome, his thin eyebrows drawn into a scowl. "Well? I thought we had a bargain."

Ransome spread his hands, did his best to hide his sudden elation. Someone was in the loft, Chauvelin, maybe, or— better still and most likely—Quinn Lioe. And if Lioe was there, and had changed the system settings, then maybe he had a second chance. "Everything was on-line when I left it. Maybe the storm's knocked it off."

Cossi's hands danced across the multileveled controls. "Nothing else is off, Na Damian. I think someone's reset."

"Lioe," Damian Chrestil said, and Ransome felt the last hope die. "It's Lioe, isn't it? You gave her a key to your loft, and told her what was going on."

Ransome shook his head. "I didn't tell her anything," he lied. "She's a Gamer, and a Republican, at that. She doesn't give a shit about politics."

"You brought her to Chauvelin's party," Damian said, soft and deadly.

Ransome shook his head again. "Yeah, I tried to get her interested in something outside the Game—she's good, too good to be stuck in the Game all her life—but she doesn't care. All she wants to do is play the Game."

There was another little silence, and then Damian Chrestil shook his head. "No. Nobody ignores politics like that."

"Gamers do," Ransome said, desperately.

"Not even Gamers." Damian Chrestil beckoned to Ivie. "Get in touch with your people up at the port. Send some over to Ransome's loft and see what they find." He looked back at Ransome. "I suppose he has security in place, so be careful."

"Fuck you," Ransome said. If Lioe was at the loft, if she had the sense to find the key that would let her retrieve the data—and she must have, if she'd blocked access to the mail system—then there was still a chance. *If Lioe can figure out what to do.* He put that thought aside. There was still nothing he could do but wait, but things were looking fractionally better than they had.

DAY 2

Chauvelin stood at the only unshuttered window, watching the wind-driven rain sweep through his garden. The bell-flower trees bent until their branches dragged along the ground, stirring the human-faced pebbles into new patterns, their flowers blown away in gusts with the wind. A few early flowers were flattened, their petals frayed to nothing against the ground. The clouds streamed in, dark overhead, darker still, almost black, to the south, so that the light was dimmed, filled with an odd, underwater quality. Ransome was not at his loft.

Chauvelin grimaced, annoyed with himself, at his inability to concentrate on anything except that useless fact, and turned away from the window to consider the double-screened workboard that lay on the wide table. Both screens displayed the transcript of the last transmission from Haas, the last that had come in before the transmitter went down for the duration of the storm, a fragmentary, garbled mess that defied the computers. He frowned again, and made himself pick up a stylus, fitting his fingers into the pressure points to change the mode. It was obvious that Haas had found at least some of what he had expected—connections between the je Tsinra-an and the Chrestil-Brisch, clients of the je Tsinra-an who did most of their business through C/B Cie.—but the overall sense of the message was so mangled that there was little he could do. Even the standard phrases certifying Haas's authority and authorizing him to act in her name for the Remembrancer-Duke had come through poorly, though there, at least, they had the Forms of Protocol to fill in the gaps. At least he could use that authority, if he had to.

And maybe he could do more. Ransome was missing; the inquiries he'd put out on the nets had brought no results, and Lioe seemed—said she knew nothing. Ji-Imbaoa certainly knew, certainly held some of the keys to this situation. If the transmission could be edited properly, he could force ji-Imbaoa's household to cooperate with him. He highlighted one section of the message, deleted the intervening words and nonsense, tilted his head to one side to study the result. The phrasing was a little stilted, but no worse than in many official documents. He finished the rest of it, editing carefully, and studied the result. The document now gave him the temporary rank necessary to resume control of the ambassadorial household, and therefore of ji-Imbaoa's household as well, on the grounds that ji-Imbaoa's carefully unspecified actions had cast a shadow on the reputation of his superiors. There was only one problem with using it: ji-Imbaoa would inevitably query it to the Remembrancer-Duke himself, and not enough of the original message survived for Chauvelin to be sure that his patron would back him in such a drastic action. He set the stylus aside, ran his finger over the glowing characters at the foot of the screen, tracing the stylized *n'jao* characters that symbolized Haas's authority. He could use this authority successfully, of that he was quite certain, but possibly at the cost of his career. *Is Ransome worth it?*

Chauvelin sighed, touched controls at the base of the workscreen to produce a paper copy and transfer the original to storage. *Is he? It's taken me most of my life—nearly thirty years—to earn this rank, starting from nothing, as a conscript, less than nothing. Even the strictest hsaia codes acknowledge that it isn't always possible to protect one's protégés.* Flashes of memory broke through his guard: Ransome newly paroled, all in grey still, the canalli brown of his skin faded to ivory; Ransome in his bed, the unexpected, wiry strength of his thin body; Ransome laughing at a party, a handful of birds, the centerpiece of a story egg, dancing in his palm; Ransome sitting on the garden wall, holding out a handful of carved stones. *And Ransome with Lioe, too, the way he watched her.* He picked up the printed sheet, rolled it carefully in the prescribed fashion, concentrating on the task so he wouldn't have to think. *If I use this, and I'm wrong—or even if I'm right and it's inexpedient—I will lose the ambassadorship. And probably my other ranks, too: there will be need to make an example of me. I'm not ready, yet, to make that choice.*

He tucked the cylinder of paper, the ends neatly folded over on themselves, into the pocket of his coat, and turned back to the window. It was raining harder now, hard enough that the rain formed a solid curtain, completely concealing the Old City in the distance below the cliffs, veiling the paths of the lower terrace. A few yard lights glowed through the rain, outlining the steps that led from one plateau to the next. He grimaced, thinking of Ransome's sculptures, and looked away.

"Sia?" Je-Sou'tsian spoke from the doorway, excitement in her voice, and Chauvelin turned sharply.

"Well, Iameis?"

"Sia, I think we've found the Visiting Speaker, or at least traced where he went."

"Good." Chauvelin reached for the cylinder of paper, touched it like a talisman. "Where?"

"He was with Damian Chrestil," je-Sou'tsian said. "He and his people, ji-Mao'ana and Magill, went to the C/B Cie. docks, and they left with him in a flyer. They headed southeast, our informant says, but I can't contact the Speaker at the Chrestil-Brisch palazze." She paused, and made a formal gesture of apology. "I regret we haven't located him more exactly, but I thought you would wish to know."

"So," Chauvelin said softly, and nodded. "Yes, I want to know." *This changes everything. He is acting irresponsibly, and he's dealing with, maybe making a deal with, a houta—Damian Chrestil is still not a person, in the law's view—and this can be construed as dishonoring his patron. That will give me just enough claim to the honorable position that Haas and my lord can afford to protect me.* He slipped the rolled paper from his pocket, touched it to lips and forehead in the ritual gesture. "As you must know, I received a last transmission from maiHu'an before we lost contact with the satellite. In it, I was granted this commission, which I now execute.''

Je-Sou'tsian bowed her head, crossed her hands on her chest, spurs downward, claws turned inward to her own body in ritual submission. ''I will bear witness, sia.''

Chauvelin nodded. ''In it, I am authorized to act as head of household, lesser father, under the authority of the Father-Emperor, father of all clans.'' The ritual phrases came surprisingly easily to his tongue, for all that it had been years since he had last used them. ''This commission supersedes all earlier claims of rank and privilege, and will do so until it is renounced or revoked.''

''I hear, my father,'' je-Sou'tsian said, ''and I witness. And I obey even to the price of my life.''

''So be it,'' Chauvelin said, and laid the rolled paper ceremoniously on the table. ''Now.'' He paused, sorting out what needed to be done. ''I want you to proclaim this to the household. Take a couple of our security people with you, just in case.''

''I don't think the Visiting Speaker's household will cause any trouble,'' je-Sou'tsian said. ''Not all of them are fond of him.''

Chauvelin smiled. ''I can't say I blame them. All right, do what you think is best about security. But I want his rooms searched, particularly for papers, disks, datablocks, anything that could prove the link with Damian Chrestil—also for anything that might tell us where he is. Keep your people on that, as well, highest priority.''

''Yes, sia.'' Je-Sou'tsian paused, seemed about to say something more, then turned and slipped away. Chauvelin stared after her, suddenly aware of the roaring of the wind beyond the window. If he could just find either Ransome or ji-Imbaoa—*when I find them,* he corrected silently, not daring to think of the consequences if he did not—he would have the tools he needed to act. But for now, all he could do was wait.

DAY 2

Lioe walked the Game nets, calling files from the libraries, moving from one familiar nonspace to the next. Images flickered in the air in front of her, bright against the dark shutters; below and to her right, where there was no danger of accidentally intruding into that space, hung Ransome's outline of Damian Chrestil's plan. From time to time she glanced at it, comparing its form to the Game scenario taking place in the working volume in front of her. The basic shape looked good, and she reached for images to complement it, trawling now through less familiar news nets and more sober datafields. She found the images she wanted after some trouble—Damian Chrestil's face, a news scan that covered the arrival of the Visiting Speaker, an old still of Chauvelin, looking younger than he had at the party—and dragged them one by one into space occupied by the *Face/ Body* program. The program considered them and produced a string of numbers; Lioe dragged those numbers into the working volume, and smiled at the result. The images attached to the character templates were not—quite—the original faces, but they were close enough to be recognized, and that was all that mattered. In some ways, it was almost a shame the scenario would never be played, she thought, studying the convolutions that formed a neat, red-branched tree in front of her eyes. *Damian Chrestil's plot makes for a wonderful Game incident. Too bad it's only made for blackmail.*

"No luck finding guns."

Roscha's voice seemed to come from a distance, and Lioe

shook her head, refocusing to look through and past the crowding images. She reached into control space to switch off her vocal link, said to Roscha, "Then there's nothing?"

"Not quite nothing," Roscha said with a lop-sided grin, and slipped a hand into the pocket of her jacket. She brought out a cheap plastic pistol, displayed it with a shrug. "This is mine. On the other hand, it's only six shots, and it's not supposed to be reloadable. I've had it modified, and I've got another magazine, but I don't know how well it will work."

"Wonderful," Lioe said.

"What are you doing?" Roscha asked. She was frowning at the control spaces, as though she was trying to make sense of the carefully focused images.

"My—our—way out," Lioe said. *I hope.* "I've pulled together a Game scenario, merchant-adventurers variant, a *jeu à clef.* I've put this whole situation into a Game—and used their faces—and I'm going to put it on the nets. If Damian Chrestil doesn't back down, leave me alone and let Ransome go, I'm going to let it run. The scenario will show up in four hours—in fact, I think I'll tell Lia Gueremei to expect it—and it will be sent on the internets as well. He'll never get rid of it, and he should have a hard time explaining why it fits what's been going on so extremely closely."

"He will be pissed," Roscha said.

She didn't sound entirely pleased, and Lioe looked sharply at her. "I wasn't thinking," she said. "Look, I don't want to get you into trouble. If you want, you can leave now. I won't mention you."

Roscha looked momentarily embarrassed. "No. I'm not leaving. Who'd watch the door? Anyway, the storm's pretty bad."

"Not that bad," Lioe said, reaching for the nearest weather station reports. Air traffic was not recommended, but the roads were still open.

"I don't want to take the bike, and I'm not leaving it," Roscha said. Face and tone were abruptly serious. "I don't want to leave, Quinn. Don't worry about me."

Lioe stared at her for a moment longer, then slowly nodded. "I'm trusting you," she said.

Roscha smiled, and turned away, settling herself against

the wall by the door. There was an intercom panel there, Lioe noticed, and for the first time became aware of a rush of street sounds—rain and wind on pavement, once in a great while the slow whine of an engine as a heavy carrier crawled along the street—that formed a counterpoint to the sounds from the net. "I've rigged the intercom," Roscha said. "At least that way we can hear them coming."

If they come in the front door, Lioe thought. "Great," she said aloud, and turned her attention back to the images that surrounded her. The scenario was complete, and again, she felt the pang of regret that no one would ever play it. All that remained was to put it on the nets, neatly packaged and ready to unfurl itself four hours from now. She had done this kind of programming before, though only for frivolous reasons, a birthday present, a joke; still, the basic technique remained the same, and the routines she used had proved impervious to the best attempts to corkscrew them open. *At least, they were impervious on Callixte.* She ignored that thought, and reached into the control space for a new set of tools. Ransome's gloves were warm against her hands, the wires tingling gently to confirm each movement.

She set a nonsense algorithm to work, let it spin its hash into the working space, then shaped the jumbled nonsense into a solid plate, turned it back in on itself, so that the algorithm constantly rebuilt, reinforced itself. It formed a virtual capsule that sealed the scenario away from the rest of the nets. She prodded at it, testing the system, and when she was satisfied with its solidity, began the trigger mechanism. The timer was easy, a standard commercial program tied to the algorithm; it would cancel the nonsense run in three hours and fifty-seven minutes. Three minutes later, the last of the nonsense wall would disappear, tidied away by the net's housekeeper routines. At last she finished, and spun the entire structure in virtual space in front of her, shaping the external presentation. The emerging image glittered as it turned, became a shape like a golden dodecahedron, each hexagonal facet marked with her Gamer's mark. That would get people's attention, if nothing else did. If Damian Chrestil didn't capitulate, it, and her growing reputation, would ensure that Gamers would copy the program to every corner of the nets. If he did give in, and she pulled the scenario—*not that hard, since I have the key algorithm; there won't be too many copies to track down*—she would lose a little status, but that was a small price to pay for survival. *And maybe not even that,* she thought suddenly. *Suppose I do what Ransome suggested, float the scenario for Avellar's Rebellion. No one could say I didn't live up to the advertising then. . . .*

But that was for later. She took a deep breath, reached out with her gloved hand, copied the dodecahedron, and shoved it into the place that was the entrance to the nets. It floated away from her, picking up speed as it went, until it vanished in a flash of black. *One away.* She copied the program and scenario again and pushed it out onto the nets, did it again and again until there were at least a dozen copies loose on the nets. Only then did she lean back a little, and reach into control space for the communications system.

She opened a space, but did not drag the connect codes into it, staring at the static-filled volume for a long moment. Then, reluctantly, she reached into the directory, rifling its files for Damian Chrestil, or the family's summer house. She found a code for the latter, and dragged it into the communications space before she could change her mind. There was a long pause, while codes streamed across the space—unusually long, nearly thirty seconds—and then the codes vanished, to be replaced by a man's head and shoulders. It was an unfamiliar, ugly face, white-skinned and broad-featured, and for a crazy instant Lioe thought of giants in the story tapes she'd viewed as a child.

"Can I help you?" the giant asked, in a voice as heavy as his features, and Lioe dragged herself back to the present.

"I want to talk to Damian Chrestil," she said. "My name's Lioe."

The giant closed his mouth over whatever he had started to say, and looked down at something out of the camera's vision. "Just a minute, Na Lioe. I'll see if he's free."

"If you're trying to set up a trace, don't bother," Lioe said. "I'll tell you where I am. I'm in Ransome's loft, and I've found what he found. You can tell Damian Chrestil that, too."

The giant's expression did not change. "I'll do that, Na

Lioe,'' he said, and his face vanished, to be replaced by what was meant to be a soothing hold pattern.

"You heard that," Lioe said over her shoulder, and Roscha answered quickly.

"Yeah. But I haven't heard anybody in the entrance yet."

"If I take too long—" Lioe began, and stopped abruptly. *If he doesn't come to talk, decides to send his people after us instead, what then? I suppose if he doesn't show up in a couple of minutes, I can cut the connection, we can head back to the port, try again from there—*

The communications space cleared abruptly, and she found herself looking at Damian Chrestil. She'd only seen him once before, at Chauvelin's party, and was surprised again at how young he was. *No older than me, if as old. Let's hope I can play this as well as he has.*

"Na Lioe," Damian said. "I'm glad to finally get to talk to you."

"I didn't think talking was what you had in mind."

Damian Chrestil shrugged. "If you'd come quietly . . . But that's old business. What can I do for you?"

"You're holding Ransome," Lioe said bluntly, and hoped she was right. "I want him back."

"You want him?" Damian's face creased suddenly into an urchin's grin. "I didn't think he was yours, too."

Lioe sighed, ostentatiously refraining from an answer.

"I'm afraid that's not possible right away," Damian went on. "I have business in train which I don't intend to see interfered with. Na Ransome will stay with me until it's finished."

"I don't think so," Lioe said. "If he's not released—and if you don't call off the goons you've got chasing me—I will spread this entire business deal onto the nets, Republican as well as Burning Brighter, and into Hsaioi-An if I can manage it."

There was a little silence, and Damian Chrestil said slowly, "I know the nets. I can kill this before it starts."

Lioe shook her head. "Not on the Game nets. The Game nets run different protocols, different rules, they serve a different clientele. I've put a new scenario in motion, Na Damian. It's a merchant-adventurer's variant, primed for release in four hours, and it's based on what you've been trying to do, from smuggling the lachesi to the high politics.'' She reached into her working space, dragged another copy into the communications space, peeled back the shell to reveal the tiny, perfect—and perfectly recognizable—characters contained in its center, held by the red webbing of the scenario's outline. ''All this has to do is come to someone's attention in C-and-I, or, I would imagine, in the Lockwardens or the governor's office, or even back in Hsaioi-An, and you're screwed. And there are enough Gamers in all those places that it's bound to happen.''

Damian Chrestil shook his head. ''Not necessarily. I admit, we may not be able to break that shell, but my people can contain the scenario as soon as it's open. It won't get that far, certainly not far enough to cause me trouble. So let's talk reasonably.''

''Once the scenario's opened, you'll never stop the spread,'' Lioe said. ''You know how Gamers are, we copy things. We share variants we like, sessions we've played, work by people we admire. And my name means something in the Game. Once that shell opens, half the Gamers on the nets will have made a copy for their own use—once they realize it's a *jeu à clef* even more of them will want it. How are you going to stop that, Na Damian?''

There was a little silence, and in it Lioe could hear a kind of choked laughter. *Ransome,* she realized, and hid her delight.

''All right,'' Damian Chrestil said. ''I'm prepared to negotiate. You're not invulnerable, Na Lioe, you crewed the ship that brought the lachesi, and that could be made to look bad for you.''

''Possibly,'' Lioe said.

''Easily enough done,'' Damian Chrestil said. ''But I'm willing to make a deal.'' He did something with controls that were out of her line of sight; an instant later, the view within the communications space widened, so that she was looking into a comfortably furnished room. The wall behind him was black—not a wall at all, she realized abruptly, but the same kind of shutter that covered Ransome's windows. Lioe tugged at the edges of her view, expanded it so that she could see the details more clearly. Half a dozen men and women waited at a polite distance, all in dockers' clothes, tough-looking people who looked like older, less beautiful versions of Roscha. The Visiting Speaker stood a little apart from them, feet planted wide apart, arms crossed on his chest, the fingers of the one visible hand working restlessly. A tiny, pretty woman—*Cella*, she realized—sat on the arm of a chair to the hsaia's right. Ransome was sitting in a comfort-able-looking chair, just outside the pool of amber light from an overhead lamp, but as she watched, he pushed himself to his feet and came to stand by Damian Chrestil. Damian looked over his shoulder, his fine eyebrows drawing to-gether in a frown, but he did not order the other man away.

"Yes, this concerns you, Ransome. Join the party, why don't you?"

"Thanks," Ransome said, and smiled.

Damian Chrestil looked back into the display space. "Since you're not a political animal, Na Lioe, I would as-sume you don't really care whether or not the lachesi gets through to my buyers in Hsaioi-An."

"Or even about your chance of being governor," Ran-some said gently, his eyes fixed on Lioe as though he wanted to convey a message.

Lioe nodded. "All I care about is your goons off my back, a job to go back to, and Ransome's freedom. That's pretty simple, Na Damian."

"I can perhaps do better," Damian Chrestil said. He paused, not looking back over his shoulder toward the Visit-ing Speaker, but the hsaia straightened anyway, both hands now poised to display claws and wrist spurs.

"We have an agreement, Damian Chrestil," ji-Imbaoa said. "If you fail to honor it—"

Damian turned on him. "You haven't yet done what you and I agreed. I'll fulfill my contracts, all right—this time—but you can go to hell." Behind him, the flat-faced giant made a gesture, and the dockers shifted position suddenly, so that they encircled the Visiting Speaker and his staff. Cella slipped easily from her place, out of the armed ring. The jericho-human made an abortive grab for a weapon hidden under his coat, and a thin woman leveled her palmgun at him.

"Enough, Magill," ji-Imbaoa said, and looked at Damian. "Very well. I have no choice. But I will ruin you for this. You and yours will never do business in Hsaioi-An again—"

Ransome said something then, in hsai, not tradetalk, and the Visiting Speaker was abruptly silent, hunching into himself as though into feathers. Ransome looked back into the communications space. "As I said to him, Chauvelin may be able to offer other connections, Na Damian. You see, I'm willing to negotiate, too."

"But will Chauvelin?" Damian Chrestil asked.

"Ask him," Ransome answered.

There was a little silence, and Lioe, still held in the chair's gentle embrace, the nets wound around her like a cocoon, held her breath. If this could work, if they could come up with a bargain—

"Be my guest," Damian Chrestil said, and gestured to the controls.

"Traitor," ji-Imbaoa said, almost conversationally, and turned his back on them all.

Ransome grinned, and reached for the control spaces. Static fuzzed a tiny circle at the edge of Lioe's viewing volume. She winced, and looked away from it, but did not adjust her own controls. An image formed, slowly at first, then flicked completely into adjustment. Chauvelin looked out at them, one eyebrow raised in arrogant question, and Lioe tugged at the image until it was as large as the other.

"Na Chauvelin," Damian Chrestil said, with a fleeting and twisted smile.

"Na Damian," Chauvelin acknowledged. "What interesting company you keep." He looked at Ransome. "I've been looking for you, I-Jay. I trust you're well?"

Ransome nodded. "Well enough."

Damian Chrestil cleared his throat. "I think we've achieved stalemate," he said. "Each of us has something the others want, and, thanks to you, Na Lioe, we have a time constraint as well."

"How so?" Both of Chauvelin's eyebrows rose.

"I've put a new Game scenario onto the nets," Lioe said bluntly. "In four hours—less that that, now—it'll be released, and every Gamer on the nets will want a copy. It's a *jeu à clef,* Ambassador, based on Na Damian's deal with the Visiting Speaker. If Damian Chrestil doesn't back off, guarantee my safety and let Ransome go, I'll let it run." She paused, couldn't resist adding, "I do think it will play."

Chauvelin was silent for a moment, his face expressionless, then looked at Ransome. "Will it work?"

"It's fucking brilliant," Ransome answered, and the amusement in his voice had a slight note of hysteria. "Oh, it'll work, all right, no question."

A faint expression of distaste flickered across Chauvelin's face, vanished as he looked back at Lioe. "I wish you had seen fit to trust me with this information, Na Lioe."

"Why the hell should I?" Lioe retorted. "I'm a Republican, you're hsaia—and I don't know you. Why should I trust my neck to you?"

"If I may interrupt," Damian Chrestil said. "I think I can offer us all a way out."

"Why not?" Lioe said, and heard Ransome laugh.

Chauvelin said, "Go on."

"Na Lioe says she wants to be left alone—my goons off your back, you said, and your job to go to. And Ransome back, which is what Na Chauvelin wants, too." Damian Chrestil looked directly at Chauvelin, his voice gone suddenly deadly cold. "Am I right in thinking you'd also like to see the Visiting Speaker's influence curbed a little, N'Ambassador?"

Chauvelin nodded once.

"Then this is what I'm offering," Damian Chrestil said. "You, N'Ambassador, will allow this shipment to proceed. Neither you nor Na Ransome will interfere with it—why should you care what happens to my money and clients, so long as ji-Imbaoa, and the je Tsinra-an, are taken down a few notches? In return, I won't act for the Visiting Speaker, or ask any awkward questions about his disgrace. As for you, Na Lioe, I want you to withdraw this scenario of yours, and to keep quiet about all of this. And I'd like you to stay away from Republican C-and-I at least until the statute of limitations runs out on any possible smuggling charges from that direction.''

I'm a pilot. That's impossible. Lioe started to protest aloud, but Damian Chrestil held up his hand.

''In return, I'm willing to offer you my sponsorship to remain on Burning Bright, as a citizen. I daresay you can find work as a notable, in the Game clubs, but if you can't, or if you don't want to—if you want to follow Ransome's example—I'll provide you with a stipend, to continue until the statute runs out.''

To stay on Burning Bright. To live as a notable, as a Gamer, my income guaranteed . . . Lioe took a deep breath, fighting for calm. This was the last thing she had expected, something outside of all possibility, that she would play this game, and win, and be offered this reward.

''That's very good, Damian,'' Chauvelin said, and there was real admiration in his voice.

''Thank you. I think it serves all our needs,'' Damian Chrestil said.

Maybe not mine, Lioe thought, indignant. *There's my piloting—I like my work—and, my God, there's Kerestel. I can't just leave him without warning.* But there were plenty of pilots in the replacement pool, good ones, too. It was not impossible, not impossible at all. *Will he keep his word? Will I find his goons still on my tail, or wake up dead some morning? Do I care? I could stay on Burning Bright, stay in the Game; most of all, if Ransome will teach me—and I think he will—I can see what else there is, beyond the Game. He and I can put an end to the Game, and see what happens then.*

''I can agree to this,'' Chauvelin said.

Damian nodded. ''Na Lioe?''

She nodded, slowly. ''I agree. But I want the money.''

''Wise move,'' Ransome said. He was smiling again, without amusement. ''And I'll agree, because the rest of you do. But you owe me something for it, Damian.''

Damian Chrestil shook his head. ''No. You're getting something already. You're getting yourself an apprentice, someone you can pass your skills to before you die. I think that's reward enough for anyone.''

There was another silence, and Lioe held her breath, sure

that Ransome would reject the offer, reject the reminder that he was going to die—*reject me*. Then, quite slowly, Ransome's smile changed, became more real. "You are good, Damian," he said.

"I'm not Bettisa," Damian Chrestil answered, and there was an odd regret in his voice, as well as certainty. There was a little pause, and Ransome nodded.

"All right. I'll agree."

Lioe let out the breath she had been holding, leaned back and let the chair tilt with her, the images moving around her to hold their relative positions. It was done, it would work— *and I will stay on Burning Bright, and in the Game. And I'll have my chance, at last, to do something no one will want to change.*

DAY 2

Damian Chrestil watched the net symbols fade and then the flicker of lights and symbols as the communications console shut itself down. It was the best he could do—*not very good,* he acknowledged silently, but at least he would be able to salvage something from the mess. *And I won't have to deal with ji-Imbaoa anymore.* He turned away from the machine, did his best to ignore Ransome, watching with his sly smile from the sidelines, and beckoned to Ivie. The flat-faced man came over quickly, his hands still curled in his pockets, caressing at least one weapon.

"Na Damian?"

Ivie was well trained, Damian thought sourly, but no one was well trained enough to keep from sounding just a little uncertain about this situation. "Escort the Visiting Speaker into the game room," he said. "And take his people with him. Be sure you search the jericho-human, though."

"A pleasure," Ivie answered, and turned away. He sounded confident enough once he'd been given something definite to do, Damian thought, and touched his remote to summon the drinks cart. He busied himself with its contents, careful to keep it and himself out of the way of Ivie's people, and saw without really looking that Cella and Ransome were being equally cautious. Cella stood well apart from the rest, still with a drink untasted in her hand, her expression remotely interested, as though she were watching someone else's Game. Damian read disapproval in her face, and looked away from it. On the far wall, the weather screen flickered soundlessly, showing the storm from various perspectives. He could hear the wind even through the heavy shutters, a numbing, constant wail that rose and fell monotonously. Out of the corner of his eye he saw Ivie say something to the Visiting Speaker, too soft and polite to be heard. Ji-Imbaoa tossed his head angrily, turning away as though he would have preferred to ignore the security specialist, and Damian Chrestil braced himself to intervene. Then, abruptly, ji-Imbaoa's resistance vanished; he made a curt gesture of agreement, and followed Ivie toward the door. Two of the guards followed, polite but obtrusive in their armed presence. The rest stayed behind, the thin woman still with her palmgun drawn and leveled at Magill. There was a little pause, and then Magill shook his head, and lifted his hands, surrendering to a search. At the woman's gesture, he and the hsaia secretary moved slowly toward the door.

"Neatly done," Ransome said. He was still smiling, but the expression was less sly, more conscious of his own failures.

Damian Chrestil ignored the irony, said, "Thank you." He was very aware of Cella's lifted eyebrow, and went on almost at random, "Make yourself comfortable."

"Consider myself a guest?" Ransome asked.

"If you must."

"Chauvelin will be grateful." Ransome pushed himself up off the arm of the chair, moved slowly across the room to stare at the weather screen. "I don't suppose there's any chance of getting back into the city."

"I wouldn't send my people out in this," Damian answered with some asperity. "You'll have to wait it out with the rest of us."

Ransome nodded, his attention still on the screen. Cella set her drink aside very precisely, and came to stand between Damian and the other man, so close that Damian could smell the faint sweetness of her perfume.

"May we talk, Damiano?"

The very reasonableness of her tone was a warning of sorts. "Of course," Damian said, and moved back into the corner of the room, far enough away from the screen that an ordinary speaking voice would not be overheard. He leaned against the side of one of the heavy chairs, still not quite willing to turn his back on Ransome, and Cella leaned close, her hip against his knee, one hand on the chair, just brushing against his thigh. They would look intimate from a distance, Damian knew, and wished for a fleeting instant that that was all she wanted.

"Are you going to go through with this?" Cella asked. She kept her voice down, but the anger was perfectly clear under the conversational surface.

Damian Chrestil eyed her for a moment, biting back his answering anger—*all the more unreasonable because I know what you're really saying, that I backed down, that I let Chauvelin win*—and said, "It's the best bet, Cella. Better odds than anything else."

"Changing horses is never a good bet," Cella answered. "The Visiting Speaker's still got power, why not stick with him? Why the hell go with Chauvelin?" She glanced over her shoulder, a quick, betraying tilt of the head toward Ransome, still staring at the screen. "And him?"

"For God's sake, Cella," Damian said. "Because ji-Imbaoa is unreliable, and because Chauvelin's winning right now."

"The je Tsinra-an have the power at court," Cella said. "I know that, I did the research for you. They're going to win in the long term, not the tzu line. You should stick with them."

"It's a little late for that."

"I could persuade him," Cella said. "I could tell him it was a bluff—"

"*Sha-mai!*" Damian Chrestil pushed her away, pushed himself up off the chair in a single motion, heedless of Ransome's frankly curious stare. "Look, Cella, I've told you what I'm doing, which is more than is really your business. You're very good at the Game, but this is reality. This is what I am going to do—this is the only thing I can do, the only way I can keep even this much—and I don't need your baroque variations to complicate it." He took a deep breath, regained his composure with an effort. "If you want to help out, yes, by all means, keep the Visiting Speaker happy. But stay out of my politics."

Cella looked at him, her face stiff and hard as a Carnival

mask, her careful makeup bright as paint against a sudden angry pallor. "I can—keep him happy—if that's what you want, yes."

"I don't really give a fuck," Damian Chrestil answered, and turned away.

"Certainly, Na Damian," Cella said, with the sweet subservience that never failed to infuriate him, and swept away toward the door.

Ransome watched without seeming to do so, all too aware of the tone if not all the words of the conversation. It was the losers who watched and listened like this, prisoners, servants, *houta. . . . Well, I've been all of those, and born canalli besides.* He fixed his attention on the screen as Cella stalked past him and disappeared into the hallway. *I can't say I'm sorry she's been taken down a peg or two.*

In the screen, waves rose and beat against the wet black metal of the storm barriers, the image dimmed and distorted by the blowing rain and the drops that ran down the camera's hooded lens. It shivered now and then, as the wind shook the shielded emplacement. The first line of barriers was almost engulfed, foam boiling against and over it; the second and third, farther up the channel, were more visible, but a steady swell still pounded against them. Ransome watched impassively, remembering what conditions would be like on the Inland Water. Even with all the barriers up, the water would be rough—the Lockwardens would have to let some of the tides through, or risk damage to the generators that powered the city and, if things got bad enough, to the barriers themselves—and the water level would be rising along the smaller canals. He had grown up on a low-lying edge of the Homestead Island District, could remember struggling with his parents to get the valuables out to higher ground without any of the neighbors finding out that they had anything worth stealing; remembered how they had piled what they couldn't carry onto the shelves that ran below the ceilings, hoping that the roof would stay intact and the water wouldn't rise too high. And hoping, too, that the overworked Lockwardens from the local station would remember to keep an eye on the block. He glanced at the controls, touched a key to superimpose the chronometer reading on the screen: still almost an hour to actual sunset, but the image in the screen was already as dark as early evening. The winds were high, but steady for now: *all in all,* he thought, *not a bad time for looting.* There would be a few bad boys in the Dry Cut and Homestead who would be risking it.

"Where's that from, Warden's East?" Damian Chrestil asked. He had come up so silently that the other hadn't been aware of his presence until he spoke.

"I think so," Ransome answered, and found himself glad of the distraction. He glanced sideways, saw the younger man still scowling faintly, not all the marks of ill temper smoothed away. *Still pissed at Cella,* he thought. *And I can't say I blame him.*

Damian Chrestil slipped a hand into his pocket, obviously reaching for a remote, and a moment later the image in the screen vanished, to be replaced by a false-color overview of the storm itself. Distinct bands of cloud curved across the city, outlined in dotted black lines beneath the flaring reds and yellows of the storm; more bands were visible to the south, but there was still no sign of the eye.

"Heading right for us," Damian Chrestil said.

"We should be here some hours," Ransome agreed, and had to raise his voice a little to be heard over the noise of the rain. Something thudded heavily against the shutters, and they both glanced toward the source of the sound, Damian Chrestil vividly alert for a second before he'd identified and dismissed the noise.

"Not too many trees around here, I hope," Ransome said, with delicate malice, and Damian's mouth twisted into a wry smile.

"Let's take a look." He worked the remote again, and the picture shifted—tapping into the house systems, Ransome realized. At least one camera was useless, its lens completely obscured by the blowing rain, so that it showed only wavering streaks of grey. Damian flicked through three more cameras, so quickly that Ransome barely had time to recognize the images—a rain-distorted view of the lawn, a camera knocked out of alignment by the wind, so that it showed only the corner of the house and a patch of wind-blown grass, more rain sweeping in heavy curtains across a

stone courtyard—and stopped as abruptly as he'd begun.
"Ah."

The camera was looking away from the wind, Ransome
realized, looking inland toward the Barrier Hills and the
low-lying trees that grew along their wind-scoured shoulders. The nearest trees were perhaps thirty meters away, up a
gentle slope. They were bent away from the house, into the
hillside, their leaves tossing wildly, thick trunks bent into a
steady arc. Ransome winced, and even as he watched, one of
the trees fell forward, quite slowly, a tangle of roots pulling
free of the wet ground. The silent fall was disconcerting,
eerie, and he looked away.

"What a lovely place to spend a storm."

Damian Chrestil shrugged, smiling slightly. "It's stood
worse."

"It wasn't the house I was worried about."

Damian shrugged again, and his smile widened. "The
odds look good to me."

And you're such a judge of that. The comment was too
double-edged, too easily turned against himself, and Ransome kept silent, though he guessed that the other had read
the thought in his eyes. He turned away from the screen,
went over to the drinks cart, and poured himself another
glass of the sweet amber wine. "Do you want anything?"

Damian Chrestil looked momentarily surprised, but then
flipped the screen back to one of the city channels, and came
to join him. "Yes, thanks, you can pour me a glass of that."

Ransome filled another of the long-stemmed glasses,
handed it to Damian Chrestil, and they stood for a moment
in an almost companionable silence. Something else fell
against the shutters, a lighter thump and then a skittering, as
though whatever it was had been dragged across the rough
surfaces. Damian Chrestil glanced quickly toward the noise,
and looked away again. He was a handsome man, Ransome
thought, attractive in the same fine-boned, long-nosed way
that his sister Bettisa had been, with the same quick response
to the unexpected. And it was good to see a man who knew
better than to follow an unflattering fashion. *And sex is the
last weapon of the weak. Not that that's stopped me before.*
He looked back at Damian Chrestil, allowed himself a quick

and calculated smile, and was not surprised when the other's smile in return held a certain interest. *But I'm bored, and he is—less than fastidious, at least by reputation. Not very flattering, I suppose. But it's better than doing nothing.*

DAY 2

Lioe lay on Ransome's neatly made bed, one arm thrown over her eyes to block the light from the main room. The walls trembled now and then in the gusts of wind; she could feel the vibration through the mattress, through the heavy wood of the bed frame. The shutter that protected the single narrow window had jammed before it quite closed off the view, and she had left it there rather than risk damaging the mechanism. The glass had seemed heavy enough, and on this side of the building, overlooking the cliff edge, there had seemed little chance that anything would blow through it. Now, feeling the building shake, she was not so sure, and looked sideways under the crook of her elbow, at the hand-span gap between the shutter and the bottom of the frame. She could see only the sky and the rain, the slate-colored clouds periodically dimmed by sheets of water blown almost horizontally past the window. She had never seen anything like this before, could not believe how tired she felt, tired of the tension, the dull fear at the pit of her stomach. Storms on Callixte were just as dangerous, maybe more so; but they swept in out of the plains with a few minutes' warning, and were over almost as quickly. There was none of the anticipation—days of anticipation—that preceded Burning Bright's storms, and certainly nothing she'd ever been through had prepared her for the steady, numbing fear. And the worst of it was that she had nothing to do—there was nothing she could do to face the storm, and nothing in the Game seemed worthwhile compared to its massive force. Once she had pulled the copies of the *jeu à clef* off the nets, there was nothing to distract her.

A noise from the street brought her bolt upright, heart pounding, an enormous ripping sound and then a crash. Roscha's voice came indistinctly from the main room. "What the hell—?"

Lioe went to join her, found the other woman standing by the main door, her head cocked to one side. The working space was opened, and the air around Ransome's chair was filled with Game images. "What was it, do you know?"

"Outside," Roscha answered. She worked the locks. "Only one way to find out."

Lioe nodded. Roscha slid back the last bolt, and eased back the heavy door. The wind caught them both by surprise, a gust of cold, wet air snapping past them into the room.

"I didn't hear a window," Lioe began.

"Sha-mai," Roscha said. "The stairway's gone."

"The stairway?" Lioe repeated, foolishly, and Roscha edged back into the loft.

"See for yourself."

Lioe leaned past her, blinking a little as the full force of the wind hit her. The short hall looked different, wrong somehow, and then she realized that the stairs were indeed gone, ripped away from the side of the building, the door hanging crooked by a single hinge. Even as she watched, another gust of wind set the door swinging, and the groan of the hinge pulling still farther out of the wall was loud even over the noise of the storm.

"The wind must've caught it just right," Roscha said.

"Is there anything we should do?" Lioe asked. She looked up and down the hall as she spoke, wondering if any of the other tenants were around, glanced back to see Roscha shrug.

"I don't know what. I don't see any sheet-board, or anything like that, and I can't see that a little rain's going to hurt this floor. There's probably a maintenance staff around somewhere, anyway."

"Probably," Lioe agreed. She was certainly right about the damage: the battered tiles had been peeling away from the floor long before the storm started. She stepped back into the loft, and Roscha pushed the door closed again. She had

to work against the weight of the wind, and Lioe leaned
against it too, to help the bolts go home.

The Game shapes were still dancing in the air around Ransome's chair. Lioe glanced idly at them, frowned, and
looked more closely. Damian Chrestil's face seemed to leap
out at her from among the busy images. "What's all this?"
she asked, and turned to see Roscha looking at her with a
mix of defiance and embarrassment. There was a little pause
before the other woman spoke.

"I was trying to remake your scenario, the one you threw
together. It was too good to waste—too good to waste on
blackmail."

Lioe ignored the deliberately provocative word. "I made
a deal," she said. "You could get all three of us killed, you,
me, and Ransome."

Roscha looked away. "I wasn't going to run it as it stood,
I was going to make a lot of changes. Enough to make a difference, I think—I know." She faced Lioe again, scowling
now. "You can't stop me."

Lioe looked at her for a long moment, weighing her options. *No, I probably could stop you. I've got the influence
on the Game nets, and I'm probably better on the nets than
you are—and Ransome will help me—but that only works
for a while. I'd have to watch you like a hawk, and I don't
have the time or the inclination to do that.* "Maybe not,"
she said aloud, "but the scenario shouldn't run, regardless of
my deal. It doesn't belong in this Game."

Roscha's frown deepened, her expression faintly interested as well as suspicious. "Why not?"

"Because this Game is over."

Roscha opened her mouth to protest, and Lioe lifted an
eyebrow at her, daring her to continue. The other woman
said nothing, and Lioe felt a thrill of excitement at the small
victory, a small, sweet pleasure at a good beginning. Was
this what Chauvelin felt, this sure power? She swept on, not
wanting to lose her moment.

"Yes, this Game is ending. The scenario I've been running is the start of it, a bigger scenario that's going to tie
everything together, all the bits and pieces, and bring this
Game to a solid conclusion, all the lines resolved in a single

grand structure. And no one, ever, is going to be able to play with it again without knowing that it's ended.'' She had not realized, until then, how important that had become to her, to write one thing, create one scenario, that could never be changed—that no one would want to change. She went on more slowly, speaking now as much to herself as to Roscha, and heard both certainty and seduction in her tone. ''It's gotten stale, it's too predictable right now. We've all felt it. So it's time to start over, begin a new Game. And that's where this scenario—'' she nodded to the dancing images, to the faces of Chauvelin and Damian Chrestil hanging in the air beside the working chair—''it and lots of others like it— that's where they come in. We can remake the Game so that it's something real, not just a distant reflection of reality, but something that changes, comments on, reshapes what's really going on. That's the Game your scenario belongs in, don't you see? Someplace where it will matter.''

Roscha looked warily at her, the frown gone, replaced by a look of uncertainty that made her look suddenly years younger, almost a child again. ''I don't play politics—''

''You could. In this Game, you could.'' Lioe smiled, suddenly, fiercely happy, the storm forgotten. ''We both can. It won't be *jeu à clef* any more, that's too easy. We can set it up so that it's an integral part of the Game, so that you can't escape it—so that no one who plays, and no one who sees the Game, hears about it, can avoid what we're doing. That's what we need, to keep us honest. To make it real.''

''That's what you need, maybe.'' Roscha shook her head. ''I'm not that good.''

''Then you'd better learn.''

There was a little silence between them, the wind a rough counterpoint, and then Roscha threw back her head and laughed. ''You're right, and I'll do it. *Sha-mai,* what a chance!''

I knew you would. Lioe hid that certainty, looked again at the busy workspace. ''Let's get on with it, then.'' She reached for the nearest of Ransome's gloves, started to draw them on.

Roscha nodded, and moved toward the other controls. ''One thing, though.''

Lioe stopped, one hand half into the thin mesh. "What?"

"A favor."

"If I can."

"I want to play the last scenarios." Roscha's face was utterly serious. "The ones that wrap this up, I mean. I want to be a part of that, too. It's—I think someone in the new Game should have been part of the old one, that's all."

I was part of the old Game. Lioe stopped short, the moment of indignation fading. *But not like her. I was looking for something else, something better, even when I didn't know it. I never was wholly part of it, no matter how hard I tried.* She said aloud, "I wouldn't have it any other way."

Roscha looked at her for a long moment, then nodded, appeased. Lioe nodded back, and reached into the control space to turn the images to herself. For a moment, she saw Roscha webbed in the Game shapes, tangled with the visible templates, and then the images sharpened, and she turned her attention to the double task of ending the old Game and creating the new:

DAY 2

The room was dark and chill under the eaves, the roof and walls trembling under the lash of the wind. Damian Chrestil burrowed close to Ransome's warmth, dragging the found blanket up over his shoulders, and wondered if it was time to leave. In the darkness Ransome's face was little more than a pale blur, but he could guess at the expression, sleepy and sated, and suspected that it matched his own. Something, not a solid object, just the wind itself, slammed the side of the house with a noise like a great drum. Damian winced, and felt Ransome shift against him, startled by the sound.

"Perhaps a downstairs room would have been wiser."

Damian shrugged, the coarse cloth of the mattress cover rasping against his shoulders. "But not nearly as private."

Even in the dark, he could see Ransome's grin. "Since when did you care about discretion, Na Damian?"

Damian Chrestil sighed. Clearly the brief truce was over—*if you could call it a truce, more like a whole different episode, something out of the Game, completely unrelated to the politics downstairs*. It had surprised him, how alike they were in bed. But that was finished. He sat up, letting the blanket slide down to his hips, and then made himself stand up, bracing himself for the other's acid comment. Ransome was watching, but idly, the blanket drawn up over his shoulder. Damian finished dressing—*not too undignified, this time, no scrambling into clothes*—and glanced back, curious. Ransome was sitting up now, hunched over a little, one hand pressed against his chest. Even as Damian frowned and opened his mouth to speak, the imagist began to cough.

Damian winced at the sound, harsh and painful even over the noise of the wind.

Ransome waved him away, got his breathing under control with an effort that seemed even more painful than the cough.

"Are you all right?" Damian asked, and did his best to keep his tone neutral. *Of course he's not all right. But that's the only thing I can ask.*

Ransome nodded, took a careful breath, and when he spoke, his voice sounded almost normal. "I'll be fine. Your thugs took my medicines, though."

"You left them," Damian said, and after a moment Ransome nodded, conceding.

"Whatever."

"Shall I have someone bring them to you?" Damian asked.

Ransome shook his head. "I'll be all right." He still didn't move, and Damian watched him warily, until at last the other man straightened. Damian Chrestil turned away, heading down the darkened hall to the stairs.

The lights of the main room seemed very bright after the darkened upper level, and he stood for a moment in the doorway to let his eyes adjust. The Visiting Speaker was back, sitting in a chair by the weather screen, a service cart drawn close beside him. Even as Damian saw him, and frowned, ji-Imbaoa rose to his feet and went to peer into the screen, the false-color image tinting his gray skin. Ivie said something to one of the men, and came quickly to join his employer.

"I'm sorry, Na Damian, but it seemed best to separate him from his security. And Na Cella's been keeping an eye on him."

Damian nodded slowly, accepting the logic of the statement. "Good enough. But watch him."

"He seems—calmer—now," Ivie said. "Na Cella's been talking to him."

Damian nodded again. Cella was sitting a little apart from the Visiting Speaker, just outside the loose ring of Ivie's security, but as he caught her eye, she rose to her feet and came

to join them, smiling gently. *I just hope she's over her snit.*
"Thanks, Almarin. He looks—at least resigned."

Ivie nodded and turned away, accepting his dismissal.
Cella said, "He still thinks he has a hand to play."

"Pity he's in the wrong game," Damian said, and was
pleased to see Cella's smile widen briefly.

"Maybe so. But I thought I should tell you."

"Thanks." There was a sound in the doorway behind
him, and Damian turned to see Ransome making his entrance, jerkin thrown loose over one shoulder. As he moved
past into the room, Damian could hear the faint rattle of his
breathing. He smiled at Cella, knowing, confident, but his
eyes slid away instantly, looking for the red-painted cylinder.

"Over there?" Cella said, and pointed to a table against
the wall just beyond the weather screen.

Ransome nodded, and started toward it, brushing past the
nearest of Ivie's people. He had to pass quite close to the
Visiting Speaker, who was still staring at something in
the weather screen, and as he did, ji-Imbaoa turned suddenly
into him, uncovered wrist spur striking for his throat.
Damian saw the look of shocked surprise on Ransome's face
as he lifted one arm in an instinctive, futile counter, and then
the spur sliced into and past the imagist's wrist, hooking him
like a fish through the cords of his neck. Ji-Imbaoa struck
again before the other could pull free, the second spur and
the clawed fingers slashing deep into Ransome's belly, and
then he'd freed both spurs and Ransome was falling, still
with the look of surprise frozen on his face.

"Kill him," Damian Chrestil said instinctively, and Cella
cried, "No!" Her voice rode through Damian's, checking
security's immediate response. Ivie glanced back over his
shoulder, flat face blank in shock and confusion, and ji-Imbaoa stepped back from Ransome's body, holding up his
bloody spurs in an oddly fastidious gesture.

"I am not under your jurisdiction. He was *min-hao*. This
was between my honor and him."

Damian hesitated, knowing that the moment for action
had already passed—had maybe never happened, the Visit-

ing Speaker had been so quick in his attack. "Self-defense," he said anyway, and ji-Imbaoa shook his head.

"Who would believe it? All the witnesses are yours."

"Na Damian?" Ivie asked.

Ransome was none of mine. I would have sold him before. And I don't know what to do. Damian said, "Cossi—?" The pilot had some medical training, he remembered.

Cossi slid the useless blackjack—her only weapon, Damian guessed—back into her pocket with a look almost of embarrassment, and went to kneel beside Ransome's body. She turned him over gently, long fingers probing at the wounds. Damian Chrestil winced and looked away. The pilot shook her head.

"Not a chance. Not even at the city hospitals."

I didn't think there was. Damian took a deep breath, looked back at the Visiting Speaker. "No," he said aloud, "it's not my jurisdiction. But it is Na Chauvelin's, and I expect—I'm certain—he will handle this appropriately. In the meantime—" He looked at Ivie. "Find someplace small, secure, no windows. Lock him in there, and keep him there until we hand him over to the ambassador."

Ivie nodded. "There's a storeroom that will do." He gestured to his people, who moved warily toward the Visiting Speaker, guns drawn.

Ji-Imbaoa looked at them, gestured disdainfully with his bloody hands. "This has nothing to do with you," he said, and one of Ivie's men hissed at the contempt in the hsaia's voice. "I have no quarrel with you."

"Go with them, then," Damian Chrestil said, well aware of the edge of fury still in his voice, and ji-Imbaoa nodded with maddening calm.

"I will do so."

Ivie's people still circled the hsaia, and Damian wished, fiercely, futilely, that he would try something, anything, that would give Ivie an excuse to act.

"This way," Ivie said, and gestured with the muzzle of his palmgun. Ji-Imbaoa nodded again, and followed him from the room.

Damian looked back at Ransome's body, sprawled now on its back in a pool of blood—*not as much as I'd expected, but then, I guess he died quick*—empty eyes staring up at the ceiling. Cossi saw him looking, and reached across to close the imagist's eyes.

"What do you want me to do with him, Na Damian?" she asked.

I don't know. Very God, I have to tell Chauvelin. Damian Chrestil took a deep breath, still staring at Ransome's body. *Not an hour ago we were in bed together—not an hour ago he was fucking me.* The room smelled of blood and shit. "Leave him for now," he began, and Cella spoke softly.

"What about one of the upstairs rooms?"

Damian looked at her blankly for a moment, then, in spite of himself, in spite of everything, smiled. "Well, he would've appreciated the irony." He looked at Cossi. "Yes, take him upstairs—get one of Ivie's people to help you. And then get a housekeeper running, get that cleaned up."

"Right, Na Damian," Cossi said.

And I will speak with Chauvelin. Damian took a deep breath, bracing himself. *Ransome dead isn't so bad, it's how he died, and where—that he died in my house when I'd made a deal with Chauvelin to keep him safe. The question now is, can I persuade Chauvelin that I didn't do it, that I didn't break our deal? And is there any way I can persuade him to turn this death to his advantage?* He shook his head, sighing. *Anyone but Ransome, that might have worked, but not when it was Chauvelin's lover. Very God, I haven't even thought of Lioe.* He pushed the thought away. *One thing at a time,* he told himself, and turned to the communications console.

DAY 2

Chauvelin had come away from the windows when the wind
got bad, waited now in one of the smaller rooms that overlooked the gardens, his back to the shuttered windows and
the storm. The walls, dark red trimmed with gold, gleamed
in the warm light; he could not feel the household generators
whirring on standby through the thick carpet, but a glance at
the monitor board told him they were ready should city
power fail. He glanced away, took a few restless steps toward the door and then back again to the desk, looking down
at the files glowing in the display surfaces. The first draft of
his formal letter to the Remembrancer-Duke waited in the
main screen, ready to be transcribed into *n-jao* script, but he
could not make himself concentrate on its careful phrases.
Damian Chrestil had given him the excuse he had needed to
break ji-Imbaoa's power. If he and the Remembrancer-Duke
played the game right, the incident could have effects as far
away as Hsiamai and the All-Father's court itself. At the
very least, the je Tsinra-an would lose face over this, a
Speaker for the court embroiled in common commerce,
tripped up by a smuggling scheme: a more than acceptable
outcome. And that didn't take into account the effects on
Burning Bright itself. Chauvelin smiled, savoring the double
victory. At the very least, Damian Chrestil would not
become governor in the next elections, nor the ones after
that; at best, he would never be governor, and the tzu Tsinra-
an would not have to contend with an ally of the je Tsinra-an
in control of Burning Bright. *And I may still be able to keep
some hold over Damian Chrestil, even after all of this is
over. That would be the best of all.*

A chime sounded in the desktop, and he reached to answer it, touching the flashing icons. ''Yes?''

''I'm sorry to disturb you, sia,'' je-Sou'tsian said, ''but it's Na Damian. He says it's urgent.''

''Put him through,'' Chauvelin said, and felt the fear cold in his stomach. *Something's gone wrong*— The picture took shape in the desktop, blotting out the open files, and Damian Chrestil looked out at him, his face strained and white.

''N'Ambassador.''

''What's happened?'' Chauvelin asked, suspecting already, dreading the answer. In the screen behind Damian Chrestil, out-of-focus shapes bent over another shape crumpled on the floor.

''I'm sorry,'' Damian Chrestil said. ''Ransome's dead.''

I knew it. Chauvelin bit back anger, the instinct that would have had him calling out the garrisons on Iaryo, on Hsiamai, to launch the missile strike that would obliterate the summer house and everyone, everything, in it. . . . ''How?''

''The Visiting Speaker,'' Damian said baldly. He was telling it badly, and he knew it. ''He attacked him. Ransome went past him, to get his medicine, and the Speaker attacked him. He was killed almost instantly.''

''Like hell,'' Chauvelin said. ''I-Jay wasn't that stupid, he would never have gone within reach—'' *But he might have,* the cold voice of logic whispered at the back of his mind. *Ransome never did fully appreciate just how much that clan line hated him. And he always underestimated ji-Imbaoa.*

''It was none of my doing,'' Damian Chrestil said.

Chauvelin looked at him for a long moment, recognizing the truth of his words in the shocked look on the younger man's face. *I-Jay's dead.* ''Where's ji-Imbaoa?''

''Locked in the cellar.'' Damian Chrestil managed a strained, mirthless grin, gone almost as quickly as it had appeared. ''I'm sorry, Chauvelin. He claimed your jurisdiction.''

Chauvelin made a noise that might at another time have been a bark of laughter. ''What a fool.'' He paused then, considering, the habit of cold calculation carrying him through in spite of himself. There was nothing he could do for Ransome, and nothing more Ransome could do for him, except that in his death he would bring down ji-Imbaoa and most of the je Tsinra-an with him. Ji-Imbaoa had overstepped himself. Even under the old codes that the je Tsinraan professed to believe in, this killing, this murder, cut across too many kinship lines, impinged on his, Chauvelin's, rights as Ransome's patron and lover. "Fool," he said again, not sure if he was thinking of ji-Imbaoa or Ransome or himself, and made himself focus on Damian Chrestil, white-faced in the screen's projection. "Hold him for me. He claims hsai law, he'll get it."

Damian Chrestil nodded. "I'm sorry," he said again.

Chauvelin said, "I'll keep our bargain, Damian. But it's because I want the Visiting Speaker."

Damian nodded again. "I accept that." He looked away briefly, made himself look back at the screen. "I've not yet spoken to Na Lioe, I don't know how she'll take it."

"I'll talk to her," Chauvelin said.

"Are you sure?" Damian asked, involuntarily.

"Our goals were the same," Chauvelin said. "I think our interests still run parallel."

Damian Chrestil flinched. "Very well," he said, and reached for the cut-off button.

"One more thing," Chauvelin said, and the younger man stopped, his hand on the key. "I want I-Jay's body. I'll send some of my household for it when the storm lifts."

"Of course," Damian answered, almost gently, and it was Chauvelin who cut the connection.

He stood for a long moment staring at the desktop, at the letter that no longer had any significance because Ransome was dead. *I knew I would outlive him. I didn't think it would be so soon. Even bringing down the je Tsinra-an isn't worth this.* He turned away from the desktop and went to the drinks cabinet, poured himself a glass of the harsh local rum, not bothering with any of the mixers. He drank deeply, barely tasting the alcohol, put the glass aside before he could be tempted to finish the bottle. *Oh, God, I know I can live without him. It's just—at the very worst, I wish it had been at my choice.*

He moved slowly back to the desktop, touched keys to

connect himself to the main communications system. He called up the familiar codes—*Ransome's codes, the codes to Ransome's loft*—and swore when the familiar message flickered across the screen: SYSTEMS ENGAGED, PLEASE TRY AGAIN.

"Override," he said harshly, and a few seconds later the screen cleared. Lioe's beautiful, strong-boned face looked out at him.

"What the hell do you want?" she began, and her frown deepened when she recognized the ambassador. "Na Chauvelin?"

"I have bad news," Chauvelin said, and knew he had not been able to hide the pain in his voice. "I-Jay—Ransome's dead."

"Oh, God." There was a long silence, Lioe's face utterly beautiful in its blank shock, and then, quite suddenly, the mask shattered into fury. "What the hell happened, did Damian Chrestil kill him? I'll murder the son of a bitch myself—"

"No." Chauvelin did not raise his voice, but she stopped abruptly, the mask reasserting itself.

"So what did happen?" she asked, after a moment.

Chauvelin swallowed hard, suddenly unwilling to speak, as though to tell the story would make it truly real. That was superstition, shock, stupidity, and he put the thought aside, went on, steadily now, "Ji-Imbaoa—the Visiting Speaker— killed him. They were old enemies, and Ransome got too close to him."

"The hsaia at your party," Lioe said.

"That's right."

Lioe closed her eyes for a moment, and when she opened them again, Chauvelin could see the tears. "Ah, sa," she said, her voice breaking. "He wouldn't've been so careless."

"Wouldn't he?" Chauvelin said, in spite of himself, heard the bitter laughter that was close to tears in his own voice.

"Yes," Lioe said, after a moment. "He would."

There was another, longer silence between them, broken

only by the howl of the wind. Chauvelin wished for an instant that he could wail with it, but hsai training prevailed. He stared at Lioe's face in the screen, wondering again just what Ransome had seen in her. *Not sex, certainly, she's not his type for that. Surely not just the Game? He meant it when he said the Game was a dead end, useless. He said she was too good for the Game, wasted on it. I wonder if he's persuaded her of that? I suppose that's one last thing I can do, give her the chance to do something more.*

"What now?" Lioe said, softly. "I—we had a deal, Ambassador, you and I and Damian Chrestil."

"The deal holds," Chauvelin said. "At least as far as I'm concerned. Ji-Imbaoa falls under hsai jurisdiction, my jurisdiction. He asked for it, in fact."

There was a note of satisfaction in his voice in spite of himself, and Lioe nodded.

"As for the rest of it," Chauvelin went on, "I'm I-Jay's next of kin, the rest of his family's dead." He took a quick breath, spoke before the full pain of it could hit him. "I'm willing to let you have the loft and its contents, tapes and equipment. No one else has a claim on them. As part of the deal we made." He made himself go on without emotion. "He would want that."

"Ah." Lioe's voice held a note of pain that Chauvelin suddenly resented. He frowned, searching for the necessary rebuke, and Lioe went on, her voice under tight control again.

"All right. I'll keep my end of the bargain."

Good. "Agreed," Chauvelin said, and cut the connection. He stood for a moment, staring at the desktop, then touched icons to close the letter that still waited for transcription. There would have to be another letter—another letter that in some ways carried better news to the Remembrancer-Duke, a bigger scandal, one that would devastate the je Tsinra-an— but he couldn't face that now. He turned away to lean against the shuttered window, feeling the force of the wind even through the spun shielding. *The price of this victory is very high.* He slammed his hand flat against the shutter, already impatient with his own grief. *He was dying anyway.*

This was quicker, maybe kinder—but I will miss him. That was all the epitaph he could promise anyone, even Ransome. He made a face, and went back to the drinks cabinet, reaching for the rum.

DAY 2

A weather screen was flickering soundlessly in the corner, the display showing the bands of clouds curving now from northeast to southwest. The winds had shifted too, and the clattering of the rain against the house was softer, less insistent. Damian Chrestil sat alone in the tiny office space, the desktop open in front of him, a small black box lying on top of the displays. The lights beneath it, shining up through the clear screen, made it look as though it was floating on a haze of blued light. Damian stared at it, not touching it or the rolled tool kit that lay beside it, too tired to do more than look for a long moment. Then, sighing, he reached for the tool kit, unrolled it, and extracted a slim hook. He worked quickly, prying open the case of the desktop's datanode—not hooked up at the moment—then fanning the stacked chips until he found the delicate nest of wires. He separated out the ones he wanted, the power feed, the direct-on-line lead, the one that fed the data to an implanted data socket, spliced the black box into them. It had been a long time since he'd done that kind of work, but it was easy enough; the skills came back quickly, like running a john-boat along the Inland Water. He eased everything, wires, box, the stacked chips, back into the cavity, and fitted the cover carefully back into place. There was room and to spare in the old-fashioned fitting.

Moving more slowly now, he rerolled the tool kit, and slipped it back into his pocket. He glanced then at the chronometer, its numbers discreetly displayed above the open file: almost midnight, and the storm would be ending soon.

Already, the winds had dropped enough to allow the Lockwardens to send out the first of the emergency repair crews, heavy-duty flyers headed for the lighter barriers west of Factory Island and Roche'Ambroise, where the news services reported some minor damage, another team headed for Plug Island to check the generators there. In another hour or two, they could leave the summer house.

He flicked a switch, reconnecting the datanode to the main system, but did not touch the waiting cord. Instead, he ran his finger over icons on the desktop, tying in to the house systems, and touched a private code. A few seconds later, a telltale lit in the monitor bar, and he said, "Cella? I need to talk to you. I'm in my office."

There was no answer—probably she wasn't wearing the jewelry that concealed the transmitter—but a moment later the telltale winked out. Damian Chrestil sighed, and settled himself to wait.

At last, the door slid open almost silently, and Cella peered around its edge. "You wanted me, Damiano?"

Damian nodded. "We need to talk," he said again.

"Certainly."

Cella moved easily into the room, seated herself at his gesture on the edge of the desktop. She was still wearing the demure, plain shirt and loose trousers, the creamy blouse improbably neat even after hours of wear. *And Ransome's death.* Damian looked down at the open files, not really seeing the crowding symbols. "You set this up," he said quietly.

Cella blinked once, her face utterly still and remote. "Ransome's death? No."

Damian Chrestil leaned back in his chair, too tired to feel much anger at the lie. "You've never had so much to say to the Visiting Speaker—to any hsaia—in your life. And the cylinders were moved, not by me, not by Ivie or any of his people. That leaves you."

"Or Ransome himself," Cella said gently. "Or the Visiting Speaker."

"The Visiting Speaker didn't have the chance," Damian said. "Ivie was watching him too closely, keeping him in that corner. And Ransome was looking for it elsewhere. You had to tell him where it was. That still leaves you, Cella.''

Cella met his eyes steadily, only the note of scorn in her voice betraying any emotion. ''Why would I kill Illario Ransome? Do you think I care if you fuck him? What's that to me, any more than any other of your minor conquests? We have a—more complicated arrangement. I thought you knew me better, Damiano.''

''I think I do.'' Damian did not move, still leaning back in his chair, his hands steepled across his chest. ''What annoys me, Cella, is your interfering in my business, screwing up a deal I had a hard time salvaging. I told you before that this was the only thing I could do to save the situation. I meant it, and I don't appreciate your trying to force my hand. You're not good enough to play politics.''

''Ransome's death is the best thing that could happen,'' Cella said. ''For you, for Chauvelin—even for the Visiting Speaker, if you wanted to play it that way; he'd be under obligation to you if you let him go. Ransome's worth a lot more dead than alive—and don't try to tell me that Chauvelin loved him so much that he'd rather get revenge than use him to bring down the je Tsinra-an. It's the best thing that could happen, if you're serious about going over to the tzu line.''

''It's not your place to make that decision,'' Damian Chrestil said. He sighed, looked down at his files again, then spun the first one so that it faced Cella. She looked down at it, her expression first curious, then angry, before she'd gotten herself under control again.

''Our arrangement is over,'' Damian Chrestil said. ''That's my assessment of your property, a fair settlement. You can take it or not, I don't really care. But I don't want to see you again.'' He pushed himself up out of the chair, took a few steps away from the desk.

''Very well,'' Cella said, her voice still rigidly controlled. ''But you won't object if I verify some of this?''

''Help yourself,'' Damian said, and heard the whisper of the interface cord drawn out of its housing in the side of the datanode. He did not look back, bracing himself, and a moment later heard the fat snap of the current as she plugged

herself into the system. There was no cry, no sound except
the buzz of the overload box shorting out, and then the
sprawling thud as she fell. The room smelled of electricity,
and then, insidiously, of scorched hair and skin. Damian
Chrestil turned then, without haste, knowing what he would
find.

Cella lay contorted by the corner of the desk, limbs tumbled, her face pressed into the carpet. Her dark hair had come
out of its crown of braids, lay in disturbed coils over her neck
and across the floor, hiding the data socket at the base of her
jaw. A thin tendril of smoke was rising from it as the implant
housing smoldered. He looked at her for a moment, but did
not touch her after all. The end of the data cord dangled over
the edge of the desk, inert: the automatics had cut the power
instantly after the massive current passed through. He left it
there, and reached into his pocket for his thin gloves. He drew
them on, ignoring the smell—burned flesh, urine, burned implant plastic, and hot metal—and used the tool kit to pry off
the cover of the datanode. The boards and wires had fused, a
ragged mess; he stepped over Cella's body to lean closer,
carefully freed the black box from the ruined node. *The mili-
tary does good work,* he thought, and gingerly stuffed the
ruined components back into the node's casing, closing it
carefully behind him. By the door, where the carpet ended
and the tiles began, he stopped, dropped the black box on the
hard surface. The casing shattered, spilling fragments; he set
his heel on them, methodically grinding them to gravel, then
swept them toward the nearest garbage slot. The baseboard
hatch slid open, and he swept the fragments into its waiting
darkness, running his foot twice over the tiles even after he
was sure he had it all. He did not look back—he did not have
to look back, would remember Cella's twisted body in absolute clarity even without a second look—but walked away,
letting the door slide closed behind him. *Power surges happen during big storms; you shouldn't go direct-on-line when
the weather's bad. Everyone knows that, and everyone does it
just the same. Poor Cella, what a shame it caught up with
you. But you shouldn't've tried to force my hand.* In an hour
or two, if no one had found her, he would send Ivie looking
for her: *until then, let her lie.*

EPILOGUE

DAY 6

Lioe stood on the midships deck, one hand on the rail to balance herself against the motion of the barge. Even four days after the storm had passed, the Water was still a little rough; it would be easier out to sea, Roscha had said, where the currents were less constrained by the complex channels. Overhead, the sky was very blue, utterly free of clouds, and the ghost of one of the moons rode the housetops over Roche'Ambroise. The sun was warm: Burning Bright was moving toward summer, Lioe remembered, and she glanced forward, wondering if she should claim a place under the thin canopy. It was crowded there, full of people in white under the white canopy, and she decided not to join them yet. There were more people in white crowding the docks, Gamers mostly, people from Shadows that she recognized, others that she didn't know, from the nets and the other clubs. White was the color of mourning on Burning Bright, and Ransome had been well respected. She smoothed the front of her own coat self-consciously, the fabric heavy over a white shirt and her most formal trousers, the breeze cool on her neck and scalp. It felt odd, not to be wearing a hat, but she was no longer a pilot, would have to get used to that. Kerestel had not been pleased, but there were good pilots available through the pools. He would learn to live with it. She glanced over her shoulder, saw Roscha coming toward her, red hair bright in the sun, very vivid against the white coat. *Everyone on Burning Bright owns one,* Roscha had said. *You never know when you'll need it.*

"It's quite a turnout," Roscha said, and leaned out over the railing to stare at the crowd on the dock.

Lioe looked with her, saw Medard-Yasinë standing with
Aliar Gueremei, a handful of Shadows' staff clustering
around them. She had seen Peter Savian earlier, conspicuous
in plain Republican shirt and trousers, a white scarf his only
concession to local custom; now he was nowhere in sight,
but instead, Kazio Beledin stood talking to a tall woman, La-
Chacalle, and a slim man with a data socket high on his face
that caught the light like a diamond. He saw her looking, and
lifted a hand in sober acknowledgment. Lioe waved back,
not knowing what else to do. LaChacalle had on a white
dress under the sheer white coat, and the others wore wide
wraps, Beledin's covering his head like a hood. "So many
Gamers," she said, and Roscha shrugged.

"Everyone knew Ambidexter. They may not have liked
him, but they'd kill to get in his games."

"Not a bad epitaph," Lioe said. *And it's not just Gamers
who feel that way.* She looked back toward the group under
the canopy, counting the political notables who'd come to
Ransome's funeral. Governor Berengaria, looking remark-
ably like her image from the parade, stood talking quietly to
a man Ransome had pointed out at Chauvelin's party as the
head of the Five Points Bank, while a detachment from the
Merchant Investors Syndicate waited for her attention.
There were representatives from all of the Five Points families, Chauvelin had said, and two of the Chrestil-Brisch. She
scanned the crowd until she found them. The head of the
family, Altagracian—*dit Chrestillio,* she remembered—was
a big man, bigger and more leonine than Damian Chrestil,
but the sister, Bettisa, had the same sharp face and fine body.
It was a little disconcerting, seeing her there, thin white coat
wrapped tight around her body, and Lioe looked away.
Chauvelin was nowhere in sight. *Probably with the ashes,*
she thought, and still wasn't sure how she felt about this ritual, the formal consigning of what was left of Ransome's
body to the seas. Death on Callixte was a private thing, and
so were funerals. There was a shout from forward, and the
beat of the engines strengthened through the deck. Very
slowly, the barge began to pull away from the dock.

"Quinn," Roscha said, just loudly enough to be heard
over the sudden rush of wind. "There's been some talk."

Lioe glanced back at her, frowned at the grim look on the other woman's face. "What about?"

"The fucking Visiting Speaker," Roscha answered. "I've been hearing from people I know up at the port—and other places, pretty much all around—that he's walking around loose. I thought you said the ambassador was going to deal with him."

"He was," Lioe answered. "As far as I know, he is. Are your friends sure it's ji-Imbaoa?"

She knew it was a stupid question even as she asked, and Roscha grinned. "Not all hsaia look alike. And he's wearing all the honors. Perii lived on Jericho, she reads hsai ribbons pretty fluently. Oh, it's him all right."

"Wonderful," Lioe said. *What the hell is ji-Imbaoa doing free? Chauvelin should be keeping him under lock and key until the next ship leaves for Hsaioi-An—*

"It occurred to me," Roscha said, "that maybe N'Ambassador wasn't all that sorry Ransome's dead."

No. Lioe shook her head, rejecting the thought even before she had fully analyzed it. *Not that I'd put it past Chauvelin to kill someone, but not Ransome. Not the way he sounded, looked, when he told me.* "There's bound to be a reason," she said, "something in hsai law, maybe."

"Maybe," Roscha said. "But the thought also occurred to me, Quinn, that maybe something could be done about it. Perii says the Visiting Speaker's been drinking pretty heavily, drowning his sorrows, she says. It'd be a shame if he didn't make it home some night—which could be arranged, Quinn. If you think it's appropriate."

Lioe stood frozen for a moment, suddenly very aware of the heat of the sun on her back, the movement of the barge under her feet. This was a power she had never expected, a direct and potent strength, the smoldering anger of the canalli channeled through Roscha, ready to hand. *That's exaggerating, sure, I don't have all the canalli—but she's offering me a means of direct action that I never dreamed I'd be able to tap. With this to back up the new Game, I've got more power than I'd ever expected.* She curbed herself sternly, made herself focus on the issue at hand. "I want to talk to Chauvelin.'' She pushed herself away from the rail before Roscha could follow.

She found Chauvelin about where she'd expected, toward the forward end of the canopy where a plain, raw-looking pottery jar stood ready on a white-draped table. He was wearing a white wrap coat, like everyone else, but had left it open, so that the wind blew it back to reveal the knots and clusters of his honors draped about his shoulders. Berengaria stood beside him, the wrinkles at the corners of her mismatched eyes making her look as though she almost smiled. Lioe sighed, and resigned herself to wait, but to her surprise, Chauvelin nodded to her, and said something to the governor. This time Berengaria did smile, and Chauvelin made his way across the last few méters to stand at Lioe's side.

''It's good to see you, Na Lioe. I'm sorry we haven't had a chance to speak before this.''

At least not today. Lioe said, ''I hear that the Visiting Speaker is back in all his old haunts, Ambassador. How does that happen?''

There was a little silence, and then Chauvelin said, ''There isn't a ship to Hsiamai for another four days. He gave his parole—his word, his promise—to give himself up when it arrives.''

''I know what parole means.'' Lioe took a deep breath, fighting back her anger.

Chauvelin said, ''It doesn't mean anything. It's his right under the law, to have this time. He'll be on the ship to Hsiamai, and the All-Father will deal with him. He miscalculated badly, it'll take the je Tsinra-an years to recover from this.''

''I can't say I find that terribly satisfying,'' Lioe said.

''You surprise me.'' Chauvelin looked at her, his lined face without emotion. ''Ji-Imbaoa is ruined. Not only that, he's ruined his entire clan. Let him have all the Oblivion he wants, it's not going to change anything. I think that's very satisfying.''

Lioe paused for a long moment, considering the ambassador's words. Yes, it was satisfying to think that ji-Imbaoa would have to live with whatever hsai law thought was the appropriate punishment for murdering an ambassador's dependent, and with the fury of his own relatives. Ransome, certainly, would have appreciated it.

"He's lost any hope of ever gaining position at court," Chauvelin said, "or of regaining what he's already lost. He'll be ostracized, completely."

"I see." Lioe looked away from him, toward the railing and the Water beyond. Traffic was heavy, as always, but funeral barges had priority, and the smaller boats gave way grudgingly, sliding to either side of the broad channel. The air smelled of salt and oil. They were coming up on Homestead Island and the end of the Water; she could just make out the blockhouses that controlled the first of the storm barriers, the stubby grey buildings conspicuous against the brighter brick behind them. According to the datastore and to the obituaries, Ransome had been born somewhere in that district, born poor, child of no one at all important. *And now his death is bringing down a major faction within Hsaioi-An. Yes, he would appreciate that.* "All right," she said, "I won't do anything."

Chauvelin lifted an eyebrow, looked genuinely surprised for an instant. Then his eyes slid sideways, and he smiled slightly. "I forgot Roscha. Careless of me. But this is a hsai matter, you can leave it to me."

"All right," Lioe said, and to her surprise, Chauvelin bowed to her.

"Thank you," he said, and turned away.

Lioe looked over her shoulder, and saw, as she'd expected, that Roscha had come up behind her, moving so silently that she hadn't heard her approach.

"Well?" Roscha asked. "What did he say?"

"We'll let it go," Lioe said. "Ji-Imbaoa will be on the ship to Hsiamai, and he'll be appropriately dealt with there."

"Do you believe that?" Roscha asked.

"Yes," Lioe answered, and managed a tight grin. "He'll get exactly what he deserves." Roscha still looked uncertain, and Lioe went on, "It's what Ransome would've wanted, I'm sure of that."

"If you say so."

"Look, this brings down an entire government," Lioe

said. "You've got to admit that's Ransome's—Ambidexter's—style."

Roscha laughed softly. "That's true. *Sha-mai*, wouldn't it make a great Game session?"

It would, Lioe thought. *It would make a brilliant one. And it's one I want to write—maybe put it at the core of the new Game, make it one of the givens, part of the background for everything. That would be a nice memorial, something else he'd approve of. And then no one could play without knowing something about him, remembering his death.* She nodded slowly. "Thanks, Roscha," she said. "I'll do just that."

DAY 6

It was midafternoon by the time Chauvelin returned to his
house, and his face stung from the combination of sun and
salt spray. Je-Sou'tsian was waiting in the main hall—like
all the household, she wore white ribbons, sprays of them
bound around each arm—flanked by a pair of understew-
ards. Chauvelin frowned, surprised to see so formal a dele-
gation, and je-Sou'tsian bowed deeply.

"Your pardon, sia, but there has been a transmission from
maiHu'an. His grace has been pleased to grant you an
award." She used the more formal word, the one that meant
"award-of-honor": she would have seen the message when
it came in, Chauvelin knew. She would have prepared the
formal package. "It's waiting in your office."

"My lord honors me beyond my deserving," Chauvelin
answered, conventionally. "Thanks, Iameis—and thanks for
that, too." He reached out, gently touched the knots of white
ribbon.

Je-Sou'tsian made the quick fluttering gesture, quickly
controlled, that meant embarrassment and pleasure. "We—I
didn't want to presume. But we regret your loss."

"Thank you," Chauvelin said again, and went up the spiral stairs to his office.

The room was unchanged, the single pane of glass that
had cracked during the storm replaced days before. Chauvelin settled himself at the desk, lifted the precisely folded
message to his lips in perfunctory acknowledgment, and
broke the temporary seal. The message—handwritten in
n-jao character and then copy-flashed; Haas's handwriting,

not the Duke's—was clear enough, but he had to read it a second time before the meaning sank in. Then, quite slowly, he began to laugh. He had done well, in the Remembrancer-Duke's opinion: this was the reward every *chaoi-mon* worked for, dreamed of, but few ever achieved. There, set out in the formal, archaic language of court records, were the certificates of posthumous co-optation for his parents and their parents, the necessary two generations that would make him no longer *chaoi-mon,* but a full hsaia, indistinguishable in the eyes of the court and the law from any other hsai. He could not quite imagine his mother's reaction, but suspected it would have been profane.

There was a second note folded up inside the official announcement, also in Haas's hand, the neat familiar alphabet used for tradetalk. He opened that, skimmed the spiky printing.

CONGRATULATIONS ON YOUR PROMOTION, AND MY SYMPA-
THIES FOR THE LOSS OF YOUR PROTÉGÉ. MY LORD IS VERY
PLEASED WITH THE OUTCOME OF THIS BUSINESS, AND IS
PLANNING TO TRAVEL TO HSIAMAI IN PERSON FOR THE TRI-
ALS. A MORE PERSONAL TOKEN OF HIS PLEASURE WILL FOL-
LOW.

Chauvelin smiled again, rather wryly this time. *I don't think I should count on that.* The Remembrancer-Duke might be less pleased after all, though on balance it shouldn't affect the ultimate outcome of the trials. He glanced at the chronometer display, gauging the time left until he would hear—*not much longer now*—and set both messages aside. One of Ransome's story eggs was sitting on the desk beside him, the case a lacquer-red sphere that looked as though it had been powdered with gold dust. He picked it up idly, turned it over until he could look through the lens into its depths. Familiar shapes, Apollo and a satyr, shared images from his and Ransome's shared culture, leaned together in a luminous forest, each with a lyre in his hands. The loop of images showed a brief conversation, a smile—*Ransome's familiar, knowing smile*—and then a brief interlude of music, the sound sweetly distant, barely audible half a meter away. *Apollo and Marsyas,* Chauvelin thought, *in the last good days before the contest.* He had never noticed it before, but the Apollo had his own eyes, and his trick of the lifted eyebrow. *Oh, very like you, I-Jay. But that's not how it was. I did everything I could to save you. You died by your own misjudgment, not by mine.*

"Sia?" That was je-Sou'tsian's voice, sharp and startled in the speakers. "Sia, I'm sorry to disturb you, but there's been an accident."

"An accident?" Chauvelin said.

"Yes, sia."

Chauvelin did not light the screens, allowed himself a smile, hearing the shock in the steward's voice.

"I'm sorry, sia," je-Sou'tsian said again, "but it's the Visiting Speaker. There's been—the Lockwardens say he fell into one of the canals, he was drunk on Oblivion, and a barge hit him."

"Is he alive?" Chauvelin demanded, and heard himself sharp and querulous.

"For now, sia. But he's not expected to live the night. They've taken him to the nearest hospital, Mercy Underface, they said."

"So." Chauvelin could not stop his smile from becoming a grin; it was an effort to keep his voice under control. "Do they know what happened?"

"Not for certain, sia. They think he fell."

"Or did he kill himself?" Chauvelin asked, and was pleased with the bitterness of his tone. *If they can believe it's suicide, that's shameful enough on top of everything else that the Remembrancer-Duke will still gain everything he would have gained through the trial.* He heard je-Sou'tsian's sharp intake of breath, wished he dared light the screen to watch her gestures.

"It—the Lockwardens asked that also, sia. It seems possible."

"Such shame," Chauvelin said, and knew that this time he did not sound sincere. "Send his house steward to stand by him, and one of us to stay with her. Express my condolences."

"I'll go myself, if you want, sia," je-Sou'tsian said.

Chauvelin nodded, then remembered the dark screen. "That would be a gracious gesture, Iameis. I'd be grateful."

"Then I'll do it," je-Sou'tsian said.

"Keep me informed of his condition," Chauvelin said, and closed the connection. It was good to have friends on the canals. He leaned back in his chair, reached out to touch the story egg again, but did not pick it up, ran his fingers instead over the warm metal of the case. *I told the truth when I told Lioe I'd take care of the Visiting Speaker. It's not my fault that she assumed I meant that I would let the law take its course. That was something Ransome would've appreciated, that double-edged conversation. And I think he would've appreciated my decision.* He smiled again, and picked up the story egg, glanced again at the bright images. The loop, triggered by the movement, showed god and satyr leaning shoulder to shoulder, and then the faint clear strain of the music as the satyr played.

INTERLUDE

They crouched in the uncertain shelter of the cargo bay, hearing the clatter of boots recede along the walkways to either side. The overhanging shelves, piled high with crates, gave some cover, but they all knew that if the baron's guards came out onto the center catwalk it would take a miracle to keep from being seen. Galan Africa/VERE CAMINESI winced as an incautious movement jarred his bandaged arm and shoulder, and stopped trying to pry the power pack away from the nonstandard mounting.

"Hazard," he said, and Gallio Hazard/PETER SAVIAN slipped his own pistol back into his belt and came to study the housing. After a moment, he pried it loose with main force, handed the two parts to Africa. The technician accepted them, prodded dubiously at the bent plugs. Hazard shrugged an apology, and drew his pistol again, his attention already turned outward toward the retreating footsteps of the guards.

Jack Blue/JAFIERA ROSCHA sprawled gasping against the nearest stack of crates, his face drawn into a scowl of pain and anger equally mixed. Mijja Lyall/FERNESA crouched at his side, digging hurriedly through the much-depleted medical kit. She found the injector at last, applied it to Blue's forearm. The telekinetic swore under his breath, but a moment later, the pain began to ease from his forehead. Lord Faro/LACHACALLE and Ibelin Belfortune/HALLY VENTURA exchanged glances, and edged a little bit away from the others, where they could exchange whispers unheard.

"What about the contact?" Desir of Harmsway/KAZIO BELEDIN said. "Where is it, Avellar?"

Avellar/AMBIDEXTER looked back at him for a moment, gave a slow, crooked smile. "Something's gone wrong, obviously. But unless you want to go back . . ." He let his voice trail off in a mocking invitation, and Harmsway looked away, scowling. Avellar's smile widened slightly, and he moved to stand beside Jack Blue. "How is it?"

Blue shrugged, made a so-so gesture with one hand. "I'll live." His voice sounded better, and Avellar nodded.

"Maybe he's losing weight," Harmsway said, too sweetly.

Blue frowned, and a cracked piece of the floor tiling tore itself loose and flung itself at Harmsway's face. Avellar plucked it out of the air before it could hit anything, dropped it onto the flooring at Blue's feet. There was blood on the tile, from where the sharp edges had cut his hand, but Avellar ignored it.

"Try that again," he said, almost conversationally, "and I'll leave you." He was looking at Blue, but Harmsway stiffened.

"Not me, surely," he said, his voice provocative. "If you leave me here, Royal, all this will have been for nothing."

"All what?" Avellar said, softly. "All this? Coming here, risking my life, planning this escape for the lot of you? That's nothing compared to what I'm willing to do to have you back at my side, Desir. But you need me just as much, if you're going to get off this planet. Don't forget that, my friend."

In spite of himself, Harmsway glanced toward the cargo door, only forty meters away across the width of the warehouse. It was even open, and he could feel that the last barrier was sealed only with a palm lock, the kind of thing he could open in his sleep . . . if he could reach it. And beyond that hatch were Avellar's people, loyal only to Avellar. His lips thinned, and he looked away.

Avellar nodded. "The ship's mine," he said. "Without me, none of you will get aboard. Hell, without me, none of you would have gotten this far."

"Without you," Gallio Hazard said, "some of us wouldn't be here at all."

"Touché," Avellar said. "But you shouldn't've left my service, Gallio."

"Avellar." Lyall's voice was suddenly sharp with fear, and Avellar turned to face her. "They've brought in a hunter," Lyall said. "And the Baron's with him."

"How close?" Harmsway demanded, and Lyall shook her head.

"I can't tell. There's—he's shielded."

"No one use any psi," Avellar said. The others murmured agreement, and he looked at Africa. "Is it finished, Galan?"

Africa shrugged his good shoulder. "I've got the connection rigged, but there's no guarantee it'll work."

Avellar nodded, and looked at Belfortune. "That leaves you, Bel."

Faro said, "Let him be."

Avellar ignored him. "Bel—"

"Avellar," Lyall said again, real horror in her voice. "He's found us."

"What?" Harmsway's voice scaled up in surprise. "Damn you, Royal—"

"Shut up," Avellar said, and was obeyed. "Belfortune. Can you stop the hunter?"

Belfortune shook his head. "I have to be close to him, I can't just reach out and take his power. It's not that easy—"

"All right," Avellar said, his voice gentle but firm, and Belfortune was silent. Faro laid a hand on his shoulder, then reached for his pistol.

"Well, Desir," Avellar said, "it's up to you and me."

Harmsway shook his head sharply, and Hazard said, "The last time, you nearly killed him."

Avellar ignored him. "If we don't work together, we'll never get out of here. You and I will both die on this wretched planet. Do you really want that, just to spite me? Or do you just enjoy it too much?"

"Yes," Harmsway said, "I can admit it. You're too strong for me, you and your crazy clone-sibs, and I like it too much."

"Would you rather be dead?" Avellar asked.

"Desir, don't," Hazard said.

Harmsway ignored him. "No, damn you. All right. I'll do it."

Avellar held out his hands, carefully not smiling, and Harmsway took them with only the slightest hesitation. There was a little silence, and then a kind of darkness seemed to gather around them. Shapes moved in the darkness, shapes that were Avellar, shapes that wore Avellar's face and a woman's body. Avellar closed his eyes, felt his power returning with Harmsway's presence, Harmsway's raw electrokinesis bridging the holes left by the deaths of half the clone. He could sense the others' presence, too: Quarta in her cell, gibbering in darkness; Secunda caught in midstride, dragged away from herself by his insistent demands; Tertius ever silent, great eyes staring at nothing. He pulled them to him, made their power his own, built a ladder with it that carried him out of the prison of his body and let him look down on the warehouse as if from a great height. He saw the world in black and white, the figures of his party and of the Baron's men clustered at the doorway pale as ghosts against the dark walls and shadows that were the piled crates. The Baron's group had stopped, huddling together around a grounded airsled. *The hunter smells something he doesn't recognize,* Avellar thought, and laughed silently. *No, you wouldn't recognize me.* He spun again, looking down from his illusory height for a solution, saw Harmsway on his knees, head bowed with strain, still clinging to his hands. Harmsway was weaker than he'd realized; Avellar allowed himself to look farther afield, saw Jack Blue now standing at Lyall's side.

Blue, he said, and felt the word fall for what seemed an eternity before it struck air and was heard. "Give me your hand."

He forced his body to free one hand from Harmsway's grip, held it out to Blue. The telekinetic took it, reluctantly, and Avellar felt the other's power join his own. He let himself rise back up the ladder, dragging Blue's talent with him, hung for a moment beneath the rafters, looking at the piles of crates through the lens of Blue's talent. Then, almost lazily, he reached out—his hand, Blue's telekinesis, moving as one, Harmsway still bridging the gaps that let him draw on his

clone-sibs, his other selves—and tipped the first row of
crates onto the baron's men. He heard screams—close at
hand, and more distant, the noise reaching his physical body
half a heartbeat later—but he closed his mind, searching for
the right point. Blue's power was fading, stuttering like an
underfueled engine, but he ignored it, and toppled a second
set of shelves, blocking any advance. Then he let himself
slide back down the ladder, feeling it dissolve behind him as
he fell, until he was back in his own body, on his knees, Jack
Blue's hand cold in his own. Harmsway was crumpled on
the warped tiles, breathing in harsh gasps, his forehead
against the floor. Blue lay open-eyed, unmoving, his face red
and mottled. Lyall crouched beside him, hand on his wrist,
and shook her head as Avellar looked at her.

"He's dead."

Belfortune laughed softly. "So that's how the great Avellar's power works. You're no more than I am, nothing more
than a vampire. At least I don't use the power I take."

"You just dine on it," Hazard said.

Faro said, "This is why I won't support you, Avellar. No
one who can do that should be emperor."

"But that's just it," Avellar said. He reached down almost absently, lifted Harmsway so that the electrokinetic's
head rested on his lap. "This power it exactly why I should
be emperor. I'm psi, yes, but it's unlimited in type, because I
can draw on all of it. But only if you let me. I can't coerce, I
can only take what's given. Jack gave me what he had, he let
me use him up, to save the rest of us. He couldn't've done it
alone, and I knew how to use what he gave me. If a psi is
going to be emperor—and you know that's inevitable,
there's no one left who isn't psi—then it should be me, because I can't do anything alone, and without consent."

Hazard nodded slowly, came to crouch at Harmsway's
side, he touched the electrokinetic's face gently, and looked
relieved when Harmsway stirred. Hazard supported him,
helped him sit upright. Harmsway's face was drawn, lines of
fatigue sharply etched.

Faro said, "The ship's waiting."

Avellar nodded, pushed himself to his feet, fighting back
his own exhaustion. "Let's go."

Two guards were standing by the cargo door, one with rifle leveled, staring toward the far door where the crates had fallen, the other babbling into a hand-held com-unit. He didn't seem to be getting any satisfactory answers, but Avellar shrank back into the shelter of the nearest stack of crates. "Faro," he whispered. "Can you take him?"

"I can take him," Faro said, and nodded to the closer guard. "But that one will spread the alarm the minute he goes down."

"Leave that to me," Harmsway whispered.

"Don't be stupid," Hazard began, and the electrokinetic shook his head, the ghost of a smile wreathing his mouth.

"The com circuit has to go, or we're all shot. Lucky you have me."

"Be ready when he takes out the com," Avellar said to Faro, and the older man nodded, his eyes fixed over the leveled gun. Africa dropped to his knees beside him, tucked the laser rifle against his shoulder.

Harmsway closed his eyes, drawing on what remained of his power. His whole body seemed for an instant to be stretched to breaking, as though the psionic stress had translated itself to every muscle in his body, and then the pain had passed. He reached along the wires behind the distant wall, searching carefully to avoid anything that was not part of the communications system, and teased his way into the handset. For an instant, he considered the spectacular, blowing all the circuits in a shower of gaudy sparks, but he no longer had the strength for that. He reached for a fuse instead and quietly poured what was left of his power through it. The cylinder melted, and he allowed himself to fall back into his body.

The guard stopped, shook his head and then the handset, and stepped forward to join the other, holding out the suddenly silent com-unit.

"Now!" Avellar said, and the others fired almost as he spoke. The guards fell without a sound. "Nice shooting. Let's go." He started across the narrow space without looking back. The others followed, crowding into the narrow space between the outer door and the ship's hatch, and Africa fiddled with the controls to close the door behind them. Avellar nodded, and laid his hand against the sensor panel in the center of the hatch. There was a soft click, and then a high-pitched tone.

"Royal Avellar," he said, and waited. A heartbeat later, the cargo lock creaked open. Familiar people, familiar faces, were waiting inside the lock, and Avellar smiled with open pleasure.

"Danile," he said, and a man—greying, thin, a long, heavily embroidered coat thrown open over expensively plain shirt and trousers—looked back at him gravely.

"I'm back, Danile," Avellar said again, and the greying man nodded.

"You're here."

"And I have Harmsway, and the others," Avellar went on. "We had an agreement, Danile."

Danile nodded again, more slowly. "Yes."

"You said," Avellar said, a note of menace in his voice, "you said you would support me, support my claim to the throne, if I brought Desir of Harmsway out of Ixion's Wheel. We're here, Danile. Are you going to keep your part of the bargain?"

"I didn't think you could do it," Danile said. "I thought—I thought I'd be rid of you. But if you can do this . . ." His voice trailed off, and he shook his head. "If you can do this, yes, you're the best choice for the position. Yes, I'll support you—Majesty."

Avellar smiled with wolfish triumph, and one of Danile's crew said urgently, "Sirs—"

"She's right," Danile said. "We have to hurry. We're cleared for departure; we'd better go while we still can."

There was a ragged murmur of agreement, and the group began to move farther into the ship, following Avellar and Danile. The cargo door slid shut again behind them, closing off their last view of Ixion's Wheel.

DAY 16

Lioe closed down the system for the last time, running her hands over the secondary controls to disconnect the monitors. She already had all the data she needed, stored in spheres until her new space was up and running—a newer building, down in the Dock Road District, closer to the clubs. A haulage company would come for the machines later, or at least for the ones she had decided to keep. It was a generous legacy, maybe too generous, especially since she was still not sure if Ransome would have wanted her to have it. She was better than he had ever been, at both games, politics and the Game itself, and once the novelty had worn off, it might have become awkward between them. But there was no point in might-have-beens. She looked around a final time, making sure she hadn't forgotten anything. There was nothing left, nothing that she wanted, and she let herself out into the sun-warmed corridor. The elevator was in use, as always; she scrambled down the new stairway, walled in storm-hardened glass, barely aware of the cityscape spread out below the cliff edge beyond her. Roscha was waiting, with a borrowed denki-bike, and the new Game began tonight. Lioe smiled, and hurried.

THE BEST IN
SCIENCE FICTION

☐	51083-6	ACHILLES' CHOICE *Larry Niven & Steven Barnes*	$4.99 Canada $5.99
☐	50270-1	THE BOAT OF A MILLION YEARS *Poul Anderson*	$4.95 Canada $5.95
☐	51528-5	A FIRE UPON THE DEEP *Vernor Vinge*	$5.99 Canada $6.99
☐	52225-7	A KNIGHT OF GHOSTS AND SHADOWS *Poul Anderson*	$4.99 Canada $5.99
☐	53259-7	THE MEMORY OF EARTH *Orson Scott Card*	$5.99 Canada $6.99
☐	51001-1	N-SPACE *Larry Niven*	$5.99 Canada $6.99
☐	52024-6	THE PHOENIX IN FLIGHT *Sherwood Smith & Dave Trowbridge*	$4.99 Canada $5.99
☐	51704-0	THE PRICE OF THE STARS *Debra Doyle & James D. Macdonald*	$4.50 Canada $5.50
☐	50890-4	RED ORC'S RAGE *Philip Jose Farmer*	$4.99 Canada $5.99
☐	50925-0	XENOCIDE *Orson Scott Card*	$5.99 Canada $6.99
☐	50947-1	YOUNG BLEYS *Gordon R. Dickson*	$5.99 Canada $6.99

Buy them at your local bookstore or use this handy coupon:
Clip and mail this page with your order.

Publishers Book and Audio Mailing Service
P.O. Box 120159, Staten Island, NY 10312-0004

Please send me the book(s) I have checked above. I am enclosing $ _____
(Please add $1.25 for the first book, and $.25 for each additional book to cover postage and handling.
Send check or money order only—no CODs.)

Name _____
Address _____
City _____ State/Zip _____
Please allow six weeks for delivery. Prices subject to change without notice.

MORE OF THE BEST IN SCIENCE FICTION

☐	50892-0	CHINA MOUNTAIN ZHANG *Maureen F. McHugh*	$3.99 Canada $4.99
☐	51383-5	THE DARK BEYOND THE STARS *Frank M. Robinson*	$4.99 Canada $5.99
☐	50180-2	DAYS OF ATONEMENT *Walter Jon Williams*	$4.99 Canada $5.99
☐	55701-8	ECCE AND OLD EARTH *Jack Vance*	$5.99 Canada $6.99
☐	52427-6	THE FORGE OF GOD *Greg Bear*	$5.99 Canada $6.99
☐	51918-3	GLASS HOUSES *Laura J. Mixon*	$3.99 Canada $4.99
☐	51096-8	HALO *Tom Maddox*	$3.99 Canada $4.99
☐	50042-3	IVORY *Mike Resnick*	$4.95 Canada $5.95
☐	50198-5	THE JUNGLE *David Drake*	$4.99 Canada $5.99
☐	51623-0	ORBITAL RESONANCE *John Barnes*	$3.99 Canada $4.99
☐	53014-4	THE RING OF CHARON *Roger MacBride Allen*	$4.95 Canada $5.95

Buy them at your local bookstore or use this handy coupon:
Clip and mail this page with your order.

Publishers Book and Audio Mailing Service
P.O. Box 120159, Staten Island, NY 10312-0004

Please send me the book(s) I have checked above. I am enclosing $ _____
(Please add $1.25 for the first book, and $.25 for each additional book to cover postage and handling.
Send check or money order only—no CODs.)

Name _____

Address _____

City _____ State/Zip _____

Please allow six weeks for delivery. Prices subject to change without notice.